ANNE T. THYSSEN

EVERNIGHT PUBLISHING ®

www.evernightpublishing.com

Copyright© 2024

Anne T. Thyssen

ISBN: 978-0-3695-0530-9

Cover Artist: Jay Aheer

Editor: Lisa Petrocelli

ANNE T. THYSSEN

THE OMEGA'S KNOWLEDGE

The Last Court of Omegas, 1

Anne T. Thyssen

Copyright © 2024

Prologue
Cartan

My mother emerged from the tent, her cries loud and distraught. She pleaded with the imposing Alpha who held me, begging him not to take me away. Tears streamed down her cheeks, but the Alpha next to her didn't even acknowledge her presence. He continued walking while cradling me in his arms. His presence had always felt safe and protective, but on that day, a strange energy surrounded him, as if an ominous presence loomed.

"Please, just give him to me," she implored. "Let him live! There may not be another!"

I was too young to comprehend her words, but the

menacing growl emanating from the Alpha holding me made it clear that her pleas fell on deaf ears. He halted, turned to her, and silenced her with a piercing gaze. Her trembling lip and darting eyes briefly met mine before she shook her head. Desperation drove her to push forward and grab his arm.

"Please, just give him to me!"

The Alpha shook her off, growling menacingly once more. Other women from the clan intervened, restraining my mother.

"No! No!" she cried out as the Alpha continued to carry me away. I peered over his shoulder, witnessing my mother's tears and her futile struggle against the other women.

"Cartan! Cartan!" she shouted after me, but I couldn't reach her, and the Alpha's strong presence, despite the underlying tension, comforted me.

More Alphas surrounded us, obscuring my view of my mother. We continued walking until her cries faded, and only a vast expanse of flat, sandy terrain stretched before us. I found the journey exhilarating, having never ventured so far from home. The aura of safety provided by the Alphas enveloped me. I had no idea of our destination until we suddenly arrived at some dark-colored rocks, a small wall that seemed out of place in the flat landscape.

Beside a massive rock, the Alpha set me down gently on the warm sand. I gazed up at him, noticing the coldness in his eyes. I couldn't recall ever seeing a different expression in them, but now there was a hint of distance I couldn't quite decipher.

"This is nothing for a true Alpha," his powerful and somber voice intoned. "Finding your way back should be an easy task."

I stared up at the Alpha before me, clad only in

pants and shoes, his tanned skin exposed to the scorching sun. His dark hair was cropped short, nearly shorn. Every aspect of him exuded power, yet I had never been afraid of him until now, until he regarded me as a disappointment.

"But you're not one," he growled. "Therefore, I leave you at the mercy of the Gods. They will determine your fate."

I blinked rapidly, not comprehending the words fully, but the underlying tone and the look in his eyes instilled fear in me. I backed against the rock, watching as the Alphas began to turn away. They moved once more as a formidable group, but with each step they took, I realized they were not taking me with them.

"Wait!" I called, pushing away from the rock, but one stride for them equaled five for me. Soon, there was nothing but sand before me. "Please!"

My feeble voice held no sway and was quickly lost in the vast landscape. Where was he? Why had he abandoned me? I looked around, hoping to find help, but there was no one in sight.

"Mamma!" I cried. "Mamma!"

But she too failed to appear. I was all alone. Frightened, I hurried back to the spot where the Alpha had left me, curling my small body in on itself. He would come back for me, I assured myself. But as time passed, the sun descended, and darkness settled in, no one returned.

Chapter One
Kiandra

"Fascinating … utterly fascinating," I mused aloud, pacing around the expansive library while clutching a large brown book in my hands. "It's completely—"

"Fascinating?" my sister, Solana, finished for me with a mocking tone.

I turned to her, finding her seated with a small pen, tapping it impatiently against a blank piece of paper while shooting me an annoyed look.

"It truly is," I replied earnestly.

"I do not see the fascination with a big, boring brown book!" she exclaimed in frustration. "And I cannot concentrate on writing my last words down if you keep prattling on about this knowledge you've acquired."

"But this is the solution. Perhaps you won't even need to write down any last words. This might be our salvation!" I exclaimed before I slammed the book down onto the paper.

Solana groaned, reclining in her chair, and then extending her hand, signaling for me to continue.

"Do you see it?" I asked, pointing to the intricate symbols and letters that swirled into the corners of the pages. To the untrained eye, they appeared as nothing more than ornate embellishments, meant to lend the pages a touch of elegance, but I saw through them. I had deciphered their hidden meaning.

"I see you getting yourself worked up over mundane letters and symbols. May I write my letter now before I get rutted on this floor by an Alpha? Or before multiple Alphas rut me?" she retorted, acknowledging the impending storm descending upon our home.

"You're not looking," I scolded her.

"I'm looking," she insisted.

"Look deeper. Into the pages. Follow the lines, do you see it?" I urged.

"I see lines."

"Solana!"

"I know you believe that somehow this library can save us from the fate that has always confined Omegas to a single role: submission to Alphas. But let's face it, this is where you've always ended up, and with the dwindling numbers of Omegas, we've known for a while that this is where our fate would lead us too. So, now I want to prepare," she informed me resolutely.

"But there may be no need!"

"Kiandra, what surrounds our walls right now?" she questioned.

"Um, Alphas."

"And not just any Alphas. That clan, the Tesarian Wolves, despite their numbers, have built a notorious reputation that has spread throughout Verocca. Even we've heard of them. They've crossed the Great Ocean and seek the Omega within these walls. Yet you believe strange letters and symbols are going to save us or our sisters from the life ahead. Who knows how many Alphas we'll have to submit to? Who knows if they won't turn this very room into a feast? We cannot escape what's about to happen. This is our future," she whispered somberly.

"But what if it didn't have to be? What if there was a way out of this?" I countered.

"Perhaps in a dreamland," she retorted, shoving my book away in frustration.

"But—"

"Kiandra, no more. I don't care!"

"But you haven't even looked."

"Fine, what is it you want me to see?" she asked, pulling the book closer once more.

"The lines aren't just lines. They are indicators of hidden tunnels."

"Hidden tunnels? Here?"

"Yes, here. They were built by our ancestors, and they made escape routes."

"Why would our father never tell us this?" she questioned.

"Maybe he never knew, but it's right here, even concealed within the text: 'When terror reigns, deep in the heart of home, you'll find the way to the light'."

"Seems like an insignificant poem to me," she replied skeptically.

"No, it's a message. I just need to decipher it."

"Oh, so you're not even certain about the existence of these tunnels?" she pressed.

"I..." I hesitated, my confidence waning.

"You don't know where the entrance is, do you, sister?" she asked me pointedly.

"Well, I'm searching," I conceded.

"It will be a miracle if those doors aren't opened later in the night," she reminded me. "They've waited us out, and we no longer have any more food. They've cut off our water supply. The city is hungry and demanding we give the Alphas what they want: us, the princesses."

"I know, but I just need a little more time," I informed her.

"There is no more time, Kiandra. Let it be."

Solana pushed back my book so she could continue writing what she called her "last words", though none of us believed anyone would ever read them. I understood that this was how my sister coped with the looming future, but I couldn't bear to see them suffer a fate they had never asked for.

I grabbed the book and left the library, my sanctuary, before walking through the torch-lit hallways. The servants' and guards' eyes followed me. It was a rare sight to see me wandering around, but I was on an important mission to find these secret tunnels. I barely paid attention to where I was going, my eyes fixed on the words and symbols before me as I mumbled to myself.

"That could be a left by the Aradia statue … or perhaps down the corridor of kings…" I turned a corner, lost in my thoughts, and passed by the beautiful portrait of our mother.

Even though I often lost touch with the world when engrossed in a book, somehow my body knew when I was passing her portrait. I froze, turned my head, and gazed up at the woman depicted in the painting. Her hair had been so blond it was almost white, and her eyes the bluest of blues. But it was her radiant smile that drew you in. Even immortalized in the portrait, her smile made it difficult to look away. For an Alpha to lose an Omega, one he loved so deeply, I knew it must have been a terrible struggle for our father to continue in this world for as long as he did. But there was no denying that after losing his Omega, his body began giving up faster. He shouldn't have left us as soon as he did, but the heart desired what it desired, and it called for someone who was no longer with us.

"I could use some guidance," I whispered as I reached out to touch the portrait. When we were younger, we weren't allowed to touch it, but after he passed away, that was the first thing I did. I touched her portrait, hoping to feel some connection, but there was nothing. I felt the roughness of the canvas, but there was no warmth as you would find in a living body.

I sighed and let the tips of my fingers graze the canvas before letting my hand fall away.

"I must do something," I murmured, my voice barely above a whisper. "I know what will happen to them. Once the Tesarian Wolves breach the city walls, it will be a swift takeover. Your daughters will be left at the mercy of those Alphas."

I knew the portrait wouldn't provide answers, but speaking to it somehow calmed my racing nerves. Despite the castle being distant from the walls, which were surrounded by tents, it felt as if the attackers had already infiltrated the premises.

Soon, this place would be overrun, and it would never be our home again. This only fueled my determination to find a solution to save my sisters. I gazed at the symbols and delicate writing, pondering the meaning of "the way to the light." It spoke of home, but what defined home besides the very walls I was already trapped within? My eyes turned to the portrait again, seeking guidance, yet there was nothing but silence from it. I returned my attention to the book, ready to resume my search through the long hallways, when an idea struck me.

"Home," I whispered, turning back to my mother's portrait. "But that's ridiculous."

The tunnels had been constructed centuries ago. Why would my mother symbolize home? Could it be that something else had once hung in this very spot? I reached out, touching the portrait again. Many of the books I had read spoke of hidden passages concealed behind seemingly ordinary covers. But would my father truly choose a picture to hide what lay beneath? Did this imply that he had always possessed knowledge of the tunnels?

Questions swirled in my mind as I slid my finger to the side of the portrait. With bated breath, I pushed, but when it didn't yield to the slight pressure, I exerted more force. The portrait tilted, sliding off the thick nail it had been hanging on. A loud crash reverberated through the hallway as it hit the floor. I let out a scream, dropping the book to the floor, as the portrait tumbled toward me. I instinctively raised my arms to shield myself, but another loud thud echoed, and I felt no pain. Slowly lowering my arms, I saw the picture hanging above me, having collided with the opposite wall instead of me. I breathed a sigh of relief, grateful not to have been crushed beneath my mother's portrait.

I bent down to pick up the book and prepared to seek help in rehanging the portrait when, as I glanced at the wall where it had hung, I noticed something unusual. It was subtle, just a small crack, but the crack was perfectly straight, making it appear out of place. I approached, running my finger along it, and then I felt it—a faint breeze coming from the other side.

I attempted to wedge my fingers into the crack, but it wouldn't give way. I placed the book down and dug my fingers into the opening. It loosened a little but refused to open further. Moving my fingers lower, I realized the crack was expanding. The wall was not made of the same stone as the surrounding area. It was covered with a thin layer of softer material and colored to blend in. I pushed lower, sliding my fingers through the crack, making it wider. When I reached the bottom, I moved upward, sliding my fingers over the top part of the door. Then, I returned to the side and began pulling. This time, the door creaked and began to open slightly. I was sweating and panting, using every ounce of my Omega strength to pry it open. Finally, it released with a pop, sending me stumbling back and nearly tripping over myself. I clung to the door to regain my balance before cautiously peering around its edge.

Inside, I found nothing but a dark, narrow corridor. It was so small that an Alpha would have to kneel to navigate it, and even then, their broad bodies might get stuck. Even a Beta would have difficulty passing through. That's when I realized the true purpose of these tunnels—they were designed to ensure that precious Omegas could escape.

I reached down and grabbed my book, flipping through the pages to the section with the lines and symbols that might help me navigate the tunnels. However, just like finding the hidden door, deciphering the guidance in this book proved to be a challenging task. I sighed in frustration, aware that time was running out before the walls would be breached.

My older sister's warnings echoed in my mind. The hungry citizens blamed us for their plight, unable to provide for them. With the water supply cut off and the sweltering heat, the people would undoubtedly seek an escape, and my sisters would become the currency for that freedom.

"Well, those who do not dare to walk into the unknown might miss the treasures lying at the end," I whispered to myself, reciting a line from my favorite fairytale. I might not be a powerful warrior queen, but I refused to be a coward. Or so I tried to convince myself as I ventured further into the darkness, clutching a tiny candleholder with a flickering flame. I closed the door behind me, concealing my secret passage for now, and then scanned my surroundings in the dim light, feeling the cool breeze brush over my skin.

"Follow the wind," I told myself, believing there must be an opening somewhere in the tunnel. I proceeded down the long, narrow corridor, goose bumps prickling my skin, and the occasional cobweb brushing against my face. I spat and grumbled, swatting them away before continuing my journey. Small droplets of water ran down the stone walls, making the air increasingly humid and stifling. I forced myself to push through the suffocating feeling and the pounding in my chest, realizing that, after walking for a while, I had no idea where I was.

"Oh, by the Gods," I whispered, my voice echoing through the echoing hallways. "No, focus on the book. You can find your way out."

I urged myself to remain calm as I studied the intricate lines and symbols. I noticed one line that started beneath the word "light" and wound its way through the letters, eventually connecting with the word "lower."

"'Lower', as in lower ground?" I wondered aloud.

I continued to follow the line as it climbed higher, connecting with the word "top." My heart pounded as I traced the line to its final destination.

"'Knowledge'. What does 'knowledge' mean in this context?"

I tapped the back of the book with my finger as I held it in one hand, carefully considering my options. My surroundings revealed a crossroads, and I glanced at the lines and symbols in the book, trying to make sense of them. One path led lower, while the other climbed higher. Following the higher route seemed promising, as it could potentially lead me to the elusive "knowledge" I needed to decipher. But first, I had to explore the lower path. I turned right and followed the tunnel, although I couldn't discern if I was truly moving belowground. The darkness and thick air seemed to consume me, making it increasingly difficult to breathe. I quickened my pace, a hasty decision that only intensified the rapid beating of my heart.

"Slow down! Slow down!" I admonished myself, desperately trying to regain control over my racing body.

My body obediently froze at my command, and I took deep, calming breaths while watching the candle in my hand flicker. The wax had been steadily dripping, a clear indication that I had been walking for a considerable amount of time. I ignored the stinging sensation on my fingers as some of the wax had hit my skin, focusing on steadying my mind and body.

"You're almost there," I reassured myself, mustering the determination to take another step forward.

As I continued down the hallway, I noticed a gradual increase in brightness. I couldn't quite comprehend how my surroundings were becoming clearer, but upon reaching the end of the tunnel, I discovered the source. High above, a clear, thick opening allowed sunlight to stream inside. It was a significantly wider crack, casting better illumination on my surroundings. I reached up, pushing my fingers through the opening to feel the invigorating breeze. Could it be...? I hesitated to complete the thought.

Instead, I pressed against the wall, grunting and exerting all my strength. The door remained stubbornly locked. I glanced down, searching for any obstacles, but nothing obstructed the path. My attention then shifted to the side of the door, where I spotted a thick iron rod wedged between two rocks. I extended my arm between the rocks and managed to grasp the iron rod. With determination, I lifted it and then slid it back, causing the lock to release.

The echoing sound of the door unlocking resonated through the tunnels. A smile crossed my lips as I pushed the door open with ease this time, allowing the powerful ocean wind to sweep me back. My long, dark-brown hair billowed behind me, and my dress fluttered in the breeze as I gazed at the vast blue sky and the waves below. I stood at a slight incline, the tunnel's exit concealed within a cave. I nodded in approval, grateful to my ancestors for their clever construction.

Chapter Two
Kiandra

My search was far from over, but with newfound answers in hand, I couldn't wait to share the news. I hurried back, nearly taking a wrong turn as I eagerly made my way toward the part of the tunnel that held the "knowledge" I sought. Fortunately, I managed to correct my course and stayed on the right path. I was determined to find my sisters after uncovering this intriguing section of the book.

As I reached the end of the tunnel leading to knowledge, I noticed that there was no crack or lock this time. I pushed against the door, but it refused to budge. Frustration welled up inside me. It seemed this door to knowledge was more mysterious or perhaps aptly symbolic—knowledge was, after all, a form of power.

In my despair, I sighed and leaned against the stone wall, resigning myself to the possibility that I might never learn what knowledge meant in this context. However, as I leaned against the wall, something gave way. The sound of stone sliding against stone echoed around me. I quickly pushed away from the wall and turned to see that one of the stones behind me had been pushed inward. Simultaneously, I heard a click, and I cautiously approached the door in front of me.

Uncertain if what I had heard indicated an opening, I reached out tentatively and pushed the door forward. To my delight, it moved, allowing light to stream inside. I stepped out and found myself in a very familiar place.

"Knowledge," I chuckled. "Of course."

Surrounding me were hundreds of ancient scrolls, books, and texts. I should have guessed that the tunnel would lead me back to my home. I turned to look at the door, which now appeared as part of a bookshelf. It was remarkably well-hidden. However, I reminded myself about the need to have someone replace the portrait to conceal the entrance again.

I hurried between the tall bookshelves, entering the front part of the library. I found Solana still hunched over her paper, diligently writing her last words. When she heard my approaching footsteps, she slowly turned, her eyes widening in surprise. She quickly glanced at the double doors in the opposite direction and then back at me.

"But how are you coming from that direction? I saw you leave through there," she pointed out, using her feather pen to gesture between me and the doors.

I smiled, my excitement bubbling over as I walked around her and slammed the book onto the table in front of her. She jumped, her eyes locked on me as if I were a madwoman.

"What?" she whispered.

"Burn the letter," I urged her.

"These are my last words. Why would I burn it?"

"Because I've found the secret tunnels."

"Not this again." She sighed, clearly uninterested.

"But it's true."

"Could you...?" Solana seemed utterly defeated, pushing my book away and resuming her writing. I looked at her with confusion, uncertain what to do next.

"Solana, I'm not lying!"

"Sure, you aren't," she retorted, her tone dismissive. "Just like when you found the ghost who haunted the southern parts of the castle."

"I was ten years old, that's unfair," I snapped, crossing my arms. "And I had read about the legend of her."

"Yes, yes," she deflected, no longer willing to listen.

"Solana, come with me, and I'll show you."

"I'd rather write in peace," she firmly replied.

"But it's true!"

"Maybe to you it is," she spat, turning to look up at me. "But that's because you won't be sacrificed like the rest of us."

"Solana, I'm trying to—"

"You're nothing but a librarian mouse, hidden away, while the rest of us will be war prizes, meant to be taken over and over, whether we desire it or not. You can dance around, be excited about your books, but some of us have other things to attend to, such as preparing for our unavoidable fate."

"Solana..."

"I just want to write in peace. Could you please?" She waved her hand dismissively, making it clear she wanted to be alone.

My heart broke. Seeing the look on my sister's face, the way she averted her eyes, I knew she was scared. Normally, Solana was so composed, and nothing made her emotions flare. But in this moment, I saw her eyes nervously shifting back and forth, and her shoulders seemed tense.

"Kiandra!" she exclaimed in frustration.

"I-I will go speak to Vivina," I said, slowly slipping out of the library, making as little noise as possible.

I glanced back, seeing my sister still engrossed in her writing. I retraced my steps down the hallways that led me to the tunnels. When I reached the spot where the portrait was being replaced, my eldest sister, the queen, stood observing the process, her long golden hair flowing wildly as she shook her head in irritation.

"Vivina!" I called, hurrying over to her.

"Do you see this?" she snapped, pointing at the portrait. "Someone pulled it off. Who dares to disgrace the former queen in such a way?"

"Well, about that—"

"Have you seen Cassia?" she interrupted.

"No, I only know where Solana is," I explained.

"That girl … did you know she has been spending time learning archery?"

"I did not know, but Cassia is strong-willed," I reminded my sister.

"But did you know it has been going on for a year?"

"No, I did not."

"She has been fearful that since our father passed away, I may not be able to take care of us."

"Well..."

"I might not be an Alpha, and I know who is banging on our doors at this very moment, but I will never allow my sisters to be hurt. If I must, I will take it all upon myself," she declared, leaving me speechless as her powerful words resonated with me.

I watched her as she turned toward the guards, who were putting the portrait back in place. She was the spitting image of our mother, yet she possessed a fire not seen in many Omegas. She stood with her arms crossed, her long, soft pink dress accentuating her magnificent figure that would make any Alpha drool. Yet her scent was as uninteresting as mine. However, she couldn't hide her dynamic, no matter how much strength she displayed or how she masked her alluring aroma.

"Vivina," I called, and she slowly turned to me, her light blue eyes softening as she gazed at me.

"Yes?"

"I … um, found something," I began, but my

sister quickly turned unfocused.

"Where did you say Solana was?" she interrupted.

"In the library."

"What is she doing there?"

"Writing."

"Writing? She is writing poetry now?"

"No, she calls it her last words," I informed her. "It's sort of strange to me. I mean, I understand she must have anger that needs to come out, but … Vivina!"

I called after my older sister, seeing her storm past me. I did not understand the sudden change and decided to follow as well. She ran back the way I had come, pushed open the double doors, and shocked some Masters working in there. However, Solana merely glanced up from the table she was sitting at, a long sigh escaping her lips.

"This place is supposed to remain quiet," she informed us.

Vivina walked determinedly over to Solana, snatched the paper from her, and forced the pen to slide, creating an awful line across it.

"Now you have ruined it," she said, her voice cold and detached.

Vivina began pacing in front of Solana, tapping a finger against the arm connected to the paper. She read what Solana had written, yet there was a strange energy in the room. I could not comprehend what was happening. Solana seemed defeated, yet Vivina appeared furious. I was about to inquire with her about the letter when she let out an angry shriek before throwing the paper at Solana.

"How *dare* you?" Vivina yelled at my third eldest sister.

She leaned forward, placing her hands on the table, her jewelry clicking together and creating an even more powerful feeling of pure rage.

"I am merely viewing this situation in the proper way," Solana spat.

"Taking your life? Is that the way to handle this?"

"It's the only way to handle this."

"Wait, that is what you have been working on?" I questioned, walking forward and snatching the paper from the ground.

I thought it was meant as a cathartic ritual. Instead, my own sister had been literally scribbling down the last words she would ever speak to anyone. How had I not noticed? I knew I could be unattached to the world around me, but this seemed almost mortifying that I could let something like this pass. I walked forward, holding up the paper.

"Have you been ingesting something?" I inquired.

"Are you calling me insane?" she snapped.

"I am merely asking if you have been taking something that would make you temporarily crazy!" I yelled.

"I have been eating what I have been served and not ingesting anything."

"Have you felt lightheaded? Confused? Is your heat close?"

"If my heat was close, then I would already be out on the other side of the walls with my legs spread and ready for an Alpha to rut me," she retorted.

"This is not the time for laughter and sarcasm!" Vivina shouted.

"Am I laughing? Has any of us laughed for weeks since this waiting-us-out siege began?" Solana countered. "We aren't laughing. We are just waiting and waiting, and I am slightly going crazy. But I would rather hang myself or throw my body off these walls than ever let an Alpha or Alphas do whatever they wanted to me. We know the stories. We know how lucky our mother was to find a proper Alpha, but who knows the wild beasts waiting out there to take us, violate us!"

Vivina sighed, and some of her anger dissipated, as did mine. Solana had every right to be afraid. Not only had the numbers of Omegas dwindled over the years, but the desperation to have one grew as well.

"Solana, we will find a solution. No one will touch you," I assured her, but she turned her head to me, glaring at me.

"It's so easy for you to say. No one outside these walls knows what the fuck you are."

"Solana!" Vivina scolded.

"No one even outside this library knows what she is," Solana continued. "While we get taken over and over, she can walk around freely. Never having to worry!"

Solana stood up, the chair scraping against the floor as she glanced between us.

"I refuse to become any Alpha's Omega, forever in service to his needs! I am my *own*!" she yelled, her voice shaking and shocking the silent Masters behind us.

She stormed past us, Vivina yelling after her, before shaking her head and rubbing her forehead.

"She will be the death of me," she sighed.

"Someone should follow her, just to ensure that..."

"I will," Vivina said and turned on her heel before stopping and gazing at me. "Find Cassia. I want her close. I want you all close."

"Yes, I will go look for her."

Chapter Three
Kiandra

The sun was setting, and an inexplicable feeling washed over me, as if it might be the last sunset I would ever witness. I recognized it as an irrational notion, but it lingered as I searched for my sister. I scoured numerous rooms, feeling like I had explored every corner of the castle before arriving at a small training ground near the vast garden. Laughter reached my ears, drawing me closer.

As I entered the training area, I saw a group of guards indulging in merriment, seemingly oblivious to the impending threat to their princess. They watched as a smaller guard expertly fired arrows at a distant target. Though their hair was tightly bound at the nape of their neck, I recognized that form and silhouette, and I instinctively prepared to mimic Vivina's stern scolding. However, I froze when Cassia's arrow struck the target's bullseye flawlessly.

"By the Gods," I murmured aloud, and the entire group turned to look at me.

I watched as the color drained from Cassia's face, leaving her pale. But she quickly regained her composure, a mischievous smile gracing her lips.

"Let me guess. The queen demands my presence?" she teased.

"She does," I confirmed.

"Well, the queen can wait. I'm practicing."

"That's hardly practice fit for a princess," I reminded her.

Cassia's smile broadened as she approached. She wasn't as tall as Vivina, but she still stood a few inches taller than me. Clad in the thick brown leather garments worn by all guards, she appeared broader as well.

"And what does a librarian like yourself know about being a princess?" she teased, her eyes challenging me.

I sighed, rolling my own. She was aware that I couldn't openly acknowledge our true relationship as sisters, but she enjoyed pushing the boundaries.

"Well?" she prodded, gently pressing the end of her bow against my chin, and tilting my head backward.

I couldn't afford to show disrespect, but I conveyed my silent message through my eyes, warning her not to push too far. She lowered the bow, her smile taking on a sweeter look. It was clear that her words and actions were all in good fun.

"I suppose I have no choice," she said and sighed theatrically.

"You can't hide."

"Not all of us can, anyway," she groaned before turning to the guards.

She tossed the bow to one of them and then began making her way toward the castle. I hurried after her, but the strength in her legs propelled her forward much faster.

"Could you slow down?" I requested.

"You tell me the queen needs me, and now you want me to wait for you?" She chuckled.

"I didn't say she needed you."

Cassia abruptly halted, causing me to collide with her well-armored back. I rubbed my nose to ease the pain as Cassia slowly turned to face me.

"What?" she inquired.

"What?" I echoed.

"So, Vivina doesn't need me?" she questioned.

"Well, she wants you nearby."

"Nearby?" Cassia laughed, a hint of mockery in

her tone. "I'm not a child! I don't need my older sister to hold my hand while we're besieged by an army of Alphas."

"I'm aware."

"I'd rather prepare to fight than sit by her side and smile, only to be forced onto my hands and knees by a damn Alpha."

"She just wants to keep all of you safe," I reminded her. "Besides, Vivina is ready to bear the burden herself to ensure none of you have to suffer."

"But we will have to. Once those doors come crashing down, we lose all power. And despite Father being protective of us, you know he would have eventually surrendered us to an Alpha. That's the way of our world—Omegas submit, and Alphas lead."

She spat out the last part, her anger obvious, and I empathized with her frustration. However, I was determined that none of my sisters would ever be forced into servitude. I had learned the secrets of the tunnels and how to keep them safe, and I was resolved to ensure their protection. Yet, I hesitated to inform them separately. Solana had already demonstrated her reluctance to listen to me, as she believed no one truly acknowledged my existence. I knew I needed to prove the knowledge I had acquired, and it would be easier to convey this information if they were all together.

"You will find a way out," I reassured her.

Cassia's voice was laced with desperation as she asked, "Do you see one? Do you see our salvation?"

I faltered, not having a clear answer. I looked around at our surroundings, trying to find a glimmer of hope.

"I..." I began, but Cassia's frustration overtook her.

"I would do anything to trade places with you.

Why didn't Father simply write us all off as stillborn babies?" she lamented.

"My circumstances were unique," I whispered, my gaze fixed on the ground.

There was a moment of silence, and then I felt Cassia's hand on my shoulder. I raised my head, seeing a small, sad smile on her lips.

"I'm sorry," she said gently.

I met her gaze and shook my head slightly.

"It was uncalled for," she whispered. "I know you never had the privilege to meet our mother. I should not have thrown that at you."

"But that doesn't mean you had her for long," I pointed out.

"I had her longer," Cassia admitted.

I nodded slightly, not wanting to delve into the painful topic of our mother.

"I just meant that things would have been easier if he had written us off as stillborn too," Cassia explained.

"You may be some of the last known Omegas," I countered. "It would have been a grave loss for him to do that to all of you."

"Nevertheless, it would have been easier," Cassia conceded.

I nodded again, acknowledging that I did not bear the same burdens as my sisters.

"Yet, we do know how to mask our scents because of you," she added, attempting to inject some humor into the conversation. "Perhaps once those Alphas barge in here and catch a whiff of our blended scent, it might give them second thoughts."

"I fear it will take more than that." I sighed.

"Maybe, but it's a great way to tell them to shove it where the sun doesn't shine, right?" She chuckled and playfully shook me. However, something had changed in

Cassia. Her grip was unusually tight, and her strength seemed to have grown. I had to reach out and grab her wrist to stop her from shaking me so hard. She looked at me, puzzled. "What's wrong?"

"You're hurting me!" I told her.

"Oh, I'm so sorry."

"What have you been doing? Or should I ask, what have you been eating? Omegas aren't normally this strong," I groaned, rubbing my sore shoulder.

"I might have done some secret training to prepare myself for the day we have to defend ourselves," she admitted.

"Does Vivina know?" I asked.

"What part of 'secret training' didn't you understand? Aren't you supposed to be the smart one?"

"Is it wise?" I inquired.

"If I must submit to an Alpha, he will see my strength first," Cassia explained with a smirk.

Cassia chuckled as she turned and walked away. I massaged my shoulder and followed her into the castle. I had been certain she was going to change her attire, but instead, she marched toward the large meeting room, believing she might find Vivina and Solana there. As expected, both were waiting, with Vivina trying to comfort Solana as they sat together at the table. Vivina's hand rested on Solana's shoulder. However, when our eldest sister noticed the armor Cassia was wearing, she leaped from her chair, anger blazing in her eyes once more.

"What in the Gods' name are you wearing?" Vivina demanded.

"Oh, this?" Cassia asked, rapping her fist against the armor on her chest, producing hollow thuds.

"Obviously!" Vivina snapped.

"It's called armor, and if you were all as clever as

me, you'd be wearing it."

"That's not suitable attire for a princess."

"Well, I'd do anything not to be one at the moment, but if I can't change my inheritance, I can at least change my appearance," Cassia retorted.

"We must stand united against this intrusion and the Alphas. We will not bow, but we cannot be seen as…" Vivina struggled to find the right words to describe Cassia, her face turning red as she held her breath and gestured wildly toward the second eldest princess.

"What? As a common guard? Maybe if they mistake me for one, I can walk right past their army," Cassia quipped.

"Guards are not women!" Vivina reminded her.

"Perhaps I should shave off all my hair then," Cassia retorted.

Vivina groaned, rubbing her eyes. "Don't you understand the importance of unity?"

"I do, I just don't see how dressing up as pretty Omega princesses and sitting around doing *nothing* will help show unity," Cassia spat.

"That's because you haven't been listening to a word I've been saying. Unity doesn't come from displaying obvious strength or power. It comes from inner strength. If we sit here, waiting for them to enter, with our chins held high, it shows we are not afraid, and unless we are forcibly removed, we will not move," Vivina explained.

"But what does my clothing have to do with us waiting on the thrones?"

"It makes you appear rebellious."

"So does my armor!"

"But we also need to be seen as composed," Vivina emphasized, glancing between Solana and Cassia, who both found it difficult to meet her eyes. "Putting on armor or writing farewell letters will not show that we are. It shows weakness because it will mean they have pushed us so hard that we find ourselves trapped. They already see us as meek Omegas. Shall we truly give them the satisfaction and confirm their belief?"

Solana and Cassia shook their heads almost simultaneously.

"No, we must show them we are not weak Omegas. We will face whatever happens with our heads held high. Are we all in agreement?"

"Yes."

"Yes."

Vivina turned to me next, and I snapped out of my trance.

"Me?"

"You are still our sister, no matter what the royal documents say," she told me, giving me a small smile.

"I will always stand by your side," I promised. "Even if I can't stand with you."

"That's good to hear," Vivina acknowledged. "But it is probably best if you find somewhere safe. I have even arranged for a guard and horse. I believe that you—"

"Run away?" I interrupted.

"You have a chance. No one can predict what will happen to the servants here. Just because you aren't regarded as an Omega doesn't mean you're exempt from harm as a woman," Vivina said.

I found her words confusing, not entirely grasping their meaning.

"It means you can still be fucked," Cassia clarified bluntly.

"Cassia!" Vivina scolded her for her crude language.

"Oh…" I mumbled, beginning to understand.

"Perhaps ... perhaps it would be best if you waited—" Vivina started to suggest.

"No! I'm with you. I will make sure no harm befalls you," I assured them.

"Kiandra, that is very sweet, but—" Vivina began to object.

"No, I have a plan."

"A plan?"

"If we prepare now, we can all leave," I explained.

"How so?"

"I found secret escape tunnels that I believe our ancestors created for emergencies, for Omegas needing to escape. They're small, dark, and confusing, but I know the way now. I have the book!"

"The book?"

"Yes, the book!"

"Not the one from the library," Solana groaned, slumping further down in her chair.

"Yes, the library. I'll go get it. I can show you everything. Just pack and prepare, and let's meet here," I urged them.

"Kiandra, I don't understand a thing."

"Listen, the tunnels lead to a secret escape point right by the ocean. We could truly disappear, and they wouldn't know what happened to us!" I exclaimed.

"She is making it up. It's the ghost again," Solana sighed.

"It's real! I have found them."

"Kiandra," Vivina began, doubt clear in her voice.

"Just let me prove it," I insisted. "Let me show you that I can be of help. I haven't spent all those years studying books and ancient scripts for nothing. Let me be of use."

Vivina looked uncertain, her eyes darting to

Solana, who shook her head. But when she turned back to me, I knew she saw the pleading gaze in my eyes.

"Let's see this book," she conceded.

"Just wait. It's going to be worth it."

Vivina nodded, yet I could still see the doubt in her eyes. However, she would not have to worry. I would make sure they were all safe. So I rushed to the library. I entered with determination, but when I reached the table where the book had been, it was gone. I looked around in panic, unsure of what had happened to it. I called out to a Master who walked over to me.

"I had a book here. An ancient book of the secret passageways of the castle," I informed him.

"It was returned to its proper place," he told me.

"But I need it!" I exclaimed in desperation.

"Then you'll have to find it."

"But I can't remember where I took it from. I barely remember which section," I said, surveying the extensive library with growing anxiety. I had grabbed the book by accident, and now it was lost in the place I normally considered my sanctuary. "Can you tell me which shelf?"

The Master led me to the back of the library, then gestured to a long row of old brown books, all seemingly identical.

"It should be here," he stated.

"But which shelf?" I demanded.

"One of these."

"How can you not know which one?"

"Because I don't know which edition you're referring to. All of these discuss secret passageways in one form or another," he explained.

All of these discuss secret passageways? I thought to myself as I gazed at the rows of books. Were the passageways not a secret after all?

Chapter Four
Cartan

I watched the towering walls in front of me, my gaze fixed on the massive gates. It wouldn't be long now. The air was thick with fear and despair, and the people within those walls were growing increasingly desperate for a taste of normalcy, yearning to escape the feeling of being hunted.

Soon, those imposing gates would swing open, and we would overtake the city without losing a single man. There was nothing more destructive than the turmoil within a person's own mind, and all I had to do was wait, watch, and be patient. I smiled as the sun dipped below the horizon, leaving only torchlight to pierce the gathering darkness. A deep silence descended upon us all.

The stillness was shattered by the sound of footsteps echoing on the well-worn path leading to the magnificent city. I turned my head, catching sight of Tyros approaching. He was dressed like any of the Tesarian Wolves, bare-chested with leather straps holding his weapons and dark pants. The weather in Verocca was chillier compared to our homeland, yet it did not bother us. We had crossed the Great Sea to find this island where the princesses were hidden, and our prize was within reach.

"High Alpha," he greeted as he came to stand beside me, his eyes fixed on the sandy-colored walls.

"Any concerns?" I inquired.

"Mainly impatience. They're growing weary of waiting," he informed me.

"It won't be much longer. I must admit they've lasted beyond my expectations. But they're tired, thirsty, and hungry. They'll give up their treasures to save themselves," I remarked.

"We're aware, but some skirmishes have started breaking out," Tyros added.

I sighed and shook my head, understanding the Alphas' pent-up aggression. If we couldn't spill blood, it needed an alternative outlet.

"Should I handle it personally?" I asked, glancing at my oldest friend, who smiled and shook his head.

"I've already dealt with it myself. I tied them to a pole at midday and let them burn," he said, making me chuckle.

"Good."

I turned my attention back to the walls, noticing the guards up there who had been observing us as we observed them. They changed positions occasionally, but their shifts had become more frequent as weariness set in. I relished the subtle signs of their vulnerability beginning to emerge.

"They are indeed a peaceful city. They even have Beta guards," Tyros remarked.

"I'm aware. They're not warriors. They have Omega leaders, after all," I pointed out.

"Perhaps some of the last Omegas left." He sighed.

"Yes, and once I bring them back with us, things will undoubtedly change."

"They certainly will. No one believed Omegas would walk on our land again. The clan leaders were certainly wrong to doubt you. So few survive the Black Desert, and even fewer as children," Tyros acknowledged.

However, there was no need for me to recount the challenges I had faced as a child. I knew what I had endured, but it had led me here. I was about to lay my eyes on the last court of Omegas. Their father had been a smart Alpha, never letting them out of his sight. But with no male heir to protect them, they were defenseless.

"It doesn't matter what I survived, as long as I continue to," I declared.

"And you will."

"Fearing my death?" I teased him, turning my head.

He smiled a little, his mouth opening as if to continue the banter when another sound interrupted us. We both turned our heads, hearing the giant brown doors beginning to open.

"It's happening," Tyros whispered.

Indeed it was, I thought.

"Go back to camp and prepare the others," I instructed. "Tonight, we celebrate."

A wide smile spread across his lips as Tyros turned away to inform the rest of the army. I strode forward, approaching a group of Beta guards who had gathered around a few elder wolves. I stopped right in front of them, looming over them all. The elders wore golden chains with a wolf pendant around their necks, signifying their importance, perhaps as advisors to the queen. But tonight, it wasn't their queen they were pledging loyalty to.

"Alpha Cartan," one of them began, bowing his head slightly. He was an elder Beta with grey hair, dressed in fine blue and white clothes. Despite his respectful words, the disdain in his eyes was evident. In their minds, I was nothing more than a barbarian. But I paid little heed to their opinions. I wanted what I had come to claim.

"Well?" I pressed.

"We ask you once more to leave our city alone," one of the elder Betas requested.

"You already have my answer. It has not changed since the last time you sent a messenger to me."

They exchanged nervous glances, well aware they had few options.

"I want the princesses," I growled, leaning forward, and watched as they all took a step back. Even their guards lacked the courage to confront me, instead following their elders. "So?"

They exchanged glances once more, but their eyes then settled on something behind me. I could sense that my army was starting to assemble. Nervous twitches appeared on their faces before they turned to each other, nodding in agreement.

"This city is peaceful. There is no need for bloodshed," the eldest Beta told me.

"Do not worry. I have done my research," I assured them. With that, I pushed past them, shoving the elder men to the side so I could enter the city.

The moment I crossed the threshold, I paused, inhaling the air and savoring the sweet taste of victory. I continued forward, with my army keeping a little distance. We strolled through the city, observing the residents poking their heads out of their homes to watch us. No one dared stand in our way, and anyone still on the streets quickly scurried indoors to hide. A smile spread across my lips as I continued through the city, following the main road that led to the castle at the far end.

The guards standing in front of the castle doors stepped aside, surrendering. They even lowered their heads in acknowledgment of their new leader as I pushed open the massive doors and beheld the magnificent interior, which was truly fitting for a princess.

However, a scream pierced the air, causing me to turn my head. I saw a servant who had dropped a basket filled with fruits and was now fleeing in the opposite direction. I knew chaos was about to erupt. As more of my army entered the castle, I felt the energy shift, a primal need to conquer and claim everything in sight.

"Gather all the servants and kill the guards," I ordered.

While I had assured the elders there would be no bloodshed on the streets, I couldn't take such risks within the castle. I couldn't be certain that the guards weren't fiercely loyal to their princesses. After all, they would have been carefully selected for their positions, so I needed to assert complete control.

All the Alphas spread out in various directions, and soon the sound of screams filled the air. I ascended the staircase directly ahead, heading for the highest floor. I wasn't entirely sure where the princesses would be, but if the rumors about their queen were true, she would be awaiting my arrival. She was reputed to be a cold beauty who wouldn't bow to any man, but she hadn't encountered an Alpha like me. I was determined to bring that queen to her knees.

I stormed down a long hallway, believing it led to a throne room. However, when I pushed open the double doors, with Tyros following closely behind me along with a few other Alphas, I was surprised to find no thrones within. Instead, there was only a simple fire burning in a lowered pit at the center of the room, along with a few statues lining the walls. In the middle stood the group of Omegas. It appeared the queen had chosen to have her sisters with her, huddled behind her.

She stood in the front, challenging me with her eyes, and I smiled at the sight of it. She was certainly full of fire and a beauty indeed. All the princesses were dressed in incredibly fine dresses, their hair colors ranging from light blond to light brown. The queen was the tallest, positioned like a wall in front of the others.

The smallest clung to her arm, while the middle child stood with her arms crossed, wearing an interestingly defiant look in her eyes too. She certainly had spirit too, didn't she? However, I would leave the task of taming her to one of the other clan leaders. They would undoubtedly have their work cut out for them, much like I did with the Omega in front of me.

I took a step closer, but before I could advance any further, I noticed something amiss.

"Why can't I smell any of you?" I snarled. My Alpha instincts grew irritated at being denied what had been so clearly described as the most heavenly scent—the scent of an Omega.

The queen raised her head high, grinning. "Perhaps you've found the wrong princesses."

I smiled a little, approaching her. She pushed her sisters back, demonstrating that she wasn't afraid to meet me head-on. My Alpha instincts growled inside me, craving her submission, but I knew it would come. I would show the headstrong queen what happened when she didn't show obedience to an Alpha.

"No, you're the right ones," I growled as I leaned forward, bringing our faces within inches of each other. "But you have done something to yourself. You think this will hide you? Somehow save you?"

She did not respond to my taunts. Instead, she simply gazed up at me with a defiant look. I let my eyes slowly move from her to the other two behind her.

"Someone is missing," I murmured. While the queen maintained her composure admirably, I noticed a slight twitch of fear in her eyes.

"Missing?" she questioned. "You have us. We are here. We are not fighters, and we will go with you peacefully."

"I know you will," I replied in a mocking tone,

then held up four fingers. "But there are supposed to be four of you."

"There are only three."

"Your mother gave birth to four Omegas," I reminded her.

"Well, if you had studied our history, you would know that the fourth Omega took our mother's life, and together they journeyed to the realm of the Gods to rest for eternity," she countered, her voice calm. Yet she couldn't completely hide the slight increase in her heartbeat.

"I have studied you. I always study my enemies, and therefore I know that while it was written that the fourth died in childbirth, the very document never received the declaration seal which confirms the truth of the words. There is a fourth, and you will tell me where she is."

"There is no fourth! We lost a sister and a mother many moons ago, and it destroyed our father's mind. You have us! That should be enough!" she yelled.

"No, no, no," I told her, shaking my head, and seeing her confidence slightly waver. "I know there are four. Four Omegas left, and I want them all. Queen Vivina, tell me now, and I will ensure the fourth is treated with respect and kindness."

"Kindness?" she laughed. "Respect? If there is one thing us Omegas have learned from our mothers, grandmothers, and ancestors, it's that there is no such thing as respect for Omegas. Not from Alphas who desire only one thing from us. From the time we overflowed these lands, we were used for nothing but pleasure and breeding, and even now, with so few of us left, we know the same fate awaits us. There is no fourth. There are only us!"

"Liar!" I growled. My voice changed again as I

circled her, making her feel like the prey she was, the small Omega. I knew it would draw out her submissive side. Yet despite her body starting to shake and her instincts begging her to surrender, she turned her head and met my eyes. She was a powerful one, and it made me snap at the air, my canines growing sharper. I growled darkly, the rumbling spreading from my chest and into my throat. But she did not want to show me her submission.

"There are three," she repeated. "Take what you can get and do not let greed overshadow true value."

I smiled a little, finding it amusing that the queen would think now was the time to provide me with a lesson. She had no comprehension of who she was standing in front of, but she would learn.

Chapter Five
Kiandra

"I found you!" I exclaimed loudly, finally locating the book I had been searching for. I descended the narrow ladder, the steps creaking and showing their age, but I had no time to be cautious. I hurried through the library, eager to find my sisters and prove to them that I had a solution for our survival. I knew a whole new world would await us once we left the safety of these walls.

I turned a corner, almost losing my grip on the worn wooden floor with my shoes, but there was no time to stop. Excitement surged through me. However, I wasn't far from the doors when they suddenly swung open. The Masters dropped what they were holding and immediately knelt in a submissive gesture to the Alpha fighters who had entered the sacred place.

The Alphas growled in satisfaction, while I let out a scream at their presence. They all turned to me, something dark flickering in their eyes as they scanned me from head to toe. My Omega instincts urged me to kneel before them and submit. They warned me that running and showing them my back would only trigger their instincts, but I couldn't help glancing behind me. If I submitted, I couldn't help my sisters.

The group of Alphas growled at me, their bodies expanding, and I took a hesitant step back. They cautioned me not to do something so foolish, but I had to save my sisters. I turned on my heel and sprinted away, and they immediately gave chase. However, I knew the place like the back of my hand and managed to confuse them as I darted through the labyrinthine bookshelves and staircases. But I wasn't naïve. I knew they would catch up to me soon.

So I raced toward the secret entrance to the tunnels, desperately searching for the handle or mechanism that would open it. I tried pressing on the stones again, but the bookshelf remained immobile. An idea struck me, and I began pulling books off the shelf, pushing them to the ground and berating myself for treating the sacred knowledge this way. But time was of the essence.

I looked back over my shoulder, hearing the Alphas tearing the place apart to find me. Just as I turned my attention back to the bookshelf, my hand grasped a book that seemed out of place. I yanked harder, and I heard a satisfying click. The bookshelf swung open. I pushed it wide and then slipped into the darkness, sealing it shut behind me.

I remained in the darkness, listening to my own breathing, while on the other side, I could hear the Alphas growling and shouting in frustration. They were baffled by how I had seemingly vanished into thin air, and I prayed to the Gods that they wouldn't discover the secret entrance.

After a while, their anger at not finding me seemed to outweigh their determination, and they left once more. I had no idea of the state of the library, and my instincts urged me to go out and assess the damage, but I knew I didn't have time. I needed to find my sisters. If the army was already here, I feared my sisters had been captured.

I turned around, but I couldn't see anything. I listened for sounds on the other side of the bookshelf, but it was completely quiet. I reached for the stone that opened the bookshelf, then poked my head out. Other than books and scattered wood, there was no sign of any Alphas. I reached for a small torch hanging on the wall before closing the bookshelf and plunging myself back into the darkness.

"You've got this," I whispered to myself. First, I had to figure out where my sisters were and then find out if I could free them. I began walking through the tunnels, gradually becoming more familiar with them. Sometimes, the sounds from outside echoed throughout the hallways, guiding me to where most people had gathered. I glanced at the book, hoping to determine my location, but my disorientation made it difficult. Instead, I searched for any openings that might reveal the world outside.

As I followed the loud echoing voices, I finally came across what I believed was another door, but I couldn't see any light streaming in. However, the edges of the door gave it away. I tried to push it forward, and it made an awful lot of noise, but the sounds on the other side drowned it out. I pushed harder until light streamed in. I cautiously poked my head out and noticed a heavy fabric covering me. I reached out and pushed it to the side, letting out a small gasp.

A whole party had gathered in one of the common rooms. Food was being served, drinks were being consumed, and some were even sparring for entertainment. However, soon, moaning reached my ears, and I turned my head to see an Alpha fucking one of the servants. They were right up against the wall, in full view of everyone, yet it didn't seem to bother anyone. I had heard that the Tesarian Wolves lived more openly, but I hadn't expected such a blatant display.

I turned my head away from the scene and moved to the other side of the fabric. From my new angle, I saw my sisters sitting on the ground in front of what was unquestionably High Alpha Cartan, with his most trusted fighters right behind him. My sisters already had chains around their necks and hands, a clear symbol of their lost freedom. Omegas weren't fighters, so the chains were entirely unnecessary. The sight angered me, but I couldn't jump out and save them. I would have to wait.

Yet Cassia's eyes shifted to the side and found me hiding in the darkness. They widened at the sight of me, and I gave her a small smile, trying to reassure her without words. Cassia nudged Vivina on her left, and she turned her head. Cassia, without looking at me, subtly nodded in my direction. Vivina glanced toward me, expressing the same surprise and then fear. I instantly understood her message through her eyes: *run*.

I shook my head and sent her a silent reply. I knew she could read me. I knew she understood that I would come back for them. She shook her head slightly, indicating that I shouldn't. I continued to smile at her as Cartan ordered some of his fighters to take the princesses to their new "chamber."

I watched as the fighters brought my sisters to their feet while I slipped back into the darkness, placing the stone door back into position. Then I began forming my plan in my head. My sisters needed provisions, clothes, money, and herbs to survive out there. I had to pack the essentials for them.

I looked at the map in front of me, trying to decipher how I could return to my room, but it seemed as if I were missing some information. Could it be the guidance for the tunnels had been divided among multiple books? The long row of bookshelves suddenly made more sense to me. Yet I couldn't return. I didn't have the time. So instead, I used the sounds, the knowledge I had of the castle, and the part of the map I had to guide me.

Chapter Six
Cartan

She thought I hadn't seen her, but it didn't escape my notice how the princesses subtly turned their heads, discreetly focusing on something further away. I didn't make it obvious as I kept my eyes straight ahead, catching a glimpse out of the corner of my eye of something moving behind the fabric in the distance. I tried not to smile, but I knew the hidden fourth Omega had shown up. Who else would be so bold or make the princesses at my feet tense in such a strange manner?

No, whoever this fourth Omega was, the only one not written or spoken about, she had found a way to reach her sisters without being discovered. Some fighters had mentioned a woman disappearing in the library where they had searched for her, yet if all the sisters hid their natural Omega scent, that must mean the fourth did as well, blending in like any other Beta servant. However, I knew the fourth one would not come out of hiding until she deemed it safe enough. Whoever she was, I already knew she was clever, and I had to lure her out with the one thing she desired—the safety of her sisters.

I ordered my fighters to take them to the dungeons, knowing the last Omega would feel too tempted not to react. I watched as the princesses were dragged through the room before I turned my eyes to the fabric. It wasn't moving anymore, and I smiled as I moved away from my spot.

"High Alpha?" Tyros called, but I ignored his words.

I walked over to where I had seen the fabric move, then pulled it away, revealing nothing but a stone wall in front of me.

"Interesting," I whispered.

"What is it?" Tyros asked.

"Do you see something?" I questioned, nodding to the wall.

He shook his head.

"I had read this entire place held hidden tunnels for escape under siege, but I thought they were merely rumors since the princesses were still here. Now I see they are indeed true."

Tyros looked confused, not understanding what I was seeing, yet I reached out and began feeling along the stones, sensing an inconsistency in the way they were shaped. However, it was clear this one only opened from the inside. Fortunately for me, I knew where the last Omega was headed. I turned to Tyros, telling him to enjoy the party and that I would soon return.

"You don't need my assistance?" he asked.

"This I can handle on my own."

"What exactly is it?"

I smiled a crooked smile, not yet ready to reveal that I had found the last Omega I was searching for. Instead, I walked away, slipping past the Alphas enjoying themselves and into the hallway. I moved underground to the dungeon and listened to the queen yelling her frustration, banging her hands against the steel door, and berating the fighters. I listened to them laughing, yet as they passed me, they inclined their heads slightly before departing. My smile did not waver, and I continued to where the princesses' cells were.

"I hate Alphas!" one of them spat.

"We haven't been around many," another countered.

"Well, I don't need to. This is enough. I will forever hate Alphas!" she growled, making my smile grow.

Whoever the clan leader that got the fiery one was certainly in for a battle. She almost tempted me to take her myself, but I remained quiet as I listened to them vent their frustration.

"We will stand tall as always," the queen said.

"Stand tall while we get fucked?" her sister retorted.

"We must show them we do not bow."

"How do we do that if we are the ones under a big Alpha's body?"

I almost wanted to laugh. *She certainly has fire,* I thought, but then their conversation took a more interesting turn.

"You know Kiandra will come for us, right?"

Kiandra, so that was her name? I mused to myself.

"I don't want her to," the queen replied.

"But she will. You know her."

"She is smart. She will know to save herself."

"Just because she can probably recite our entire library doesn't mean she understands the consequences of real-life choices. Father and you have sheltered her!" the third one joined in.

The queen did not respond, but that was not necessary. Their conversation had already piqued my interest in this fourth Omega, the youngest of them all. I wasn't even completely certain of her age, but she had to have just reached her twenties or so, and the little one was determined to save her sisters all on her own.

I slipped into the darkness, hiding behind a corner not far from where the princesses' cells were, and then I waited.

Chapter Seven
Kiandra

I took a few wrong turns, but eventually found my bedroom on the lower floors. I couldn't sleep near the real princesses. I slipped into the hallway leading to my bedroom, then crossed it and quietly entered behind the wooden door. I closed it silently, listening for any commotion happening on the other side, but it was dead quiet.

I breathed a sigh of relief before turning to my room. It was a mess, with papers and books stacked everywhere. I knew that taking books outside the sacred library was strictly forbidden, but I might have taken a few for some late-night studying. My cheeks flushed with embarrassment at my obsession, but I quickly snapped out of my trance. I grabbed some small satchels and packed them with clothes. They appeared to be simple servants' attire in dull, brown colors, but it would help them blend in.

I also packed a cloak for each of them, then stuffed a few purses with gold coins and added herbs to mask their Omega nature. When I had everything packed, I slung the bags over my shoulders and grabbed the torch and book once more. I cautiously poked my head into the dimly lit hallway, glancing around, but the festivities had drawn the attention of the guards to the floors above. I retreated into the tunnels, heading even further down than the ground floor.

A chill seemed to creep into my bones as if something haunted this place. I knew I was entering a part of the castle I had never ventured into before. Our father had forbidden it, believing it was no place for delicate Omegas. I scoured the area for the door that would lead me into the dungeon's hallways when I heard the undertones of Alphas' voices.

I froze, waiting for them to pass by before resuming my search for the door. It proved challenging to locate, as the walls were made of stone arranged in a random pattern. I pressed my hands against the stones, hoping to find a hidden handle, and finally noticed something to my left. I turned and held up the torch, revealing a small iron handle protruding from the wall. A smile crossed my face as I walked over to it.

I pulled on the handle, hearing the stone slide away, and silently thanked my ancestors for constructing these secret passageways. I poked my head into the dark, eerie hallway, glancing around, but there were no guards in sight. I hurried down the corridor, following the sound of my sisters' voices until I reached the cell that held them. I unlocked and opened the door.

"Kiandra?" Solana asked, astonished.

They all turned their heads to look at me.

"Come!" I urged them, waving for them to join me.

They hurried over and hugged me tightly.

"That was foolish!" scolded Vivina, though a smile played on her lips. "You should have escaped."

"I couldn't leave you all behind. Here," I handed them the bags I had packed.

"There are only three," Solana pointed out.

"I will stay."

"Why?"

"I am not known to the Alphas. I could be of use here. I can protect our home until you're ready to return."

"Kiandra, that is utterly insane. You cannot stay. You're coming with us!" Vivina told me.

"No, go to the tunnels. Just walk straight ahead. It will take you to your freedom," I said, pulling my sisters out of their cell. "You have everything you need in the bags."

"I am not leaving you behind! You're coming with us!" Vivina insisted.

"That she is." We all spun around, seeing a dark figure emerging from around the corner. Even through the thick, rotten smell down here, his Alpha scent overpowered it. He came closer, stalking us, making us feel like the small Omegas we were.

"Run," I told them.

"Kiandra!" Vivina exclaimed.

"Now!"

The Alpha came toward us, but instead of running with my sisters, I ran to him. He had not expected that. He froze before he crashed into me. Despite never having met Alphas, I had studied them. I understood their weaknesses and how an Omega could even tame an Alpha to her will.

As my sisters ran toward the tunnels, I placed myself on my knees in front of the Alpha, letting my instincts guide me. It gave them the head start they needed while I remained submissive to the Alpha before me, bowing my head and tilting it slightly to the side. I felt his sharp eyes on me, trying to decipher my behavior, but I simply remained in place, waiting.

His hand shot out, wrapping around my long braid and pulling it back, forcing me to look up into his eyes. They had turned completely black, the pupil consuming the brown color, showing his instincts were playing and taking over, enjoying my submission. But then he forced his Alpha nature back, his eyes returning to their brown color, and his growl turned angry.

"Well played," he snapped before he leaned down and picked me up, throwing me over his shoulder.

"Hey!"

He hurried down the hallway where my sisters had gone, reaching the tunnel. When I glanced behind myself and saw my sisters were nowhere in sight, I smiled. However, I was quickly placed on my feet, and an angry Alpha towered over me, pointing to the open tunnel while a growl surged from his chest.

"Where does it go?" he demanded to know.

I lowered my eyes, maintaining my submissive demeanor, but I would not reveal to him where my sisters had gone. His growl turned darker, and his hand moved to my throat, squeezing. I knew he barely put any power behind it, yet I could feel a constriction in the air in my lungs. I tried hard to stop my instincts from going crazy, urging me to fight him. However, I knew disobeying him would only make him tighten his grip. Alphas loved the smell of fear, even in their Omegas.

"Answer me!" he growled, yet I remained quiet.

He pulled me closer to him, bringing our faces within inches of each other. His growl was so powerful that I could feel the vibrations running through his arm and into me. I felt an immediate shift in my own body. Shamelessly, it reacted to his display of power, and I squeezed my thighs together to ensure my slick wouldn't drip uncontrollably to the floor.

I knew Omegas were meant to please Alphas, but I hadn't expected such a fast and powerful reaction. The Alpha began sniffing the air around me, and not even my long, dark clothes could hide the fact that I was reacting to his dominant nature.

His growl changed rhythm and became one of satisfaction. The sound made my body react even more powerfully, as Omegas were designed to submit. We were made to find the strongest Alphas and provide them with pleasure beyond their belief, so they would stay and protect us, ensuring our survival. My body was responding as it was meant to, but it did nothing to cool the heat in my cheeks.

He leaned closer, burying his nose in my neck, his entire body expanding. Yet his growl turned angry again, and when he pulled back, he still looked furious.

"Bland," he growled. "Yet I can smell your desire."

I swallowed hard, trying my best not to move and to let him handle me as he wanted. It was the best way to deal with an enraged Alpha—to give him exactly what he desired. His eyes glanced down, and he reached for my dress, pulling it up. It took everything in me not to pull away, and his nostrils flared as he raised my dress, releasing the scent of my arousal into the room.

He slipped his hand inside, grazing over my thigh, and my eyes rolled back. The simple touch from him was enough to send me into a frenzy of need, and my body released more slick, ready to receive him. He ran his fingers over my inner thigh, almost grazing my pussy before he pulled his hand away. I opened my eyes, shocked that he did not simply take me, but instead, he brought his fingers to his lips, tasting me, and I whimpered at the sight. I had never imagined that an Alpha would want to lick my desire off his fingers, and he even looked incredibly pleased by what he tasted.

A dark smile returned to his lips afterward before he pushed me up against the wall, my sisters now long forgotten as he shoved my dress higher, getting on his knees. Why was he kneeling? A scream of delight erupted from my lips as he pushed his face between my thighs, his big hands wrapping around my legs and pulling them apart to create space for his enormous body.

Pleasure, unlike anything I had experienced before, exploded in my body as he almost drank the slick dripping out of me, and I only seemed to get wetter as his warm tongue licked over my entrance, pushing inside. I felt myself squeezing around him, wanting him deeper inside me, wanting to feel his knot sealing us together. He chuckled darkly against my wet and sensitive skin, sensing the desperate need my body had for him. I tried pushing up on my toes to get away from the powerful sensations. I couldn't think when he did that, and I always needed to think.

A clear mind was important, but one of his hands moved higher, grasping my hip, and keeping me in place as he continued to pleasure me. It felt like something hot was building in my lower belly, and it frightened me because of the power it seemed to have. I reached out, trying to shove him away, yet my hands seemed to have a will of their own, grasping his hair and pushing him closer instead of away. It elicited another dark chuckle, the vibrations teasing me, before he latched onto the most sensitive part of me.

He sucked hard, making my eyes roll back again, but this time, pure delight exploded within me, and I screamed so loudly it echoed through the tunnels as I rocked my hips against his face. He continued to apply more pressure to that sensitive part, driving me wild as I experienced pleasure beyond my wildest imagination. I had thought with an Alpha, it was all about pleasing him, yet I found no struggle in surrendering to the Alpha before me. When he finally pulled back, my Omega instincts told me it was time to show what I could do for him.

He stood, moving closer to me, still pressing me against the wall. He studied me, a look of confusion on his face as if he were trying to make a connection. I couldn't comprehend what was going on, but it didn't stop me from attempting to reach out and touch him. All I desired was to trace every contour of his hard body with my fingers and let my tongue follow their path.

This wasn't like me. I had never experienced such overwhelming desires before. All I needed in the past were my books, but the Alpha before me seemed to radiate an irresistible allure. I yearned to taste him, but he wrapped his hand around my throat once more, keeping me at bay as he growled menacingly. I whimpered, pushing my hips forward, pleading with him to take me, to claim me like an Alpha would an Omega.

I watched as he shook his head, appearing perplexed and unable to maintain his focus. I called out to him again by pressing myself closer, and his growl darkened further before his free hand went to his pants, starting to undo them. He freed his hard cock, a sight I had rarely witnessed, and my eyes widened with fear. Was I supposed to take that inside me? Even in his large hand, it appeared massive, hard, and desperate for release.

He pushed me down until I was on my knees once more, then tore the front of my dress open, freeing my breasts. He reached down, grasping one of them firmly, making me whimper as he continued to stroke his own cock, which grew larger before me. How was that even possible? I understood the biological process, but the reality before me was harder to comprehend.

He groaned and growled as he fondled my breast, which just barely filled his hand. His body tightened, and the sight before me was simultaneously terrifying and an exquisite visual feast. Just as he was on the verge of climaxing, he wrapped his hand in my hair and began releasing his seed all over my chest and breasts.

It seemed to satisfy some primal urge in him as he continued to expel large amounts of white liquid all over me, and I was astonished to find myself growing wetter, drenching myself simply from feeling it on my skin. How had I been reduced to this? This was precisely what my sisters and I had been warned about—the power an Alpha could have over an Omega. I knew Omegas could enchant Alphas, but I was shocked by how little control I had over my body.

Even after he had finished climaxing, he began to stroke his hard length again, still craving more. I whimpered, yearning for him as well, but then his hand abruptly stopped the playful caress, and he growled darker than ever before as he tugged himself away and then pulled me to my feet. He pressed me into the wall by gripping my arms, and I noticed he was attempting to speak, but all that emerged were animalistic sounds. He shook his head, trying to clear his mind before finally speaking.

"You will pay for this, little Omega," he growled as a warning before he grabbed me by the nape of my neck and dragged me along.

Chapter Eight
Cartan

I had declared the eldest sister would be mine, that I would tame the fiery Omega queen and compel her to submit to me as she took my cock into her mouth and sucked with vigor. But when that little, delicious, and curvy Omega appeared in the darkness, carrying small bags and a big brown book with her, something within me seemed to stir. I couldn't quite pinpoint what it was, but it distracted me, allowing things to carry on for far too long.

I hadn't anticipated that it would be much of a problem to let her open the cell, but the young Omega was smarter than I had expected. Instead of running, she toyed with my Alpha instincts, diverting my attention from the real task at hand. It demonstrated how Omegas could truly be the downfall of an Alpha if he was not careful, and I had allowed it to momentarily make me lose my composure.

However, I managed to see through some of my Alpha instincts and realized that I couldn't become completely consumed by this Omega's body. Three others had escaped me, and that was a shameful realization. Nothing had ever caused me to lose focus before! So how had this Omega managed to turn me into an animal?

It infuriated me think about, and I found myself wanting to release even more of my cum onto her. However, I needed to maintain my focus, so I dragged her along with me instead.

I was heading for the party where my army was celebrating, but I had barely left the dungeon when I felt an intense anger at the thought of returning her, half-naked and covered in my cum, to the other Alphas. Something within me screamed that I had to gouge out the eyeballs of anyone who saw her naked, which was exceedingly confusing.

The clans of the Black Desert had no issue with displaying their pleasures openly. It was part of our culture, a natural need, yet I couldn't bear to expose this Omega to anyone in the state she was in. I turned to her, seeing her gaze up at me with those soft brown eyes that appeared even larger after I had pleasured her and released all over her.

I noticed fear in her eyes as well, but I knew that if I pushed her to her knees and demanded she pleasure me next, her Omega side would take over, and she would eagerly take me as deep as she could. My whole body shook with desire, and for a moment, my instincts took over again, craving exactly that. But a rational voice stepped forward, reminding me that I had three runaway princesses to recover.

I pulled the fourth one with me, heading to one of the larger bedrooms on the upper floor. I pushed her inside, and I saw her stumble backward before regaining her balance. She turned to me, shock evident on her face, her breathing rapid, pushing her breasts toward me. Shit, what an invitation they were, and my mouth watered at the thought of sucking on them until they were raw, with a simple flick of my tongue causing her to drip her wonderful slick. Why could I smell her desires, yet I couldn't detect her natural scent? What had she done to herself?

However, slowly, the last princess was regaining some sense of the world around her, and she pulled her ruined dress together. I growled, warning her not to hide her wonderful body that I desired nothing more than to lay claim to. She forced her arms down, surprising me by not resisting like her other sisters had. What was it about this one that made me want to engage in wicked deeds with her? I had no real desire to focus on the other princesses. No, I had something better in front of me, and I took a step forward, wanting to devour the sweet prey before me. But I quickly shook my head, reminding myself that now was not the time. I pointed at her, struggling to regain my ability to speak.

"*Do. Not. Move!*" I managed to utter.

She nodded, surprising me even more by not resisting me. How was it that the one princess who had been hidden from sight desired to obey me? She had managed to free her sisters, yet now she surrendered? Did she simply see the futility in resisting, or was her clever mind playing games with me? I did not trust her at all.

So, as I turned away, I slammed the door shut and locked it, taking the key with me as I returned to the festivities. I knew I was exuding a heavily aggressive energy, which alarmed the other Alphas, causing them to growl and step out of my way. Tyros noticed me approaching and came closer.

"What happened?" he inquired.

I couldn't speak at first. I simply growled, which surprised him. I knew he could see the way my pupils had consumed the color of my eyes. I could feel how little control I had left, all because of the fourth princess. That Omega had been plucked from any Alpha's dream, yet the thought of someone else desiring her as his own caused me to growl once more.

"What is going on with you?" Tyros asked.

"*We ... are ... going ... hunting,*" I snarled.

"What?"

"*The princesses ... have escaped.*"

"How?"

I simply didn't have the strength to tell him or provide even half an explanation. I shook my head, gestured for him to follow, and he called a group as we left the room. The princesses couldn't have gotten far, and after recapturing them, I intended to return to finish what I had started with Kiandra.

Chapter Nine
Kiandra

It took me a while before I could pull myself out of the trance my own instincts had ensnared me in. It was incredibly fascinating how easy it was to succumb to the allure of an Alpha. I understood the dynamic between the two, having read numerous books about what an Alpha and Omega pairing meant, and how Alphas born from an Omega and Alpha union were considered true Alphas, more powerful than any others. Like Omegas, there were few left in the world, but I wouldn't doubt it if Alpha Cartan was one. His power, enormous build, and everything about him screamed dominance, turning me into nothing but an animal in heat. Fortunately, I hadn't entered my heat cycle yet, but I knew the herbs I had taken wouldn't be able to block it, and once I entered it, I would be at the mercy of any Alpha who wanted me.

There was a reason we locked ourselves away during our heat cycles, but as I looked around, I knew there would be no escape for me this time. I still had a few weeks before it returned, but I wasn't sure I would get through the night without at least being claimed once. I needed to ensure I maintained a clear mind. Omegas held power too through the pleasure they could provide. An Alpha would become fiercely protective of the Omega he deemed as his, so if I did not want to be rutted and used by multiple Alphas, I had to lean into my instincts and use whatever tricks I had up my sleeve. Yet I was very inexperienced. Could I truly please Alpha Cartan, or would I not be able to trick him into offering his protection?

My head began to ache, a headache creeping in as I paced around in the bedroom that belonged to my sister

Cassia. However, as I realized whose room it was, an idea formed in my mind. I ran to one of her chests, opened it, and found only dresses inside. I happily pulled out a white and golden dress, using my ruined one to clean off the Alpha's seed, and then put on my sister's. It was a bit too long, so I tied it up on the side.

Then I went on a hunt for any weapons she might have hidden. I knew they wouldn't be lying out in the open, as the servants would inform Vivina about it. So, I searched every chest, every drawer, and every closet. At the very bottom of one of those chests, hidden beneath what looked like maps of every land and island out there, I found something odd. The chest seemed large on the outside, yet the bottom reached much higher than made sense.

I knocked on it, hearing the hollowness, and I noticed a small hole in the side. I pulled on it and saw the bottom came off. I placed it aside, then found numerous weapons hidden inside, including knives, smaller daggers, and whips. I pulled one out, sliding my hand over the leather. Did my sister know how to wield one, or was she interested in learning? I stood up, letting the leather strip fall to the ground. I tried swinging it, but the small snap it gave out startled me, and I dropped it.

"Not for me," I murmured before packing it away. Then I retrieved one of the smaller knives, which had a golden handle and a curved tip. It was indeed beautiful, and I stood up again, briefly pointing the tip at the door as if the Alpha were truly standing in front of me. My hand shook a bit, yet I sighed and lowered the knife. I realized I wouldn't enhance my security by threatening him.

Besides, I knew he could easily disarm me and take control if he wanted to. A shiver ran through me, but to my surprise, the thought didn't bring disgust, as it usually did. I never understood the carnal needs residing in wolves. I understood the biological aspect, but these feelings within me were completely new. Did I secretly wish for the Alpha to claim me right on the very bed behind me? I glanced over my shoulder and then shook my head.

That was my sister's bed. It felt strange, but when I shifted my gaze to the floor beneath me, and wondered if he would take me there, I felt a pulsing between my legs and was reminded of when his tongue had swiped over that area. It had brought me immense pleasure, and I instinctively squeezed my thighs together, cursing at myself for surrendering so easily. I wasn't planning to fight him, but it shocked me how easily I had fallen into the spell of my own instincts.

The thought of it made me pace the room as I tried to figure out why I had reacted this way. I didn't seem to want to submit to any of the other Alpha fighters who had attacked me, and yet I had gone right on my knees before Alpha Cartan. I had done it to distract him, but I found it strangely easy to remain on my knees, showing him submission. Why was that?

My fingers itched to get ahold of more books that could help me understand this reaction, but I had heard the heavy lock turning. I wasn't leaving this room, and when he came back, I knew what would happen next. Could I handle it? Would he not hurt me by pushing himself into me? I knew Omegas were meant to please and take their Alphas, but it seemed completely unrealistic, yet my body seemed to be begging for it.

"None of this makes sense!" I groaned, frustrated that I couldn't find anything logical to hold onto in my frightened condition. I had thought I would be better prepared to handle the Alpha, but he had shaken me completely. I went to sit on the big bed, sighing deeply as

I fell back onto it. I looked up at the high, white ceiling, wondering how far my sisters had gotten by now. Had they been able to procure a boat? Were they already off the island? Or had they decided to stay? I had many questions, but I knew I would not find any answers. All I could do was pray to the Gods that they had managed to escape.

Chapter Ten
Kiandra

It was close to morning when I was woken up by the heavy lock turning. I had fallen asleep on my sister's bed, and I quickly sat up as I watched a furious Alpha enter the room, slamming the doors shut behind him. His eyes still held that dark color, showing me he was in a horrible mood.

I scrambled from the bed, trying once more to allow my instincts to guide me in handling the Alpha who was storming over to me. I got on my knees on the floor, focusing on the ground. When he stopped in front of me, I almost felt a shove from the enraged energy he displayed. However, I couldn't help but smile. I knew he must have left to go hunt my sisters, and if he was in such a foul mood, then he couldn't have found them yet.

He reached out, grabbing a fistful of my hair and pulling my head back. With his other hand, he began working on his pants again, pushing them lower. He brought me closer, so his hard cock was only inches from my face, and the powerful raw Alpha scent made my head spin with delight. I pushed closer, wanting to taste and lick him, my instincts screaming that was what I was supposed to do, but he held me back, and it made me hiss a little. He noticed, and a dark smile spread across his lips as he began stroking himself again. Yet this time I felt angry at the sight, as if I were being denied something.

"Where are they?" he growled at me as he continued to stroke that magnificent cock. I just wanted to taste it! Yet I remained still, causing his grip to tighten. "Where?"

I shook my head as much as he allowed me to, and he began pumping himself faster. I whimpered, shoving forward, but he held me back, and I hissed from the pain in my scalp. He stroked his large hand up and down, liquid sliding from the tip, and I licked my lips, watching it. He chuckled darkly, seeing the change in me, yet he didn't allow me any closer.

"Tell me!" he demanded.

I whimpered my denial, and his growl turned even darker. He shoved me backward, turning me so I was on my hands and knees before he began ripping my dress apart until I was completely naked. I had expected this. I knew it was going to happen, and so I pushed back toward him, offering myself to him. I felt my body doing its trick, simply reacting to his scent that filled the room, and I grew wetter, gushing out slick to be able to take him. Yet as I felt the broad head right at the entrance of my pussy, I knew it was going to be a battle to take.

"Where?" he growled, reaching out to fist my hair again as another powerful and warm hand landed on my hip.

I shook my head, and then I felt the undeniably sharp stretch. I whimpered, pushing forward as he entered me, but he pulled me to him, impaling me on his cock. I let out a scream as he shoved all the way in, yet his growl overpowered my sounds as he felt pure pleasure from entering me.

He gave me no time to relax, simply began slamming his cock in and out of me, bending me to him and having me in any way he desired. I thought the whole act was going to be uncomfortable as he took up so much space just from entering me, but the uncomfortableness only lasted a moment, then I felt that fire spread again. I began whimpering for new reasons, pushing against him, and meeting his thrust after thrust as my walls tightened and squeezed around him. It was indeed bliss beyond comprehension.

The way he took me made me scream for more, wanting him as deep as he could go, and the Alpha grew crazier from the pleasure I was bestowing upon him. He pulled me up against him, taking me even deeper as he wrapped his arms around me while he shoved into me.

I couldn't stop the fire from exploding. I leaned my head back, resting it against his shoulder as I came apart once more, yet it seemed even fiercer this time. I couldn't even scream, the sound stuck in my throat as my whole body wept, drenching us both in my own release. It seemed to please Alpha Cartan greatly as he fucked me even faster, growing desperate, his thrusts losing their rhythm, and I knew he was going to experience the same bliss soon.

Yet I began feeling something new. I was being stretched once more. His knot preparing to lock us together. I began whimpering from that new sting, but he didn't stop pumping into me even harder, going as deep as he could until my pussy locked around him, welcoming his knot. He let out such a dark growl, the walls shook around us as he began emptying his seed into me, filling my womb and ensuring not a drop escaped.

Luckily, my herbs prevented pregnancy too. While it was unlikely that he could get me pregnant outside of my heat, it was still comforting to know the herbs would be there to protect me. Yet strangely, I felt a sting in my heart knowing he wouldn't succeed. Why was that? I understood I needed his protection, but why was the thought of creating a life together suddenly on my mind?

As Cartan rested, coming down slowly, his panting filling my ear, I woke up a little from the trance my instincts seemed to put me in every time he was close. I leaned my head to the side, burying my nose into his neck and nuzzling it. I knew Alphas would purr for their

Omegas, the ones they wanted to protect and breed with, and to my delight, I began hearing the soft rumble.

Yet I had not expected how much the sound would affect me, as if I had been missing something profound all my life. Our father had purred for us as well, only their younglings able to elicit it too, but this was something even better. It filled me with a true feeling of safety, one I had never experienced before, and in that safety, I realized what I had to do to ensure that purr, body, and protection never went to anyone else—I had to mark him.

Only an Omega could ensure the marking process began. It was the only true power we had, and this was the weapon I had to take into use. I felt my canines tingle as they elongated, and then I shifted as much as his tight knot would allow me. I reached out to push him closer, and then I heard a powerful roar as I sank my teeth into that delightful spot that smelled even more of him.

I bit so deeply his blood filled my mouth, but it was the most delicious thing I had ever tasted. I swallowed a mouthful of it, his cock spurting more of his release into me, and I felt him shiver beneath my hand, wanting to mate with me as I marked him, but he could not move yet. It allowed me to fully mark him without struggle, claiming him as mine.

Chapter Eleven
Cartan

I had never been so foolish as to underestimate an enemy. I always made sure to learn about them, to be prepared for anything they might throw my way. I hadn't reached the top, claiming a seat among the clan leaders, by being so reckless as to think a smaller opponent would not pose a threat. Yet this tiny Omega in my arms, with a body seemingly molded by the Gods themselves, had managed to surprise me time and time again. Not only had her body tightly embraced my cock, driving me to experience pleasures that should be beyond mortal capacity, but she had also marked me as hers.

This experience had led me to a more intense release, and I couldn't help but climax inside her once more, even while fully knotted. My desire to mate with her again was overwhelming, especially after she had marked me. However, I remained still, aware that moving would harm her delicate skin.

As the marking spell wore off after she withdrew her teeth, the reality of the situation struck me. What was I going to tell the other clan leaders now? The princesses were not meant to be claimed so soon, yet here I was, having claimed one for myself—or rather, she had claimed me. My frustration surged, and I pushed her forward, my knot finally releasing her.

She gasped as I withdrew and turned her over, pushing her onto her back. I watched as my cum and a trace of blood flowed from her, confirming her untouched status. Why did this please me so? Despite my anger, I couldn't deny that this Omega kept me on edge. While I had no intention of mating with her again, I couldn't resist the overwhelming desire that gripped me, like the need for air itself.

She gasped as I entered her once more, arching her back to meet my thrusts. I restrained her hands above her head, pressing them down as I leaned forward to suck on one of her breasts, teasing her nipple. Her moans drove me to madness as I continued to move inside her.

I cursed myself for bringing her pleasure when she had disrupted so many things. Here I was, making her moan and writhe beneath me, when I should be punishing her. I pulled back, wrapping my hand around her throat and ceasing my thrusts. She whimpered, gazing up at me with needy, glassy eyes.

"What have you done?" I growled. It took her a moment to snap out of her frenzy, but when she did, she smiled up at me. She didn't utter a word, and her attempt to play games with me infuriated me. I thrust into her deeper, tightening my grip on her throat as I released her wrists, all while increasing the pace. She began whimpering, her nails digging into my hand as I let her experience my anger and forced her into submission through her own pleasure.

She cried out, trembling beneath me as she climaxed once more, tears streaming from her eyes. I continued to possess her, refusing to grant her the respite she needed. She tried to push away, seeking a break, but I persisted with my torment, feeling my knot expand once again. This intensified her sensations, and she dug her nails even deeper into my skin, drawing blood as I latched onto her and reached another ecstatic climax. How could anything feel so incredible? Yet this small Omega had taken control, making my entire body quiver with pleasure as I filled her repeatedly.

"P-Please, release me," she whimpered, her voice fragile, and my grip had tightened too much on her delicate throat. I hadn't realized how fragile she could be.

Yet her voice had a certain allure, awakening something within me. I loosened my grip, allowing her to gulp in mouthfuls of air. It was then that I recognized the feeling that had surfaced in me.

As I released my grip, I felt my canines tingle, urging me to mark her in the same way she had marked me. However, that would only complicate an already difficult situation. How dare this Omega play these games with me? Nevertheless, I found myself oddly intrigued by her.

"Where are they?" I questioned her once more. Her smile returned, and I slid my hand into her hair, pushing her closer to me. She gasped, fear flickering in her eyes, causing her smile to waver.

"Where?" I growled, feeling a roar building within my chest.

"I don't know," she admitted, and I noticed her heartbeat remained steady. It had quickened due to exhaustion and fear of me, but it did not change as she spoke.

"You know these lands."

"We know nothing of these lands. I have only studied them, but my sisters do not know them," she revealed.

"And you thought it was wise to let them go on their own?" I retorted. She narrowed her eyes slightly, but I growled, and her eyes dropped in submission. She was adept at acknowledging who the Alpha was, giving me what I desired. Still, she had managed to infuriate me more than anyone else, even more than my own father who had abandoned me as a small child. Why was this Omega so perplexing?

"They will manage. It's better than being tied to an Alpha," she whispered.

"And yet you marked me."

"Survival. They are free, but I am not."

"So perceptive. You're not a simple princess, are you?" I spat.

"I do not exist," she replied cryptically.

"You feel very real," I mocked, lifting my other hand and running my thumb across her sweet, pink lips. I found myself wanting to see those lips wrapped around my shaft as I filled her mouth. Surprisingly, she parted her lips slightly, and I slipped my thumb inside. She sucked on it, sending shivers of delight through me. How was she able to affect me this way? All I could think about was mating with her.

I knew this was going to complicate matters since I was returning with only a single princess, one I had claimed for myself. But for some reason, I didn't care. I should care! For the Gods' sake, I ordered myself to care. Instead, I withdrew my finger and pushed the Omega back to the ground. My knot slowly released her, and I flipped her onto her stomach before plunging into her once more, both of us groaning in pleasure as I fully enveloped her on the floor. Her cries of pleasure echoed throughout the room, and I felt like I was losing my mind.

"You think your mark will save you?" I growled in her ear, and she glanced over her shoulder, smiling once more.

"You haven't stopped mating with me," she pointed out. "You will never stop now."

"And you sound more delighted by it than I am," I countered.

"You will take me away from everything I know," she panted, squeezing her eyes shut as she felt another climax building. "I am just one Omega in a big world. All I can do is find the Alpha I think will best protect me."

She whimpered, biting down on her lip as she

came, tightening around me, leaving barely any room to move. Her climax triggered my own release, and I growled as I claimed her once more, filling her completely.

We both breathed heavily as we rested, and I nuzzled closer to her neck, searching for the Omega scent I desired. Yet it wasn't there on her neck. I could only smell her arousal, and I realized that if I hadn't triggered it, I wouldn't have been able to track her, which was why her sisters had not been found yet.

"Why are you so smart, little one?" I whispered in her ear. "What have you done to yourself?"

"Knowledge is power," she breathed before pushing up and nuzzling into my chest.

I hadn't anticipated the effect her movements would have on me, and I began purring again, hearing a sweet sigh escape her lips. I was ... purring? I knew Alphas had the ability to do it, but the sound seemed to come from me instinctively, as if I needed to calm her and make her feel safe after knotting her. It intrigued me and slightly unsettled me. This Omega was going to be a challenge to handle, but she would not hold the power. It was time she learned that.

Chapter Twelve
Kiandra

Alpha Cartan had moved us from the floor to the bed, but he showed no signs of stopping our mating until the sun's rays streamed through the windows. By then, I was utterly spent, my muscles trembling, and my strength depleted. Still, I couldn't resist burying my nose in his neck, searching for that powerful Alpha scent. He remained nestled between my legs, knotting me so deeply it felt as though I could barely breathe. However, his purring filled my ears, providing a sense of calm and security that I craved.

I had no idea what the future held, where we would go next, but I knew Alpha Cartan wouldn't stay on the Rocky Island. He belonged in a much warmer climate, among the clan leaders and in the Black Desert. So, I felt content with my choice. If I had to belong to an Alpha, he seemed like the right one. He had led his army, and he would return without having lost a single Alpha. He had conquered our city, claimed an Omega, and mated with her—a rare and sacred achievement that would likely earn him great respect among the other Alphas. Yes, he was undoubtedly the right choice.

However, I could use a small break. I wasn't sure how I would keep up with Alpha Cartan's stamina. He seemed only more ravenous after each release, and I wasn't sure how much more I could take.

"Tell me what you did to your scent," he growled, pulling back to look at me.

I met his gaze but remained silent.

"Now!"

His demanding tone left me with no choice. I realized that his Alpha instincts felt cheated because he couldn't properly scent me.

"Herbs," I finally replied.

"What kind?"

I hesitated, biting my lip, and he growled once more.

"What kind?"

"They are called Dark Lilacs. They mask our scents," I explained.

"Does it wear off?"

"It will within three weeks if I don't ingest more," I revealed.

He nodded in approval, then fixed me with a dark glare. "Do not take more. I want to be able to smell my Omega," he ordered.

I nodded, agreeing outwardly, but inside, I couldn't promise to honor my word. Those herbs also ensured I wouldn't get pregnant. I had no intention of carrying this Alpha's child, and considering his insatiable appetite, I knew he would want me as often as possible.

Alpha Cartan pulled away from me abruptly, and I gasped as our bodies disconnected, feeling his seed sliding out of me and making an even bigger mess on the already dirty sheets. He retrieved his pants and left me on the bed, my strength drained, and I had no energy to rise. I let my head fall back and finally closed my eyes.

I couldn't discern how long I had slept, but eventually, the doors opened once more. I quickly covered myself, but it was just a group of young Beta servants who had come to help me prepare for our departure. They assisted me out of bed and into a room with a small pool. They bathed me, gently washing away the remnants of last night's activities, and the warm water provided a welcome relief to my aching muscles.

Alpha Cartan hadn't bitten me back, marking me as his, but he had left swallow marks with his teeth wherever he could. I was uncertain why he held back. I couldn't recall in any books that an Alpha didn't want to fully seal the mating bond, but somehow he had restrained himself.

As I left the water, another servant stood ready with a dress more my size and shoes for me to wear. They got me dressed before ushering me from the room and leading me down the lengthy hallways. It was an interesting experience to suddenly walk around as if I truly were a princess now.

However, it seemed I couldn't hide anymore. Yet as we descended the floors, I paused on one of them, realizing the library was not far away. My own desires couldn't be controlled, and I slipped away, hurrying to the room and wondering what I should take with me. I knew I couldn't bring everything, but I should have the most essential things, should I not?

However, just as I reached a ladder so I could take one of my favorites with me, a powerful voice cleared itself behind me. I turned around, seeing Alpha Cartan there, his eyes narrowed as he ran them up my body.

"Were you not informed to come straight to me?" he asked, his voice dark.

"I can't leave yet."

"That is not for you to decide," he growled.

"But I—"

He stormed forward and easily grabbed me by the waist, pulling me down from the ladder.

"Just a few!" I pleaded.

He shook his head, then took hold of my arm and led me away.

"When I give you an order, even if it doesn't come from my lips, you follow it," he snarled.

I discreetly rolled my eyes, but his keen senses noticed it, and he stopped abruptly. He turned me to face him, gripping my jaw with his large hand and moving closer.

"You do not roll your eyes at your Alpha," he warned in a low voice. Yet I could barely hear his words as my gaze fixated on his lips, remembering how they had felt on my body. It was shameful to admit how quickly my body reacted, but it recognized all too well what the Alpha in front of me could do.

Cartan noticed the change in me as he smelled the air, and he pushed me against the wall behind me before turning me and pulling my hips toward him. None of us said anything, but words weren't necessary. We couldn't resist the sudden need to be together, and when he thrust inside me, I cried out in a mixture of delight and pain. It felt so good that tears welled up in my eyes. I was thoroughly used, and yet I seemed to crave more.

Alpha Cartan picked up the pace, his hands gripping my hips so hard that he tore my dress slightly, but he didn't stop. His thick cock continued to slide in and out of me, creating wicked noises, while he leaned closer to bury his nose in my neck. I knew he sought my scent, but there wasn't much to find, and it only fueled his punishing thrusts. However, that seemed to tear an even more powerful release from me, and I dug my nails into the wall, feeling like I could barely see as the pleasure stormed through me, reducing me to a quivering mess held together only by Alpha Cartan's powerful grip. He wasn't far behind me, my body urging him to come, and he thrust into me a few more times before knotting himself to me, making me gasp at the sensation.

We remained locked in that passionate embrace as we both recovered from the intense mating. Through the one-sided bond, I felt Cartan's hunger growing. How was it possible for him to desire me even more? Yet it was a thrilling sensation, and I squeezed around him, eliciting a groan from him. He wrapped an arm around me, burying his face even deeper in my neck, trying to capture any small trace of Omega scent into his nose. It made me shudder with delight, and I mewled, shocking myself with the needy sound.

"High Alpha," a voice called, and I let out a small scream as I noticed someone else in the hallway with us.

A dark, threatening growl rumbled from the Alpha behind me, and I saw the other turn his side to us, sighing a little as he did so. I placed my hands over my face, feeling so embarrassed, but Alpha Cartan was firmly knotted to me, and neither of us was going anywhere.

"What?" he growled, his voice slightly changed.

"We are ready to depart. You can continue on the ship," the other Alpha informed us.

I could sense a sharp, powerful anger coursing through me, and it stung so badly. Omegas weren't accustomed to such rage, and I lowered one of my hands to rub over the spot where my heart was, but it wouldn't dissipate. What was wrong with me?

"Go. We will follow," Alpha Cartan ordered.

I listened to the other man leave before one of Alpha Cartan's hands snaked around my body, one of his fingers finding the sweet spot.

"Time to release me, little one," he purred in my ear as he played with my clit.

I moaned, wanting more and forgetting about the mortifying incident, but then I felt my body grow more relaxed as Alpha Cartan released himself from me before pulling away and getting dressed. I let my dress fall as well, slowly turning toward him. Such a confusing mix of emotions flowed through the one-sided bond, and I didn't know how to handle them, so I constructed a mental bridge between us to try to calm the storm. It worked somewhat, yet the Alpha kept scrutinizing me. He looked at me as if he were ready to devour me on the spot.

"Weren't we leaving?" I asked.

His whole body seemed to tense, but then he made a curt nod and grabbed my arm once more. Despite his grip being so firm it almost hurt, there was a strange sense of satisfaction that spread through me from feeling it. Was it because it almost seemed to be a possessive act? I knew his signs of possessiveness would ensure even more protection, but why did I feel this satisfied? I couldn't forget what he had done to my home and family. If he thought I truly wanted him, he was sorely mistaken. This was purely for survival.

We walked outside where a group of Alphas was waiting for us. As Cartan took the lead, they followed behind us, all of them watching me with intrigue in their eyes. However, one growl from Cartan and they all found other interesting spots to focus on as we walked through the city. I saw many of the people there, poking their heads out of the windows or backing away from the streets when they saw us approaching. I knew they had no idea who I was, but I had completely forgotten to question how Cartan knew of my existence. He didn't appear surprised to see me with my sisters. How much did the Alpha beside me truly know? I was about to ask when I noticed the angry look on his face, and I knew it was better to wait.

We continued out of the city, the old Beta advisors standing by the gate and bowing their heads to him as if he were not the one who had taken over everything and left with one of the Omega princesses. I wanted to curse at them, and I knew Cassia would have said something before spitting at them, but I was not as fiery as her. Instead, I allowed the Alpha to lead me away from everything I knew. Glancing behind me as we reached the harbor, I gazed up at the castle. This was likely the last time I would ever lay eyes on it, so I absorbed the sight for as long as I could.

Even as I was directed onto the ship, I remained where I could still see my home in the distance. Luckily, Alpha Cartan kept himself occupied with getting the crew to work, allowing me to stay on the deck near the edge of the ship, watching as my home gradually disappeared from view.

Chapter Thirteen
Cartan

She had not moved since we boarded the ship, left the harbor, and started our journey back to the Mainlands. The princess remained in her spot, gazing at the castle. I watched her the entire time. Even as I gave orders to the men, ensuring everything proceeded smoothly, I positioned myself so I could still see her. I knew she wanted to keep her eyes on her home for as long as possible. Even after it disappeared, she continued to look back in its direction. It was fascinating how focused she could remain, unwilling to shift her attention.

However, as Tyros came to stand beside me, my own focus shifted, and I turned to him. I could see the concern etched on his face, a concern that had been present earlier. I shared that same feeling, but I also felt a twinge of frustration at him almost catching a glimpse of my Omega in her most vulnerable state. No one else should witness her in such a way. Luckily, her dress was long and slightly puffy at the end, providing adequate coverage.

"You haven't taken your eyes off her once, and you let her distract you," Tyros pointed out.

I groaned, rubbing my eyes, feeling annoyed with myself. "I didn't expect it to be like this," I murmured.

"I thought you had selected the queen as your own. Wasn't she the one you intended to request from the other clan leaders? You were confident in your choice," he reminded me.

"She was my initial choice," I confirmed.

"What happened then?"

"I wish I knew. The moment that Omega knelt before me, something stirred within me."

"Stirred?"

"Dormant and potent instincts. Whenever I'm near her, all I can think about is being between her thighs and making her come," I groaned.

"Then she shouldn't be the Omega you choose. She makes you lose focus. She was able to assist the other princesses," he pointed out.

"Trust me, I understand what we've lost, but I'll find them again and bring them to the clan leaders. However, it's too late for me to make a choice now. The Omega chose first, and it's well within her right," I snapped.

Tyros glanced at the mark on my shoulder. Whenever I looked at or touched it, I felt immense pride. It wasn't that I didn't desire the Omega's mark. It was a sacred gesture to be chosen by one. But the Omega had claimed me too soon. It would be seen as an insult, a selfish act by the other clan leaders, and it would create significant problems for me.

"Why did she choose to mark you so early?" Tyros inquired.

"Do you not believe I am a capable Alpha, deserving of such a mark?" I snapped, straightening my posture to stand tall, even towering over Tyros, who was no small Alpha.

He quickly shook his head. "Of course not, High Alpha, but based on what I know about Omegas, a marking only happens when an Omega feels safe and comfortable enough with the Alpha."

Yes, I was aware of what led an Omega to choose their Alpha. But I understood her tactics. I could almost respect her clever move if it weren't for the complications it would now create. I could already hear the other Alphas' complaints and how they believed I had completely disregarded all my promises to them.

"I'm well aware of what triggers an Omega's choice," I snapped.

"Still, I'm sure the others would be eager to know how you managed to make the Omega feel so comfortable with you so quickly," he pointed out.

I was certain they wanted answers, and if I had a straightforward response, I would have provided it. However, I couldn't reveal the true intentions of the young Omega. So, instead of addressing Tyros's question, I walked past him, descended the small staircase leading to the deck, and approached my Omega, who still had her gaze fixed on the horizon. She sensed my presence drawing near, turning her head slightly, only to avert her gaze from me again. Her long hair danced in the wind, a tempting invitation for me to run my fingers through it once more and feel the soft strands, but she caught me off guard with her words as she continued to focus on the land she had left behind, "You weren't surprised when you found me."

"You are correct," I replied.

"How did you know?" she inquired.

"I never embark on unknown territory without acquiring knowledge of its history," I explained.

"I'm supposed to be dead," she stated before turning her head to look at me.

"You are," I affirmed.

"Many believe I am."

"Indeed, many do," I acknowledged.

"Yet somehow you knew."

"All reports of born Omega children are sent to the High Citadel in the King's Land. However, your report was never official. It lacked the required stamp," I disclosed.

"But you don't reside in the King's Land."

"No, I do not," I admitted.

"Yet you go there to study your enemies?" she questioned.

I nodded. "I have a connection to the king, and when you promise him the chance of an Omega, he becomes very accommodating."

"It will be difficult now that you have no Omegas except me, and I've marked you," she countered with a smug smile.

I moved swiftly, catching her by surprise as I approached from behind, my hand entwining in her hair and pulling her head back. She gasped, and the sound sent a shiver down my spine, causing my cock to grow hard. This little Omega had an extraordinary power over me. A mere whimper from her lips was enough to drive me wild.

"I know exactly how this appears," I growled into her ear. "But I left some of my fighters behind. They will meticulously search every corner of that island. Should your sisters have ventured to the Mainlands or anywhere in Verocca, I will track them down and present them to the other leaders and the king."

"Will there be enough of us, or are we to be shared?" she taunted, provoking me further. My grip tightened on her hair, and she whimpered again under the intense pressure. If she dared to disrespect her Alpha, she would face the consequences.

"That decision is mine to make," I asserted.

"Yours?"

"I found you, claimed your land, and took you. I have the authority to determine what comes next," I snarled.

"And me?" Her voice trembled, revealing her apprehension and fear of being mated by multiple Alphas. However, the mere thought of other Alphas touching her sent me into a primal frenzy.

"You already know what will happen to you. You didn't choose me for nothing," I whispered darkly, burying my nose in her neck to capture any lingering hints of her Omega scent. However, unless I aroused her, there wasn't much to detect. If I wanted to lose myself in her scent, I would have to do so with my face buried between her thighs—something I didn't mind in the slightest.

"I don't know what your bestial nature may compel you to do, even with my mark on you," she countered, her fear apparent despite her attempt to sound strong.

"How were you able to hide with such a defiant mouth?" I whispered.

"Answer me first," she retorted.

I bit her neck as punishment for attempting to give me orders, and she whimpered again.

"Never forget that I am the Alpha here," I growled.

"Yes, Alpha," she replied, making me groan as she uttered the words in the sweetest tone. However, as I pulled away to gaze at her, a smug smile played on her lips once again. She was well aware of the power of her words, skilled in taunting and pleasing me simultaneously. *What a cunning Omega,* I thought, though my desire to be enveloped between her thighs remained undiminished. I yearned to make her writhe with pleasure and replace that smirk with tears of ecstasy.

Focus, I told myself.

"Will I share you?" I mused tauntingly, observing the fire ignite in her eyes, the smile faltering slightly. "Hmm … that depends."

"D-Depends?" she stammered.

"On how well you please me," I informed her.

I had no intention of sharing the little Omega. She

was mine now, but if she believed she could play games with me, she had another thing coming. I felt her shudder, attempting to turn slightly, but I wrapped my arm around her waist, keeping her securely against me.

"H-How do I please you?" she inquired, causing me to growl in satisfaction.

God, I loved hearing her ask that question. In my mind's eye, I could only see her naked, on her knees before me, her tongue and lips lavishing attention on my throbbing cock until I spilled everything I had over her chest once more. Would it be so wrong to relinquish control to Tyros for a moment?

However, my rational side reminded me that it wouldn't be just a moment. Once I was buried within Kiandra once more, I would be a lost Alpha, consumed by the need to mate with her. If the intensity outside of her heat was this overwhelming, I could only imagine what it would be like to serve her through it. It piqued my curiosity about the little Omega.

"When is your heat?" I asked, dismissing her question about pleasing me.

"W-What?" she stammered.

"When is it?" I repeated, searching her eyes for an answer. She blinked rapidly, struggling to comprehend why I was inquiring about her heat. "I am your Alpha. I should be aware. Or do you plan to spend it with someone else?"

I knew that wasn't going to happen, but I couldn't resist taunting her a bit.

"Only if you plan to share me," she retorted, swiftly coming up with a response.

I smiled, seeing through her playful ruse before slowly releasing her hair. She turned to face me, and I kept my arm around her, my hand resting on her round ass. I knew I had left a few marks there, attempting to satisfy the need to claim her by leaving temporary imprints. Once I had resolved the conflict with the other Alphas, my Omega would be ready for my next step. There wouldn't be a shred of doubt about her belonging to me. Even now, with her so close to my body, the need surged within me. She felt incredibly soft, perfect beneath my touch. It was challenging to pull away from her, and I didn't do so immediately. I rested my hands on the railing, caging her in but no longer touching her.

"When?" I pressed.

"Sometime within the next month," she replied.

"Perfect."

I stepped away, and she gazed at me with puzzled eyes.

"So, will you?" she inquired as I turned to leave.

"What?"

"Share me?"

Instead of responding, I smiled, keeping her in suspense. I noticed frustration rising within her as she crossed her arms. The little Omega despised being left in the dark, and her irritation was evident as she called after me.

"Well?" she demanded.

I offered no reply and returned to my position beside Tyros, who was shaking his head slightly, recognizing the complexity of the situation. There wasn't much I could do now except prepare for what lay ahead.

Chapter Fourteen
Kiandra

I was in a state of disarray, overwhelmed by the multitude of unanswered questions swirling in my mind. I despised not knowing, and my usual refuge was immersing myself in books to gain a comprehensive understanding of a world I had never seen. However, I had no books, and the Alpha had astutely discerned my attempts to extract answers from him, his silence leaving me to feel only agitated. He had gone so far as to order one of his fighters to escort me to his cabin, where I spent the entire day pacing anxiously. Although food had been brought to me, I had not touched a morsel. The longer I dwelled on the unanswered questions, the more concerned I grew, wondering if my mark would truly ensure my safety.

Perhaps Cartan felt nothing from a one-sided marking. Maybe he was nothing more than a primal creature who would willingly offer me as a feast to the other clan leaders. This thought did nothing to silence my fears, and I continued to move around.

When Cartan finally returned to his cabin late in the evening, I could barely endure the uncertainty any longer. I needed answers, and he had informed me that only by pleasing him would I receive his protection. As he entered, I began removing my dress, taking solace in the fact that he did not find me repulsive.

His desire to mate frequently was apparent, and as I loosened the thick fabric and let it fall, I positioned myself on the floor on my knees with my legs slightly apart so that he could scent me. I kept my eyes lowered and heard his pleased growl, which elicited a physical response in my body, causing me to grow wet and yearn for him. I heard fabric tearing, and then his fingers firmly gripped my chin, pulling me to his hard cock.

This time, he did not deny me the taste of him as he thrust deep into my throat. I emitted muffled sounds but he quickly withdrew, gripping my hair as he guided me up and down his length. I was surprised by how aroused it made me, and I eagerly sucked and used my tongue to pleasure his cock, learning what elicited that contented rumble from him.

However, just as he began to quicken his pace, he suddenly slowed down while keeping me in place. I continued to suck on the tip, and he groaned before removing me from his cock. I gazed up at him, bewildered, but he wore a pleased smile on his lips.

"You haven't eaten," he observed.

At this moment, I cared little about food. My safety and securing his protection were far more crucial. I attempted to move closer to his cock, but he held me at bay once more. Reaching over me, he picked up some pieces of meat from the plate above me and offered them to my lips. However, I pressed them together, lacking any appetite.

"Eat," he commanded.

I obediently parted my lips, understanding that resisting him would only provoke his anger. He inserted the food into my mouth, and as I felt his fingers inside, I began sucking on them, eliciting another contented growl from him. He withdrew them, and then his grip relaxed, allowing me to return to pleasuring his cock, driven by an insatiable need.

I ran my tongue along its length, demonstrating my gratitude. He shivered under the sensual caress before pulling me back once more and offering me more food. I soon realized his strategy, and if indulging him meant I could also satisfy my hunger for him, I willingly consumed the food.

However, it wasn't long before his urgency for release took precedence, and he forcefully thrust his cock deep into my mouth. I whimpered in delight and eagerly sucked, allowing him to dictate the pace. I sensed the rhythm falter slightly before he began pumping his release into my throat. I hurriedly swallowed it all, but a small amount dribbled from my lips.

Once he had finished, he pulled me away and tilted my head back. He reached out and ran his finger over my skin, feeding me the remaining liquid on them. After I had licked him clean, he helped me back onto my feet and turned me around. He bent me over the table and spread my legs wider. I pushed back, ready for him, but instead of his cock, I felt the gentle swipe of his tongue. I screamed in pleasure, and he repeated the action before positioning himself over me and thrusting his cock into me, stretching me wide once more. My eyes rolled back as I moaned like a wanton woman.

Cartan showed no restraint. He withdrew until only the tip remained inside me before driving deeply again, maintaining the almost punishing rhythm. I was uncertain why I was being subjected to such an intense experience, but the pleasure surged through me at an agonizingly slow pace. When I finally reached the peak, I was trembling and crying out in ecstasy.

Alpha Cartan held me down on the table, ensuring I remained under his control, as I felt the waves of my release washing over me. Yet my inner walls clamped down on him so tightly that he had no choice but to expand and hold me firmly, locking us together as his hot seed poured into me.

His purring commenced immediately after, and I sighed contentedly before feeling something press against my lips once more. I realized it was more food, but I accepted it, allowing him to feed me what remained. When I had consumed the last morsel, I turned my head slightly, granting me a view of the dominant Alpha behind me.

"Have I pleased you?" I inquired, noticing a wicked smile spreading across my lips.

"For now," he replied.

I groaned, resting my forehead against the cool wooden table. I tapped it lightly, and as I did, I felt something soft against my skin. I pulled back slightly to see Cartan's large hand where I had been tapping my head. I turned a bit, and he shook his head.

"Don't harm yourself," he ordered.

His words caught me off guard. After all, I was just an Omega for him to use as he pleased. Despite having marked him, he didn't necessarily need to care for me beyond the minimum required to ensure my continued existence. Yet, despite the faint hint of warmth I felt, my burning questions continued to plague me, driving me to the brink of madness.

"Then answer me," I demanded, eliciting a warning growl from him. "I can't take it. Don't torture me."

"You simply can't stand not knowing, can you?" he chuckled.

"I can't! It's the worst. I need to know!" I exclaimed.

"Knowledge isn't always power as you claim."

"It certainly is! I could not have been prepared for what you were going to subject me to unless I had knowledge about Alphas and Omegas."

Cartan tilted his head slightly to the side, studying me intently. "How much knowledge do you have?"

"A significant amount. I've studied it all, despite never being meant for an Alpha."

"Why study it, then?"

"My sisters were certainly going to be tied to Alphas at some point," I explained.

"And what about you? Why were you hidden from the world?"

I sighed, lowering myself further onto my forearms, still feeling his knot keeping us securely connected. It seemed like his body was determined not to release me this time, a thought that strangely brought me comfort, though I quickly pushed it aside.

"Opportunity," I replied.

"What kind of opportunity?"

"For freedom. Everyone knew about my sisters, their dynamics, and what would eventually become of them. Our father passed away too early to find suitable Alphas for them, but their fates were clear. However, when I was born, people initially thought I was dead. I was nothing but a small, lifeless thing, not making a sound while my mother took her last breath. However, the moment my father held me in his hands, ready to lay me beside my mother, I woke up. I gained color, and I found my voice. But he was alone when I took my first breath, and he realized the true protection he could provide me was through anonymity."

I glanced at the Alpha behind me, noting the intrigued expression on his face.

"But as you grew older and they could determine whether you were truly an Omega, your scent must have given you away."

"My father chose only the most loyal people to serve at the castle, and I was clever from birth. I found ways to disguise myself using Beta clothing, and later, with herbs."

"Which you shared with your sisters. Your father didn't see it as an offense?"

"He certainly didn't like it, but he understood the safety it could bring. My entire life was spent in that library, you see, and that's how I remained hidden."

Cartan ran a warm hand down my back, making me sigh as his purring grew louder. His knot continued to hold us tightly, and he needed me to relax so I wouldn't grip him so tightly. He slid his hand around me, stroking my clit.

"Oh, yes," I panted, unable to contain my pleasure.

He growled deeply when he finally slipped from me, then he pulled out and lifted me, carrying me to a bed further away. He gently laid me down on the furs, spreading my legs wide before entering me again, going as deep as possible and delivering intense pleasure as he took me vigorously, almost howling like a wolf as he reached his peak.

Chapter Fifteen
Cartan

My little Omega lay soundly asleep in my arms, my continuous purring never ceasing, and my knot still firmly connecting us as I cradled her in safety. It bestowed upon me an overwhelming sense of tranquility, a sensation I had never thought I would experience. While I possessed the ability to remain patient, all Alphas were inherently burdened with a potent aggression that demanded release.

But there was no need for me to leave the bed, pace anxiously, or monitor the world's happenings. I could simply lie there and gaze upon the small Omega before me. Regardless of the outcome with the other clan leaders, I knew that no one was permitted to even cast a lingering or lustful glance in her direction. I would not hesitate to tear them apart if they dared.

I was aware of how an Alpha could become entranced by their Omega, which was why I had already chosen one before encountering her. I had believed it would bring a measure of control. But the youngest princess had an inexplicable allure that drew me in, making me believe that nothing else could compare.

Nevertheless, maybe I should attempt a comparison. Maybe I should seek out a distraction from this intense connection with the enigmatic Omega in front of me. The idea did not particularly appeal to me, but we had brought servants and entertainment with us for a reason.

As my knot released Kiandra, I carefully slipped out of bed without disturbing her, dressing in my pants and boots. I ventured outside, taking in the invigorating sea air, and Tyros soon joined me. He had been assigned as the night's guard to ensure everything ran smoothly.

"You seem troubled," he pointed out, though the unspoken words hung heavy in the air.

"I am aware of what she is doing to me, but I will regain my focus," I pledged.

"Was it not painful to tear yourself away from her?"

"She does not possess that level of control over me."

"Yet," he added.

I emitted a low growl, warning him not to overstep his boundaries. I needed to appear composed when meeting the other clan leaders in a few weeks. Hopefully, by then, Kiandra's herbs would have lost some of their effectiveness. However, I was astounded to find myself displeased at the thought of others being able to detect her scent as well.

"Perhaps you should demonstrate that she does not truly dominate you," Tyros suggested, voicing the same contemplations that had been swirling in my mind.

The idea itself was simple enough. I could easily find a Beta woman to divert my attention, to momentarily liberate my thoughts from the Omega. Yet, actualizing the notion felt insurmountable. What troubled me even more was how firmly rooted to the spot I remained. This should not be happening. I was certain I would never be so utterly captivated by an Omega, but there I stood, my mouth watering at the mere thought of tasting her again. The way she whimpered and moaned when her pussy was pleasured was enough to awaken the primal animal within me, the one that only knew the art of mating.

"Shit," Tyros muttered, taking a cautious step to the side.

"What?" I snapped at him.

"Your scent is so overpowering. I can hardly

stand being this close to you. I'm surprised you haven't marked her yet," Tyros observed.

"It's close," I growled, the shift in my tone lending it a predatory edge.

"You must refrain from doing so, considering how it might appear to the other clan leaders—"

"I know!" I interrupted, my voice resonating over the expanse of the ocean. "I understand the implications."

"You've worked too hard to let it all crumble," he cautioned.

"What do you want from me?" I demanded.

"Go distract yourself. Do not succumb to her allure again," he advised.

I shook my head, feeling irritation welling up within me. My instincts screamed at me to eliminate my oldest friend for attempting to keep me from my bonded Omega. Though I had yet to mark her, she remained undeniably connected to me. No one should be able to prevent me from being with her. Nonetheless, I comprehended the significance of his words.

With a curt nod, I turned away and made my way back below deck. I navigated the corridors filled with moaning sounds, but they held no allure for me. I lacked the enthusiasm to entertain the thought of engaging with a Beta. I had barely taken a step forward when I abruptly spun around, my body aware of precisely what it craved, and it was not behind any of those doors.

Returning to my cabin, I immediately noticed Kiandra sitting up, reclining on her elbows. A strange intuition told me she had discerned the turmoil brewing within me, drawing conclusions that were highly plausible. She was far too perceptive for me to hide anything from her.

"Did it work?" she spat out, her voice dripping with venom, which oddly gratified my instincts. Had my

Omega already become possessive of me? Why did that sense of possessiveness feel so satisfying? I began undressing as I advanced toward her, my cock already throbbing and eager for more. She tightened the furs around her, glaring at me, convinced that I had spent my time elsewhere. How had she pieced it all together so swiftly?

"Did what work?" I taunted her.

"Don't come near me!" she hissed, displaying her small teeth as she retreated against the wall. Nevertheless, I continued to approach her. She attempted to jump from the bed, but I seized her ankle, yanking her back and forcing her onto her hands and knees once again. She continued to hiss at me, but her body betrayed her, releasing her sweet slick. Leaning down, I lapped it up, causing her to shudder beneath me and push back, eager for more. I began sliding my tongue over her drenched folds, gripping her hips firmly as I feasted on her, driving her to a fevered state of arousal.

"That's it, my little Omega, come for your Alpha," I growled darkly. She climaxed at my command, crying out and pushing back, but in her haze, I withdrew and thrust into her, eliciting a small scream from her at the intrusion. I pulled her back against me, our bodies molding together as I continued to thrust, feeling her walls clench around me, drawing me deeper.

I leaned in close to her ear and whispered, "Can you smell anyone but your Alpha?"

She grew strangely still, but I persisted, driving more sounds of pleasure from her lips.

"Well?" I pressed.

She turned her head, burying it in my neck, which prompted a contented growl to escape me as I continued to claim her. She nuzzled even closer, wrapping an arm around me to keep me near as I continued our passionate mating until we were both drenched in sweat, completely entwined, and having reached our climax. Kiandra didn't pull away from my neck, and I began to purr.

Yet her soft whisper reached my ears, "You may want to share me, but I've already claimed you."

She hadn't explicitly expressed a desire not to share me, but her unspoken words were clear.

Chapter Sixteen
Kiandra

Something peculiar had transpired since the onset of our voyage. I found myself confined to the cabin, permitted only to venture onto the deck under vigilant guard. Cartan would return in the dead of night, and the mere sensation of the bed shifting or the sound of the door closing would render me wet and yearning for him. We would engage in frenzied mating, our bodies communicating what words could not. He would purr me to slumber, only for me to awaken in the morning, bereft of his presence.

The bed felt empty without him, especially since it was designed to accommodate an Alpha's form. I despised the fact that, after merely two weeks at sea, I had grown to miss him. I loathed the intensity of my yearning, but I consoled myself, recognizing it as an inevitable consequence. According to my extensive studies, an Omega spending an extended duration with the same Alpha would inevitably form a profound attachment. Familiarity would breed a sense of security until she could no longer resist the urge to claim him.

Yet Cartan had not marked me, intensifying my unease about whether I was adequately safeguarded from being shared among the other clan leaders. This distance he had imposed between us only exacerbated my apprehension. Additionally, each time I did encounter him, all we could think of was mating, as we had been separated throughout the day. Somewhere within the recesses of my mind, I understood why we were ensnared in this pattern, yet the specific terminology eluded me. Without my books, I was unable to pinpoint precisely what was transpiring between us.

I was aware of the innate attraction, the magnetic pull between Alphas and Omegas, but it seemed our capacity for rational thought diminished with each day spent apart. Why was this the case? I knew the answer. It was on the tip of my tongue.

"Come on, Kiandra, think," I admonished myself as I sat by the sizable window overlooking the ocean. I hoped the tranquil seascape might help my contemplation, but my thoughts incessantly gravitated toward Cartan. His golden complexion, marked by the scars and battles he had endured, only accentuated his allure. I delighted in running my fingers through his short, dark hair, tracing the sharp contours of his jawline, and feeling the texture of his closely trimmed beard. However, what brought even greater pleasure was when my fingers descended to explore his bared chest and abdomen, igniting a fervor within me.

"Gods," I moaned, shaking my head. I was supposed to discern an explanation for my loss of control, yet I was spiraling further into my desires. This was unlike me, and I stood up, pacing the room. I wore no clothing because on the second night, Cartan had returned and ripped my dress before mounting me, our union culminating in a blissful, ecstatic entwinement.

"Again!" I exclaimed, throwing my arms wide, utterly at a loss. I needed to regain my focus, to decipher how to emerge from this bewildering haze. Perhaps my heat was approaching sooner than I anticipated. Maybe it had been influencing me all along. That had to be the explanation, right? Cartan appeared to have no trouble distancing himself from me, as he carried out his duties on the ship. Yet, I found it impossible to divert my thoughts from him even for a brief respite.

In my frustration, I leaned forward, placing my hand against the glass, and looking at the powerful waves. The serene view provided some measure of solace, and I inhaled deeply, trying to banish all thoughts of the magnificent Alpha.

"Think of your sisters," I whispered to myself, and I did, finding relief in envisioning them. I fervently hoped they had successfully escaped, vanishing into the vast, unfamiliar world beyond. Despite my desire for their freedom, Cartan had raised a disconcerting point: how well would they fare in the unknown place?

I could picture Cassia rallying a band of outlaws, ruling them with an iron grip, making the roads perilous for travelers. A smile graced my lips at the thought of her as a formidable bandit. Vivina, on the other hand, would undoubtedly be tirelessly working to reclaim her throne, amassing supporters through the sheer force of her eloquent persuasion.

As for Solana, she had teetered on the brink of despair when we were surrounded from all sides. How would she navigate this harsh world? Were they sticking together, or had circumstances driven them apart? The thought of their separation weighed heavily on my mind.

"Oh no," I groaned, sensing my thoughts gaining newfound dominance. Once again, I found myself ensnared by the enigma of my sisters' well-being, an agonizing unknown that tormented my psyche. As these thoughts intensified, an insatiable yearning for Cartan welled up within me. I wasn't entirely taken aback by my response.

My instincts wanted to restore balance, yet it troubled me that I was gravitating toward him. My purpose had been to wield power, to show that Omegas possessed a degree of control. However, I began to doubt whether my knowledge could be effectively applied in the real world. While some aspects seemed to align, my current behavior defied reason. How could I yearn for someone who had taken so much from me?

I should have been consumed by nothing but disdain, and yet an inexplicable warmth stirred in my lower abdomen, while my slick coated my thighs and pussy. How could this be happening to me? I sought refuge in the notion that it was my impending heat, but I couldn't deny the sudden and profound need that had arisen.

I craved Cartan, but he would not return until nightfall. My eyes roamed the room, desperately seeking something to help my yearning. They landed upon the furs, and an unusual compulsion overcame me. I approached them, irresistibly drawn to bring them to my nose and inhale deeply. As the scent enveloped me, my body quivered with delight.

A compulsion to gather the furs and create a pile seized me, akin to … I recoiled, hissing, and cast the fur in my hand to the floor. Colliding with the table at the center of the room, I abruptly comprehended what I had been doing—I had been trying to nest! Panic set in as I stumbled to the floor, clutching my head. If I was nesting, my heat had to be close, right? It couldn't possibly be because I yearned for the security of Cartan's presence, driving me to create a private place for us, could it?

I groaned, my body quivering as I rocked back and forth. What was happening to me? I was not this primal creature. I could be slightly clumsy, somewhat disconnected from the world beneath my feet, but I was in control, intelligent, always composed. Yet now, my body constantly betrayed me, yielding to instincts and reducing me to precisely what I vehemently resisted—nothing more than an Omega. It was a harrowing thought.

Chapter Seventeen
Kiandra

I remained awake this time, acutely aware when the door creaked open in the dead of night. The room was in utter darkness. Heavy footsteps traversed the chamber, heading toward the bed, but Cartan soon detected my absence. I watched him turn, then heard him inhale deeply, his nose savoring the potent fragrance that had intensified as the herbs gradually waned. He had taken to burying his nose in my neck or running it along my back while mating me from behind, an act that seemed to ignite his primal instincts.

However, at this moment, it wasn't the wild, untamed creature I sought in my proximity. I didn't wish to react to him, but as his footsteps drew nearer, an inexplicable longing to reach out for him surged within me. After all, he represented safety. Yet when his hand stretched beneath the table and gripped my leg, I hissed and kicked out, though my resistance merely earned a dark chuckle from him. He effortlessly hoisted me off the floor, depositing me onto the table and enclosing me with his powerful and broad arms. Every facet of him exuded Alpha dominance, stoking the flames of desire within me.

"Why are you hiding, little Omega?" he inquired, his dark voice caressing my skin like a seductive melody. I parted my legs invitingly, and he accepted the unspoken invitation, positioning himself between them. However, he still wore his pants, maintaining close proximity without further contact. "I sense your worry, your fear, but it's not directed at me."

He inclined his head slightly, scrutinizing me as his face drew nearer. I found myself leaning in, irresistibly drawn to the Alpha before me. Without restraint, I pressed my lips to his in a brief kiss. He appeared taken aback by the gesture but responded by gripping my hair and claiming my lips in a far more assertive manner.

He dominated the kiss, his tongue delving into my mouth and igniting an intense heat that felt like a consuming blaze. One of his hands ventured to my breasts, caressing and squeezing the sensitive flesh, eliciting a whimper from me. However, his ministrations and possession abruptly ceased as he pulled back, lips glistening from our passionate exchange.

"Don't stop," I implored, yearning for his touch to quell the turmoil within me.

"Tell me what troubles you first," he demanded.

"You already know. You're the one who's keeping me confined," I retorted.

"You're free to venture outside."

"Under guard, and even then, I can't. I have no clothes. You tore them apart."

He smiled, visibly pleased with himself, which incited another hiss of frustration from me, yet he found my irritation amusing.

"I prefer you this way," he growled darkly, allowing his eyes to roam freely over my exposed form. I reveled in the intensity of his gaze and pushed out my chest, the sensitive skin grazing against his hand, though he refrained from further engagement.

"Yes, keeping me as your personal plaything, trapped, always ready to receive you, must bring you great satisfaction, while I slowly descend into madness in here," I snarled.

He growled back at me, not appreciating my tone, but I couldn't suppress my frustration. When I wasn't consumed by yearning for him, my thoughts spiraled out of control, intensifying my desire for him.

"Do you understand that in order for an Alpha to retain his sanity, he must ensure the happiness of his Omega?" I challenged, his eyes narrowing slightly, though I possessed the most profound understanding of our dynamic. I had studied it thoroughly. "I am not happy."

"Then tell me what you need. I might have initially arrived to collect you and your sisters as offerings, but you are not our prisoners. If you desire something, all you must do is ask," he declared, surprising me with the simple prospect of making a request that would be fulfilled.

"Clothes," I began.

"Some will be delivered to you in the morning," he assured me.

He lifted me and placed me on the bed before disrobing himself.

"Books!" I quickly added before the allure of his Alpha physique drew me in.

Leaning over me, he smoothly joined me on the bed, nestling between my legs.

"In the morning," he replied before capturing my lips in a fervent kiss. I moaned into his mouth, my nails digging into his shoulders.

Reaching between us, he positioned himself, taking his time to slide in, as though savoring every inch of our connection. I pulled back, gasping for air, but he was not willing to let our lips part, claiming me once more with a forceful kiss. His tongue delved into my mouth as he slowly penetrated me, his deliberate pace driving me to the brink of desperation.

When he eventually quickened the rhythm, thrusting into me with urgency, my entire body erupted, and I tilted my head back, crying out in ecstasy. He leaned down, kissing and nipping at my neck while maintaining his relentless pace. His movements grew more forceful, his groans louder, until he finally knotted me, releasing inside me.

As I panted, slowly descending from my climax, I became aware of how serene I felt, and how the bond between us exuded tranquility. I had to shut him off for the day, as he was constantly consumed by aggression, but these moments were characterized by pure peace.

I reached up, running my fingers through his hair, causing his entire body to relax. It was a weakness of his, and it brought a smile to my lips. I was becoming accustomed to him. This thought sparked my concern once more, but he distracted me by gently biting my neck before soothing the sting with his tongue.

"What troubled you today?" he inquired once again.

I hesitated to reveal the task I had nearly completed earlier in the day, so I redirected his attention to another pressing concern that weighed heavily on my mind each day.

"I've been worrying about how my sisters are faring," I whispered. "It's been two weeks."

He lifted his head and regarded me intently, the faint scar on his cheek barely discernible in the darkness. I reached up, tracing it with a finger, and he seized my hand, kissing my wrist.

"You were the one who set them free," he reminded me.

"They deserve their freedom," I asserted.

"Yet they are wholly unprepared for the world beyond, and you are aware of this. Who knows what might befall them now?"

I understood his intentions—to torment me with the consequences of my choices and make me suffer for complicating his mission. I groaned and averted my gaze, but he caught my chin and compelled me to meet his eyes.

"Of course, you could tell me their whereabouts, and I could ensure their safe transport to the other side," he proposed.

"I don't know where they are," I replied.

He growled darkly, tightening his grip on my chin, causing me to wince slightly.

"I don't know!" I exclaimed.

"They are your sisters. You set them free!"

"Exactly! I released them into the wild, that's it!" I informed him, feeling his grip loosen slightly as his eyes searched mine.

"Do you truly have no idea where they are heading?" he questioned.

"I do not."

"Then you're even more foolish than I thought."

I hissed at him, but he merely smiled.

"You didn't even provide them with a safe destination. Now they are at the mercy of the Gods," he reminded me, making me glance down as I realized the truth of his words. Without proper guidance or understanding of the land, how would they fare out there?

As I had packed my bags, it hadn't even crossed my mind to ensure they had a map or know where to seek refuge. The realization hit me hard, and I began to squirm beneath Cartan's firm grasp. However, we were still locked together, and I couldn't risk hurting myself. But I couldn't endure this uncertainty, knowing my sisters were truly at the mercy of fate.

I reached out to Cartan, urging him to alleviate my anxiety by teasing the mark I had given him. He growled darkly, a delightful tone that made my body tingle. His hips responded, yearning to continue our mating. I needed the same, something to calm my fears, but then his large hand tangled in my hair, pulling my head back.

"Where are they?" he demanded, surprising me with his words.

"I thought you believed me."

"I do believe you aren't aware of their exact location, but they are your sisters, and it's evident who possesses the sharper mind," he said, making me hiss again as he insulted my sisters. He smiled and leaned closer to me, his intoxicating scent surrounding us. I pressed against him, offering my breasts to him, which he eyed with hunger, but he resisted, denying us both what we desired.

"Where would they go?" he asked, changing his approach, his eyes locked onto mine.

"I..." I felt tempted to divulge all the places I believed would be safe for them to seek refuge, hoping they were considering the same options. However, my inner voice screamed that I hadn't freed them only to be the reason for their capture. I clamped down hard on my lower lip, refusing to speak, and Cartan growled again, pressing me to tell him.

"Where?" he tried once more.

I shook my head, but as he felt his knot release me, he flipped me onto my stomach and pressed me into the bed, sliding himself deep inside me. It was an agonizingly pleasurable torment. I relished the sensation of his massive Alpha cock stretching me in the most exquisite way, providing me with immense pleasure, but the knowledge that this was all I would ever be infuriated me.

I clawed at the furs, trying to ignore his expert movements. I knew I couldn't prevent myself from climaxing. It felt too incredible. Still, I attempted to remain silent. But just as I teetered on the edge of release,

Cartan withdrew, spilling his seed across my back and ass. I gasped at the sensation of it smearing my skin, yet strangely, I had an overpowering urge to coat myself in his scent.

It's just my heat, I reassured myself, trying to suppress my mounting desires. But before I could resist any further, Cartan was back inside me, thrusting forcefully, causing my body to jerk forward. He gripped my shoulder to hold me in place. I was on the brink of climaxing, feeling my nipples rubbing against the bedding as his cock found an exquisite spot within me.

However, Cartan was not focused on my pleasure. He rushed to reach his climax, locking us together before leaving me panting and unsatisfied. I groaned, pounding my hand into the bed, uncertain why he had denied me. He always made me climax, even when he interrogated me or left me alone for the entire day. Even the first time he claimed me and when I marked him, he had provided me with incredible pleasure. So why was he doing this now? I turned my head, glaring at him, and saw him smiling.

"Where?" he asked once more.

"Please," I whispered, attempting to shift slightly, only to gasp at the sensation of his knot securely keeping me in place.

"No moving," he commanded.

"Please!"

He leaned over me, pressing his hand into my shoulder, ensuring I remained still. His warm breath caressed my neck as he buried his face in my hair, inhaling deeply.

"It's coming back," he murmured, referring to my scent gradually returning. Soon, I wouldn't be protected against any potential pregnancy, and given the frequency with which Cartan took me, I wouldn't be surprised if I ended up pregnant before my heat arrived.

"Now tell me where they are, and I will give you what your little Omega body craves from her Alpha," he taunted.

"No..." I whimpered, struggling to resist.

"Your sisters need protection too. Remember what you said the first time I took you. You're just one little Omega in a vast world. You need an Alpha."

"My sisters are free!" I groaned, yearning to move to find some friction.

"And how long will they remain free? They may be able to hide their Omega scents, but they are ill-prepared for the harshness of the outside world. Do you think concealing their scent will save them from being taken advantage of? Do you believe it will spare them from being forced onto their backs or trapped in someone's house, made to serve? You've been sheltered your entire lives. You aren't prepared for the true brutality that exists."

"The brutality of Alphas!" I snapped, and Cartan gripped my hair with his free hand, pulling my head back.

"You're mistaken."

"History has shown that you treat us as nothing more than slaves," I spat.

"That's where you're mistaken, and someone as intelligent as you knows there's more to it than that. Besides, we learn from history. There will be no savage hunts or auctions for you. You will be taken care of."

"But owned," I snarled. "Perhaps even shared."

He growled in anger and then sank his teeth into my neck in a sharp bite without marking me. I hissed, but he ran his warm tongue over the sting afterward.

"*Mine*," he growled in my ear, causing me to shudder.

"Am I?"

His grip on my hair tightened even more, and he turned my head forcefully, claiming my lips in a searing kiss that made my toes curl. I moaned against his lips, and he slipped his tongue into my mouth, stroking mine with his. However, the intense kiss didn't last long as he pulled away, fixing me with his stern gaze.

"You belong to only one Alpha," he asserted.

"Yet he has played games with me, made me believe I might be shared, and he won't mark me. So who's to say I won't suddenly find myself yielding to an entire camp of Alphas?"

His growl deepened, and he pushed me harder into the bed as his knot began to release me. Then he positioned my ass in the air this time as he took me.

"Gods," I moaned into the bed, on the brink of climax. He only teased me before withdrawing and turning me over, gripping my hair and commanding me to pleasure him with my mouth.

I took him in as deeply as I could, and he tried to push a bit further, causing me to gag briefly before pulling back and controlling the pace. Even having my mouth filled with him made me wetter, feeling fire between my legs. I moaned around his hardness, my nails grazing his thighs as I lost myself in the sensations of pleasuring my Alpha. He was undeniably perfect. I begrudgingly admitted it to myself—he was everything I could desire, given that I had to submit to one. I truly hoped he meant it when he said I only belonged to him, because I didn't want anyone else.

Cartan's grip tightened further, and he thrust into my mouth faster, intensifying my moans and whimpers. My fingers ventured between my legs, but his primal growl warned me not to touch myself. It was torture not being able to relieve the throbbing ache of my clit, desperate for attention. However, Cartan continued to use me for his own pleasure before climaxing in my mouth.

Chapter Eighteen
Cartan

I couldn't deny that I would rather have known the whereabouts of the other princesses immediately, but I had to admire the strength of my determined little Omega. She was a challenge to unravel, and I found great pleasure in it.

Never had a woman made me yearn to remain between her legs until the sun ceased to burn or to pleasure her with my tongue for an eternity, surviving only on the sweet slick she was producing. But that was precisely what my Omega reduced me to.

I had assumed it might become easier, but it seemed that each time we mated, the longing grew stronger. Moreover, her enticing scent was gradually returning, driving me into a maddening frenzy of desire. I longed to bask in its heavenly sweetness while keeping it all to myself.

It would be challenging to allow other Alphas near her, but I couldn't let her continue taking the herbs. I craved her scent, feeling entitled to it, and it was finally making its way back to me. However, I couldn't be a selfish Alpha. I needed to learn the whereabouts of those princesses.

I knew I was close to breaking Kiandra. Her concern for her sisters was evident, and every time I fucked her and purred, she understood just how secure she could be with an Alpha. Her resolve was slowly weakening, and I just needed a bit more time.

So I returned the next day, repeating the same questions, denying her any pleasure. When I came back on the third day and followed the same routine, taking her three times and leaving Kiandra a trembling, panting mess, sprawled beneath me and tearfully begging to be allowed release, I heard her mumble something.

"What?" I whispered.

She took deep breaths, attempting to compose herself. I pulled back slightly, gazing into her tear-filled, sweet brown eyes. She just wanted her Alpha to grant her release, but she had to earn it first. However, she looked incredibly alluring in her disheveled state, with wet cheeks and trembling lips. I struggled to resist the temptation to taste her tears with my tongue.

"Geylash," she finally managed to say. "It's … it's a smaller city on Rocky Island. It would be a wise place to seek help. Our father loved the city, but also…"

"Also?" I inquired, urging her to continue.

She bit her lip and shook her head slightly, as if she couldn't muster the strength to utter the words. I leaned in, nuzzling her neck, and began purring for her. She let out a contented sigh, immediately relaxing against me. However, it still wasn't enough to prompt her to reveal more. I slipped a hand between our bodies, finding her needy clit and tracing slow circles around it, making her whimper.

"Alpha," she panted, and I relished the way she addressed me.

"Where else?" I whispered in her ear. Strangely, I didn't enjoy using her pleasure as leverage. Every fiber of my being urged me to bring her to climax repeatedly, so she would understand that no other Alpha could make her feel this way, and she would need only me. However, it was a cunning strategy to break her, and as she started to quiver in anticipation of her release, I slowed down.

"No…" she whimpered.

"Where else?" I questioned.

"Velisha!" she cried out.

I stopped teasing her clit, and she began sobbing

once more.

"No, don't stop!" she pleaded desperately.

"Velisha is nothing but a small farming town, with little of value," I reminded her, locking eyes with her.

She sniffled and nodded. "Our mother lived there."

"Your mother was originally from the Mainlands," I corrected.

Kiandra nodded, taking deep breaths to compose herself. "Yes, that's true. She was born there but fled the place when her father intended to tie her to an Alpha she hadn't chosen herself. She took a ship to the Rocky Island and ended up in Velisha. That's where our father found her after hearing about the constant attacks they faced. He saved her, and they fell in love. My mother cherished the simplicity of Velisha. Maybe..."

"Maybe they went there," I finished her thought. "Nostalgia can be a powerful force."

She nodded, biting her lip, and I could see the guilt in her eyes for revealing this information. Nevertheless, my little Omega would be rewarded for her honesty. I began stroking her clit again, and she moaned loudly, tilting her head back to accept everything I offered. It took only a few strokes, and she trembled, climaxing beneath me. She clung to my body, her pussy contracting around me, as if trying to milk every drop of cum from me.

As she reached her peak, my knot began to release her, and I continued thrusting through her orgasm, pushing her into another intense climax that had her panting my name repeatedly. She was undoubtedly a gift from the Gods, enough to drive me utterly insane.

"Is there anywhere else? Could they have left the island?" I asked, feeling the buildup of an orgasm inside me, my balls heavy and ready to release once more.

"I…" My little Omega whimpered again, succumbing to another climax, her nails raking down my back, which only intensified my pleasure.

I claimed her lips, forcing myself to slow down again, despite her protests and her biting down on my skin. I felt a slight sting, and then she began sucking on my bottom lip, savoring the blood that trickled from it. It drove me even wilder, and I thrust into her without restraint, unable to focus on anything else. She wrapped her legs around me as tightly as she could and allowed me to enter her repeatedly, giving me immense pleasure. The walls seemed to shake from my roar as I climaxed, knotting us together once more and emptying myself completely inside her.

We both collapsed onto the bed, thoroughly content, and she nuzzled against my neck, prompting me to purr for her immediately. She sighed so contentedly that it sent shivers of delight down my spine, and I held her close, covering her body with mine.

"Anywhere else?" I inquired once more. "Could any of them have decided it was better to flee the island?"

"Cassia," she whispered, breathing me in and becoming intoxicated by my scent.

"The second eldest?"

"Yes. She is fierce, she enjoys combat."

"An Omega who fights?" I questioned.

"She has trained with the guards. She is skilled with weapons. She might see this as her opportunity."

"Would she be audacious enough to attempt to rescue you?" I asked, thinking there might be one Omega I wouldn't need to search for.

"Perhaps," she replied, her voice revealing the impact of the orgasms and our bond.

"What about the eldest?"

"She will most likely stay. That is her home," Kiandra informed me.

"And the third eldest? Where might she go?"

Kiandra fell silent, which puzzled me. I pulled back, seeing her blink rapidly, as if emerging from a trance. I reached out, cupping her jaw in my hand to ensure she stayed focused on me.

"Well?"

"I-I'm not sure," she whispered, glancing down and displaying her submission.

"Why not?"

"She…"

"Yes?"

"She would rather die than belong to an Alpha," Kiandra admitted, sending a chill down my spine. These four Omegas could be the last ones left in the world, unless others were hiding using the herbs as well. But we couldn't afford to lose any more. We needed to locate the third eldest as quickly as possible.

"How can you be so certain?"

"She wrote a goodbye letter before your attack," she revealed. "Our sister scolded her for taking such a drastic step, but she's terrified."

"And you don't know where she might go?"

Kiandra shook her head. "Solana is complex. I can't decipher her thought process."

"Take a guess. The world can be a harsh place. If fear has driven her to the edge of desperation, it's crucial that you think now, Kiandra."

My serious tone caused her eyes to widen, and I could see her sharp mind working quickly. She understood that her sister wouldn't fare well in the outside world. If the Omegas didn't stick together, I needed to explore every possible hiding spot.

"Maybe the High Tower. It's an old library in the

West," she whispered.

"I'm familiar with it."

"If she hasn't left the island, she could be there."

"And if she left?"

"Search any place with art and poetry. She enjoys those, or anywhere she might find supplies for drawing and painting," Kiandra explained.

"She's on the run. Do you think she would take the time for that?"

"When we are frightened, we seek the things that bring us solace. Why do you think you have brought me to such distress? I want my books!" she snarled at me, surprising me with her strength. But I smiled and claimed her lips in a passionate kiss. She moaned against me, surrendering to my embrace.

"You will have your books. Even more when we reach the Mainlands."

Chapter Nineteen
Kiandra

I felt a mixture of guilt and an unusual sense of relaxation. While I remained under guard and restricted to the ship's deck, I had at least been provided with some form of entertainment. Perched on a small stool by the ship's side, I delved into a tiny book about the Mainlands. There wasn't much reading material available on the ship, as it hadn't been a priority for their journey, but Cartan had managed to provide me with this small diversion.

He, on the other hand, was occupied in a large room, engrossed in conversations with other Alphas about matters I was not privy to. It grated on me that I appeared to be nothing more than a source of pleasure for Cartan. I understood what I had agreed to—the surrender of myself to him in exchange for the protection I knew I would need. Yet, it didn't diminish the feeling of being used.

I even began to doubt if my confusing behavior had anything to do with my heat. When Cartan wasn't nearby and other Alphas were around me, yet kept their distance to avoid angering him, I felt nothing. There was no sense of safety or longing. I could simply look at them and shrug. Why was that? I pressed two fingers to my forehead, desperately searching my mind for the answers I knew were buried within.

"Come on," I urged myself. I knew the answer was there somewhere. It wasn't just a result of the time I had spent with him. The powerful reaction had been immediate. I tapped my finger against the book, momentarily abandoning my reading about the Mainlands. The book wasn't providing me with much new information anyway. My thoughts were consumed by the enigmatic Alpha who had been claiming me every evening and throughout the night.

Perhaps that was why my memories eluded me. Whenever he was near, he would possess me with such intensity that rational thought became a distant memory. I needed proper rest to figure this out, but sleep was elusive unless Cartan was close by. My Omega instincts had grown accustomed to his presence, finding solace and safety in him. His purr was a soothing melody to my ears, and his scent was both dark and delightful, making me want to bury my nose in his neck all day.

I was getting distracted again, a clear sign that something wasn't right. Was it solely my heat, or was there something deeper drawing me to him? Why couldn't I think clearly? I groaned and leaned my head back, gazing up at the boundless blue sky above. I hadn't taken the time to appreciate my surroundings.

The fear of leaving my home, the small island where I had grown up and the familiar library I knew, had overwhelmed me. But now, out on the open ocean, heading to a new place filled with new knowledge and experiences, I realized I had overlooked the beauty around me. A small smile tugged at my lips as I tried to find a positive aspect in all of this. Yet, my thoughts soon circled back to what I had revealed to Cartan.

He now possessed knowledge of places where he might have a chance to find my sisters. Regret gnawed at me. I shouldn't have divulged anything. My sacrifice appeared to have been in vain, but my worries for my sisters still lingered. How would they fare out there? What if I had unwittingly exposed them to new hardships? Perhaps belonging to an Alpha wouldn't be the worst fate in the world.

There might be some silver lining in it all,

especially if I could convey to my sisters how marking an Alpha could shield them from unwanted advances. Cartan, despite not having marked me, exuded an unmistakable possessiveness, and I hoped that would deter anyone else from desiring me. Maybe this was the way to safeguard ourselves. I just needed to find a way to communicate this message to my sisters, wherever they were.

I returned to my book, attempting to immerse myself in its words to distract my mind from the multitude of unanswered questions and concerns that plagued me. However, before long, the door to the cabin that Cartan had entered opened. The other Alphas exited, and Cartan's gaze immediately found me. He motioned for me to join him, and I rose to my feet. The dress I wore was unlike anything I had ever donned before. We were heading toward warmer climates, so the fabric was lighter, but the wind tugged at it, brushing over my nipples and sensitive skin, intensifying my awareness of the fact that I was walking toward the Alpha my body yearned for.

I ascended the small staircase to reach him, and it was evident that Cartan could sense the change in me, detecting my need for him. Still, he only smiled. He didn't seize me and take me with wild abandon. Instead, he guided me inside, where I spotted a large map spread out on a massive brown table.

Cartan urged me forward, his warm hands resting on my hips, and I struggled to stifle a moan. He halted us in front of the map, which depicted the entirety of Verocca. I had seen numerous maps of this land before, but none as grand as this. I even noticed how the edges extended beyond the table, hinting at additional undiscovered territory. I spotted more landmasses and islands that had previously escaped my attention.

"There's more here," I whispered.

"Some maps don't show the entirety of Verocca. I found very old ones that depict it all," Cartan explained.

My fingers traced the uncharted regions, and my eyes gravitated toward our current location. There was a tiny ship icon in the midst of it all, positioned close to the Mainlands. From there, I could see our journey would take us to the Black Desert, Cartan's home, and the domain of many tribes.

Verocca was inhabited by various Alpha tribes, but these Alphas had managed to establish a treaty and operate as a unified entity. It was an impressive feat, but Cartan diverted my attention as he took my hand and guided me around the table. We stopped by the Rocky Island, and I observed the numerous cities and towns listed on the map, a rarity in cartography. Most maps I had encountered only mentioned the most significant locations, those integral to trade and commerce.

"Incredible," I whispered in awe.

"Velisha," he said, pointing to the small town where my mother had sought refuge.

I nodded, uncertain about his intentions.

"Do you see all this forest surrounding it?" he questioned.

"Yes," I replied.

"And do you notice this town here?" he asked. He pointed to a much larger town outside the forest and closer to the other side of the island.

"I do," I confirmed.

"Do you know in that town, slavery is still legal?" he revealed.

"What? No, it can't be," I protested. "That's a matter for the Mainlands."

"In some places, yes, it's still perfectly legal, including this tiny town here," he said, tapping the location on the map.

"But my father wouldn't have allowed it," I argued.

"It's such a small town, much like Velisha. I believe he may have overlooked it, and the laws there are somewhat … questionable," he explained.

"How so?" I inquired.

He flashed a smile and retrieved a rolled-up paper, spreading it out in front of me. His warm body pressed against mine as he held the paper open, making it challenging for me to focus.

"These are some of the town's regulations," he clarified, and I read through them.

"But it clearly states that buying people is illegal," I pointed out.

"Yes, it does. However, it is not illegal to sell them or even to own slaves. The legality only pertains to purchasing, creating a loophole that they exploit," he informed me, causing a lump to form in my throat. He took the paper away and once again pointed to Velisha. "You mentioned that the town was once terrorized, and your father protected its people?"

"Yes," I affirmed.

"From what I understand, it should be relatively peaceful now. But look how close these two places are. If Velisha is nothing more than farmland with no real protection, how easy would it not be to capture a beautiful princess disguised as a mere Beta woman and turn her into a slave?" he insinuated, sending shivers down my spine.

"Why are you telling me this?" I whispered, slowly turning toward him.

He lightly tapped my head with the paper before taking a seat in one of the chairs around the table. He stretched his long, leather-covered legs in front of him, watching me intently.

"To show you how ill-conceived your plan was," he stated.

"You're trying to teach me a lesson?" I retorted.

"Indeed, I am. Omegas like you belong with Alphas," he asserted.

"Oh, yes, what a promising future, always there to please so many Alphas. So you intend to throw me to the wolves," I snapped, and Cartan growled darkly before standing up. He took a single, menacing step toward me, seizing me by the throat and pressing me firmly against the table.

"I told you, you belong to only one Alpha," he growled.

"Yes, and he refused to mark me in return, leaving me vulnerable to others," I reminded him.

Cartan shook his head, his eyes turning completely black before me.

"No other Alpha gets to touch," he snarled, his voice taking on a more animalistic tone. The bond between us radiated with his emotions, filled with the pain of being unable to mark me. He wanted to, but something held him back. I knew I needed his mark to seal our connection, leaving no room for others. I wondered if I could extract an answer from him or provoke him enough to lose control. I reached for my dress and began to lift it, inching it up over my legs. Cartan's gaze dropped, noticing how the soft blue material ascended higher. His nostrils flared, detecting my desire for him. Another growl escaped him, this time a gratified one. If he could use my pleasure against me, then I could do the same.

"Do you truly want others to have me?" I whispered, feeling his grip on my throat tighten. But I didn't stop lifting my dress until it was bunched around my hips. I reached between myself, sliding my fingers through my wetness, and then brought those fingers up to trace across Cartan's lips. This made him snarl, his fangs revealing themselves. "To let someone else taste me?"

Cartan roared, yanking me higher up and spreading my legs wide. His head descended between my thighs, his short beard grazing my skin, and I cried out in pleasure. His wicked tongue licked along my wet pussy and pushed inside me, teasing my core. I was spread wide for him as he feasted on me, causing me to unravel in moments. I lifted my hips, and he growled in satisfaction as I offered myself to him.

He sucked on my clit, pushing me over the edge before moving up my body, pulling me to the edge of the table, and yanking down his own pants to enter me. He thrust inside, making me gasp as he buried his entire length, causing my nipples to become incredibly sensitive. I wriggled out of the top part of my dress, and the moment my breasts were exposed, his mouth latched onto one of them, sucking hard. I cried out again in ecstasy, and he sucked harder until it almost bordered on pain. Then he switched to the other breast, subjecting it to the same treatment while his hips moved faster, driving his cock deep inside me with each thrust.

I reached for Cartan, gripping his hair and pulling him closer. I made him bury his nose in my neck, right where he was supposed to mark me. I felt his canines graze my skin and pushed him harder against me. However, he growled his disapproval, pulling out of me and turning me around.

My toes were barely touching the floor before he was thrusting inside me once more. He took me without restraint, his hand around my neck, pressing me against the table. I saw stars, and my entire world dimmed with blinking lights as I climaxed harder than ever before, unable to even scream. My voice was trapped while he continued pounding into me, losing himself in the moment. His grip tightened so much that it became painful as he released himself inside me, his knot stretching and locking us together. But then we were both panting, trying to catch our breath.

"You won't deceive me with your sweet scent and pussy," he warned me. "I will mark you. No one else will even entertain the thought, but it will happen when I decide."

"Why? What's so important that you're willing to leave me vulnerable to someone else? Just because I've marked you doesn't mean another Alpha couldn't decide to kill you and claim me for himself or even attempt to force his own mark on me," I challenged him.

Cartan simply chuckled darkly, his hand sliding into my hair, his fingers gently grazing my skull, sending pleasurable shivers throughout my body.

"You think another Alpha can kill me?" he taunted.

"There's always a greater opponent out there," I replied.

This time, his grip tightened painfully, and I whimpered.

"Do not underestimate me, little Omega," he snarled in my ear. "I am your Alpha, and anyone who dares to look at you for a moment too long, I will tear them apart and feed them their own eyeballs. Do you understand?"

Surprisingly, my body responded by tightening around him, making him chuckle again as my physical reaction answered him.

"Good," he whispered before a soft purring began, and I sighed contentedly as a silence enveloped us.

However, I soon felt Cartan's hand slide beneath to touch my stomach, sending shivers down my body.

"You're not pregnant yet," he observed.

"I told you when my heat is," I replied.

"Yes, but I've taken you many times by now," he noted.

I gulped, trying not to appear too obvious, but I couldn't hide anything from the Alpha behind me. He grabbed my chin and turned my head.

"You're keeping a secret from me," he declared.

"I..." My eyes darted to the side. I was a terrible liar.

"What have you done, little Omega?" he inquired.

"N-Nothing," I stammered.

"Answer me. Why aren't you pregnant yet?" he pressed.

"You won't mark me, but you're more than willing to get me pregnant?" I attempted to deflect from his question.

"That pup would be the first true Alpha to have been born in decades in The Black Desert. It would be the greatest honor. So why aren't you pregnant yet?" he questioned.

"I am not in my heat yet!"

"No, there is something else," he snarled. His thoughts were racing, and I knew it wouldn't take him long to piece it together. Admitting my secret would likely lead him to go easy on me.

"The herbs..." I whispered, my gaze shifting downward.

"The herbs. Of course. So they not only mask your scent but also prevent pregnancy?" he demanded.

"Yes..."

His growl resonated with dark aggression, causing me to whimper, even though his grip wasn't overly tight.

It frustrated me that my body only grew wetter in response to his anger, even though it was directed at me.

"In less than a week, they will wear off, and when they do, you will take nothing to prevent a pup from being conceived. I will keep you bound in my tent until you're with child," he threatened. With that, he withdrew from me, pulling me upright before escorting me back to his cabin, where he locked me inside.

Chapter Twenty
Kiandra

I gazed out at the vast ocean before me, perched by the expansive window once more, and let out a deep sigh. I knew my confession would likely infuriate Cartan, but I hoped that by coming clean, I had at least lessened some of his anger. His warning had sent shivers down my spine. The prospect of being reduced to a mere breeding vessel was dreadful, even though my body seemed to relish the idea of constant mating and pleasure. I, however, had no desire to be just another Omega breeder.

In the days of old, that's precisely what we were—Omegas hunted and claimed like wild animals. Cartan's words lingered in my mind. He spoke of learning from history, a sentiment I couldn't disagree with, yet he didn't seem to have learned. However, with fewer of us now, some believed it was divine punishment, retribution from the Gods for not cherishing the profound bond that could form between an Alpha and an Omega.

"A true bond!" I exclaimed, rising from the chair I had been occupying. The revelation struck me, simultaneously frightening and settling.

I scoured the books I had at my disposal, but none delved into the intricacies of the bond between an Omega and an Alpha. So, I turned to my own memories, recalling what I knew about the concept of a true bond. My parents had shared one—a deep, instantaneous connection reserved for the most perfect pair of mates. It was said that such a bond between an Alpha and an Omega was unparalleled in its intensity.

If this was what existed between Cartan and me, I had to concede that it was indeed remarkable. Yet, it was also daunting to consider the implications. Cartan would be possessive beyond measure, all while he continued to impose his lessons on me, making me feel like a powerless Omega subject to his will. It angered me because I felt enslaved by our bond, unable to harness the influence I should rightfully have over an Alpha.

"Gods," I groaned, rubbing my eyes. I wondered if I could somehow lessen the overwhelming connection that bound us. Cartan's emotions were already difficult to handle. Perhaps once we reached the Mainlands, I could find a solution—something to restore my sense of empowerment and enable me to make Cartan bow to me, instead of remaining a submissive Omega under his rule.

****

Later in the evening, Cartan returned, but he didn't bother to disrobe us. Instead, he settled into a chair and had me kneel before him, releasing his hard cock and guiding me onto it. He used me solely for his pleasure, climaxing down my throat before adjusting his clothing and abruptly standing up. I gazed up at him with a perplexed expression, my body tingling with the usual desire, yearning for his touch and the feel of him inside me.

"Until I'm certain you can conceive, I won't be fucking you," he growled, leaving the cabin without further explanation.

I hissed in frustration, baring my teeth at the closed door, before storming over to the bed and sitting down with an angry huff. I thought I had felt used before, but this was an entirely new level. I angrily grabbed my hair and noticed the furs on the bed were disheveled. I began arranging them, only to catch myself attempting to create a nest once again.

"Shit!" I yelled, pushing away from the bed.

My body trembled from denying the comfort of nesting, a preparation not only for my upcoming heat but also for a refuge during times of confusion. These furs were enticing, as they held my Alpha's scent, but rather than providing comfort, that thought fueled my anger.

Instead, I fetched some clean clothes from a nearby chest and laid them out on the floor, fashioning a makeshift bed. Lying down, however, felt utterly wrong without the reassuring purr and scent of my Alpha. I tossed and turned, unable to settle, my frustration mounting. I clenched the clothes, trying to wrap them around me in a makeshift nest-like manner. It sort of worked, tricking my mind into a sense of correctness, and I drifted into an uneasy slumber, far from restful.

Morning arrived, the sunlight streaming into the cabin. I slipped out of my makeshift nest, glaring at it as it failed to provide the comfort I craved. I cast a sidelong glance at the distant bed, my hands itching to rearrange the furs and sheets into a comforting sanctuary. However, I resisted the urge, turning my back on it.

Soon, though, my irritation waned as a meal was brought into the cabin. I eagerly focused on eating, pushing my nest-related frustrations aside. But once the distraction was gone, my attention returned to the bed. I shook my head, making my way to the cabin door. Outside, I encountered one of my guards and requested access to the deck.

Carrying my book with me, I tried to distract myself outdoors, but it was challenging to concentrate when I observed Cartan working on the ship. He effortlessly ascended the tall ropes, moved confidently among his crew, and sometimes even took the helm himself. He looked so commanding, steering the ship with a composed expression and his gaze fixed firmly ahead.

Gods, it took very little for my focus to waver, and I forced myself to avert my gaze from him, turning so I could present him my back. I stared intently at the words on the pages, reading about the Mainlands once more. However, I caught myself repeatedly glancing at Cartan—issuing orders, conversing casually with his men, or even skillfully navigating the ship. He appeared so impressive, commanding everyone with an air of calm and determination.

But it didn't take much for me to lose my concentration entirely, and I struggled to avert my gaze from him. I forced myself to focus on the book, but it offered no new insights. Time passed around me, and I suddenly sensed a powerful presence behind me. Looking up, I noted that the sun was on its way down before I glanced over my shoulder and saw Cartan standing there.

With a single nod, he signaled for me to stand, and I complied. We returned to the cabin together, and once more, he had me kneel before him, taking him into my mouth. This time, my body quivered from being denied his touch, and tears welled up in my eyes when he finally stood. However, he didn't leave immediately.

Instead, he returned with food, placing it on the table and then sitting down. He beckoned for me to come closer while I still sat on the ground. I rose and when I was near enough, he reached out, placing me on his lap. I wrapped an arm around his neck for support, and he began feeding me. It was the first time he had done this, and the gesture took me by surprise. I remembered my sisters telling me that our mother was not allowed to eat or feed herself.

Now, Cartan was tending to another of my needs, but I understood why he did it. Since he was refusing to touch me, he found different ways to keep me emotionally bound to him, making me crave his presence.

I turned my head stubbornly away from the food before me, and it elicited a growl of warning from Cartan. Despite the powerful alarms in my head telling me not to provoke the Alpha, I ignored them.

"Are you challenging me, little Omega?" he questioned.

"I will not eat from your hand," I retorted.

"I am your Alpha, and therefore you will," he asserted.

"An Alpha who once again uses the Omega he has been given," I spat.

Cartan grabbed my chin, turning my head, and pressed a piece of meat to my lips, but I kept them firmly sealed together.

"Things are different now," he assured me.

"How? You said we learn from history, but you will gladly tie me up in your tent to be used. How is that different from how Omegas were treated in the past?" I demanded.

"You're right. In the Mainlands, where they used to flourish, they were treated poorly, but it wasn't the case throughout Verocca. In the clans, they were revered. Among my people, they were respected, and I know they were on the Rocky Island as well, although they never had an abundance of Omegas. However, because of those cruel acts, we all paid," he replied. He surprised me with his words as if he wanted to rewrite history and save the Omegas who had suffered. "The clans want a different way now."

"And what about the king? His family used to indulge in Omega companions," I spat, prompting a smile from Cartan.

"He wants a different approach as well. As I said, we learn, and we strive to do better. Now, I simply need to locate your sisters."

"Yes, perfect, wonderful! So they can be tied up in tents as well. How can you be certain that some Alpha won't want them all for himself, or even the king?" I challenged.

"First, eat, and I will answer," he proposed.

"Manipulative."

"It's called negotiation, Princess," he countered, making me eye the food in his hand before finally relenting. I took the piece of meat from his hand, and as I did, the tips of his fingers brushed against my lips. I noticed how he tensed at the contact, giving me an idea of something I could use against him.

"Now," I pressed.

"We can't afford to be selfish," he explained. "Not when there are so few of you. Therefore, through our treaty, we have agreed that Omegas will go to each of the clan leaders."

"But there are many clan leaders."

"But only five in The Black Desert," he reminded me.

"That still leaves one out, plus the king."

"The king will receive an Omega. I will find a solution for that, but my allegiance is to the clans."

"That still leaves one out," I insisted.

Cartan smiled, which puzzled me. He shook his head but then brought more food to my lips. This time, I sucked on his fingers, drawing them in deeper, and I heard him growl as his body tensed beneath me. When I leaned back, it was with a satisfied smile. He warned me with his eyes not to push him, but I had no intention of heeding that warning.

"So?" I pressed. "You're leaving one out."

"He cannot be satisfied with any of you females."

"What? What does that mean?" I asked. Cartan

leaned back and gave me a smug look, leaving me to figure it out on my own. It didn't take long, and I let out a slow, "*Oh*. He prefers males."

"He does," Cartan confirmed.

"Male Omegas are even rarer. I don't even know if there are any left," I remarked.

"We are aware of this, and he has made it very clear he has no intention of claiming any of you."

"So that just leaves the king out. Won't he be displeased?" I pointed out.

"No, I will find a solution for that."

"You sound quite confident."

"I found you," he reminded me, his grip on my body firm as he watched me with his intensely powerful eyes.

He was right. He had indeed found me, even after I was officially declared dead. However, my sisters and I might very well be the last of our kind. How could he fulfill the king's desires?

That's when a thought crossed my mind.

"You're not offering our first daughter to the king!" I snapped at him, observing the myriad of emotions that flickered across his face, too numerous to decipher.

"I most certainly am not," he finally replied. "Anyone who desires our daughter will have to face me in combat."

I rolled my eyes, but he held me tighter against him, and I noticed a smile form on his lips, which took me by surprise.

"What's so amusing?" I inquired.

"I like that you specified 'first', indicating there will be more. Perhaps you don't mind being kept in my tent, constantly breeding and mating," he purred, stirring a longing within me that I resented.

"I do. I'll go insane, much like being confined to this cabin is driving me crazy."

"It will come to an end soon," he reassured me, feeding me more food as I continued to press him with questions.

"How will you determine which Omega goes to whom?"

"Well, I had the first pick for locating all of you," he informed me.

"Was that a mutual decision or your decision?" I asked, seeking clarification.

He smiled, and his answer became apparent.

"Did you already have your eye on me, or...?" I started.

"I initially chose your eldest sister," he confessed. This ignited a burning rage within me that revealed my own possessive feelings toward the Alpha before me.

Cartan leaned in closer, taking in my stronger Omega scent, and chuckled contentedly. "Don't worry, little Omega. There is only you now."

His words instantly soothed me, but they didn't diminish my curiosity.

"So, how will you decide?" I inquired.

Cartan shrugged. "We'll hold a meeting and determine who goes where."

"Will we have any say in the matter?" I asked.

He merely raised an eyebrow, indicating that we wouldn't. I groaned and tried to wriggle free from his grip, but he held me tighter, preventing me from escaping.

"How can you simply decide our fates?" I snapped.

"You would all be paired with strong and honorable Alphas," he reassured me.

"Do you not understand that it's the Omega who

has the final say?" I argued.

"I'm aware, but I also know that Omegas can grow comfortable with an Alpha over time, forming a bond," he explained.

"It wouldn't be the same," I murmured, glancing away. My parents had a true bond, and now I had one too. No matter how much power it had over me, I couldn't deny it was special.

"Even though a bond can form, it doesn't guarantee compatibility or that they won't drive each other insane," I reminded him. "The Omegas should choose."

"Would you?" he challenged.

I bit my lip, knowing we would do everything in our power not to. My decision to accept the mark had been a strategic move to protect myself, but maybe my sisters could also see its value.

"I believe we would. I've realized the importance of it," I admitted.

"How would you decide?" he inquired. "You mentioned Solana's fear of Alphas."

"Maybe they could spend time with each of them," I suggested, but Cartan shook his head. "Why not?"

"The Alphas would grow impatient, angry, possessive. They would want to claim the first one they spend time with because they would fear none of them would choose him," he explained.

"So, we have no choice?" I protested.

"You will be protected and kept safe," he replied.

"I think my sisters can keep themselves safe. I should never have told you anything. They will most likely stay together, and with their combined skills, they will manage," I stated, crossing my arms, only to have more food brought to my lips, which I ate.

"But none of them are prepared for the real world," he reminded me.

"Cassia will be the fighter, as always, and Vivina is a natural leader. She'll make smart decisions even under pressure."

"And Solana?"

"She is calm, sweet, and she will surely make valuable connections," I explained.

"Or she could be seen as easy prey. Perhaps they all could be," he countered.

I glared at him, resenting how he used my fears to make me vulnerable, all the while providing me with food and a sense of security.

Chapter Twenty-One
Cartan

We were three days away from the Mainlands, and my Omega's herbs would be out of her system in just one. She was growing needier for me, whimpering every time I released into her throat. Yet it seemed she could almost climax just from the taste of my cum on her tongue. The intensity of our upcoming mating was going to be fierce after this denial.

As her Alpha, it was my duty to fulfill all her needs, a responsibility ingrained in me. But I was punishing her for keeping this secret from me. How dare she manipulate me with her exquisite body in such a cruel manner? Every aspect of her was remarkable, meant to be cherished by an Alpha and filled with his seed to create powerful Alphas and Omegas. Only an Omega could give birth to another Omega, which was why their numbers were now so scarce. So why would my Omega try to prevent more of her kind from existing? It made no sense, but it would soon be over.

Her scent had become so overpowering that every time I entered the cabin, I was instantly aroused. It permeated every nook and cranny, driving me wild. One more day, and I would have my cock buried so deep inside her pussy she wouldn't know where she ended and I began. My body thrummed with desire as I stood gazing at the horizon, but I had decided it was best to wait until tomorrow morning to see her. I wasn't sure I could resist her if I caught another whiff of her sweet scent.

So I kept myself occupied throughout the day and into the night, but my blood pumped faster, my cock remained perpetually erect, and thoughts of having Kiandra again consumed me. When the faintest hint of dawn broke the darkness, I could no longer contain myself.

I turned abruptly, charging below deck and down the long corridors until I stood outside my cabin. I unlocked the door, not wanting my Omega to leave until I could claim her once more. However, when I stepped inside, I froze, the door closing behind me. Something was different.

I scanned the room, trying to discern the change. Kiandra wasn't in sight, but instead, my eyes landed on a massive pile of furs meticulously arranged together. It took me a moment to recall what I knew about Omegas, and the realization hit me hard: Kiandra was nesting.

Nesting could only occur for two reasons—either her heat was imminent or she was creating a secure haven for us, indicating her comfort with her Alpha. It could be either reason. I was aware her heat was approaching. I could smell it, feel it, and my body was preparing for the impending rut. However, once her heat subsided, I would soon discover whether she would nest again.

The sight before me pleased me immensely, my Alpha instincts swelling with pride at what Kiandra had constructed. I hastily discarded my clothes, overcome with the urgency to be with her. The pile of furs covered her completely, but I knew it wouldn't quite accommodate both of us. There were not enough layers, but I was willing to provide her with as many as she needed to create a larger, more permanent nest in my tent.

I located the small opening and pushed my way inside, entering this sacred space. Kiandra was already awake and hissed at me as I joined her in the nest. Yet as I settled in behind her, she began rubbing her round ass against me, a clear indication of her desire. Despite her anger, she wanted me there. I pulled her closer to me, sliding my hand down her stomach until I found her wet pussy. Her skin was swollen, and she moaned like a female in heat, but I had no intention of denying her my touch or my cock any longer.

My fingers traced along her wet flesh, causing her to grow louder and press against me. Just as she began trembling, indicating her need for more, I lifted her leg and entered her, making her gasp. I wrapped an arm around her, holding her close as I began to thrust, my mind lost in the moment as I penetrated her slick channel.

"What a beautiful nest you've made, little Omega," I purred in her ear, and she whimpered louder, clearly enjoying the praise. I bit her earlobe, driving myself deeper into her, and she cried out in release, her juices flowing over us and making the furs beneath us even wetter. I pushed her further into the bedding, using my body to subdue her. She climaxed again almost immediately, clutching the furs tightly as she moaned and convulsed around me.

I couldn't hold back for long, feeling my knot expanding and locking us together as I spilled into her. This time, there was a genuine possibility of impregnating her. It filled me with joy, and I rolled us to the side, purring contentedly. Kiandra turned her head as much as she could, nuzzling into me. However, I detected a faint sharp note in her sweet Omega scent.

"Why are you irritated?" I asked. "You just came so intensely that you drenched both of us."

She hissed, too frustrated to articulate her thoughts, and the sight amused me as it reminded me of a kitten baring its teeth. I couldn't understand why there would be any emotions other than contentment in this nest, which was an Omega's safe haven. I chose to ignore it for now.

We were both sated and spent, and I lazily played with one of her nipples, my focus now entirely on her.

She mewled in delight, pressing herself against my hand.

"You're satisfied yet angry," I murmured in her ear. "Are you not content with the nest? Or are you angry that you won't be using your herbs anymore?"

"I knew I wouldn't be able to keep taking them. I've accepted that fate," she replied.

I growled slightly, disliking how she spoke of it as if she were facing her own execution.

"What troubles you then?"

I moved my hand to her other breast, teasing the erect bud, and she moaned again.

"I don't like it," she whimpered, causing me to freeze in my movement.

"My touch?"

"The need to nest," she murmured, and I began stroking her nipple again before squeezing the soft, thick flesh.

"It's natural," I reminded her.

"I'm doing it because you've made me so frustrated and confused, yet I still want you in here," she muttered angrily.

I smiled, nuzzling her neck and kissing her skin as I continued to purr for her. "I want to be in here too."

I knew she wouldn't admit it, but she found solace in hearing it.

"How long have you felt this way?"

She turned away from me, not wanting to reveal her thoughts, which meant it had been a while. After being denied her own pleasure for so long, she had given in to her need for comfort. I kissed her neck again and buried my face in her soft, fragrant hair, inhaling her intoxicating Omega scent. No wonder it couldn't truly be described in any book. It was meant to drive an Alpha wild, and it was undoubtedly true. My body shook with the need to mate once more, but I had to wait until my knot released her. I slid my hand lower, teasing her clit and hastening the process.

"So, it's not just your impending heat that makes you want to nest?" I asked, recalling the other reason for nesting and what her words implied.

She tensed against me, but my mate was terrible at lying. She was honest to a fault, and I cherished that. I wanted truthfulness, and she had chosen not to answer me, but it was evident that even her instincts had selected me as her Alpha, and she wanted to create a home with me. Warm feelings I wasn't accustomed to surged within me, yet there was no reason to let it unsettle me. Kiandra belonged to me and no one else.

Chapter Twenty-Two
Kiandra

The port to the Mainlands dwarfed the one on the Rocky Island, bustling with numerous ships navigating the far side of the land. I leaned further over the railing, straining to see where it ended, drawing a growl from Cartan behind me as our ship began to slow down upon approaching a long bridge.

Cartan grabbed me, pulling me closer to him, ensconcing me in his firm embrace as we slowly came to a halt. A smaller drawbridge was lowered to provide us with a means of disembarking. I couldn't help but anticipate some kind of welcoming party, but there was none. The soldiers worked swiftly and gather by the bustling harbor, occupying a considerable space. Cartan never released me, instead instructing the Alphas to proceed toward the far end of the city connected to the harbor.

In the distance, I could make out the castle where the king resided, but we veered down different roads, distancing ourselves from the castle and heading for the exit. I noticed many of the Alphas carrying satchels, clearly prepared for a journey. According to the maps I had studied, the trip should take no more than three days on horseback to reach the clans, but when we reached the end of the bustling city without any horses in sight, it became clear that we would be traveling on foot.

As I gazed down the busy road ahead, I noticed that in the far distance, a desert stretched out, its dark sand a stark contrast to the lighter-colored ground. Cartan lifted me into his arms, taking me by surprise as he began walking while carrying me. It was a sweet gesture, but I was no fragile Omega.

"I can walk," I informed him.

"You're not accustomed to the long distance we'll be traveling," he replied.

"Long?"

"We won't rest until nightfall."

I stared at him in disbelief, knowing it would take at least a day just to reach the edge of the desert, and who knew how far we had to go to reach the clans. Therefore, I decided against complaining and simply allowed Cartan to carry me. I noticed many people stopping to watch, but as we left the city behind, our encounters with others became infrequent.

The army marched without complaint, and when I glanced over Cartan's shoulder, I could see the extensive line of soldiers. It was fascinating to witness, as my father had been the city's sole true warrior. He had trained a few Alphas and kept them close, but after his death, they had vanished, not staying to serve the Omegas. It was an Alpha's honor that had bound them to our father, so we bore them no ill will for disappearing. We had wanted no wars, but one had come to us, and now I found myself in the arms of our conqueror.

Therefore, being carried felt peculiar, but it afforded me ample time to take in my surroundings. I could still see the city, home to one of Verocca's grandest libraries. Unfortunately, I had been given no opportunity to explore the place. Cartan was determined to return me to his territory as swiftly as possible, and given that he had not yet secured my sisters, I surmised he needed to strategize how to keep the other clan leaders patient and waiting.

I was unsure whether I wanted my sisters to be found. I knew they didn't desire to be owned either, and it was clear from what Cartan had told me that we wouldn't have much choice in who we belonged to. But I worried about them, and I began to doubt if I had made the right choice in helping them escape. I just hoped they stayed together and found a way to manage on their own.

Cartan didn't say much either. Sometimes I noticed him talking quietly to another Alpha beside him, one who had seen me getting knotted by Cartan in the hallway of my home. It made me unable to look at the other Alpha for long, and as the day grew late, fatigue set in. I sought my Alpha more and buried my face in his neck. This seemed to please him immensely as he kept me close to his warm body.

The heat of the sun beat down on my delicate skin, and I knew I would need better protection. I wasn't accustomed to such intense sun, and in the desert, it was supposed to be even hotter. How did all those Alphas survive out there? I wondered. I knew their tanned skin offered a slight shield, but what about water? Where did they find that source and food? They had cut off our canals and entrances to weaken us, but I wondered where they had access to these vital resources. My curiosity was piqued, and I couldn't wait to explore the dark sandy landscape.

As expected, we reached the first small dune of dark sand in the evening, where the army quickly set up camp, creating fires and preparing food. I stood in the midst of it all, uncertain about what to do. While I had studied survival skills, their methods were different from what I had read. Their tents were unique, bound together with thick leather straps and cone-shaped rather than rectangular. They seemed smaller, and I couldn't help but observe how quickly Cartan set up his. A smile played on his lips when he noticed me scrutinizing the details.

"Omega," he called.

"Done with calling me Princess?" I taunted.

"You aren't one anymore after stepping foot on

this land. Now come here."

I followed his order, knowing he could easily lift me and carry me to his spot. As I stood in front of him, he grabbed me and positioned me so my back was against his front.

"Have you ever set up a tent before?" he questioned.

I shook my head. "I've only read about survival skills, but yours are different from what I've learned. The tents my father had were larger."

"That's because these are primarily traveling tents, smaller and easier to transport. You'll see larger ones when we arrive at my clan, and even grander ones in the central meeting areas. There, we all work together to ensure everyone stays alive and well."

I nodded, listening intently to his instructions. He showed me how to fasten the side of the tent to the sandy ground, stretching it out securely to prevent it from collapsing. Cartan arranged his belongings inside, and even though I had to crouch down to enter the small space, there was just enough room for sleeping.

However, as soon as Cartan began laying out furs for sleeping, my Omega instincts kicked in. I reached out and snatched one from his hand, and he chuckled, handing me the rest. I gathered them all in a big pile in my arms before I started tidying up the space. Cartan ran a hand through my hair, almost petting me, before leaving the tent to allow me to create a temporary nest for us.

I didn't even think, I just worked on it, but I wasn't satisfied because I didn't have enough to work with. I ended up sitting back on my legs, looking at the small, inadequate nest. It was all wrong, with barely enough room for my Alpha, and it brought my mood down. However, I quickly snapped out of my sulking and slapped my cheeks.

"No, no, no, this safe place is just for you," I murmured to myself, then heard Cartan calling out to me.

I looked at the nest, feeling nervous and ashamed that it wasn't better. My instincts told me it needed to be perfect, but Cartan's voice made it impossible for me to stay. I slid out of the tent, and Cartan was standing by a fire, waving me over. I walked to him, and he picked me up before carrying me to the fire where the other Alphas were sitting.

He settled down with me on his lap, and food was quickly served. I had eaten a few dinners with my family, but this was different. I had never sat with so many people, never so many Alphas, and I hardly knew any of them. It made me seek comfort in my Alpha's body, which Cartan didn't seem to mind as he conversed with his men. It was clear they all shared a tight bond. Some even moved from fire to fire to talk to others, and I watched in awe.

Cartan noticed me observing and turned his gaze to me, a small smile on his lips.

"What?" I asked.

"I see your curious mind at work," he replied before reaching out to stroke my cheek. His fingers trailed lower, and his thumb slid over my lips. My tongue darted out, gliding over his thumb and tasting the saltiness of the cooked meat that still clung to his skin. His growl deepened, his body reacting, and then he hoisted me over his shoulder, carrying me away to his "lair."

"Cartan!" I exclaimed. I was pounding my hands against his back in embarrassment, but his hand came down on my ass, delivering a sharp spank that silenced me. I squirmed a little, finding a strange liking for the sting that followed, and I knew he could sense my reaction.

He carried me into the tent, and I grew more nervous as we entered because it reminded me of the poorly made and incomplete nest. As he lowered me to the ground, I placed my hand over his eyes, which confused him, but a mischievous smile played on his lips.

"What are you doing, little Omega?" he asked, amusement in his voice.

I bit down hard on my lower lip, unsure of how to explain to him that I didn't want him to see the temporary nest I had created. However, as Cartan gently took my hand, I allowed him to lower it. He watched me with intrigue, noticing how I nervously chewed on my lower lip.

"What is it?" he inquired.

"I-I don't like the nest," I admitted, glancing down at the imperfect arrangement of furs. "I can't make it the way I want to."

I curled up, bringing my legs closer to my chest, but Cartan lifted my chin and pressed his lips to mine in the softest kiss he had ever given me.

"It's all right, little Omega," he whispered. "When we get home, you will create the most beautiful nest, and I will ensure you have everything you need for it."

His words sent shivers of delight through my entire body, making me feel hotter and needier than ever before. I knew I shouldn't react this way. I needed to maintain some control. But I had been so nervous about the nest, and the Alpha before me had dispelled all that worry with just a few sentences.

I quickly reached for the straps of my thin dress, wriggling out of it as fast as I could. Cartan watched me with hungry eyes as I got naked and pushed the dress aside before I reclined, resting on my arms. I spread my legs open for him, offering an unmistakable invitation, and he growled darkly before his mouth descended on my eager pussy. I couldn't hold back, screaming in ecstasy as his warm mouth feasted on my sensitive skin. He showed no restraint, relentlessly sucking on my clit until I came apart, calling out his name and rocking my hips against his face.

He swiftly shed his own clothes and then took me, thrusting into me with perfect timing, and I cried out again, feeling every sensation heightened to an almost overwhelming degree. It was incredible how in sync our bodies were, delivering pleasure beyond imagination. I barely registered the cheering from outside, as my own cries grew louder, forgetting we were no longer confined to a cabin.

I couldn't focus on anything but the intense pleasure as I climaxed, feeling a fire spread through my veins. Then, Cartan had me on all fours, pounding into me even more vigorously, his growls turning into triumphant howls as he knotted us together. That's when I realized the echoes of appreciation reverberating through the night, and my cheeks burned with embarrassment. I covered my face with my hand, shaking my head slightly, while Cartan trailed his lips down my neck and shoulders.

"They heard me," I murmured.

"Good. It means they know your Alpha is taking good care of you," he whispered before gently nipping my skin.

"I can never leave this tent." I sighed, hearing him chuckle.

Cartan leaned over me, purring again, and the vibrations calmed me. Once I was a bit more relaxed, he turned my head and kissed my lips.

"Our union is cause for celebration," he explained.

"How so?" I inquired.

"Because it signifies the potential start of the next generation of Alphas and Omegas. It's a sacred event, a reminder of the connection between us," he continued. "To us, that is something worth celebrating."

I understood the reasoning behind it, but it didn't alleviate my concerns about facing all those Alphas tomorrow. Yet Cartan distracted me from my thoughts as he began mating with me again.

Chapter Twenty-Three
Cartan

My Omega had an insatiable hunger for knowledge, and I made it my mission to keep her mind engaged, except for those moments when our primal desires took over. During our mating sessions, I would ensure her thoughts were filled with a longing for her Alpha. However, watching her explore the land around us, becoming curious about every little detail, every bug, every animal, and the intricate patterns on the ground beneath our feet, brought me great pleasure. Something deep within me rejoiced in the knowledge that my Omega appreciated my homeland and had a thirst for understanding it better. There was much for her to discover in this wild and perilous land, but I would never let her out of my sight.

I had noticed her fair skin taking on a slight reddish hue, so I took extra care to provide her with shelter from the sun. In time, she would acquire the natural golden glow of one accustomed to this environment, and I wouldn't need to worry about her suffering from sunburn.

"What do you eat?" she inquired, her attention momentarily drawn to a large hunting bird soaring overhead. With swift precision, it snatched a black snake slithering across the ground. "Oh, did you see that? It spotted the snake despite its camouflage."

I chuckled and glanced at Tyros, who seemed uplifted by the Omega's cheerful curiosity. They said that an Omega brought peace to both people and the land they inhabited, and it appeared to be true.

"Do you consume snakes?" she suddenly turned to me and asked.

"Some," I replied, and she shuddered, eliciting a smile from me.

"What else?"

"There are many creatures in these lands. They often emerge at night when the sun's warmth has faded."

"So you hunt during the night?" she inquired.

"Mostly from evening into the night."

"What do you do during the day?"

"I ensure the safety of our people, work on the tents, construct whatever we need, and fashion weapons. There are myriad tasks to keep us occupied."

"Do you sleep?" she probed, prompting another chuckle from me.

"We take turns hunting. With all the clans now gathered, we have even more hands."

"And more mouths to feed," she astutely observed, displaying her quick intellect.

"Correct."

"What's the most common food source here?" she asked, her gaze never fixed on me, but rather on the world around her.

"Boars."

"They inhabit this place?" she inquired, her surprise evident.

"They dwell in the caves, feasting on creatures that venture out from the sands at night. Haven't you studied these things?" I teased her gently.

"Our library was not extensive, and it mostly covered the Rocky Island. I have some knowledge of Mainlands' history, Omega history, and my own family's history, but there are many topics I couldn't explore. Plus, we were rarely allowed to leave the castle, especially not me."

I knew precisely how to delight my Omega. I needed to provide her with her own private library, where she could immerse herself in knowledge. I couldn't wait to have her back in my tent, where she could create her own little haven, and I could savor her body repeatedly.

"Where do you source your water?" she inquired, noticing one of the Alphas taking a drink from a flask hanging from his hip.

"There are water holes, but we also have a source by the clans. This desert may not seem abundant, but it harbors numerous secrets," I explained.

"Not seem abundant?" she questioned in disbelief. "I've never felt a stronger desire to explore a place!"

The sight of her smiling as she surveyed her surroundings sent my long-dormant heart racing. In that moment, I realized that all I wanted was to see my Omega smile. She looked remarkably beautiful when she did.

As evening descended, we made camp once more. This time, Kiandra was more inclined to engage with the others, asking questions and learning about the army I had brought with me. She was intrigued by the fact that the army comprised Alphas from various clans, all working together under my command. However, when she attempted to sit closer to some of the others due to her excitement and curiosity, I swiftly pulled her to me, issuing a growling warning. Yet she responded with a small smile and a quick kiss, which nearly drove me to madness. I knew she did it to soothe me, but the moment her lips met mine, I was ready to claim her right there in front of the other Alphas.

However, I couldn't bear the thought of the other Alphas seeing my Omega in the nude. So I carried her back to my tent, one hand gripping her firm ass.

"We were eating!" she reminded me.

"I want to feast on something else."

My Omega responded immediately, her body

aroused by the idea of her Alpha pleasuring her, and I swiftly ushered us into the tent. However, she grew restless once more, wanting a more comfortable nest. I understood her frustration. She couldn't create a better resting place, and this forced her to continually rearrange the furs. At the moment, there was no remedy for her restlessness other than to use my Alpha powers to subdue her. It was the only way to distract her and ensure she rested. I reached out and seized her by the neck, gently pushing her to the ground and raising her sweet ass into the air before tearing her dress from her body.

She gasped and wriggled beneath me, but she also arched her back and pushed her rear higher, offering herself to me. A soft whimper escaped her lips as her pussy glistened, and slick trickled down her thighs. I reached out with my other hand, scooping up the wetness and feeding it to her, relishing the sensual sounds emanating from her as I pleasured her with my fingers.

She began to moan and pushed back, craving the deeper connection. I withdrew my fingers, hearing her protest as she longed for my touch once more, but I was on my way. I tore through my own clothing, grasped her hip firmly, and thrust into her tight, welcoming heat. She clamped down around me so tightly that moving was almost impossible, but this was an Omega's body, designed to satiate an Alpha beyond comprehension. With both hands gripping her hips, I thrust deeper and began to pound her vigorously. Kiandra's cries grew louder, and our union was once again celebrated by the Alphas surrounding us. A new era was dawning with us.

Chapter Twenty-Four
Cartan

When I awoke early the next morning, my body feeling invigorated, I sensed an unusual chill in the air. I opened my eyes, only to find Kiandra was not sleeping beside me. My arm was wrapped around a bundle of fur, but not my precious Omega. I brought the fur to my nose, inhaling her delightful scent, which had kept me oblivious to her absence. A surge of hot rage and worry coursed through me, prompting me to swiftly dress. I stepped outside, prepared to track down my Omega or kill whatever had taken her, if that was the case. However, the moment I emerged from the tent, I was greeted by an enchanting sight.

Other Alphas who had also awakened were observing the same scene as me. We had camped near a small water hole, a place often frequented by wildlife. However, it was not the animals that had our attention. Instead, we all beheld a captivating sight. Kiandra was standing by the water, her hand gently caressing the neck of a white mare. The horse was undoubtedly wild, and its herd stood farther back, observing the pair as well. Many wild horses roamed the desert, but approaching them was nearly impossible. Yet somehow, my Omega possessed the ability to do just that. She stood there, smiling as she stroked the mare's long neck and appeared to be conversing with it.

The power of Omegas to bring peace became even more evident, as I had never witnessed anything quite like it. Horses, though prey animals, were capable of kicking and biting, and they could be lethal. Yet the white mare seemed tranquil and content in Kiandra's presence.

I walked a bit closer to Tyros, who turned to me with a smile.

"We found her like this," he explained. "It must be a sign from the Gods."

Tyros was a staunch believer, more so than myself, but I could not deny the significance of such a direct message. It was clear that the Gods favored the presence of an Omega in our territory. Despite her birth on a cliff overlooking the powerful ocean, she belonged here.

"The white ones are often considered messengers," he reminded me, and I nodded. However, I noticed the herd growing agitated.

Emerging from behind the pair, a dark panther was stealthily advancing across the dark sand toward my Omega. I growled in fury, drawing the knife from my belt, and hurried toward Kiandra, calling out to her. She turned her head just as the panther lunged, but the white mare grew frantic, defending my mate.

With a powerful kick, it sent the panther tumbling backward. I reached my Omega's side, pulling her to safety, while the herd of horses grew increasingly wild. They converged, rearing up and neighing in anger, attempting to drive away the predator. The panther was kicked again, and I ushered Kiandra back, watching as the panther retreated across the dark sands. The white mare, clearly the herd's leader, turned her gaze toward us before letting out a resounding neigh and then galloping away with the rest.

My Omega wore a large smile, her excitement obvious beneath her shaking skin. I could sense her eagerness, and I knew that if I were to release my hold on her, she might dash after the horses. However, witnessing her in this state brought me immense joy. She seemed so attuned to the land, and it filled me with a profound satisfaction. Yet, I chided myself for not keeping a more vigilant watch. Kiandra was undeniably enchanting, and it was all too easy to become distracted. But I resolved that from now on, my Omega would remain by my side, never to stray.

"Come. We still have quite a distance to cover," I urged.

"I adore this desert," she whispered, her words warming my heart even further.

I ran my hand tenderly through her hair before guiding her along with me. We efficiently packed up the camp, and soon enough, my Omega was nestled securely in my arms. Although many of the women in the larger camp were accustomed to long walks, I saw no reason for my Omega to endure the same. She would always be safely sheltered within the camp, and I had no intentions of arguing otherwise. Yet, Kiandra seemed content being cradled in my arms, granting her ample time to observe her surroundings.

"Is it true that some of the storms here are so powerful they alter the landscape?" she inquired.

"Where did you read that?" I asked.

She shrugged. "I can't recall. I believe I skimmed it in some book a while back, but I never delved deeply into Mainlands studies. I just vaguely remember reading about it."

"The storms here are indeed powerful. The rain can turn the sand into mud and create quicksand. You wouldn't want to get caught in it."

"What happens if you do?"

"Escaping becomes nearly impossible without assistance, and the more you struggle, the faster you sink. But we always survey the area to locate all the hidden spots."

"They're hidden?"

"The surface might appear to be regular sand, but it's not. Additionally, when it doesn't rain, the sky occasionally lights up with lightning and thunder, creating a spectacular display. Nevertheless, it's best to stay indoors during such storms," I cautioned.

"I'd love to see it," she breathed, completely ignoring my warning. Despite her disregard, I couldn't help but find her enthusiasm endearing.

I leaned closer to my Omega, prompting her to turn her attention toward me. "No more venturing outside the tent without me."

Her expression shifted to one of slight discontent. "Why not?"

"This land is dangerous, as you witnessed today. You need to stay close to me."

Kiandra furrowed her brow, looking away and prompting me to growl in warning. She turned to face me once more.

"Little Omega, I won't debate this with you. You are unfamiliar with this desert, while I grew up in it. It's my world, and you must heed my advice."

Although she didn't appear particularly pleased, she eventually nodded in acceptance of my directive.

Chapter Twenty-Five
Cartan

As we approached the camp, an obvious excitement coursed through the army. My Omega seemed to notice the Alphas growing tense around her, interpreting their behavior as a potential threat, and she nuzzled closer to me. Although the presence of other Alphas still unnerved her, I welcomed her proximity eagerly. I longed to keep her near me at all times, and thus far, she had adhered to my command of not leaving the tent without me. However, I shared in the Alphas' excitement as the first tents of the camp began to come into view, and news of our return rapidly spread. People rushed to greet us, families reuniting after weeks of separation.

I eventually set my Omega down, drawing the attention of those present who recognized her for what she was. However, I knew that the other clan leaders would soon realize that only one Omega had returned with me. I would search for the others later, but for now, I had a single, thoroughly claimed Omega by my side. With my arm around her waist, I guided her through the main parts of the camp.

"Where are we headed?" she inquired, her gaze wandering as she observed the people and structures around her. "Do any of these tents belong to you?"

"This is the main gathering point. Do you see the large tent over there?" I asked, and she nodded. "That's where meetings between the High Alphas are held, with all the clan leaders. However, each section of the camp belongs to one of them. Do you notice the different colors on the tents?"

She nodded again.

"Each color represents the pack to which they belong. In the old days, we each had our own territory, and conflicts would erupt if one crossed into another's territory. These are new times, where we are all united, but we still value having our own space, which is why there are designated sections with space between each camp," I explained. Her eyes grew even wider, and I could see her mind racing with questions.

Many eyes were fixed on us as we strolled through the camps, though my Omega seemed oblivious to the attention.

"Which color is yours?" she asked, and I appreciated that she inquired about mine first.

"The red one," I replied, watching her swivel her head in every direction, searching for it.

"I don't see it," she remarked.

"That's because our section is all the way over there," I explained, pointing it out.

My Omega was too small to see it from this distance, and I could sense her frustration as the other tents obstructed her view. However, we were nearing our destination, and when she finally spotted the first tent with a red line encircling the top, her excitement grew.

"Is this your part?" she inquired, casting a glance behind her. "But we've almost left the others behind."

I nodded but refrained from explaining why my section seemed more isolated. I felt her gaze on me, yet she didn't press me for further information. Instead, more people approached, blocking our path as they welcomed their High Alpha back. When they spotted Kiandra beside me, their excitement escalated, as they were eager to get acquainted with her. My little Omega wasn't accustomed to such attention, having been confined to a library for years.

Nevertheless, she endeavored to appear open and

kind, a gesture I truly appreciated. After allowing my clan to bask in my Omega's presence for a while, I guided her through the crowd, allowing them to reunite with their Alphas.

Kiandra and I proceeded toward the largest tent at the far end when she turned her head to scrutinize another rather large one nearby.

"Why does that one have two colors?" she inquired.

Beneath the red line, there was also a black one, and I smiled, leaning in closer to her ear. "Those are pleasure tents."

She turned her head, gazing up at me in shock. "Like ... brothels?"

"Oh, so you do know what that is?" I teased her, noticing her cheeks flush.

"We have those in the city," she murmured, looking away.

"Well, these she-wolves don't get paid. They simply enjoy intimacy," I clarified.

Kiandra's eyes widened, and she quickly focused on something else, making me chuckle.

"Is that one yours?" she asked, pointing at the large leather tent, and I nodded. "It's much larger than the traveling tent. But then again, all of these are, but yours is so much bigger."

My Omega began to ramble excitedly, filling me with warmth. She was so full of enthusiasm that I nudged her forward, allowing her to run ahead. There were no immediate dangers on the way to the tent, and when she sensed the signal, she sprinted off. However, my Omega couldn't help but scrutinize every detail, starting right at the front of the tent. She stopped, grasping the fabric that covered the entrance and studying how it was fastened before moving around the side of it. I chuckled softly as she began to talk to herself, her fingers tapping nervously against her thigh. It became evident that something was bothering her.

"Do you take a lot of notes?" I inquired.

"Loads!" she exclaimed, completing a full circuit around the tent. When she returned, I had gone inside, placing our belongings down, and then I emerged with a pen and paper for her. She gasped in excitement, taking both items from me and laying a hand on the back of the paper before she began scribbling. I watched her with amusement, seeing the excitement on her face.

Soon, she ventured inside, discovering that the place was divided into different sections, with long leather curtains used to create separate rooms. She started with the main room, which had a small iron fireplace in the center and an opening at the top for the smoke to escape. Then she ventured deeper, noticing it was circular in design, allowing one to move in a full circle to access each room without turning around. She eventually stumbled upon my desk, standing in one of the rooms that had been transformed into a private library of sorts. She began picking up book after book, studying them intently.

"I've never seen any of these before. The words are completely unfamiliar to me!" she exclaimed.

"It's the Old Language of the Wild Wolves, the clans that used to live here in isolation. This place used to be considered cursed, and no one dared approach it. However, the language is nearly extinct now, spoken only during ceremonies," I explained.

"I must learn it!"

I was fluent in the language, and I was delighted that she wanted to explore it as well. However, Kiandra took the book as she continued her exploration. Her enthusiasm brought a smile to my face, and I was more than willing to let her keep the edition. She ventured on without the pen and paper, entering another section, which was designated for relaxation.

Next was a place for my weapons, and finally, she arrived at the room where I expected to find her most often: our bedroom. She noticed the numerous furs and pillows spread across the floor, creating a plush sleeping area. I sensed the moment her focus shifted away from exploration. Her instincts had been triggered, and she dropped the book to the ground. I realized that if she had been in her right mind, she would never have treated the work that way.

However, her nesting instincts had been delayed, and it had clearly frustrated her. When her instincts sensed a suitable opportunity to prepare not just for her heat but for both of us, she set to work. It was incredible to watch how she meticulously arranged everything. She was an Omega in her element, and I felt privileged to witness it.

Yet I quickly learned that I needed to maintain a considerable distance from her and the furs, as she hissed at me when I came too close to her unfinished work. It only increased my desire for her, but I forced myself to remain still, observing her until she gave me the signal that she was finished.

She had created her own little sanctuary inside our tent, a comforting and secure space for her to rest, seek refuge when I was not around, and eventually give birth to our pups. I even noticed her sniffing some of the furs that still carried traces of my scent. However, it wasn't quite enough, and after Kiandra had removed her dress to add to the nest, ensuring it carried her scent as well, she literally crawled toward me.

I could smell her powerful scent, and I knew we were just days away from her entering her heat, if it hadn't already arrived. She was sweating, panting, and trembling, leaving a trail of her juices on the ground. When she reached me, she began tugging at my pants. It became apparent that she wanted the garment to contribute to the nest's scent, and after I removed them, she quickly snatched them away before sliding into the furs to enhance their aroma with mine.

I let out a dark growl, my eyes fixated on the inviting sight of her round, upturned ass as she disappeared into the nest. My cock throbbed and leaked, craving her, and I knew she needed to complete her task quickly because I was desperate to mate with her.

However, a sharp whistle interrupted my desires, and my growl grew even darker. I wasn't in the right state of mind to leave my mate right now. The whistling grew louder, demanding my attention. I felt torn between two needs: one urging me to prioritize the clans, and the other insisting I stay with my Omega. If she was on the verge of entering her heat, I needed to be there, ready to claim her. I also wanted to mark our little nest with both our releases.

Yet, the whistling became more insistent, and I noticed that my Omega had fallen silent, hiding in the nest. She understood that an intruder was too close, and she remained in the darkness, showing her understanding that her Alpha needed to assess the situation first. This pleased me greatly, as it demonstrated her trust in my ability to protect her.

I quickly found some clothes from a chest, wrapping a long piece of dark linen around me. I left the tent with only that covering me, and a relentless erection that yearned for my Omega's touch. However, when I stepped outside, I saw Tyros waiting at a respectful distance from the tent, giving me and my Omega the privacy we needed.

"You'd better have a good reason for calling me,"

I growled, my voice filled with a primal intensity I couldn't hide.

"The other High Alphas have already called for a meeting," Tyros replied.

That sobered me up a bit. Now that I was out in the fresh air, away from my Omega's influence, my mind began to clear.

"I've just returned," I pointed out.

"They were eager for those princesses. They doubted you could accomplish it, and the fact that you've returned with all Alphas alive speaks of your triumph. They want to assess the goods you've brought back."

"But we both know I haven't brought anything back for them," I snarled.

"Yes, rumors have spread regarding that as well, which is why they are even more insistent. They want to know why only you have obtained one Omega," he reminded me.

I groaned and ran my hand through my hair. I could sense my Omega calling to me, longing for my presence, and I had to suppress the connection. There was a reason I hadn't fully embraced it, and I knew that the sooner I could appease the other clan leaders, the faster I could mark Kiandra as mine and fully connect with her.

"Did you send messages to the Rocky Island to search for the princesses?" I inquired.

"I did, and to the other places they might go. But you know if the king finds them first—"

I shook my head, interrupting him. I was aware of the king's pursuit, but the clans took precedence, as they always did. Nevertheless, I owed the young king a debt of gratitude. I would never have been able to leave this land without him.

"All right, let's go talk to them," I conceded.

"You need to bring her," Tyros insisted.

"No!" I growled in response.

"Cartan, you have to," he told me, using my name, a privilege he rarely exercised and only in complete privacy, like now.

I groaned, disliking the idea of any Alphas being so close to my Omega when she was clearly on the brink of her heat. However, I knew I still had some time before she fully entered it.

"Fine, I'll bring her. But this meeting better be over quickly," I growled.

"Don't count on it."

Chapter Twenty-Six
Kiandra

I felt an intense warmth coursing through my body. My pussy was aching and swollen, yearning for my Alpha. I knew I was dangerously close to succumbing to my heat, where all I would understand was the primal urge to mate. I buried my face in his pants, reveling in his scent that enveloped me. It took me a moment to snap out of that heat-like state, to remember who I was and what I was doing. I quickly sat up in the nest, which I could barely recall having built, and shook my head.

"Omega," I heard a dark, aggressive voice call out.

Cartan was clearly upset about something, but I couldn't quite grasp what it was. Was it the nest? Had I not constructed it properly enough? My instincts went haywire, and I anxiously started fiddling with some layers of it, thinking I needed to redo it. However, just as I neared the entrance, a hand firmly grabbed my ankle, yanking me out. I hissed and kicked out in defense, but my Alpha growled at me, forcing me to freeze.

His eyes were completely dark as he stared down at me, and as I lay on my back, my Omega instincts told me there was only one thing to do—spread my legs, opening myself up to him. His eyes seemed to darken even further as they locked onto the glistening skin further down my body. However, my Alpha didn't mate with me. Instead, he shook his head, released my ankle, and stormed away in anger. I looked after him with confusion and hurt, not understanding why he had rejected me. He had never said no before, and it stung to see him leave.

"No, remember who you are," I whispered,

shaking my head.

This was not good. I was teetering on the edge of madness due to desire, surrounded by Cartan's scent, in his home, on his land, and the overwhelming thought thrilled me to no end, leaving me dizzy and unable to collect my thoughts. However, my attention was diverted when a young woman entered, carrying a small child in a sling on her chest. It was like a splash of cold water, and I quickly covered myself with a fur nearby. She smiled at me, holding something in her hand.

"I've come to help you get dressed, High Omega," she told me.

"Oh…"

I noticed she wasn't wearing the same type of dress I had been, and the one she held in her hand was also different. She was dressed in leather clothes, a long leather skirt, and a top that barely covered her breasts. Yet I could understand the choice of minimal clothing, considering the high temperatures.

"Come, let's get you ready," she said, approaching me, and I stood up.

"Are you close to Alpha Cartan?" I inquired as she helped me into the stola, glancing at the small child on her chest.

She was clearly a Beta woman, not much older than me, and I had lived through twenty-one summers. I knew Alpha Cartan was around twenty-seven. However, the child had a tiny speck of dark hair, and this woman was blond.

"I have known him for a long time, yes," she replied.

"Oh?"

I knew Cartan couldn't have lived like a monk, and the thought of other women being with him now angered me. However, the Beta woman must have noticed the look on my face and began laughing.

"I was in the same clan as him before he was taken away. When he came back, I immediately joined his side. We've known each other since we were children," she told me. "I am Mara, mated to his oldest friend, Tyros."

I knew who Tyros was and realized that I had been acting possessive without reason. Mara began braiding my hair, but not into a single braid. She created one long braid down the middle while leaving smaller ones to incorporate into the larger one. It was beautifully done, much like her own hair.

"I'm sorry we don't have more time for a more complex hairstyle, but a meeting has been called," she explained.

"A meeting?"

"The other clan leaders are eager to meet you," she informed me, but I sensed a tension in her demeanor, which raised some concerns.

Mara led me out of the tent again, walking alongside me toward the large meeting tent. The sun was descending, casting a warm glow across the camp, and torches had been lit around the meeting area, creating an inviting atmosphere despite the late hour.

"This gathering isn't a good one, is it?" I inquired, and Mara shook her head, offering me a small, knowing smile.

"You see that this camp is situated a bit farther away from the others?" she pointed out

I nodded in acknowledgment.

"That's because Cartan has a more complicated history of unaccepted Alpha blood," she continued.

"What do you mean—"

"His past," she interjected, signaling that she didn't want to delve into Cartan's history. "In any case, he has worked diligently to reach his current position, but even now, he is seen as an outsider. To prove his worth, Cartan promised all clan leaders Omegas. Yet, do you see many Omegas here?"

"Is that why he came to our land?" I asked.

"No one was even certain if you truly existed," Mara replied. "Your father kept you hidden, allowing very few to see you. You became almost like legends, especially you. No one knew of a fourth one except Cartan. However, it was agreed that he would find all of you, bring you here, and then decide which clan leader each of you would be given to."

"He mentioned that to me."

"You weren't supposed to be claimed until it had been decided who you would belong to."

"But I claimed Cartan," I pointed out. She gave me a look that conveyed the complications I had created by doing so. It suddenly dawned on me why Cartan had held back from marking me, and why the act had angered him.

"Here, the clans always come first," Mara continued. "To ensure our survival and the well-being of our pups, we work together as one big clan, despite the different colors and sections. A leader cannot be selfish, putting himself first."

"So, when I marked Cartan, it seemed like he was prioritizing himself?"

She nodded, and I let out a string of curses under my breath. "I only did it because—"

"No need to explain yourself. Our High Alpha is a remarkable Alpha. Why wouldn't you want to claim him right away?" she asked, reassuring me.

I didn't correct Mara, refraining from revealing the real reason I had initially claimed Cartan. I simply followed her as we approached the entrance of the large tent, pondering what would transpire during this meeting.

"Do you think the other Alphas will demand that Cartan hand me over to one of them?" I asked as we neared the tent's opening.

"They might, but it's unlikely to happen. Our High Alpha has clearly staked his claim on you, even without his mark," she assured me.

I blushed slightly, realizing that his scent probably clung to every inch of my skin. When was the last time I had taken a proper bath? I shivered at the thought, but that would have to wait. First, I needed to understand what would transpire at this meeting.

"I don't know," I murmured, gazing through the dark opening.

"What?" Mara inquired.

"If Cartan truly wanted me, then why bring me to a gathering of enraged Alphas who also desire me, or at the very least, an Omega?" I whispered, fearing that Cartan may have lied to me and intended to share me.

"He had no other choice," Mara explained.

"How so?"

"They demanded to see you as well."

"Great," I mumbled, biting down on the soft skin on the inner side of my cheek.

I didn't want to enter the tent, but Mara gently pushed me forward, encouraging me to go.

"Should I remember anything? Any specific way to behave?" I asked.

"An Omega knows how to conduct themselves around Alphas," she replied before walking away.

"Wonderful," I whispered, my voice tinged with anxiety, as I stepped into the tent.

Chapter Twenty-Seven
Cartan

The other clan leaders stood around a small, flickering fire in the center, having taken their seats among the low pillow-filled benches. Their collective gaze bore into me as I stood by the staircase leading down into the sunken area where the seating arrangement had been made. I didn't sit down, nor did they expect me to. I waited for my Omega to enter, and I could sense the moment she did. So did all the other Alphas, their interest piqued as they caught sight of this concealed princess.

Kiandra froze for a moment upon seeing the other Alphas, and their low growls greeted her hesitation. This prompted me to emit a deeper one in response, my protective instincts on full display. I didn't like the way they were scrutinizing her. When they turned their attention away from her, I waved her closer, and she heeded my call, descending the steps and stopping beside me. Her focus remained on the ground in front of her feet, avoiding eye contact, and she displayed her submission. While I understood that it appeased them, I couldn't help but feel a twinge of discomfort seeing her submit to anyone other than me. However, her instincts demanded it.

"Welcome, Omega," High Alpha Seran greeted her, causing Kiandra to slowly raise her gaze.

"Thank you," she replied, her voice timid and small. I sensed her seeking closer to me, her hand brushing against mine, which seemed to calm her. Every Alpha in the room noticed how she gravitated toward me, and I couldn't help but smile, knowing none of them would ever lay a finger on her. She was mine, entirely *mine*.

"Are you the third one?"

"The fourth princess," she corrected.

"So it's true," High Alpha Recor chimed in. "There really was a fourth?"

"Yes," she affirmed.

"Why were you hidden?" High Alpha Kylos inquired, the only one in the room not overtly displaying an interest in my Omega, as she wasn't his type.

"I was declared dead when I was born," she explained. "However, I miraculously survived, but my father saw an opportunity to keep me even more hidden."

"But you chose to reveal yourself to High Alpha Cartan?" Alpha Recor probed.

"No, he found me."

"How did he find you?" Alpha Kylos asked.

Kiandra shifted nervously, her hands clasping together in front of her. I could tell she didn't want to discuss how she had distracted me, but there was no need to keep it a secret. I only had one princess with me now.

"She was familiar with the secret tunnels in the castle. She had studied them and used those tunnels to reach her sisters," I explained.

"And yet, you somehow managed to capture this one," Alpha Seran said, the long scar across his face adding a menacing edge to his features. While others might find it frightening, it thrilled me, as I was the one who had given it to him.

"I was about to catch the rest, but it's no exaggeration when we are warned that an Omega can be quite distracting to an Alpha. At this very moment, all of you are likely pondering what it would take to kill me and claim her," I pointed out. I saw them exchange glances, except for Kylos, who smiled. High Alpha Peros had yet to speak, but he rarely did. Still, I could sense his displeasure in his eyes, and the way he watched my

Omega. He appeared to be the closest to making a move, and I glared at him, warning him not to try. I would rip his throat from his body before he could get near her.

"So what? She dropped to all fours before you could catch the others?" Alpha Seran taunted.

"Close," I admitted, causing Kiandra to gasp and turn to look up at me. Yet I wasn't lying. She had knelt down.

"A rather feeble excuse," Alpha Seran growled. "You promised Omegas for all of us, and yet you return with one who has evidently laid claim to you."

"I am searching for the other princesses. They are unfamiliar with the many lands and can't hide forever. You will have your Omegas."

Seran didn't appear satisfied and shifted his attention back to my Omega, making her take a step back.

"Why did you choose him?" Seran asked, and I tensed a little.

Both Kiandra and I understood why she had chosen me. While I admired her intelligence and choice, I was fully aware that her answer would intensify the other Alphas' desires to take her from me.

"Perhaps we shouldn't question their connection so directly," Kylos suggested, the calmest one among us. "You're clearly putting High Alpha Cartan on edge, and it's unsettling his Omega. Soon, this floor will be stained with blood, and I'd prefer not to have the room reek of it."

Seran crossed his arms, looking irritated, but he redirected his attention away from my Omega. Instead, Kylos leaned forward, resting his arms on his knees.

"He is only asking, Omega, because anyone here would consider themselves worthy of an Omega mate. It's a simple curiosity, not a challenge," he explained, but his gaze turned to me when he mentioned the challenge part. "Just answer honestly."

I felt my Omega's eyes on me, scrutinizing me from head to toe. I knew what she had to say, and I welcomed her honesty. I turned to her, silently encouraging her to speak her mind. To my surprise, she didn't avert her gaze from me.

"It was instinct," she replied. "There wasn't much time to think, but it just felt right."

I knew my Omega was incapable of falsehood, and while her words didn't convey the full truth, they held sincerity. It filled me with pride, and I turned back to the other Alphas, wearing a reassuring smile.

"Have you interacted with any other Alphas before?" Recor inquired, drawing Kiandra's attention to him.

"Only my father."

"None outside your family?" Seran pressed.

"My father had a few Alphas around him, but I mostly kept to myself or spent time with my sisters in private," she explained.

"So that's a 'no'," Seran concluded.

"But I've been with the army on this journey. I've spoken to many Alphas from each of your clans. Nevertheless, I still want the Alpha I've marked," she assured them. I couldn't help but notice the way they tensed, emitting low growls. However, an Omega's mark could not be coerced. She had chosen me, and they had to accept it.

"It doesn't change the fact that you've acted selfishly," Peros finally spoke up, his eyes on me. "No one was supposed to be marked until they arrived here, even if you only brought one."

"She hasn't been marked," I revealed, then grasped Kiandra's hair, causing her to gasp as I forced her head back. "There is no mark."

"But you're marked," Seran pointed out.

"That's not what we discussed. Moreover, I've found the Omegas and brought one here. This very Omega claimed me as her own. None of you can say you have achieved the same, despite calling yourselves High Alphas," I retorted, my words inciting growls throughout the room. "I will bring the other sisters here. I have a good idea of where they might be, and then you will have what I promised you. However, this Omega chose me, and nothing prohibited her from doing so."

They exchanged glances once more, with Kylos continuing to find amusement in the unfolding drama. However, he had nothing to worry about. Kiandra would never be a desirable prospect for him. Should I ever come across a male Omega, he would be the one to claim them.

Recor's voice took on a snarl, and I instinctively pushed Kiandra slightly behind me while growling in response to the other Alpha's aggression. He rose from his seat, matching my fury. I could sense this confrontation was distressing my Omega, but I couldn't allow anyone to challenge the fact that Kiandra had chosen me. The moment I could, my mark would be on her neck, and every part of her would belong to me.

"I have unequivocally acted in the best interests of the clans," I retorted, my voice strong and unwavering. "I swore upon the blood in my veins that I would bring the Omegas to the Mainlands or find suitable ones for you. However, I will not tolerate being called selfish or accused of acting solely in my own interests. It was always understood that I had the first choice. More importantly, I have already begun the process of mating with the Omega. We will be the first pair to bring a true Alpha or Omega into the lands. I will not stand for my honor to be insulted."

Growls continued to reverberate through the

room, the tension escalating to alarming levels. I found it perplexing because I believed my words were reasonable. Then, I noticed that the only Alpha in the room who should not be affected by my Omega's scent had eyes as dark as night. At that moment, an alluring aroma filled my nostrils, and I glanced behind me, discovering that my Omega's eyes had shifted to a slightly golden hue. Omega eyes turned golden only when they entered their heat.

"Fuck," I groaned in realization. In an instant, the first Alpha leapt over the fire. I swiftly pushed my hand into his chest, propelling Seran right into Recor, causing them to tumble to the ground. To my surprise, Kylos, influenced by my Omega's heat as nature dictated, managed to hold back Peros, who was growling and struggling beneath Kylos's restraint.

"Go! Now!" Kylos ordered.

I didn't hesitate. Kiandra bowed forward in pain as the first waves of her heat washed over her. I scooped her up and threw her over my shoulder before sprinting from the scene. I stormed through the camp, which had luckily quieted down due to the late hour, but I knew my Omega's scent would soon send the place into chaos.

Fortunately, I made it back to our tent, placing my Omega on the fur-covered ground. She was deep into her heat by now, her normal bodily functions shutting down to sustain her throughout the week-long cycle. She struggled to control her limbs and remove her dress, while my rut-driven instincts made me growl ferociously with a burning desire to claim her.

She tried to crawl away from me, hissing in fear, but she couldn't escape. My rut had taken hold of me, and the sight of my Omega fleeing from me only fueled my anger. I grabbed her leg, pulling her back to me, and then tore her clothes from her body. She thrashed against me, whimpering as I handled her roughly, flipping her over and presenting her enticing ass. I ripped my own clothes apart in my desperation.

Her pussy wasn't just wet. It was swollen, red, and dripping slick in long, sticky lines. It was the most exquisite little cunt I had ever seen. I thrust into her wet passage, howling in ecstasy as she wiggled and whimpered beneath me, clamping down tightly around me. Her response only spurred me on, intensifying my determination to mate with her. I pounded into her mercilessly, thrusting over and over, her wetness coating both of us and making our coupling delightfully slippery.

She whimpered, cried, and begged me to knot her. The way she tightened around me during her second climax made it impossible for me to hold back any longer. I thrust a few more times, and then my knot expanded and locked us together. I released every drop of my cum inside her, marking her on the inside before leaning over her and sinking my teeth into the sweet spot on her neck.

Chapter Twenty-Eight
Cartan

She was the first Omega I had ever bedded, and only Omegas experienced heats. These heats were often described as the most incredible experiences in the world, and an Alpha serving an Omega during their heat would forever be connected to that female. I used to think that a description could do justice to the reality, but it was obvious nothing compared to being with my Omega. She was like an enchantress who had one purpose—to mate with me.

She would do anything to capture my attention, ensuring that I remained completely focused on her, often neglecting rest and sustenance. She would ride me so vigorously and swiftly that I would climax without knotting her at times. Her sweet giggles at the power she held over me would frequently prompt me to turn her around and mount her, plunging into her with a passionate intensity that left her docile and submissive. Yet, she always returned to me, seeking more.

If I attempted to close my eyes for a moment, thinking she was resting, she would start to trace the mark on my neck with her tongue before letting it glide down my body and slide along my cock. Her mouth would take me as deep as she could, and I would often pull her away at the last moment before releasing my cum all over her.

My little Omega would drive herself wild with desire for my scent, smearing my seed over her breasts and chest before licking her fingers clean. The sight would ignite my need, and I would find myself pushing her onto the ground, spreading her legs wide, and thrusting into her with a desperation bordering on madness. Our clan would howl in celebration of our union, and their joyful sounds filled the night. This was truly a momentous occasion for all of us.

As her heat progressed, my mate grew bolder and more daring. She would signal her desire for me to mate with her, often touching herself right in front of me. Sometimes, she would entice me, only to slip away from my grasp, forcing me to chase her. She never strayed far, never leaving our bedroom, but I took her in our nest many times, often with her on her back, so I could watch her golden eyes gaze up at me with pure lust and desire. She would call my title, screaming "Alpha" in her heightened state of pleasure, but she couldn't manage any other words. She was an animal in need of carnal satisfaction and nothing else.

While I reveled in every moment when I regained some semblance of consciousness, her heat pushed me into a relentless rut. I remained constantly aroused, yearning to be inside her at all times. However, as my awareness grew, I began to remember my responsibilities as her Alpha. During her heat, she didn't require much sustenance, as her bodily functions had slowed, but she still needed some energy and water to prevent complete exhaustion. Fortunately, both provisions had been made available to us, as her heat had struck suddenly, and I had been unprepared.

As Kiandra finally managed to rest a bit in our nest, I began to pace around, and that's when I discovered the food by the entrance. I brought it back to her, and she was already stirring, sensing her Alpha's absence. She crawled out of the nest, remaining on all fours, and as soon as her golden eyes locked onto me, she whimpered. She leaned back, resting a hand behind her and sliding another down her body. She began to touch herself in front of me, and I growled darkly, urging her to stop so I could feed her. However, she simply smiled at me and continued to tease herself.

She trembled right in front of me, deriving pleasure from my presence, and in my frustration, I accidentally dropped the food from my hand. I pushed her to the ground in a fit of powerful need to dominate and took her from behind, thrusting hard into her. She let out a small scream from the intensity, but her cries only grew louder and filled with delight as I fucked her vigorously. She shivered all over, her inner muscles tightening around me until it felt like she was strangling my cock. My knot eventually locked us together, and I climaxed with a powerful roar.

When my desires were finally satiated, and I had made my mate submit once more, I noticed the food lying on the ground. I shook my head and gave my mate's ass a light spank. She gasped and shifted forward slightly, but I pulled her back to prevent any tearing, plunging my cock even deeper. She groaned, leaning forward to present her ass, offering herself to me again. However, I couldn't forget my duty as her Alpha.

When my knot finally released her, I brought Kiandra over to the food and seated her on my lap. She initially thought I wanted her to straddle me, but I held her in place, preventing her from descending onto my hard cock. Confusion and frustration flickered across her face as she couldn't comprehend why I was denying her the one thing she craved above all else at this moment. Nevertheless, I smiled at her and brought a piece of dried meat to her lips, but she hissed and turned her head away.

A low growl escaped me in response to her defiance. My little Omega, driven by her instinctual need for my cock, didn't realize she required nourishment. An idea crossed my mind, and I loosened my grip slightly. As soon as Kiandra recognized that she could ride me, she bestowed a sweet smile upon me and impaled herself on my throbbing length.

I groaned, struggling to maintain my self-control as her intoxicating warmth enveloped me. I needed to focus on feeding her, even though her incredible pussy threatened to drive me to madness. When she was fully seated on me, I gripped her firmly once more, eliciting a hiss of annoyance from her as I denied her movement. Nevertheless, I presented the food to her lips once again.

"*Eat*!" I commanded in my primal voice.

She regarded me with curiosity, not comprehending my words at first, but then her gaze shifted to the food. To my delightful surprise, Kiandra traced her tongue along one of my fingers, the same finger that held a piece of meat, before she took both the food and my fingertips into her mouth. She moaned sensually, and I teetered on the brink of climax from this simple act. At least she consumed the food, and I reached for more. She repeated the process, and my grip slackened slightly. With subtle movements of her hips, she began riding me achingly slowly, all the while I continued to feed her small morsels of sustenance.

My body had never felt so taut, and I had never denied myself release for this long, but I needed to ensure Kiandra ate as much as possible. She gradually increased the pace, testing my restraint, a smug glint in her eyes suggesting she knew she was pushing me to the edge— and she relished every moment of it.

Getting her to drink water was more challenging than feeding her, as she couldn't suck on my fingers while taking in the liquid. So, when I brought a small cup of water to her lips, she regarded it curiously, ceasing her rhythmic movements. I growled, urging her to continue, and then I presented the cup to her once more.

Initially, she didn't quite grasp the concept and

instead ran her tongue from my wrist up my hand. In response, I entwined my fingers in her hair, gently pulling her head back to hold her in place as I offered the cup once again.

"Drink, and I will knot you, my little mate," I offered, and it wasn't until a small amount of water trickled past her lips that she understood the contents of the cup.

Her primal instincts kicked in, and she emptied the cup with urgency. After ensuring she had ingested some liquid, I was incredibly aroused and overwhelmed with the need to knot her. However, Kiandra dismounted from me, prompting an angry growl from me. She shifted her position, swinging her leg over mine and placing the other on my left side, facing away from me. Her juices coated me as she slowly took me inside her once more. Both of us trembled with pleasure, and she moaned loudly as I filled her completely.

Then, without warning, an orgasm overcame me, and I climaxed inside her, sinking my teeth into her shoulder in the process. She whimpered but remained still as I released myself inside her. The release had occurred so swiftly that I hadn't even knotted her, and she hadn't experienced her climax yet.

My instincts were not satisfied with this, and I repositioned us so that we were lying on our sides. Kiandra looked back at me, and I claimed her lips as I began thrusting into her, one hand sliding down her body to tease her clit. She called out my title as she convulsed, shaking violently in my arms. It was a mesmerizing sight. Right there, with my Omega, I felt like I could die happily. There would never be anyone else for me, I was certain of it. She was mine, and no one else would even be allowed to gaze upon her without my explicit permission.

****

As we approached the end of Kiandra's heat, she began to sleep more, and the golden hue in her eyes gradually faded. My instincts still roared with desire for her, yearning to knot her, but the little Omega was growing weary. With each yawn and desire for rest, she increasingly relied on my purring to soothe her. Although I remained on edge, I found immense contentment in merely holding her close. It felt as if she had always belonged by my side, and since I required very little sleep during my rut, I could take my time watching over her.

She possessed the sweetest, small, pink lips and had a straight nose with a few freckles adorning it. Her skin had already taken on a gentle sun-kissed hue, yet her body remained gracefully curved and tantalizing, an exquisite canvas for admiration and playful teasing.

My fingers caressed the contours of her body, aching to press into her skin as I prepared to claim her once more. However, I summoned every ounce of self-control, compelling myself to remain still, awaiting the reawakening of my Omega. It was as though she possessed an innate understanding of my desires, for her eyes fluttered open, the once-prominent gold now giving way to the return of her rich brown irises.

Nevertheless, she graced me with one of her enchanting smiles, reminiscent of the expressions she wore when engrossed in a book or captivated by a newfound discovery. In that moment, it occurred to me that perhaps I could make this Omega love me, for in her world, knowledge was the most precious treasure, and she regarded me as something equally precious.

She pressed her nose to my skin, inhaling deeply before her hand trailed down my stomach. My cock throbbed, craving her touch, yet she barely grazed its tip before pulling away, giving me her back. A growl of frustration escaped me, but my Omega turned around, glancing over her shoulder, and flashing me a teasing smile. I grabbed her leg, pulling it over mine and aligning myself with her, sliding into her slick heat. She whimpered as I entered her, her body welcoming me eagerly. I quickly wrapped my arm around her, but as my hand brushed her stomach, I felt something peculiar. Uncertain if I had sensed it correctly, I moved my hand back, searching for that tingling sensation.

It was a subtle electric feeling, but it was unmistakable, right on her lower abdomen, reacting to my own Alpha powers. It was then that I realized I had overlooked something in my fervor to mate with my Omega. Leaning closer to her, I inhaled her intoxicating scent, and there it was—the sweet aroma had become nearly addictive, triggering my protective instinct, and alerting me that something just as precious was now growing inside her.

I had thought I was a doomed Alpha before, but the knowledge that my Omega carried my child, my heir, drove me to the brink of madness. I held her even tighter, pressing her against my body, but I refrained from moving as I immersed myself in the unfamiliar warmth that welled up within me. I had never felt this way before.

Kiandra grew restless with just my throbbing cock inside her but no rhythmic motion. She whimpered and wiggled on my cock, but I withdrew from her. She mewled, calling out for me. I turned her onto her back and slowly eased back into her, savoring the exquisite expressions of pleasure that illuminated her face as I took my time with her. Her melodious sounds filled the air, and I maintained a leisurely pace, cherishing her, all the while knowing we were building a future together.

Chapter Twenty-Nine
Kiandra

Often when I awoke from my heats, I would find myself feeling exhausted, sticky, and somewhat disoriented. Initially, my recollection of events would be hazy, but the memories would gradually resurface, and they weren't always pleasant. However, this time was different. I felt a comforting warmth all around me, securely enveloped in the strong arms of an Alpha. Despite the lingering stickiness, there was no confusion. I felt safe and content, soothed by the deep purring that filled the air, prompting me to seek the source by nuzzling my face against a broad chest.

"You've returned to me, my little Omega, haven't you?" a dark, velvety voice purred into my ear.

His voice sent shivers through my entire body, and I could feel myself grow wet once more. It had never happened so swiftly before, but I was engulfed in his potent Alpha scent, and his voice invoked memories of his commanding presence growling at me while he claimed me with fierce passion.

I sensed him inhaling deeply, savoring my scent, which elicited an appreciative sound from his lips. In no time, I found myself on my back, with Cartan positioned between my legs. I willingly spread myself for him, craving his closeness. As he entered me, I gasped at the sensation of him filling every inch of me, setting a frenetic pace that had me crying out while clinging to his powerful form.

We climaxed together swiftly, his knot locking us together, and while I was left thoroughly satisfied, I continued to bury my face in the crook of his neck, my hands tracing his form. Every inch I touched confirmed his strength, and I hummed in delight.

"You drive me to madness, little Omega," he whispered, his voice husky with desire. "I almost forgot to feed you."

I smiled, unfazed by his oversight. I had never felt this invigorated after a heat before. In the past, we had always been isolated when our heats approached, as the mere presence of an Omega in heat could drive any nearby males into a frenzy, making them willing to fight to the death for a chance to mate with me or my sisters. While it had kept us safe, it also left me with a lingering emptiness. Only now did I realize what I had truly needed, and I yearned for more.

Wrapping my legs around my Alpha, I elicited a low growl from Cartan as our connection deepened. I began teasing his skin with my teeth, sensing him trembling beneath my touch. Yet, as I became more aware of my surroundings, a strange sensation crept over me. I pulled back, my Alpha's heightened senses detecting my unease. He lifted his head, though his smile remained reassuring rather than concerned. Nonetheless, I knew something was amiss, something that felt different, though I couldn't quite pinpoint it.

"I feel strange, Cartan," I whispered, casting my gaze around our dimly lit nest, with the only source of light emanating from the entrance.

Cartan's purring grew louder, comforting me, but I couldn't shake the sensation of something being wrong. His hand glided down my body, coming to rest on my stomach, and when our unborn child sensed their father's powerful purring too, they stirred within me. I gasped, looking up at Cartan, who smiled at me with genuine affection, a look that surprised me. He had never regarded me in such a way, as if I were the most precious thing in existence.

"Am I pregnant?" I inquired.

Cartan nodded, leaning down to kiss me passionately. His tongue melded with mine, and as his knot receded, he began mating with me at a slower, more tender pace. It was then that I noticed our bond seemed to have grown stronger. He had marked me!

"You're safe, little Omega," he whispered soothingly. "I won't let anything harm either of you."

His words filled me with a delightful sense of security, and as an orgasm rippled through me, he continued to fuck me until he found his release as well, refraining from knotting me. The sensation of emptiness lingered, but Cartan assured me he needed to fetch us some food.

Left alone in our nest, I realized how reliant I had become on him. In his absence, a sense of unease washed over me, and I wrapped myself in the layers of fur that now carried his powerful scent. Completely surrounded, I felt calmer, as if he were still present, protecting me from all sides.

I listened to his approach, yet I remained still, cocooned in the warmth of the furs. His deep chuckle resonated through the room as he noticed how tightly I had wrapped myself up. A hand slipped beneath the furs, finding my calf and gently tugging. I hissed softly, reluctant to move from my comfortable spot. My body felt wonderfully used, but any sudden movements caused discomfort. I preferred to stay in the nest, but Cartan was insistent. He pulled me out and lifted me into his arms. I instinctively wrapped my legs around his waist, and his lips met mine, coaxing me to relax against him.

"Let's get you cleaned up," he murmured against my lips. He carried me to the adjacent room where a large tub awaited, already filled with warm water. I hummed in delight as the warmth eased the tension in my shoulders.

Cartan's skilled hands moved over my body, washing away the remnants of our passionate encounter, and I leaned into his touch. With him so close, I could take my time to truly observe him, paying attention to the small details. A faint scar by his eyebrow, another along the left side of his jaw, and three long ones on his shoulder, as if someone had tried to rip his arm away. My fingers traced the marks as he scrubbed something fragrant into my hair, filling the air with a pleasant floral scent.

"How did you get this?" I whispered, referring to his scars.

"A panther," he replied.

"When?"

"When I was just a kid."

"How did you survive it?"

Cartan shrugged, as though surviving such an attack was a simple feat. However, his response piqued my curiosity, especially considering what Tyros's mate had told me. I realized how little I truly knew about my Alpha, so I leaned toward him, resting against his chest. A smile played on his lips as I snuggled closer.

"Tell me something about you," I urged. But his smile faded, and I sensed tension in his body beneath my touch.

"What do you want to know?" he asked, his voice strained.

"Everything."

His eyes widened, and I offered a reassuring smile before scooping up some water and letting it trickle down his sculpted form.

"Now that we have fully marked each other and created something," I continued, "shouldn't I get to know my Alpha?"

Cartan relaxed and turned me so that my back was pressed against his front. His purring reverberated through me as his hand rested on my stomach, and I gasped at the strange sensation that radiated from the tiny presence within me in response to its father.

"My story isn't important," he whispered in my ear.

I turned to look at him, puzzled by his words.

"Of course it is," I insisted. "Every story is."

He shook his head, his thumb gently stroking the extra protective layer on my stomach. "My future is important. My presence. My Omega and child. Nothing more."

His words left me feeling perplexed. I cherished stories and history, and I was eager to know his past. However, it seemed Cartan was fiercely protective of his own. Nonetheless, I was determined to uncover the truth.

"The other Alphas," I began cautiously, sensing his tension returning, "did … you kill them?"

I was aware of the power an Omega's heat held, but I couldn't recall the details.

"You don't remember?" he asked.

"I only remember you talking, arguing about my sisters and the others being dissatisfied because you hadn't given them the Omegas you promised," I explained.

"Yes, they were quite dissatisfied, but they are not dead."

"No?"

"Kylos helped, and I managed to get you out of there before anything terrible happened. Nevertheless, there was quite the commotion in the camp, but they found alternative outlets for their pent-up aggression."

"The pleasure tents?" I inquired, catching the hint of a chuckle in his voice.

"That, or they turned to physical combat. Surprisingly, Tyros informed me that no deaths occurred."

A shiver ran down my spine, the thought of Alphas succumbing to madness during an Omega's heat making me uneasy.

"It was a mistake to take you there," Cartan sighed. "I knew your heat was imminent. I shouldn't have risked it."

"They demanded my presence. I don't believe you had much of a choice. Couldn't they have forced me to go?" I pondered.

Cartan's growl rumbled through the air, but the sound didn't incite fear. It brought me comfort and I couldn't help but smile.

"No one lays a finger on you," he snarled. His hand splayed protectively over my stomach, extending his vow to the tiny presence growing within me.

"I was merely posing a question," I teased, and he nuzzled closer to my neck, inhaling my scent. "The most important thing is that no one was harmed, but yes, next time we should probably stay in the tent."

His purring resumed, this time louder, and I could feel his cock pressing against my lower back. It sent a warm shiver through me, and I subtly moved against him, teasing his hard length.

"I like the way you speak of a 'next time'," he groaned, his pleasure evident.

"Won't you be there?" I joked, but Cartan swiftly grasped my throat, exerting gentle pressure as he turned me to face him.

"There will be no one else there but me," he growled, his tone shifting.

I smiled up at him, elated by the knowledge that only he would be with me. I pressed up to kiss him, and Cartan seized me, turning me around before impaling me on his hard shaft. A gasp escaped me as I leaned my head back in ecstasy.

"You need no one but me," he declared.

"Oh, Gods," I whimpered. He compelled me to move fast up and down on him, the impending orgasm building with intensity.

"I am your Alpha. Say it," he ordered.

I nodded fervently as pleasure surged through me.

"Say it!"

"Yes, you! You're my Alpha!" I screamed as the climax washed over me, my toes curling in ecstasy. He continued thrusting into me from below, his movements driving me wild, until he locked us together and found release as well.

Chapter Thirty
Cartan

I sat with my Omega nestled on my lap at the desk inside the tent, feeding her small morsels of food. My arm remained securely around her, my hand gently resting on her stomach. The little life growing within her seemed brimming with energy now that she was fully awake. Removing my hand would only result in my mate growing restless and placing it back on her stomach.

She was still acclimating to the power inside her, and I couldn't help but be intrigued by the tiny presence growing within her. Would it be an Alpha or an Omega? Regardless, it would mark a significant event, the first true Omega or Alpha in the desert in a long time. I cherished this peaceful moment as my Omega grew fuller and started feeding me morsels as well. It provided ample opportunities to trace my lips and tongue along her skin, teasing her until she was wet and ready for me. Our bodies had become so accustomed to each other.

However, the tranquility was suddenly interrupted by a whistle, signaling Tyros's approach. Even before he appeared, a growl rose within me. I had little tolerance for other Alphas around my Omega, especially now that she was pregnant.

Nevertheless, Kiandra simply kissed my cheek and wrapped her arm around my neck while placing her other hand on my chest. Her touch immediately calmed me, and the growl subsided just before Tyros emerged. He smiled at both of us but avoided keeping his gaze on Kiandra for too long.

"High Alpha, may I have a moment?" he requested. I sighed, reluctant to let go of my Omega, especially when she seemed to need me more at this moment. Yet my obedient mate slipped off my lap to let me stand. I pulled her close, planting a kiss on her lips, and instructed her to wait for me. She sat back down in my seat, looking small and delicate as she continued to eat, even grabbing a book.

Outside, the bright sun shone, and the dry, fresh air was a welcome change from the confines of our tent. I hadn't realized how much I craved the outdoors while indulging in my mate's pleasure. She had a way of making me forget everything else. I found myself constantly glancing back at the tent, prompting Tyros to whistle again to regain my attention.

"What?" I asked, noticing the amused smile on his lips.

"I'm glad I already have a mate, and who is not an Omega," he chuckled. "At least that means I still have my head."

I groaned and scratched my neck before forcing myself to show him he had my full attention.

"The other Alphas wish to speak with you now that you're out of your rut," he revealed. I began growling once more, causing him to take a step back as the intensity caught him off guard.

"Just you," he hurriedly clarified. "Everyone knows she is fully claimed now, and they wouldn't dare challenge you for her."

"Good, because I would tear them apart. No one gets close to her, especially not now," I snarled.

Tyros watched me for a moment before his smile returned. "Is she pregnant?"

I nodded, feeling the warmth in my heart spreading once more. This strange feeling was perplexing.

"Then it truly settles the matter. The others might be uncomfortable with her claiming you first, but they can't change what this pregnancy will bring. It's a new beginning," he pointed out.

"I'm aware," I said, glancing back at the tent with a longing to return. However, the other Alphas had called a meeting, so I had to attend. "Well, let's go then."

I started walking across the hard ground, with Tyros following beside me. Yet, I could sense there was more he wished to convey.

"What?" I asked.

"There is someone else who wants to see you, and he is at the meeting."

"Who?" I inquired.

"The king."

"Great," I groaned, running a hand down my face. Dealing with the king on top of everything else was not something I looked forward to, but I hadn't fully explained the situation to him yet, and he deserved to know what was transpiring.

I walked with Tyros toward the tent, but he remained outside. The king's guards were stationed near the tent as well, giving me a wary glance as I entered. I detested how he had brought other Alphas into our land, and I knew the High Alphas felt the same way, but the king was not someone to be trifled with. He may not have grown up in our world, but he was far from a weak ruler.

Inside the tent, the Alphas were in conversation, but upon hearing me enter, only the king smiled. It surprised me that he wasn't angrier. I descended the small steps, and he approached me while the others took their seats.

"The first Alpha to mate with a true Omega in decades," he celebrated, though I could detect a condescending tone in his voice.

He took a sip from his cup, his light-blue eyes shimmering with anger. I was certain the other Alphas had filled him in on the situation.

"I allowed you to traverse my land with your army. I permitted you to use my ships, my harbor, and what do I discover?" he said, coming closer to me. I remained on edge and issued a warning growl.

He stopped at a certain distance, tossing the remainder of his drink into the fireplace before responding with another powerful growl of his own.

"You have *one*!" he shouted. "One you've claimed for yourself! Did I not assist you? Do you not owe me an Omega in return? Yet you lay claim to the only one you managed to capture."

"She is *mine*!" I snarled, and the sheer aggression in my voice was unmistakable. If anyone, even the king, thought they could take her from me, they were gravely mistaken.

"You have become attached," he observed.

"It happens to Alphas who spend a lot of time with an Omega."

"No, this is deeper. It appears you've lost yourself in her. Could it be a true bond has formed?" he suggested, catching me off guard as I hadn't considered it myself. It would explain the constant surprises, the powerful attraction.

Suddenly, many things began to make sense, but I was taken aback that the king had reached this conclusion. Did he desire a true bond himself? When he spoke of an Omega, I saw dark desire in his eyes, a craving to possess something rare and delicate, but not necessarily a desire for a deeper connection. That's why I wasn't particularly eager to provide him with an Omega.

"My guess is that it has," he snarled before shaking his head in frustration. "Where is she?"

"Not here, and you won't see her," I warned as I stepped closer to him.

I was broader and slightly taller than him, but he didn't allow that to intimidate him. Normally, I would have been impressed by his confidence, but this was about my Omega, and no one would ever feel entitled to her.

"You owe me something. I want to see this rarity," he insisted.

"I will get you an Omega like the rest, but the fourth princess remains mine, and I have no obligation to show her to you. Not unless you want those pretty blue eyes to suddenly disappear from your skull," I retorted.

The king glared back at me, but then a small smile crept onto his lips. He seemed amused, which left me feeling confused.

"I suppose that's what Omega pussy does to you," he mused aloud, making me growl in irritation. The king, however, didn't seem to want to push the issue any further.

"Just remember, you wouldn't even have had the chance to find your little princess without my help. Do not disrespect that kindness," he warned.

"I will remember, but she is mine, and you cannot demand to see her. You will receive what I promised you, but until then, stay away from my Omega," I growled.

The king smiled faintly again, shook his head, and then walked past me. A strong flowery scent trailed behind him, annoying me. He smelled like a pampered, luxury-loving male. However, the other Alpha soon departed, and I turned to face the other clan leaders. They appeared less angry now, understanding that there was little they could change about the fact that Kiandra was mine and would remain so. Yet this time, I also had good news to share.

"You shouldn't make an enemy out of him," Kylos cautioned. "He has more Alphas under his command than there are in this entire camp."

"I'm aware," I sighed.

"He merely wanted to see your Omega," Recor pointed out, but I began growling again and shook my head.

"Why is that an unreasonable request?" Seran asked, not comprehending until they had Omegas of their own. It was an instinctual reaction, but I felt they needed a brief explanation for my strong response.

"She is pregnant," I revealed, and the others exchanged glances.

The room fell silent for a moment before Kylos clapped his hands together and stood up. He approached me, placing a hand on my shoulder and offering a smile.

"Congratulations. This is wonderful news. We will celebrate tonight," he announced.

I nodded, and Kylos turned to the other three, who also stood up, joining us by the fire. They each placed a hand on my shoulders, offering their congratulations, and at last, I was allowed to return to my Omega.

Chapter Thirty-One
Kiandra

The words were so foreign to me. My tongue curled, pressing against my teeth as I attempted to pronounce them properly, but I seemed to fail miserably. It made me pace around the room, trying to dispel this strange, restless energy within me. I had never experienced restlessness like this before, and it left me feeling anxious for my Alpha. However, I distracted myself by focusing on the unfamiliar words before me, determined to find the right way to pronounce them. I was so engrossed in my task that I didn't hear Cartan re-enter the tent. I just kept pacing, my mind consumed by the Old Language.

Finally, I felt an arm wrap around my waist, pulling me into the embrace of a strong, comforting body. It brought a smile to my face, his powerful scent filling my senses as his hand rested on my stomach, instantly calming me.

"Is this how you work? Pacing?" he inquired.

"I do pace a lot, and mumble," I admitted.

"You shouldn't tire yourself," he gently scolded.

"I am not a wounded animal, and this is difficult," I explained. "I have never struggled like this before."

Cartan chuckled and kissed my neck. "Which word is troubling you?"

"This one? Why does the letter swirl?" I pointed to a particular word in the text.

"Because it's meant to be elongated. The Rs are longer, almost like a growl, and the Ls are soft," he patiently explained.

"That is incredibly complicated."

"I thought you enjoyed a challenge, little one," he

teased.

"I love completing a challenge," I corrected.

"Then you will find a way to conquer this one too."

Cartan scooped me up and carried me back to the bedroom, making me giggle with delight. As he placed me among the furs, he attempted to unclasp the locks on my dress. Yet I held up the book before him.

"What about this word?" I asked. "What does it mean?"

He sighed, not particularly interested in the Old Language at the moment.

"It stands by itself," I pointed out.

"It's an old form of 'loved one' or 'dear one'. It's a term often used for a mate," he told me before setting the book aside. I reached for it, but he pressed against me, kissing me passionately, and I melted under his touch.

"Can you say it?" I whispered, seeing a smile play on his lips.

"Herlas," he purred, making me shiver with delight. He finally managed to remove my dress and pushed me onto my back. He kissed his way down my body, paying attention to my nipples before descending to my most sensitive areas. His warm tongue expertly pleasured me, and I ran my fingers through his short hair.

"Who taught you?" I panted, feeling pleasure build within me. But he growled in response, not wanting to engage in conversation now.

I tried to tease him by pushing him away, but he grabbed my thighs, pulling me closer before returning to pleasuring me with renewed vigor. He sucked on my clit until I exploded, crying out his name. Cartan quickly rid himself of his pants and entered me as he moved up my body. I felt a powerful surge through our bond, an intense need to claim me as if he couldn't bear not being knotted to me for another moment. It made me cling to him, surrendering to the storm of emotions within him. Through the bond, I finally understood my Alpha on a deeper level. It wasn't just desire that fueled him. There was a possessiveness, a primal need to claim and own, appeasing all my Omega instincts. It led to a second climax before he knotted himself to me, his seed marking me as his once more.

We both collapsed onto the furs, my body humming with satisfaction. I began playing with his hair, and he relaxed against me, utterly content.

"Who taught you?" I asked again, hearing him groan softly as he kissed the mark he had left on my neck.

"I'm knotting your pussy, and all you can think about is the Old Language?" he groaned.

"No, I'm wondering about my Alpha and who taught him the language," I chuckled.

He nuzzled my neck, making me whimper and hold him closer, but he pulled out of my grip slightly and then grabbed a strand of my hair, teasing my skin with it.

"I grew up hearing it," he explained. "It was taught to me alongside the common tongue."

"Why?" I inquired.

He closed his eyes with a tired expression, but my curiosity was insatiable. Now that I wasn't holding up the same defenses, I simply craved to know everything about him. Cartan was an enigma. All the High Alphas were, in fact. Meeting them had made me realize there were still so many things I didn't know, and I yearned to ask questions and seek answers.

"Because my father thought it was important for me to know both," he finally revealed.

"Your father? Is he here in the camp?" I asked, but Cartan let out a dark growl that surprised me, and I lowered my eyes in submission.

"He is … gone," Cartan confessed. As his knot began receding, he mated with me again, this time with harder thrusts, hitting that wondrous spot that made me arch my back and cry out in release.

Cartan pulled out and turned me around. He pushed the front of my body down, my ass in the air, and entered me again. His powerful hands gripped my skin firmly, almost to the point of stinging, but I relished the sensation as it mixed with the pleasure of being dominated so thoroughly. My Omega instincts reveled in delight as I came once more.

Cartan continued to mate with me, and I sensed him struggling to hold back, not wanting to stop. It frustrated my Omega side, and I clenched around him, urging him to climax. However, that caused him to pull out and deliver a hard spank to my backside. I hissed and started to push up, but he kept me down, thrusting into me once more as his hand slipped around my waist. He expertly stroked my clit while driving into me deeply, leading me to another climax before he followed suit, knotting us together and releasing himself into me.

I felt utterly sated, barely able to keep my eyes open, with Cartan's past long forgotten in my mind. Instead, I felt the soothing embrace of darkness as I drifted into a peaceful rest.

I woke later in the evening as I heard people entering the tent. It made me sit up in my nest and realize that Cartan was gone. I curled up in the darkness, hoping the strangers would leave or that my Alpha would return soon. However, a soft voice broke the silence, "High Omega?"

My anxiety lessened upon recognizing Mara's voice. Slowly, I emerged from the nest, finding a group of Beta women in front of me, all smiles. I held a fur close to me, perplexed by their presence, but then I heard the distant, rhythmic sound of drums.

"What's that?" I inquired as I stood up.

"We are celebrating, of course," Mara told me. "So let's get you ready."

"Ready for what?" I asked, but my question went unanswered. Instead, the women giggled and proceeded to wash and dress me. They adorned me in a dark green stola, sandals, and braided my hair before applying a light-red hue to my lips and dark lines around my eyes. It seemed they were having their own party while preparing me, and I had never worn makeup before. While my sisters had been forced to dress up and attend important events in the castle, I had always stayed in my library. So I welcomed the assistance.

When they were satisfied with their work, they brought a mirror to me, displaying my reflection. I appeared somewhat older and more serious, but I didn't dislike it. It also made me look very desirable, and I nodded approvingly. They pulled me from my seat and led me out of the tent. We walked for a while until we reached the main gathering area, where a grand celebration was in full swing. It was like nothing I had ever seen before. We had never had parties like these in the castle, and not even the street festivals I had observed bore any resemblance to this extravagant affair.

The scene was wild and untamed, with people dancing to the powerful rhythm of the drums and grinding their bodies together. Some were even mating openly, shocking me with their audacity. Yet out here, such behavior seemed perfectly normal, a clear celebration of desire. Food stalls had been set up, and numerous fires blazed, casting flickering shadows across the ground. Laughter and conversation filled the air, but anyone I passed bowed their heads, even the Alpha women offering me a nod of respect, though submission was far from their natural instinct.

Mara guided me to one of the food stalls, offering me a skewer with freshly cooked meat smothered in delicious sauce. I devoured it greedily before the women ushered me to the next stall and handed me a goblet of wine. As I loosened up and allowed myself to immerse in the festivities, the primal beat of the drums began to course through me, stirring a peculiar sensation.

"Can we dance?" I inquired.

Mara laughed and shook her head. "Not unless you want your Alpha to slaughter everyone in sight. You could ask him, but he won't let you go alone."

"Why not?" I pressed.

"I'm sure it's quite evident," she replied, gesturing toward the wild and explicit dances taking place. However, that only intensified my desire to join the crowd, my heart pounding with an unfamiliar exhilaration. Then, I noticed a peculiar echo to the rhythmic pounding, and it dawned on me that my heart was racing not just because of the drums but also due to another presence.

My gaze scanned the crowd, locating my Alpha among the other High Alphas. He was watching me with an intense, unwavering gaze. I could see the others attempting to engage him in conversation, but he remained fixated on me. I heard murmuring voices around me, but their words held no meaning. All that registered was my Alpha, the way he stared at me with eyes that had turned entirely black, brimming with desire.

I sensed his silent urging through our bond, but I was unable to move. My entire body quivered beneath his intense scrutiny, rendering me powerless, and so my Alpha began moving toward me. With each step he took, he seemed to grow fiercer, more imposing, a force of nature, and I felt myself grow wet between my legs at the sight of his commanding presence. The other women quickly made way for him, moving aside as he positioned himself in front of me. The moment he could, he seized me, pulling me into his embrace, and I moaned in delight. He inhaled my scent, detecting my arousal, and pressed me tightly against him, making me aware of the effect I had on him.

Leaning down, he whispered in my ear, "You don't deny your Alpha when he calls for you."

I quivered against him, my hands sliding down his bare chest and stomach, feeling the deep rumble beneath his skin.

"Touch me," I whimpered, guiding his hand higher toward my neck.

I wrapped my arm around his, drawing him closer, and pressed my lips to his. He groaned against my mouth, allowing his hand to descend further until it rested on my breast, his thumb brushing over my hardened nipple. I had lost all awareness of the world around me. All that existed were the sensations of my Alpha and the relentless rhythm of the drums. If he were to command me to kneel and pleasure him or to disrobe for him to mate, I would obey without hesitation. I had never experienced a connection more powerful than the one we now shared.

"Touch me," I whispered again, pressing my breast into his hand. His kiss grew more demanding, more insistent.

He wanted me too, so why was he holding back? However, the loud whistling and cheers suddenly reached my ears, pulling me out of our intense moment. I pulled away and noticed that many wolves of the desert were watching us. My cheeks burned with embarrassment, and I buried my face in my Alpha's chest as I heard him laugh. His hand came to rest on my ass and gave it a playful squeeze. I pushed him away, which only seemed to amuse him further.

"Did you not want me to touch you?" he teased.

"I didn't realize where we were," I mumbled, still trying to regain my composure.

"An old tradition dictates that an Omega is always claimed by the Alpha in front of the Alpha's clan to demonstrate their union," he growled into my ear.

I pulled back, looking at him in shock. Was he going to mate with me right here, in front of everyone? And why did the thought only make me wetter? Cartan shook his head.

"I don't share you," he stated firmly. "Your magnificent body is for me and me alone."

"Then why did you say that?" I wondered.

"I was merely explaining their joy at seeing us together like this," he explained before pulling me back into his embrace, holding me as close as possible.

"High Alpha, are you going to keep your Omega all to yourself?" a Beta woman shouted playfully, joined by other wolves who teased us.

Cartan groaned, clearly wanting to keep me with him, but I smiled up at him and took his hand, leading him over to the others where we indulged in pleasant conversations and wine.

Chapter Thirty-Two
Cartan

Witnessing my Omega's radiant happiness filled me with a joy that words couldn't adequately express. I longed for that smile to grace her lips continuously, and I was willing to do whatever it took to ensure her ongoing happiness. It was the most precious thing in the world to me, second only to her body and the tiny life growing inside her. That life was becoming more robust with each passing moment, drawing energy from my Omega. It meant I had to make sure she kept eating, even if it was just a little. As the party continued and people consumed more drinks, the presence inside her seemed to become increasingly aware. I observed this intriguing change in Kiandra, although I wasn't sure if she had noticed it herself as she remained engrossed in conversation with the others. She was a remarkably curious creature, and I couldn't help but adore her even more.

When another Beta male nearly brushed against her, I sensed a surge of tension within my mate, prompting me to pull her closer and position her in front of me, protecting her from unwanted attention. Kiandra merely smiled up at me, seemingly viewing my response as a slight overreaction.

However, I had discerned that it was not her but the tiny life inside her that had reacted to the proximity of another man's scent. This gave rise to a theory in my mind, but I chose to keep it to myself for now. Kiandra was relishing the evening, getting to know our customs and the people, and she appeared to be fitting right in. Once I located her sisters, I hoped she could guide them into accepting this as their perfect home. She would ensure they found their place here by their Alpha's side.

Suddenly, Kiandra turned in my arms, her eyes fixed on me with a request in her gaze. "Can we dance?"

I growled softly, aware of how close she would be to other Alphas and their scents of arousal in the dancing crowd, and shook my head.

"Why not?" she questioned, her eyes slightly glazed, possibly from a bit too much indulgence.

"Because I'd have to kill my own clan members for letting their scent rub off all over you if we did," I replied.

"But I want to try." Kiandra moved sensuously against me, swaying her hips beneath my hands and pressing herself closer. She was a bewitching temptress, and I was thoroughly enchanted by her. However, I couldn't allow other Alphas to inadvertently touch her, especially with that little life growing inside her. I had become even more protective of her. If she wished to dance, I'd let her put on a private performance just for me. So, I lifted her up, and our lips met in a passionate kiss. Kiandra believed I was taking her to the dance circle, but I had other plans. I carried us away from the festivities, my control slipping.

My little Omega pulled away, realizing we were heading in the opposite direction. "That's the wrong way," she pointed out.

"No, it's the right way," I assured her as I brought her back to our tent. She wriggled in my arms, attempting to break free and return to the party. When her feet touched the ground, she ran for the opening of the tent. Her determination to tease me amused me. I followed her, catching her just outside the tent and hoisting her over my shoulder.

"No! Cartan! The party!" she protested, kicking her legs in the air.

"We'll return once I've marked you. My scent

isn't even on your skin anymore."

"What? You want me soaked with your seed before we go back?" she teased.

"Definitely," I replied, guiding her back inside. I led her to where my desk was, causing papers and books to scatter in all directions before I gently placed her on its surface.

She looked up at me with a seductive smile, her long hair cascading down the edge of the desk. Her hair, styled in the traditional manner of the Tesarian Wolves, added an exotic allure to her appearance. Each clan had its own unique way of doing their hair, and the Tesarian style suited my Omega perfectly. It only fueled my desire for her, and I lifted her dress, eager to be inside her.

Her small hands worked on the strings of my pants, and together, we got them lowered before I slid inside her. Her body resisted my intrusion at first, not fully prepared to accept me, but I slipped a hand between us to tease her clit. Her moans filled the room as she leaned her head back, and I penetrated her fully. As I began thrusting into her wetness, she clamped down around me so tightly that it almost took my breath away, and we had barely begun.

My Omega was incredibly sensitive, her own desires urging her on despite her longing to return to the party. I adjusted our position, standing up and wrapping a hand around her neck while continuing our passionate mating. She trembled and cried out my name, the desk creaking beneath us due to our combined fervor and my powerful thrusts. She was beyond my wildest dreams. Initially, I thought I needed an Omega merely to produce strong heirs and validate my worth, but my Omega had filled a void I hadn't even realized existed. Her presence completed me, and I was eternally grateful for her. I allowed my instincts to take over, marking her inner walls so she would bear my scent completely before we returned.

"Now we can go back," I murmured, but my mate's hands continued to explore my body. Then, she dug her nails into my ass and pulled me closer, causing a deep growl of pleasure to escape my lips.

"Go back where?" she inquired, her tone filled with innocence, and I smiled against her neck, showering it with kisses. The thought of returning to the party was quickly fading from both our minds.

****

When I woke in the middle of the night, it was the sensation of coldness against my skin that roused me from slumber. An immediate sense of unease gripped me, and I hastily opened my eyes, only to discover an empty space beside me. Panic surged within me as my Alpha instincts roared in anger at the absence of my mate, who should have been nestled at my side in our shared nest.

We hadn't returned to the party as planned. Instead, we had spent the evening engaged in passionate mating before drifting off to sleep. The fact that my Omega had left my side now filled me with dread. I knew she needed me close at this moment, and I feared the worst as I reached for a long, dark linen fabric to wrap around my waist. Storming outside the tent, I grabbed a knife along the way, prepared for whatever I might find.

As I stepped outside, I was met with a breathtaking sight that left me stunned. The same horse that Kiandra had been gently stroking by a small water hole had returned, and this time, my Omega was riding the horse in the nude, right in front of our tent. She wasn't going fast, and her soft laughter reached my ears, causing my heart to race as I beheld the surreal scene before me. I had never seen anything more beautiful. Did she even realize what she was doing? It seemed she was in some sort of dreamlike state as she clung to the horse's mane. Her behavior was unlike anything I had ever witnessed from her. However, the mare eventually slowed down, and Kiandra leaned over its back, embracing it, before her eyes locked onto mine.

She pushed herself up, waving at me with a smile before gracefully sliding off the horse's back. Tenderly, she stroked the animal's skin and planted a kiss on it before the white horse galloped away through the camp. I walked over to my mate, enfolding her in my arms, thankful that no one else had witnessed her vulnerable state.

"This is a very peculiar dream, but I rather like it," she told me, her words revealing her belief that she was still in a dream.

I kissed the top of her head before scooping her up. She giggled happily, wrapping one arm around my neck while gazing at me with affection.

"What did I say about leaving the tent without me?" I teased her, watching as she bit down on her lower lip.

"Not to," she replied.

"Exactly. And what did you do?"

"I left the tent," she confessed, her breathing quickening slightly.

"Without any clothes," I added.

"Are you going to punish me?" she inquired, her eyes filled with anticipation.

"I most certainly am," I declared, carrying her to our bedroom. I placed her down gently, and she attempted to slide into our nest for protection. However, I swiftly grabbed her leg and flipped her onto her stomach before delivering a playful swat to her behind. She gasped, her arousal intensifying, and my own desire surged instantly. I gave her another playful spank, the sound echoing in the silent night, and she groaned but pressed back, eager for more. It appeared my mate enjoyed a bit of pain, and I wasted no time in shedding my own clothing before positioning her on her hands and knees. I administered a few more spanks, causing her dripping core to clench and yearn for something to fill it. Sliding inside her, I heard her emit a sweet whimper.

"Alpha," she panted, and I wrapped a hand in her hair, pulling her closer as I began thrusting into her luscious body. Her cries grew louder, waking the people nearest to us, but the union between us was celebrated as they cheered for their High Alpha and High Omega.

Chapter Thirty-Three
Kiandra

With our bond fully established, understanding Cartan had become easier compared to the initial one-sided connection. The earlier bond had felt untamed and perplexing, while the current one brought a sense of tranquility because Cartan could now empathize with my feelings. He had grown increasingly protective of me, swiftly responding to any distress I experienced. If a troublesome word or an infuriating book crossed my path, he would gently remove them from my hands, soothing my agitation with his touch and passion. He would purr throughout the night, calming the restless presence within me. Such was the routine of our days, but Cartan's indulgence had extended too far. One morning, I awoke to find him absent from my side.

I searched the tent for any sign of him, but it was evident he had been gone for quite some time. I attempted to reach out to him through our bond, but he had intentionally closed off our connection. Irritation surged within me, and I returned to our nest, wrapping myself in furs and linen to quell my unease. The inner presence mirrored my discomfort, growing increasingly restless without the soothing influence of their father.

Why had he left me? I experienced a strange, unwarranted sensation of betrayal. How had I become so dependent? I had initially resolved not to be the typical Omega reliant on their Alpha's constant presence, yet I had unwittingly fallen into that very pattern. Now, in his absence, I found myself adrift, uncertain of how to occupy myself without him. Frustrated with my own vulnerability, I unwrapped from the furs only to be greeted by the entrance of Mara and a few others.

"Good morning, High Omega," Mara greeted me.

"Just Kiandra," I corrected her, dismissing the formal title.

The usage of titles had always felt foreign to me. While I occasionally employed my sisters' titles, they had always referred to me simply as Kiandra. However, my preference appeared to discomfort the Beta women.

"Or High Omega," I added softly, noting the smiles on their lips.

"We're here to assist you in dressing for the day and offer you an opportunity to explore the camp," Mara explained.

"Am I finally going to see the entire camp?" I inquired, my excitement growing.

"Yes," she affirmed, prompting me to lead the women further inside as they assisted me in getting ready. I requested to be dressed like them, as I wished to blend in rather than stand out. Although they hesitated due to their orders, they ultimately acceded to my request. Leather straps bound my breasts, and a lengthy leather garment was secured around my waist, with a high side slit that would not offer much coverage while walking. They intricately braided my hair in the customary style with smaller braids interwoven, and then we were prepared to explore.

Stepping into the sunlight, I inhaled the dry air, relishing the stark contrast from the denser and more humid air near the Rocky Island. My anticipation swelled as we ventured through Cartan's clan's section. They guided me through the working tents where weapons, baskets, and clothing were crafted. Passing by Beta women laying out meat to dry in the sun, we received friendly waves from them. I observed women collaborating to supervise older children who were not yet old enough to contribute but had outgrown being carried around. It brought a smile to my face, deepening my curiosity about every aspect of their lives. Viewing the camp in daylight revealed an entirely different perspective, and Mara did her best to explain their ways.

"But they weren't always connected," I pointed out, seeking to learn more about their history.

"No, they were not. The unity of the clans is a relatively recent development, occurring only about a decade ago, thanks to the High Alphas you see now. However, they didn't achieve this on their own. It was a shared vision by their fathers, but to ensure it could become a reality, they needed to prove they could work together. So, the clans gradually moved closer to each other to allow the young heirs to become accustomed to one another. With time, they were pressed even closer together, eventually leading to what you see today," Mara explained.

"So Cartan grew up with these Alphas?" I inquired.

"No," Mara replied tersely, her gaze drifting to a spot further away.

"But you just said—"

"Have you ever woven a basket?" she interjected.

"Um, no," I admitted.

She took hold of my arm, leading me over to a spot where a blanket had been laid out on the sandy ground, sheltered by a half-roof constructed from leather and wooden poles.

"Why didn't Cartan grow up with them?" I persisted, though Mara tried to show me how to make a basket.

"See, you fold—"

"Mara!" I called, catching her hands as she gestured in front of me.

The other women in the group fell silent, and I

glanced around, but none of them appeared interested in our conversation. Turning my attention back to Mara, I pressed her for answers.

"It's his story, High Omega. You should talk to your Alpha."

"It's not really talking he's interested in," I murmured, prompting giggles from the other women.

"If your Alpha doesn't wish to discuss it, then let it be," Mara advised, but that wasn't my nature.

I hungered for answers, and my curiosity only intensified. If Cartan hadn't grown up with the other High Alphas to learn cooperation, then where had he been? I attempted to focus on Mara's instructions for weaving a basket, but my mind was elsewhere, and my efforts became tangled and awkward. Eventually, Mara had to take over once more while I lost myself in contemplation. There was so much about Cartan's past that I yearned to understand.

As the women chatted among themselves, I seized the opportunity to slip away unnoticed. I walked through the camp, observing the various activities and structures. We had only covered a fraction of what there was to see, and I was eager to explore further.

I strolled through the camp, witnessing everyone hard at work. In the distance, on a rocky hill, a group of Alphas had gathered, overlooking the camp from a higher vantage point. It was clear they were guarding the area and remaining vigilant for potential threats.

Continuing my exploration, I passed a large pleasure tent where the sounds emanating from within were vibrant and lively. The tent bore the distinct scent of Alpha females, indicating they were the ones occupying it instead of the Beta women.

Further along, I encountered another group consisting of both Alpha females and males. They appeared to be preparing for a hunt, sharpening their weapons, and discussing their strategies. I smiled as I watched them, eavesdropping on their conversation before my curiosity led me elsewhere.

I ventured through different sections of the camp until I stumbled upon an enclosure filled with horses. I approached, observing the Beta women caring for the animals, ensuring they had enough food and water. Leaning against the wooden barrier surrounding the enclosure, I suddenly felt the presence within me grow restless. I couldn't quite comprehend what was happening before a powerful figure came to a stop beside me. Turning my head, I saw one of the High Alphas, though I couldn't recall his name. He was the most imposing among them, radiating an aura so potent that I instinctively took a step to the side.

"Do you know where they are?" he inquired. He turned his piercing green eyes upon me, their intensity causing me to avert my gaze, focusing instead on the ground.

"Who?" I replied cautiously.

"Your sisters," he snapped impatiently.

"I do not possess the exact knowledge of their whereabouts. I have shared with Cartan all that I know," I explained, my voice steady despite my unease.

"The king suspected that the two of you shared a true bond, which might explain why he allowed your sisters to escape," he noted, his tone contemplative. "Yet I harbored doubts about whether it was right to let him go. He has always struck me as a weak Alpha."

My anger rose at the slight to Cartan's honor, and I couldn't hold back my fury any longer. I hissed at the High Alpha, my sudden show of aggression entirely unlike the typical demeanor of an Omega.

"Weak? And yet he returns with an Omega," I

retorted, my tone defiant.

"Exactly. One Omega. He promised at least three. He has failed to deliver," the Alpha clarified with a hint of dissatisfaction.

"I did that. I freed them," I retorted.

"And have you faced any consequences for your defiance?" the High Alpha inquired, his words laden with insinuation.

I stared at him in shock, unable to fathom how seeking the freedom of my sisters could be construed as deserving punishment.

"W-Why would I be punished?" I stammered.

"You defied your Alpha," he pointed out matter-of-factly.

"He had not yet claimed me, and I had not claimed him," I snapped back.

"You are an Omega," the Alpha reminded me, crossing his arms. "You were always meant to belong to an Alpha, and you were aware he could have been among the Alphas attacking your city. You defied him and allowed your sisters to defy their Alphas. Let me make it clear that the moment I get my hands on the Omega that is mine, she will undoubtedly be disciplined."

I stepped closer to him, my anger fueling my defiance, my voice a low growl as I confronted him. "Then I hope you never find her, because if you lay a hand on one of my sisters—"

"Then what, little Omega?" he interrupted, a challenging glint in his eyes. "If you step out of line, it is expected that Cartan will put you in your place."

I stared up at the High Alpha, my eyes narrowed with determination, and he continued to wear a self-assured smile.

"He won't hurt me," I asserted firmly.

"A punishment is supposed to hurt," he replied

coldly. "And if he will not do it, it just proves he is as weak as we have always thought. He has been tamed by you then."

"An Alpha honors his Omega, he doesn't hurt her."

"The pain is honoring her. It's to remind her where her place is," he told me, making me shake my head.

"If anyone here is undeserving of an Omega, it's you," I retorted heatedly before turning away, dismissing the conversation.

"If Cartan were truly an Alpha deserving of you, he wouldn't tolerate you speaking to me like that," the High Alpha called after me, his words trailing as I walked away.

I chose not to engage further with the other Alpha, recognizing that nothing positive would come from continuing the argument. The conversation had already stirred my emotions, causing the presence within me to become restless. All I yearned for now was to return to our nest, enveloped in my Alpha's scent, the only balm capable of calming my turbulent emotions.

Chapter Thirty-Four
Cartan

I whimpered, my shoulder throbbing with searing pain, the infected flesh burning from the panther's claw. I knew I was teetering on the brink of death, my strength drained, every fiber of my being aching. When had I last eaten? I had survived on the meager sustenance of a small water source within the cave where I had taken shelter, but even the cave had its own inhabitant, which resented my presence.

My location remained a mystery, except for the endless expanse of sand that stretched as far as the eye could see. Collapsing onto the unforgiving ground, my knees buckled beneath me, and I cried out as my injured arm bore the brunt of the fall. Tears welled up in my eyes, mingling with the sand beneath me. This was to be my grave, abandoned by my father to meet my end. Why had he forsaken me?

Curling into myself, I felt the unforgiving sun scorching my skin. I yearned for it all to end. Then, a faint sound reached my ears—a beautiful voice, lighter than air. I lifted my head slightly, peering through my blurred vision and the swirling sand. Amidst the desolation, I spotted something—an elegant figure adorned in a flowing white dress with hair of the same hue.

A woman stood in the distance, her gaze fixed upon me. Who was she? Surely, this was a dream, wasn't it? My head grew heavy, and I lowered it once more, too weak to hold it up. I closed my eyes, only to sense something—a gentle hand caressing my cheek. I opened my eyes once more, beholding the enchanting woman.

"What is such a young Alpha doing out here?"

she cooed.

I could not muster words. Instead, I wept, and she consoled me, soothing my anguish with tender strokes and cooling touches on my scalding skin. I had lost track of time during my ordeal, but my famished stomach and weakened limbs indicated it had been a considerable duration. But who was this enigmatic woman?

"Do not fret, Cartan. You are not meant to perish here," she assured me.

I wanted to inquire how she knew this, but her gentle touch was more comforting than my mother's had ever been. She continued to caress me until my eyes closed once more, and I drifted into slumber.

The sound of boots roused me from my restless sleep, and I glanced upward to witness looming shadows enveloping me. Horses nearby grew unsettled, their movements punctuating the quiet desert night. Powerful hands seized me, lifting me from the ground, enveloping me in a familiar presence that once evoked a sense of security. However, I hesitated to place my trust in another Alpha again.

"Cartan?" I turned my head to find Tyros emerging behind me, his expression marked with concern.

"What is it?" I asked, puzzled by his worried demeanor.

"Are you all right?" he inquired. "You've been staring into the desert for quite some time, motionless."

I had been oblivious to my distant gaze, as my mind seldom wandered in such a manner. My Omega had been growing increasingly curious about me, which pleased me. However, it also stirred memories of the past.

"I'm here," I reassured him. He nodded, then gestured to the young Alphas we were currently training.

"They want to witness your skills," he informed

me.

Just as I was about to turn toward them, I sensed something unusual through the bond—a sharp surge of fear, followed by anger. My mate was never given to anger, but this was not my own emotion. I was certain of it. I had closed off my end of the bond to avoid distraction from Kiandra's sweet call, but hers remained wide open, flooded with turbulent emotions. It put me on edge, as I could not fathom why my Omega was so distraught. Her anger soon morphed into something more bitter and overpowering, and it was evident she needed me.

"Keep an eye on them. I'll be back," I instructed Tyros.

"Alpha!" he called out as I turned to depart.

"Something is amiss with my Omega," I declared, knowing it was reason enough for my sudden departure. The training grounds lay just beyond the camp, so my return would not take long. However, my mate's tumultuous emotions seemed to intensify with each step, leaving me concerned that something dire had transpired.

Nevertheless, the fragrant scent of her filled our tent, indicating her presence. I listened for any signs of her, hearing her soft breathing emanating from our bedroom. I entered that section, but my mate was nowhere in sight, which meant she had taken refuge within the nest. While I was relieved that she sought comfort there, I grew increasingly troubled by the escalating intensity of her emotions.

"Little Omega?" I called out, but another surge of fear reverberated through our bond. Why had my mate suddenly grown fearful of me? Even when I touched her for the first time, there was no fear. She had always been remarkably astute, surprising me and even occasionally outshining me in the most endearing way when she marked me as her own.

Therefore, I struggled to comprehend why my voice had suddenly become a source of unease for her. We needed to resolve this. Her emotions were causing my head to spin, a sensation I was not accustomed to, and shutting her out via the bond was not an option. As her Alpha, it was my duty to ensure her well-being, which meant eliminating any distress or fear. However, for her to heal, she had to come to me.

"Kiandra," I tried, but she remained motionless.

I reached inside the nest to touch her, but as my fingers grazed her ankle, she hissed and curled into a defensive posture. Anger surged within me as I delved deeper into the nest, determined to get a proper hold of her. To my surprise, she thrashed and fought against me, ensnared in the tangle of furs that tightened around her with every struggle. This allowed me to easily extract her from the nest and place her on my lap.

I brushed aside her disheveled hair, noticing a few braids intertwined, but the largest one had come undone. I was aware that the others were scheduled to show her around the camp today, so why was she back in our nest in the middle of the day? She had even discarded her clothing, and beneath the furs, I could feel the warmth of her skin.

However, as I attempted to slide a hand underneath to rest on her stomach, she pushed it away. I growled, warning her not to deny my touch, particularly because I sensed turmoil within our pup. What had agitated our child to this extent? Something must have threatened them for their distress to be so obvious. But what was it? When I attempted to make contact with her bare skin once more, she tried to evade my touch. I growled again, tightening my grip around her, and then holding her chin to make her focus on me.

"*Stop!*" I commanded, and my Omega whimpered, growing still upon hearing the authority in my tone. I couldn't communicate with her if she remained upset and refused to meet my gaze. I had not seen her all day, so how could she harbor anger toward me? Once my Omega ceased her restless movements in my arms, I began purring to help her relax. Strangely, this seemed to distress her even further, and she struggled to move away.

"Stop that," I admonished her.

"Let me go!"

Once again, I grasped her chin, forcing her to look at me. Her breathing was heavy, and the furs had started to unravel slightly, revealing one of her breasts. My eyes briefly glanced at the soft flesh, my hand yearning to touch it, but instead, I withdrew it and placed it gently on her stomach. I resumed purring, and as the presence within her began to calm down, my mate's breathing eased.

It was evident that both were agitating each other, and I could not converse with her until the storm inside her had subsided. When our pup sensed that someone was there to protect their mother, they grew completely still, and Kiandra let out a shaky breath, relaxing in my arms. She was an Omega and was not meant to harbor such anger. It was clearly disconcerting for her.

I pulled her closer to me, pressing her nose to my neck, and she inhaled my scent, finding comfort in it. I removed the furs covering her, allowing us to be skin to skin, and her legs encircled my waist, seeking my warmth. However, it was not long before I felt her tense again, as if my scent was no longer what she desired.

"Why can't I calm you anymore?" I inquired.

"Just release me," she pleaded.

"Not until you give me a reason to."

"I want to return to my nest."

"It's not the nest you need," I reminded her. Nevertheless, she obstinately pushed away from me, prompting me to guide us back into the shadows. I covered her body with mine, ensuring she felt the full presence of her Alpha.

She looked up at me, desire in her eyes, but an almost imperceptible barrier seemed to exist between us. She was resisting our connection, leaving me perplexed. However, I had a hunch about what was transpiring within her.

"I didn't like leaving you this morning," I reassured her. Her eyes widened, and I thought perhaps that was what had provoked her anger. However, her tumultuous emotions showed no signs of abating. Our pup seemed to feed off her turmoil, and I had to reach down to stroke her stomach to reassure our child that everything was fine. I maintained my hand there while resting on my other arm, hovering over my Omega.

"Why are you so upset? Why are you rejecting my touch?" I inquired.

"Your touch," she scoffed.

I growled, disliking the way she spoke those words.

"Will your touch hurt me too?" she whispered, a defiant look in her eyes.

"Why would my touch hurt you? Do I not make you feel good, little Omega?" I knew I did, but I wanted to understand if there was something that made her uncomfortable.

"I didn't comprehend it at first, but I've been contemplating its importance," she replied, evading my question.

"You're speaking in riddles," I told her.

She pushed up slightly, her face drawing nearer to

mine.

"What happens when someone in the clan steps out of line?" she asked.

Chapter Thirty-Five
Cartan

I gazed at my Omega with a puzzled expression but provided her with an answer, "They are punished to ensure they remember the consequences of their actions."

"And what if their actions unintentionally put someone else in danger?" she inquired.

"We have strict measures to ensure the safety of everyone here. In this harsh environment, even a small mistake can have dire consequences. Therefore, we need to ensure they remember," I explained to her, and she nodded in understanding.

"That's what I thought," she whispered, and I could hear the pain in her voice as she placed a hand over mine on her stomach. "You're going to hurt me, aren't you?"

"What? Why would I do that?" I questioned, genuinely concerned. "Have you done something, little Omega?"

Fear gripped me for a moment, fearing she might have committed some transgression that warranted punishment. Perhaps that was why she was here, seeking refuge from the potential consequences. When she nodded and wiped her tears with her free hand, my apprehension grew.

"Tell me what you've done, and we'll find a way to address it," I urged, gently stroking her belly.

Kiandra sniffled again, her tears flowing more freely now. "I-I freed my sisters. I interfered with your plans, and I allowed them to escape into a dangerous world."

I instantly felt a wave of relief wash over me, understanding it was concern for her sisters that had overwhelmed her. It had been some time since we last discussed them, and as she found her place within our clan, it was natural for her to miss them. I purred louder, shifting to my side and pulling Kiandra closer, but she remained wary of being pressed against me, fearing that the warmth she craved would transform into pain.

"It's okay, little Omega, I won't hurt you," I reassured her, my voice soft and soothing. I pressed her closer to me, and eventually, she began to nuzzle against my body, allowing herself to relax. I ran my fingers through her hair, feeling her tension melt away as she turned her head to gaze up at me once more.

"But I defied your authority," she pointed out. "I made the other Alphas lose respect for you."

"While you certainly made things more complicated, you've already told me where I can locate your sisters, and three Omegas can't hide for long," I reassured her. "Moreover, the way others perceive me is not your responsibility. Those judgments have been formed over many years."

She shook her head, and her persistent sadness baffled me. "Little Omega, I can't comprehend your emotions. Why are you so distressed?" I inquired, growing frustrated by her fluctuating feelings.

"You must punish those who step out of line," she explained. "You never punished me for my actions. I deceived you."

"Do you doubt my ability to locate your sisters? I may be physically present here, but that won't hinder me from finding them," I stated firmly.

Kiandra shook her head and wiped her cheeks. "No, I don't doubt you. I knew right away you were the perfect Alpha for me."

Her words filled me with immense pride, but she still appeared troubled by something.

"But I still did it. I still helped my sisters escape, Omegas destined for other Alphas, and now they are upset with me too," she whispered. "They think you should punish me, but I don't want you to hurt me. I'm scared."

Her words took some time to register fully, making me comprehend what had upset Kiandra. I growled darkly as I wrapped a hand around her throat in response. To my surprise, my Omega responded positively to my Alpha powers, and the scent of her arousal filled the nest. However, I did not tear off my clothes or flip her onto her back. Instead, I focused on calming her.

"Did you leave the others?" I inquired, and Kiandra gulped, her body trembling beneath my hand.

"Yes," she whispered.

"Did you venture out on your own?"

"Y-Yes."

I turned Kiandra, placing her front down on the ground, and kept one hand on her back while the other rested on her ass. I felt her shiver beneath my touch, but I was determined to teach my mate a lesson. It wasn't about making her fear me, as she believed, because my touch would never cause harm. Rather, I intended for her to remember this. I delivered a firm spank to her rear, causing her to whimper, but I immediately soothed the stinging sensation with my palm. When she relaxed enough, I repeated the action.

"Whom did you speak to?" I asked.

"I can't remember which High Alpha it was," she confessed, and I spanked her ass again, prompting her to moan. As I smoothed away the sting, she began to push back against me, clearly ready for more.

"Do you recall which clan you visited?"

"Um ... Ah!" I struck her again, and she gripped

the furs tightly before nodding. "The color was yellow! Yellow!"

"Peros," I snarled before delivering a series of harsh spanks, one after another. The punishment was brief, and once I believed this memory had been etched into her consciousness, I turned her to face me once more. She did not gaze up at me with fear, but her eyes were still filled with tears.

"What did he say to you?"

"J-Just that you shouldn't have allowed me to step out of line. A true Alpha guides his Omega, ensuring she knows her rightful place. And because I deceived you, they believe I deserved the painful sting of a punishment," she whispered, her voice trembling. "He questioned your strength, which I vehemently disagreed with, so I, well, I confronted him, defending your honor. He interpreted that as further proof of your inadequacy as my Alpha."

My mate spoke with such urgency that her words required a moment to fully penetrate my consciousness. A brief silence hung between us as her revelation sank in. When the truth became clear, I reached out and gently touched her tender ass, eliciting a hiss of discomfort from her.

"Does it hurt?" I asked, my concern evident.

"A-A little," she admitted.

"Do you despise my touch?" I inquired, leaning down to lick her now-hard nipple, which had become erect from her punishment.

"N-No," she stammered, her breath coming out in pants.

"Do you want your Alpha to fuck you?"

I sucked hard on her nipple, causing her to whimper. I released it with a satisfying pop and looked up to see her nodding. Pleased, I swiftly removed my clothes and positioned myself between her legs. Sliding my cock through the wetness pooling between her thighs, I aligned myself and thrust into her tight, eager channel.

We both groaned in response to our union, but I granted her no respite. I began to fuck her passionately, driving into her like a wild beast. She clung to me, crying out with sweet abandon until she climaxed underneath me. I continued thrusting into her with forceful, punishing strokes, and she wrapped her legs around me, urging me deeper until my knot expanded and locked us together.

After fulfilling her needs, my little Omega was nothing but a sea of calmness, and I could feel it through our bond. I leaned down to lick her other nipple, teasing it with my tongue, and she moaned in delight.

"I would say you've admirably accepted your 'punishment', and there's no need to be scared anymore," I told her, locking eyes with her. She blinked in confusion.

"But you didn't punish me," she whispered. "You made me feel good."

I smiled and moved up to her face, kissing her gently. "Doesn't your ass hurt?"

"It stings a little, but you've spanked me before. How's that a punishment?" she questioned.

"Will you try to trick me again?" I asked, growling lightly. She shook her head quickly, and her eyes held determination. "Will you wander off on your own again?"

"I was still in the territory," she pointed out, and I growled again, making her shake her head even more vigorously. "I won't go exploring without someone with me."

"Good. And will you remember this moment?"

Her cheeks flushed a deep pink, and she nodded.

"A punishment doesn't have to cause searing pain. It should teach a lesson that will be remembered."

"What?" she asked, intrigued.

I smiled, enjoying her curiosity. "Let me give you an example, little Omega. There was a young Alpha once who wanted to tame one of the wild horses we had recently acquired. He sneaked into the enclosure with his friends to prove himself. However, things didn't go as planned, and the horse threw him off, injuring its leg in the process. Do you know what his punishment was?"

She shook her head, eager to hear the outcome.

"He had to take care of the injured horse until it was better. Now that horse won't let anyone else ride it," I explained.

Her eyes widened in understanding, and she began to bite her lower lip in deep thought. "Alpha Peros made it sound like—"

"Are you his Omega?" I interrupted her with a firm tone, shifting my hips slightly so she could feel the knot inside her.

She gasped and shook her head vigorously. "No."

"Whose are you?" I inquired, my voice laced with authority.

"Yours," she whispered with a sweet, pleading tone.

"Then isn't it up to me to decide how you should be punished?" I asked, a playful tone in my voice.

She smiled teasingly and nodded. "Yes, Alpha."

"And if I say that you have been punished, haven't you been punished?"

"Yes," she breathed, now sounding needy. Her fingers roamed along my body, seeking contact with me, and I obliged, drawing closer to her and grazing her lips with mine.

"You're *mine*, Kiandra," I asserted, my voice

husky. "I would never hurt you. I might tease your body, leading it to that sweet edge between pain and pleasure, but I will always bring you pleasure. So much that you'll beg me to stop."

I growled, feeling my knot begin to recede, and I quickened my pace, making her pant and writhe beneath me. We shared a powerful kiss, a reminder of who she belonged to.

Chapter Thirty-Six
Cartan

I was consumed by anger, even as I looked down at my mate, who lay peacefully asleep after our passionate mating. Despite my desire to remain in the nest with her, keeping her satisfied, I knew I had other responsibilities that demanded my attention. However, before leaving, I tenderly kissed her stomach, where our precious treasure was growing.

"Watch over her for me," I whispered, gently enveloping my mate in a fur to preserve my scent around her.

After leaving the nest, I dressed once more and stormed outside. Tyros approached me, clearly displeased that I hadn't appeared sooner, especially as the sun was setting, signaling the end of the day's training.

"Cartan, what's going on?" he snarled.

I brushed past him, aware of his concerned gaze. He quickly caught up with me, his curiosity apparent.

"Where are you heading?" he inquired. "You missed training. You've been slacking off this past week. You were supposed to demonstrate your commitment to the clans."

"I am!" I growled at him before coming to a sudden halt and seizing the leather strap that held his knives across his chest. I gripped it tightly, pulling him toward me, and he stared up at me in astonishment. "But when someone makes my own mate fear me, they deserve to face the consequences."

"What?" he questioned, clearly baffled.

"My own mate was afraid of my presence today."

"I don't understand. You weren't even with her," he pointed out.

"Exactly. Someone manipulated her fragile mind today, and the only one who has the right to play with her is me," I sneered before pushing him back slightly.

Now, Tyros was intrigued, and he followed me as I made my way through the clans. The people sensed my anger and quickly cleared a path for me, but they were not my focus. When I finally located Peros with Seran and another group of Alphas, who appeared prepared for a hunt, I let out a deafening roar before launching myself at Peros. We both tumbled to the ground, and I swiftly delivered a few punches before seizing his throat. Peros growled up at me, attempting to pry my hands away. We grappled for a moment, with him landing a few punches before I pushed him off. At that moment, Seran intervened, seizing Peros, while Tyros stepped closer to me and placed his hand on my chest after I stood up.

"What the fuck is going on?" Seran demanded to know.

Peros spat out blood, and I licked a wound on my lip.

"Stay away from my mate!" I snarled at him, observing him narrow his eyes.

Seran slowly turned to Peros. "Did you touch her?"

"Of course not," Peros quickly replied. "It seems my words upset her, and soft Alpha Cartan here has rushed to defend his mate's delicate feelings."

I growled menacingly, surging forward, and Tyros had to plant his feet firmly in the ground to prevent me from doing something regrettable. There was a fundamental rule we upheld for the sake of peace: no killings within our territory. Fighting for sport or training purposes was allowed, but any intent to cause harm was strictly prohibited. Tyros understood the real source of my fury and made every effort to restrain me.

"So Peros said a few foolish things, is that really a surprise?" Seran inquired, causing Peros to huff.

"He didn't just say a few foolish things. My own mate feared me when I returned today," I snarled, watching as Seran turned his attention to Peros.

"What did you say?" Seran pressed.

Peros shrugged dismissively. "I merely mentioned that Cartan is weak."

"You implied that I would harm her."

"It's your responsibility as her Alpha to keep her in check."

"My mate is pregnant. The moment she saw me, she submitted to me, falling to her knees in acknowledgment of me as her Alpha. She has never strayed from her path, but you made her doubt that."

"She manipulated you. She tricked you. Your Omega controls you," Peros retorted.

My growl grew even darker, and this time, Tyros couldn't hold me back. He stumbled, and I slipped past him, but Seran positioned himself in my way.

"He does have a point," Seran stated, drawing my ire.

"Do you doubt my ability to keep my Omega in check? Has she done anything to endanger this pack?" I challenged.

"She did set her sisters free."

"But she did it out of love. She is gentle, as Omegas are meant to be," I reminded them. "Our Omegas are not like the Alphas we train or the Beta women who serve us. They are different, and you would understand that better if you were bonded to one."

"But you messed that up, didn't you?" Peros spat. "Because you allowed an Omega to deceive you."

"And yet she chose me. She wants nothing to do with any of you," I retorted with a smile. "That's what truly irks you, isn't it? But in case you doubt my ability to manage my Omega, I can assure you I've already dealt with her. Her cheeks are still wet with tears. Are you satisfied? Because you will never come close enough to even look at her again."

The group fell silent, and I turned to Seran. "The Omega is mine. We are the first true pair in decades. I don't care about your jealousy. None of you will speak to her again, and it's a pity, considering the unique power she possesses. The serenity she imparts to anyone in her presence is unlike anything else. That's the essence of an Omega—harmony, and none of you will get to experience it. Perhaps I'll even arrange for the other princesses to be claimed by Alphas from my clan."

Both Seran and Peros growled in response, and I took a step back to observe them both. "Are you going to challenge me again over my Omega? Are you going to suggest that I can't control her? Are you going to upset her once more?"

Both remained silent, and my words seemed to instill a measure of fear in them. They had been promised Omegas, and while they could search for them on their own, only I and a select few from my pack knew their possible whereabouts. It was entirely up to me whether they would have an Omega to call their own. Consequently, they dared not challenge me. Satisfied with their subdued response, I left them to their own devices.

Tyros followed me, a faint smile playing on his lips. "Did you really punish her?" he asked in a low voice.

"Of course I did," I replied, though the smile I gave him caused him to chuckle softly and shake his head. "Just in my own way."

Chapter Thirty-Seven
Kiandra

My mate returned to the tent late in the evening the next day, covered in dark sand, and I swiftly prepared the tub with warm water before inviting him inside. He observed me with desire in his eyes as I straddled him and cleansed his powerful body with the cloth in my hand. However, when I leaned forward to rinse his hair, he shifted, capturing my nipple with his mouth and sucking fervently. I gasped and threaded my fingers through his hair, gently tugging, but he refused to let go.

"Cartan, I'm trying to clean you," I chuckled, and his warm tongue glided over the hardened nub.

"I'm taking care of you," he responded, sucking again.

I attempted to focus on my task, but it proved challenging with the sensations he was evoking between my legs. He maneuvered me, and when I descended once more, his cock was there, sliding into me leisurely. I gasped in delight as I took him in fully, and he trembled beneath my touch, yet he didn't move or shift me in any way. He seemed content to have me wrapped around him.

"Carry on," he instructed. I shot him a scolding look before resuming washing his body, admiring his well-defined muscles, and loving his magnificent physique.

"Will you ever tell me anything about yourself?" I inquired. "A'has."

His eyes widened when he heard me use the Old Language to address him as my Alpha.

"You're learning," he praised.

"Slowly," I replied, seizing his hands and placing them on my breasts. He began kneading and teasing them before moving closer to suck on one of them again. I shifted my hips slightly, and he growled in satisfaction. "You know these will be filled with milk at some point."

Another pleased rumble escaped his lips before he switched to the other nipple, sucking vigorously.

"Nothing will prevent me from savoring them," he assured me before running his tongue over the nipple, sending shivers through me as I continued to rock my hips slowly.

His hands settled on my hips, letting me move while maintaining a firm grip that showed his power.

"We are building something together, but you won't share anything about yourself, and neither will the others. You have very loyal clan members," I panted, increasing my pace as I chased my climax.

"I hope you haven't been seeking answers from the other High Alphas," he warned.

I shook my head and leaned toward him, resting my hands on his shoulders. "No, I promise I spent the day with the others."

His hand slipped to my ass, gripping the sensitive flesh firmly. "Otherwise, you know what will happen."

I chuckled at his teasing threat, but he gripped me even harder, causing me to hiss. Then he took control, making me ride him faster. Orgasm overtook me suddenly, and I arched my back, crying out my release before I felt his knot expanding, stretching me wider. I continued to move atop him until he held me tightly against him, locking us together, and then he released inside me, leaving us both sighing contentedly. I rested my body on top of his, and his hand began playing with my wet strands.

"Tell me something," I implored, realizing that his walls had come down after our intimate encounter. Perhaps having me wrapped around him had helped him speak.

"You truly want to know my story, don't you?" he mused.

I nodded. "I don't like being in the dark."

He smiled. "I know, little Omega."

"Tell me about your past. I know you didn't grow up with the other Alphas."

"Ah, so they've let something slip."

"Just tell me, please," I pleaded, his wet fingers tracing my shoulder and arm.

"My father took me from my mother's arms and left me to die in the desert."

I stared at him in shock, but he met my gaze with a calmness that made it seem like what he was saying was entirely ordinary.

"W-What?" I stammered.

"It's quite common to test your Alpha sons in this way," he explained.

"Common?" I repeated incredulously.

"It's an ancient practice to ensure their strength and resilience. However, their fathers typically retrieve them after a few days."

"Days?" I exclaimed, pulling back and placing my hands protectively over my stomach. "If we have a son, we are not sending him out into the desert!"

He gently placed his hand over mine on my stomach, his expression slightly cool.

"Cartan!"

"The other High Alphas went through it as well," he explained. "The difference is that their fathers actually came for them, and they were older."

"How old were you?"

"I was five," he replied.

"What? We are not subjecting our son to that!" I retorted vehemently.

"Well, the tradition has been fading away more and more. It might be considered outdated," he admitted with a faint smile.

"Very outdated," I stated, crossing my arms and hearing him chuckle.

"It's okay, little Omega. If you don't want it to happen, it won't. Normally, they are older, prepared for the challenge, and trained for it. They aren't left with nothing, and they are always retrieved. I wasn't."

"Why weren't you?"

"My father believed I wasn't growing fast enough. He thought I was too weak to become a true Alpha."

"I don't understand. A true Alpha has an Omega mother and an Alpha father, but you mentioned that such pairings haven't occurred in decades."

He nodded. "You're right. They haven't, but that's because not everyone knows my story."

I moved closer to him, placing my arms on his chest, and looked up at him with curiosity. He chuckled at my inquisitive expression, encouraging him to tell me more.

"My mother was a Beta woman, and she couldn't conceive."

I stared at him, puzzled. "That doesn't make sense. How could she be your mother, then?"

"It's said that my father disappeared in the desert for a while. They went out on a routine hunt, but it went wrong. He vanished among the rocky terrain, and they couldn't locate him. They were certain he was dead, which led to a power struggle within the clan to determine the next leader. Many Alphas perished in the process, but not long after, he reappeared, looking perfectly fine. It was a mystery, but he claimed that an Omega found him and nursed him back to health. Some believed he had been hallucinating or delirious, but the fact was their Alpha had returned, so they didn't care about the how. Then, several moons later, on the quietest night anyone could remember, the camp was filled with the cries of a baby."

"A baby?" I questioned.

"Yes, and right outside my father's tent, he and his mate found me. Everyone was perplexed, except my father. He claimed me as his own, but no one understood why or how. Some thought he accepted me solely because he wanted an heir, but my Beta mother explained the unique bond between an Omega and an Alpha. Yet she swore she loved me as her own."

"You remember her words?" I whispered.

"I remember them vividly. Naturally, my father had expectations for his son, particularly a true-born one, but I failed to meet them."

"How could you? You were just five."

He sighed, his fingers tracing patterns on my skin again. "It doesn't matter. I should have been stronger. I should have been able to endure more, but instead, I almost perished out there."

"How did you survive? On your own?"

"No, there are other Alphas in these parts, smaller groups that keep their distance from us. They follow different ways of life, and one of these groups found me. I was raised there," he revealed.

"But now you're here."

"Yes, I am."

When he didn't offer more details, I applied gentle pressure to his chest, and he chuckled.

"Fine, but this will be the only time we discuss this," he conceded. I shook my head in disagreement, which elicited a growl from him. I leaned in closer, kissed his jaw, and then his lips, showing my submission to him once again. "I returned and ended my father's life when I was sixteen. I assumed control of the clan at that point."

"What?" I gasped, pulling back from him, my shock evident. "W-Why?"

"I wanted the clan. It was rightfully mine, and I needed to prove I wasn't weak."

"Cartan…"

"But people don't forget easily." He sighed, and I moved closer to him, placing my hands gently on his cheeks to make him focus on me.

"You are the most formidable Alpha I've ever encountered. You possess not only physical strength but also intelligence and quick wit. When you touch me, I lose all sense of self. I knew immediately that you were the perfect Alpha for me, regardless of my initial reasons for choosing you. You were the one I desired," I whispered, watching his eyes darken as his instincts stirred.

He effortlessly lifted me out of the tub and set me down on the furs before laying me on my back, resuming our mating. This time, it felt as though he were branding me with each long, deep stroke, and he reached his climax first, knotting me deeply before his fingers skillfully teased my clit, sending me shivering as I unraveled in pleasure. However, being knotted to him, I could only surrender to the blissful sensations.

Once we had both calmed down, his eyes had returned to their deeper brown, and I smiled up at him.

"What about your Beta mother?" I asked. "Is she here with us?"

He shook his head. "After I was taken away, she managed to conceive and carry a child for a while, but the birth came too soon and claimed both their lives."

A pang of sorrow gripped my heart as I realized

that the one parent he had truly known had died before he could return to let her know he was alive.

Cartan pressed his lips to mine. "Don't be sad, little Omega. It's just the past."

"No, the past is history, and history is important. You know this," I reminded him, and I saw a smile curve his lips.

"My clever little Omega," he praised, kissing down my neck and causing me to sigh.

I tried not to let his past weigh too heavily on my emotions. It was evident my Alpha didn't want to dwell on it or discuss it further. He didn't even appear particularly angry about it, although he saw himself as a weaker Alpha in the past, which I vehemently disagreed with. He was far from weak, then or now, and his power far exceeded what I had initially realized.

"Cartan?" I called out, and he pulled back to gaze at me.

"If you're born a true Alpha, why don't the others see you as a worthy one? None of them have Omega mothers, do they?"

He shook his head. "No, but hardly anyone believes I wasn't born to my Beta mother. They don't buy into the story of some mysterious Omega living in the desert."

I pondered his words, running my fingers through his dark hair. "And what do you believe?"

He smiled, appreciating my sharp mind. "I believe when you find an Omega, you don't let her go."

I chuckled, shaking my head. "Come now, you must have your own theories?"

But Cartan simply shrugged before capturing my lips once more, and we continued to mate throughout the night.

Chapter Thirty-Eight
Kiandra

I sat among the other Beta women, weaving a basket and shielded from the scorching sun. However, an inexplicable feeling of being watched had me turning my head repeatedly in search of the source. Despite my intuition, whenever I looked in the direction of the gaze, no one appeared to be observing me. It left me deeply perplexed, and I began to slow down in my weaving, eventually directing my attention to Mara.

"Mara, do I have something on me?" I inquired, gesturing to my clothes, which were akin to those I had worn the previous day.

"No," she replied.

"Is there something on my face?"

She shook her head. "No, you look fine."

Mara's son, nestled in a sling on her body, began to stir, and she lowered her leather top to nurse him.

"Then why do I feel like people are staring at me?" I pondered.

"Oh, that could be because High Alpha was so furious with High Alpha Peros yesterday and even confronted him," Lura explained beside me, and I turned my head.

"He confronted Peros?"

"Yes, he did, High Omega," she responded, offering me a small smile. "And he told them that due to High Alpha Peros's behavior, none of them were allowed near you again."

My mouth fell open in disbelief at this unexpected revelation, and I blinked rapidly before shaking my head. "But the others didn't do anything wrong. It was just Peros."

"He upset you, High Omega," Mara chimed in. "High Alpha Cartan had every right to defend you. He wouldn't be a good Alpha if he didn't. Perhaps with time, he will permit the others to approach you again."

"Shouldn't that be my decision?" I inquired, gesturing to myself. However, the others erupted in laughter, as if I had made a joke. "I'm serious!"

But their laughter persisted as they resumed their work. This left me feeling somewhat frustrated. I understood Cartan's possessiveness, and I was perfectly fine with not speaking to Peros again. However, what about Kylos? He had even helped Cartan when I went into heat. It seemed absurd that I couldn't communicate with any of them due to Peros's aggressive behavior. All I wanted was to find Cartan and inform him that he couldn't control me in this manner.

The women around me noticed my silence and stopped working, turning their puzzled gazes toward me.

"Is everything all right, High Omega?" Mara inquired. "Are you feeling unwell?"

"Unwell?"

"Because of the baby."

She gestured toward my stomach, but I shook my head. I hadn't begun experiencing any sickness yet, but my anger appeared to intensify with each passing moment. It was baffling. Why was I so furious? I understood that my Alpha's behavior might be somewhat vexing, but the longer I stewed in this frustration, the more powerful my anger grew. Could it be that the little life inside me was reacting to my emotions? Suddenly, a realization dawned on me, and I placed my hand over my stomach.

"High Omega, what's wrong?" Mara inquired, but I wasn't ready to share my thoughts just yet.

"Perhaps I am feeling a bit unwell. Does anyone

have any water?" I asked, diverting the conversation from Mara's question.

A waterskin was swiftly brought to me, and I drank eagerly before handing it back, focusing once more on my weaving. I had a few matters I wished to discuss with Cartan when he returned, but for the time being, I was rather delighted with the discovery I had made.

****

My Alpha found me later in the evening, returning from the training grounds, and discovered me dining with some of the other Beta women. He approached where I was seated, encircling me with his arms and effortlessly lifting me off the ground. Laughter rippled through the group, but I pounded my hands on his back in protest.

"Cartan!" I exclaimed, and he responded by smacking my ass playfully before whisking me away to the tent.

He set me down just inside the tent's entrance, and the instant my feet touched the ground, he noticed what I was wearing. His eyes roamed over my attire twice before locking onto mine, and they were nothing but pools of inky black.

"What?" I inquired.

"Why aren't you wearing your stolas?" he snarled, circling me like a predator.

He tugged at my skirt ever so slightly, causing a little squeal to escape my lips as I instinctively moved away. His fingers then moved gracefully to toy with the delicate string securing my top. The knot came undone, and I hastily pressed my arm over my chest, desperately trying to maintain the modesty of my attire.

"Cartan!"

I turned to face him, but he leaned closer and growled.

"I could bend you over so fast and have my way with you," he uttered. His words ignited a spark of desire within me at the thought of my Alpha unexpectedly claiming me out of sheer need. But I shook my head, reminding myself of my irritation with him.

"These are traditional clothes. Am I not supposed to blend in with the rest?" I countered.

He shook his head vigorously. "No."

"Why not?"

"You're not like everyone else," he snapped, causing me to roll my eyes. This prompted him to seize my jaw and draw me closer.

"Did you just roll your eyes at me?"

I gave him a sly smile, the little growing being inside me granting me the strength to challenge Cartan. He growled deeper, but my inner resolve held firm, and I maintained eye contact.

"*Do not toy with me. These clothes are too revealing, and they offer easy access!*" he asserted.

"Well, you've made sure no one dares to look at me, so I don't think there's a problem," I retorted.

"What?"

"Your orders about the High Alphas not being able to approach me have made everyone too afraid to get near me," I explained.

"Good," he replied. "You're mine."

"I'm yours, yes, but I won't be locked away in a castle again, left with nothing but books and you!" I exclaimed, causing Cartan to pull back, looking stunned. My own words surprised me. I hadn't realized I had been holding these feelings inside until I uttered them.

"Do you feel lonely, little Omega?" he inquired.

"I didn't realize I did until you brought me here,"

I whispered. "I would gladly submit to you on my knees and please you right now, but I won't tolerate you isolating me."

Cartan regarded me intensely before his thumb began to stroke lightly over my jaw, and he nodded.

"I won't isolate you. I am protecting you," he explained.

"The clan is afraid to approach me. I only have Mara and a few others. I don't want that. Can you take back your orders?" I asked.

Cartan released me, crossing his arms, still appearing somewhat displeased.

"How about just allowing Kylos to speak to me?" I proposed.

Cartan seemed more amenable to this idea and nodded. "Only Kylos, but you don't go to his section unaccompanied."

I nodded, and Cartan smiled before reaching out and removing my top, tossing it aside. Then, he pointed to the ground. A small smile graced my lips as I obediently knelt before him and began to undo the string on his pants. He tightened his grip on my hair, holding me close.

"And you will wear the dresses," he growled.

I shook my head, prompting him to grip me tighter, but I believed we could find a compromise.

"I'll cover up more. I see they have longer tops," I told him, pushing down his pants to free his hard cock.

"Agreed," he replied as he pulled me closer.

I licked along his hard shaft, teasing the tip, and he growled darkly.

"Besides, don't you appreciate easy access?" I teased, and he pushed into my mouth, eliciting a slight gag from me. However, I was prepared for his rough handling. I knew the effect I had on him, so I relaxed my throat and began moving up and down on him, driving him wild with desire. Yet he didn't allow me to bring him to completion with my mouth.

Instead, he withdrew and stroked himself until he came all over my chest and breasts. He then turned me around, tearing my skirt from my body. His tongue glided over my wet skin, and I moaned in response, eagerly pressing back to receive more. He delved deeper, caressing my clit with the tip of his tongue before thrusting it inside me. I groaned as my inner walls clenched around him, and he returned to sucking on my clit until I cried out in ecstasy, drenching both of us in my juices. Cartan pulled away, seizing my hips, and then entered me.

Right there in the tent's entrance, a mere piece of fabric separating us from the outside world, he claimed me. I couldn't remain silent. I knew they all heard me, and they celebrated their Alpha pleasuring his Omega. In this newfound realm, I had come to relish these moments.

Chapter Thirty-Nine
Kiandra

We were back in our intimate nest, Cartan knotted to me, and I cherished the opportunity to explore his taut and warm skin, while he leisurely toyed with my hair, gently tracing my nipple with a strand, keeping me in a heightened state of arousal. He appeared utterly captivated by me and the way I responded to these subtle caresses, but how could I not react? Every gesture, every touch from him sent waves of pleasure coursing through my body, and I couldn't help but moan and cry out when he fucked me.

However, amid this tranquil moment, an important revelation weighed on my mind.

"I learned something new today," I confided in him.

"Did you study the Old Language?" he inquired.

"No, I was weaving baskets. I'm still terrible at it. Mara always takes over," I admitted, eliciting a chuckle from him.

"But that's not what I meant. I think I may be carrying an Alpha," I whispered, placing his hand on my stomach. His expression remained calm, a serene smile gracing his lips.

"You don't seem surprised," I observed.

"I had a suspicion," he revealed. "I noticed you becoming unsettled whenever I wasn't in contact with you. Alphas emit a more assertive energy, and it can confuse your Omega senses."

His insight struck a chord within me. I had indeed felt more agitated than usual, which allowed me to meet Cartan's gaze without hesitation.

"The first true Alpha in a long time," he

251

murmured, his hand gently caressing my stomach. I leaned closer to him, our breaths mingling, and I felt his body tremble beneath my touch. I knew he yearned to mate with me once more, but his knot remained securely fastened.

"Others may not see it or may even deny it, but I do," I whispered.

"See what?" he asked.

"Something that sets you apart from the others," I told him.

"Having an Omega?" he queried.

I chuckled softly. "No, it's something deeper within you. You've not only survived immense brutality but also recognize the significance of unity and tradition. While the other High Alphas find you lacking, something tells me that if you were to lead your entire clan and depart, you would flourish. That's not just power. It's the mark of a true Alpha who knows how to care for his pack properly."

Cartan's eyes widened slightly, revealing his intrigue. He reached up to cup my cheek, and I hummed at his touch.

"You're incredibly perceptive, my dear Omega," he whispered before claiming my lips in a tender kiss.

"My father valued peace, yet he was a fighter in his own right," I shared. "But he didn't need to conquer territory or assert dominance through brutality. His strength lay in maintaining peace. You exhibit the same trait."

"He was a true Alpha," Cartan murmured.

"He was. He believed my mother would be the last Omega on the island, but then he rescued her, and our family was blessed with four siblings."

"Indeed a true blessing."

The intensity with which he uttered those words

set my heart racing, and I eagerly closed the gap between us, capturing his lips in a fervent kiss. As his knot slowly receded, allowing for movement, we once again became lost in the passionate embrace of our connection.

Chapter Forty
Kiandra

I had donned a lightweight jacket over the simple top that barely covered my breasts. Cartan had insisted I wear something more concealing before allowing me to leave, and even then, he preferred me to be in the tent, unclothed and ready for him. Despite being his Omega, I believed in contributing to the community's well-being, just as everyone else did. Work was a shared responsibility that ensured happiness and safety for all. However, on this particular day, I had some damage control to address.

I made my way from Cartan's territory to Kylos's, accompanied by Mara, as Cartan preferred me not to move alone. Many eyes followed me, but none dared hold my gaze for long. It was a strange sensation, one that left me slightly bewildered.

"Is something amiss, High Omega?" Mara inquired, carrying her infant son with her.

"I can't help but find it ridiculous that no one dares to look at me," I sighed.

"You're a unique presence," she responded.

"No, it's Cartan they fear, not me."

Mara walked alongside me, saying little. I smiled to myself, slowly turning to her.

"Cartan told me his story," I revealed.

"He did?"

"I can see why you're all so loyal to him. He's an extraordinary Alpha," I commented, my smile growing as I spoke of him.

"He is, and now he has a worthy mate by his side. No Alpha or Beta woman would ever have sufficed, though many tried," Mara teased, causing me to roll my eyes and chuckle.

I didn't concern myself with Cartan's past. We were building a future together, and that was all that mattered. However, as we entered Kylos's section, I wasn't sure where to find the High Alpha.

"Do you see him anywhere?" I inquired, placing my hands on my hips.

"He's probably working somewhere," Mara speculated.

"Probably, but where?"

"He has a fondness for crafting weapons," she explained. "Let's check the forge."

We headed to a larger tent with a gaping entrance, smoke billowing from the top. Inside, a small group of Alphas was diligently forging metal into weapons for their use. The largest among them, Kylos, stood at the far end, hammering away at glowing metal. All eyes turned toward me the moment we entered, and I offered them a warm smile before approaching Kylos. He glanced up as he heard my footsteps, shaking his head. His bare chest was drenched in sweat, and loose strands of dark-brown hair clung to the sides of his face.

"Do you wish me dead, Omega?" he teased as he plunged the searing metal into cool water, causing it to sizzle and emit steam.

"Fear not, I've spoken to my Alpha, and you're on the 'good Alpha' list," I joked, prompting a chuckle from him.

"Only because he doesn't see me as a threat."

"If you're thinking it's due to your preference in mates, I don't believe that's the case," I explained.

"No?"

"It might play a part, but Cartan and I recognize your honor. You're the one who treated me with the least hostility, and I hope to forge a friendship with you."

"Really?" he asked, sounding somewhat incredulous.

He set aside his tools, crossed his arms, and scrutinized me with a smile. "I'm not so different from the others. I simply don't see the point in fighting for something I have no interest in. But I concur with the rest of them. It was selfish of Cartan to let you mark him and consequently lose the other princesses. They were promised Omegas and should have them. So, tell me again if you're still interested in forming a friendship with me."

"Do you think they deserve Omegas?" I inquired.

"I do."

"Even Peros?"

"Even Peros. He may appear harsh, deeply rooted in the old Alpha ways of this region, but you haven't witnessed the good he's done or the sacrifices he's had to make to become the High Alpha he is," Kylos explained.

I contemplated his words, unsure if I shared his perspective. However, a voice of reason reminded me that while I initially regarded Cartan as a beast, I had come to understand him better through his past. Perhaps there were hidden facets to Peros that I had yet to discover.

"Very well, I'll take your word for it," I conceded, noting the surprised expression on Kylos's face.

"You will?"

"You know these Alphas better than I do, and the first time I met Cartan, I didn't think much differently about him than I do about Peros now," I explained. "But don't view Cartan as selfish. I marked him."

"But he allowed you to. If he had been vigilant enough, he wouldn't have permitted it."

"I marked him before he had a chance to object."

"As an Alpha of the Black Desert, he should have

been vigilant, and I believe he was. His instincts craved it. Every Alpha desires an Omega's mark. It's a great honor. Therefore, he was selfish."

"I'm not entirely sure I agree," I shot back, crossing my arms.

"Little Omega, it's not that we don't understand why it happened. Even if you hadn't marked him, and he had brought you back for us to decide, it's obvious you would have belonged to him. You share a true bond, don't you?" Kylos questioned.

"I believe so."

"When did you realize it?" Kylos asked.

"Probably the moment I marked him. I'm sure you understand I had different reasons for doing so, but everything in me told me it was a good choice. Now I realize my Omega side chose him because he was the perfect fit for me. It was, in some way, about survival, as it always is for Omegas. I just didn't realize how deep it went," I revealed.

"But your instincts knew."

"Yes, and with time, I came to see it too. But you must understand we've been taught how dangerous it is for Omegas out there. Our own mother fled her home because she was promised to a brutal Alpha she knew she could never love," I informed him, and Kylos nodded. "I freed my sisters, thinking their fate might be the same. Now I do worry if I made the right choice."

"I appreciate your honesty, little Omega, but hopefully, we find your sisters before anything happens to them."

I nodded. "I hope so too. I never realized how wonderful this is, but the four walls of the library were sort of all I knew."

"And you can't learn everything from books."

"Debatable," I teased, making him chuckle before

we walked out of the tent together.

"Has your Alpha provided you with enough to read, or are you interested in more?" he questioned.

"Do you have something for me?"

"Well, if we are to form a friendship, it's about give-and-take, right?" he pointed out.

"I think just give," I teased, seeing him smile as we walked to a tent located further away from the working tents.

Like Cartan's tent, Kylos's was stationed on the outer skirts of the territory, marked by the blue circle around the top, representing the color of his pack. However, as I was about to step inside, Kylos held out his arm, not touching me but signaling me to stop.

"What?" I asked.

"You can't come inside, Omega," he chuckled.

"Why not?"

"Because Cartan might have allowed us to talk, but if you enter my tent, I'm certain he does not care about my preferences. He will kill me," he informed me, and I tilted my head to the side.

"I don't see why."

Kylos didn't offer further explanation. He simply walked inside, laughing, which piqued my curiosity. I wanted to see how his home was decorated and how different it was from the rest of the territory. I could already observe variations in clothing and hairstyles among the pack members. Many of the males had long braided hair, often with just one braid, while the women wore leather dresses instead of two separate pieces. They adorned their single long braids with stones and jewelry. Kylos also had one long braid, with the sides of his head shaved, giving him a distinctive rugged appearance. I appreciated their unique style and wanted to see more.

I took a step closer, but Mara reached out,

grabbing my arm and holding me back.

"High Omega," she scolded.

"What?" I asked, feigning innocence.

"You can't. High Alpha Kylos is right. If High Alpha Cartan found out you had entered his tent, he would burn the whole territory to the ground."

"It can't be that serious."

"Were you not taught anything about Alphas?" she questioned.

"I was taught about the dangers they pose."

"Then you must know that entering his tent would be a grave offense against your Alpha," she reminded me.

I sighed, crossing my arms, but then Kylos emerged from his tent, carrying a few books. Excitement welled up within me, and as soon as he offered them to me, I snatched them from his hands, making him chuckle.

"Oh, Cartan doesn't have these!" I exclaimed.

"They are books about our history, and that one is about the former Omegas who resided in the Black Desert," he explained, pointing to a white book with browned edges. I eagerly flipped through it, feeling my heart race with excitement, as some of the Omegas had also been depicted. It was a feast for my mind, and I turned to Kylos, who was smiling at me. Then, to his surprise, I wrapped an arm around his neck and hugged him.

"High Omega!" Mara exclaimed, terrified, and she pulled me away.

"What?" I asked. "It's a kind gesture between friends."

Both Kylos and Mara shook their heads, and Kylos turned to Mara.

"You saw I didn't hug her back," he told her, and Mara nodded.

"I'll come by tomorrow as well. Then you can

show me more about your pack," I informed him.

"I'm guessing the books are more interesting at the moment."

I smiled teasingly at him before waving goodbye and walking back to Cartan's section with Mara.

Chapter Forty-One
Cartan

I returned to my Omega, finding her in the tent amidst a sea of furs and sheets, and the unmistakable scent of Kylos clung to her. It provoked a deep growl from my throat as I snatched the book from her hands.

"No!" she complained, attempting to reach for the volume as I held it just out of her reach, almost taunting her.

"Why do you smell so strongly of Kylos?" I demanded.

"He gave me some books."

"I can see that. This one is not in my collection. *The Omegas of The Black Desert*," I read aloud, comprehending why this book held such fascination for my Omega. However, it did not explain why she reeked of Kylos.

I leaned in closer, burying my nose in her hair and neck, and the scent grew even more potent. I growled again and wrapped my hand around her throat.

"Why do you smell of him? Did you enter his tent?"

"No, I wasn't allowed to," she explained, a teasing smile playing on her lips as if she relished seeing me so on edge.

"Then why?"

"I hugged him."

"You *what*?" I exclaimed, then tossed the book aside.

"Hey!" She pushed my hand away and tried to reach for it, but I swiftly encircled her waist with my arm, keeping her pressed against me.

"You reek of him," I snarled.

"It was just a friendly hug."

"No one touches you," I stated and reached for the string on her skirt.

She began rubbing her backside against me, desiring me as well and recognizing the need to appease her Alpha after touching another male and bringing his scent back with her.

"Technically, I touched him," she teased.

"Then you do not deserve the pleasure of my touch," I informed her, hearing her whimper her protest.

I unwrapped her from her skirt and discarded the material before pushing her forward, causing her ass to arch up in the air. I swiftly lowered my pants to free my throbbing cock. I tantalizingly brushed my cock against her wet entrance, letting the tip become slick with her juices. She moaned and pushed back, eager to take me inside her, but I withdrew and began to stroke myself.

Kiandra turned her head, observing me as I teased myself, and I knew it infuriated her Omega side, which longed to be the one bringing me pleasure. She tried to rise, but I placed a hand on her back and continued to stroke myself, watching my beautiful mate. Her pussy clenched in desperation for me, and she hissed when I persisted in denying her my thrusts. Her act of defiance only served to quicken my impending orgasm.

A guttural grunt escaped my lips as I ejaculated, my hot seed spurting all over her ass and lower back. I smeared it across her skin, covering her in my scent.

"Please, Alpha," she pleaded, shaking her ass as she presented herself to me. I responded by smacking her rear, causing her to gasp.

"You brought another Alpha's scent in here. Why should I reward my Omega for that?" I taunted her, a devious smile playing on my lips as I savored her desperate and vulnerable state.

Her juices trickled down her thighs, her pussy aching for my cock. All she yearned for now was to please me after having teased me, but I wasn't granting her that satisfaction, and it was clearly frustrating her.

"Well?" I questioned, delivering another swat to her ass, causing more of her slick to drip from her.

"It was just a hug," she panted.

"You do not go near other Alphas. They have not earned the privilege of your perfect touch," I growled before I leaned down and spread her thighs wider.

My tongue traced up along her right inner thigh, then I swept it over her delectable spot. She cried out, arching her back to seek more, but I withdrew.

"Gods! Please!" she begged.

"It isn't the Gods you should be praying to," I taunted.

"I'm sorry, Alpha. I won't do it again. Just please," she moaned.

I licked over her wet skin once more, causing her to shiver and have a small climax. While I relished teasing her, driving her utterly wild for me, her enticing scent began to fill the tent, and I couldn't resist the allure of my mate's body any longer. I positioned myself and thrust inside, making her gasp as I filled her completely. I gripped her hips roughly, taking my mate hard and punishing her with her own pleasure for even entertaining the thought that another Alpha deserved her touch. She belonged to me and no one else.

"Oh, Gods!" she cried out again when she climaxed around me, her inner walls contracting and squeezing me tightly.

I groaned, trying to maintain control. I wanted her pleasure to border on exquisite agony, and when she came again immediately after the first climax, she attempted to reach back to slow me down. However, I continued to pound into her through her orgasm, reaching my own release just as her screams neared a higher pitch. I roared as I knotted myself to her, experiencing an explosive climax.

We both panted as we came down from our peak, but my mate had gone utterly limp, her body still trembling beneath me. I smiled at the intoxicating sight and began leisurely teasing her clit.

"Please, Alpha," she moaned, not yet ready for a third orgasm.

"Will you go and reward another Alpha with your sweet touch?" I asked.

She shook her head, her desperation evident.

"Who is the Alpha deserving of you?" I inquired.

"You!" she cried out, shaking her head in her desperate state. "You are, Alpha."

"Will you tease your Alpha like this again?" I asked, deriving immense satisfaction from her acknowledgment of my worthiness.

"No! Please!" she pleaded.

Her body trembled once more, and I granted her another wave of pleasure, causing her to clutch at the furs and let out a small scream. I gradually slowed down, and she looked over her shoulder with such a ravished expression that my desire for her surged to new heights. I leaned closer, claiming her lips, and she moaned into my mouth.

"My touch, my scent, my body—everything you need is right here," I whispered, and she mewled in agreement, affirming my words.

Chapter Forty-Two
Kiandra

I sensed an unusual breeze caressing my skin, an unfamiliar chill that usually never troubled me with my Alpha's protective embrace. Confusion washed over me as I felt the cold touch of the wind, prompting me to blink open my eyes. A hint of worry tingled within me as I glanced around, but Cartan was nowhere in sight. This was unsettling, as he rarely left me alone at night and hesitated to let me go even in the mornings.

"Cartan?" I called out, but there was no response. Instead, a soft, distant sound reached my ears, like a faint whisper that I strained to decipher.

I decided to leave the nest, donning one of the stolas nearby before making my way to the front of the tent where a small fire was burning. My calls for Cartan went unanswered once again. The gentle whispering persisted, sounding like a voice, though the words remained elusive.

With curiosity gnawing at me, I pushed aside the fabric covering the entrance of the tent and found myself face to face with an elderly woman. Her hair was as white as the dress she wore, and she stood serenely in the midst of it all, her gaze fixed upon me.

"Hello?" I called out, my voice tinged with uncertainty.

A serene smile graced her lips. Initially, I couldn't pinpoint what it was about her, but I felt an overwhelming sense of safety in her presence. Drawing nearer, I soon realized the source of this feeling—she was an Omega.

"Who are you?" I inquired.

She remained silent, continuing to smile as she

reached out to touch my cheek. My sisters had often described our mother's touch as the most soothing sensation in the world, yet I had never experienced it. However, the touch of this older Omega seemed to come close, filling me with an inexplicable connection. Why did I feel such a strong bond with her?

"You're an Omega," I whispered.

Her reply was equally quiet. "So are you."

"Do you live here?" I questioned, my mind racing to connect dots that I knew were likely inaccurate. How could an Omega survive alone in the Black Desert?

"You're a good Omega," she praised. "Smart, strong, and kind. You're good for him."

"Cartan? Are you...?" I started to ask, but she raised a finger to her lips, silencing me.

"No matter where you go, he will find you. So don't be scared."

"Scared?" I whispered. "What am I scared of?"

"I believe there may be little for you to fear, but fear always exists. Wherever you go, your Alpha will come for you."

"I don't understand any of this," I whispered, growing frustrated that her words were not making sense to me.

"Just trust your Alpha," she advised. "He won't rest until he has you."

"Has me? Cartan never lost me."

The older Omega continued to stroke my cheek, soothing my entire being. I felt an overwhelming sense of comfort, like being wrapped in a protective cocoon. My eyelids grew heavy, and although I didn't want to stop gazing at the older Omega, the world began to blur and fade into darkness.

My body jerked awake, a sudden sense of suffocation overwhelming me. I was trapped in darkness, disoriented, and alarmed. Frantically, I groped around, my hands encountering something rough, but I couldn't find an escape.

"Hey!" I shouted, panic rising within me. "What is this? Let me out! Let me out!"

Tears welled up in my eyes as I struggled to comprehend my situation. Where was I? What had happened? I attempted to take deep breaths to calm my racing mind, but the air felt oppressive, as though I had been cut off from the fresh wind.

"Calm down, Kiandra," I whispered to myself, trying to control my hyperventilation. "Just calm down and think."

Gradually, I began to discern peculiar details. The sound of hooves reached my ears, and I felt the swaying motion of a wagon, all while surrounded by absolute darkness. I extended my hands again, encountering the rough texture of fabric and exploring its contours. It felt like a burlap sack or some equally coarse material. I had been placed in a bag! But why? Who had taken me? I couldn't fathom that Cartan was merely playing a game with me, especially after our intimate encounter last night. No, this was something altogether different.

I sniffed the air, but it offered no clues, being dense and humid. A slight jolt indicated that we were traversing a rough road. How long had I been asleep? Did Cartan know I had been taken?

A multitude of anxious thoughts raced through my mind, and I dreaded the worst. There had been a time when Omegas were more plentiful, sold as commodities, mere breeding stock. I wondered if that might be my grim future. I could already envision myself with a price tag around my neck.

Gods, I prayed that such a fate wouldn't befall me. I'd rather endure anything than be sold off like chattel. A surge of longing for my Alpha overwhelmed me, and my heart ached for Cartan. But then I remembered the woman from my dream—the one who had assured me that wherever I went, Cartan would find me and urged me to trust in him.

I knew she was right. Cartan was no weak Alpha. Deep in my heart, I recognized him as a true Alpha, one who would stop at nothing to find me, even if I were taken to the farthest reaches of Verocca, under the control of a cruel Alpha or Beta lord. I could withstand any torment, confident that Cartan would come to rescue me.

Suddenly, I felt a sharp pang in my heart, an intensity of aggression beyond anything I had ever experienced. I smiled and withdrew from Cartan's aggressive emotions, unable to bear such intensity. He had learned of my disappearance, and his fury knew no bounds. *He is coming for me*, I thought, placing a hand on my stomach.

"It's okay," I whispered, feeling our unborn child's fierce energy. "Your father is on his way."

Chapter Forty-Three
Cartan

One thing I despised more than anything was leaving the warm embrace of my Omega early in the morning. Tyros often roused me, either with a long whistle or by calling my name to signal the beginning of the day. This time, he had chosen to wake me even earlier for a hunt, and I groaned in displeasure. My cock was hard, my body yearning for another round with Kiandra, but I knew one round would inevitably lead to three more, and I'd never leave her side.

I buried my nose into her soft skin, savoring her scent. Reluctantly, I withdrew from her, my growl low and frustrated as I began dressing. Leaving her side was always a painful experience. Kiandra was the missing piece of my soul, and parting from her tore at my very core. But as the High Alpha of our clan, I had responsibilities to uphold.

Emerging from the tent, I seethed with anger, my hard cock replaced by an intense desire to kill something. Tyros chuckled but kept a safe distance as we made our way through the camp to meet the other Alphas joining us on the hunt. Among our group, two women matched the aggression and energy of the male Alphas.

We discussed our hunting strategy before embarking on our journey into the unforgiving expanse of the Black Desert. We trekked for quite some time until we reached a series of small stone cliffs housing a tiny cave. I knew it harbored a boar, and we encircled the area, waiting for the creature to emerge. The sun began its ascent as we patiently bided our time.

I started hearing the grunting sounds of the boar within, and soon enough, a rather large male appeared to forage for a late snack. Without hesitation, we hurled our spears at the unsuspecting beast. The first missed, landing in the sand, and causing the boar to panic. But my throw hit home, piercing its neck, while the others found their marks in its back. The boar's life was extinguished in an instant.

Joyous sounds filled the air as we secured our bounty and checked the remaining caves. Soon, we began the journey back to camp, with three boars in tow. We left the caves inhabited by mothers and their young undisturbed to ensure the species' survival and maintain a stable meat supply.

As we returned to camp, the sun had risen higher in the sky, and the camp had sprung to life. People greeted us warmly, and we distributed the meat that would be shared among the clans. Though we had our own territories, resources, and working power, we believed in the importance of collective sharing. This approach ensured balance and the survival of all clans.

With the hunt concluded and no longer distracted, my thoughts turned to my Omega once more. She occupied my every waking moment, and while it was slightly disconcerting, I wouldn't trade her for anything in this world. Having an Omega was the greatest blessing an Alpha could receive, and I couldn't help but cast a glance toward my tent. But once again, Tyros appeared at my side, slapping my shoulder, and reminding me that we had tents to prepare and build.

I nodded and was about to follow him to our task when a peculiar sensation seized my heart. It was a sharp feeling, distinct and powerful, pulsing alongside the steady rhythm of my heartbeat. I recognized this feeling. I had tried it once before when Peros frightened my mate, but this sensation was even sharper. It cut through me with such intensity that I almost fell to my knees.

"Alpha?" Tyros called out, his voice an echoing murmur. I whipped my head toward my tent. My instincts roared with fury, and without saying a word, I sprinted toward my sanctuary. Others followed, sensing my distress, but I couldn't divulge the cause. Upon entering my tent, I rushed to our bedroom, but the faint scent of Kiandra indicated she hadn't been there for a while. Yet that wasn't what filled me with dread. What elicited a dark growl and a torrent of anger was the scent of a stranger in our sacred and intimate space.

I searched our nest in vain for any sign of her, but I knew she wasn't there. My nose twitched, detecting the smell of the invader as I made my way to the entrance of the tent, but it vanished amidst the familiar scents of the clans. I couldn't track him.

"High Alpha?" Tyros called.

"*Someone ... took her!*" I roared, my voice nothing but a primal growl.

"Who would be so foolish?" Tyros snarled, echoing the sentiments of the other Alphas who shared my fury. An idea sparked in my mind as Tyros asked the question that had just crossed my thoughts.

With long, furious strides, I stormed through the camp, leaving my territory and entering Peros's. I found him emerging from one of the pleasure tents, still fastening his pants. He barely had a chance to turn his head before I grabbed him, propelling him backward into the tent. We tumbled inside, landing beside another couple engaged in their own passions. I pinned him to the ground, my hands closing around his throat, and he growled back in defiance before I delivered a punishing blow. He retaliated, pushing me out of the tent.

A crowd began to gather as we lunged at each other, neither willing to yield. Blood flowed from both of us, and it was evident this confrontation would end in tragedy if allowed to continue. Yet neither of us showed any inclination to stop. It took the combined efforts of the other High Alphas, Recor and Kylos, to pull us apart. Peros sported a swollen left eye, a broken nose, and long, bloody scratches across his chest and stomach. I knew I looked just as battered, but I felt no pain. All I could sense was a seething, dark rage that consumed me.

"What is the meaning of this?" Recor demanded.

"Ask Cartan, he attacked me," Peros growled.

"Cartan?" Recor turned to me, but I couldn't form words. All that escaped my lips were guttural growls. I yearned to explain the situation, to clarify my actions so I could tear Peros apart and then go in search of my Omega, still covered in his blood. But my vocalizations remained unintelligible.

"Cartan?" Recor pressed, but Tyros stepped forward.

"Our High Omega is missing. Someone entered our High Alpha's tent and took her."

Peros wiped away blood from his face. "And your first assumption was that I had taken her?"

A deafening growl erupted from me, stunning everyone. I couldn't think clearly. Peros seemed less enraged by my outburst and deep in thought as he contemplated the situation.

"I did not touch your Omega," he said solemnly. "I haven't been near her since you ordered us to stay away. However, we did have visitors at the border."

"Why didn't you inform us of this?" Recor inquired.

"Why should I? The matter was resolved swiftly. If I had allowed them into the camp, it wouldn't have happened without your knowledge."

"*Who*?" I snarled.

"Soldiers from the king's realm arrived,

demanding to see your Omega. I informed them of your directive, that you would not permit it," he explained. "Perhaps I made some comments to your Omega that she found displeasing, but I would never jeopardize her safety, nor that of your child. She is a member of our clans now, and I would never put her life at risk."

Hearing the sincerity in his voice calmed me somewhat, and Recor and Kylos gradually released their grips. I took a deep breath, piecing together the situation. It was evident who had taken her, but the question that nagged at me was how he had infiltrated the camp without our knowledge. Then it dawned on me.

"It's trading day," I muttered, my voice slipping back into a growl. I scanned the group of wolves that had gathered. *We fucking allowed him inside.*"

My voice became a series of growls once more, and the other High Alphas cursed softly.

"At least we know where she is," Recor pointed out.

"I want as many Alphas as possible. I am getting my Omega back!" I declared.

"We will help. Kylos and I will accompany you," Peros offered. I nodded, not caring who joined the rescue mission. All that mattered was reclaiming her and our child, safe and sound. If anyone had harmed her in any way, I would tear them limb from limb.

Chapter Forty-Four
Kiandra

I wasn't sure how long we had been traveling. I dozed off multiple times, but when I finally roused, weakened by days without food or water, I heard the unmistakable sound of voices outside. The voices were deep, signaling that they belonged to men. After a while, the wagon started moving again, and I had a sense we were approaching something, although I couldn't quite discern what it was. The road became rougher, and the sounds around me grew more numerous, indicating that we were in a place with more people, possibly a bustling city. I struggled to calm my racing heart and the fiery determination inside me, attempting to grasp the situation. Before I could make sense of it all, the wagon came to a slow halt, and I heard more voices, some of them sounding rougher and possibly in positions of authority.

I didn't get a chance to process what was happening before I heard something being opened. Light filtered through the tiny holes in the fabric, and then hands reached in and grabbed me. I hissed and struggled, but I was still confined within the bag. More voices conversed around me, but my agitation prevented me from comprehending their words. Then the wagon started moving away while I was carried by strong hands. Some of those hands ventured where they shouldn't, and I wriggled and hissed in response, but laughter followed.

Soon, I heard the opening of doors and the sound of boots echoing down hallways. Where was I being taken? Another pair of doors opened, and I felt myself being lowered until my bag touched a cool stone surface.

"What is this?" an unfamiliar voice inquired.

"The Omega."

"Why is she in a bag?"

"The most secure way to transport her."

I heard a deep sigh, as if the person found this mode of transport absurd, and I couldn't help but agree. It had been suffocating.

"Release her," the voice commanded, and the tie above my head was loosened, allowing fresh air to rush in.

Desperate to escape, I scrambled free of the bag, kicking it away before I started assessing my surroundings, trying to make sense of where I was. My gaze first fell on a pair of imposing Alphas standing behind me, adorned in golden armor, appearing to be guards. I then turned my head in the opposite direction and locked eyes with a pair of striking azure orbs.

My mouth fell open in astonishment as I beheld the handsome face before me. His features were impeccably sculpted, with a dark smirk playing on his lips. He wore a golden crown upon his head and sat on a grand, ebony throne adorned with gold accents. His attire was elegant, reminiscent of what my father had worn, although he had never favored such vibrant colors or excessive gold. There was only one person who would flaunt their wealth to such an extent, and the realization sent shivers down my spine.

"Welcome, Omega," the King of the Mainlands greeted me.

"W-Why am I here?" I stammered, my voice quivering.

"I apologize for the rough transport, but you now have a fierce Alpha guarding you," he replied.

"You took me!" I exclaimed.

"I simply wished to meet you."

"You took me!" I repeated.

"Your Alpha was unwilling to allow me a meeting with you. I had to take matters into my own hands."

"Why?" I inquired.

"Because your Alpha would not have been able to cross the ocean without my harbor or my ships! I possess the only place large enough to accommodate the army he needed to bring with him. Do you know what he promised me in return?"

"An Omega," I whispered.

"Indeed, and that promise went unfulfilled. Now he has the audacity to deny me a meeting with the last remaining Omega in these lands," he stated, gesturing toward me. "I believe it is only fair that I borrow his Omega for a while."

"B-Borrow?" I stammered, uncertain of the meaning.

The king smiled and rose from his throne, causing me to retreat, but I bumped into the legs of the guards behind me. The king halted in front of me and extended his hand, though I stared at it with trepidation.

"I apologize for the rough treatment, but there's no need to fear," he reassured me.

Unsure if I believed him but feeling I had little choice, I reluctantly accepted his hand. He helped me to my feet, and when I tried to withdraw, his grip momentarily tightened before he released me.

"Are you hungry?" he inquired.

"Hungry?" I echoed in disbelief.

"Yes, I'm aware that you're eating for two. I'm sure you must be famished, and I am sure you wish to bathe as well," he pointed out with a knowing look.

"You know I'm pregnant?" I inquired, surprised.

"Well, the news spread quite fast, but also, I can smell it," he replied matter-of-factly. I momentarily forgot just how keen an Alpha's senses could be. The king might not have the rough appearance and imposing stature of the High Alphas, but I couldn't underestimate him. He was no weak Alpha, and I needed to be cautious around him until Cartan arrived to retrieve me.

"Well?" he prompted.

"I could eat," I replied, attempting to appear amiable and accommodating.

"Wonderful," he responded before gesturing for me to follow him.

I trailed behind him, leaving the guards behind as we exited the grand throne room. I stumbled slightly, feeling a bit unsteady on my legs. The king reached out to assist me, but the moment his hand touched me, I instinctively pulled away. I couldn't bring myself to trust him at all.

"I don't want you to fall," he said softly. "You're carrying something precious."

I didn't like the way he phrased it, but I forced a small smile onto my lips as we walked through the sprawling castle. I was well aware of his family's history, and they were notorious for their harsh rule. I had to maintain my distance from the king to ensure he wouldn't subject me to the same fate as the Omegas who once resided here.

The king led me to a room bustling with servants whom he instructed to clean and dress me in fresh garments. I couldn't contain my excitement, given the state of disarray my attire had been in after the arduous journey. There had been no breaks to relieve myself, leaving me to soil clothes. Once I had emerged from the chamber, the king motioned for me to follow him, guiding me to a magnificent dining room where an opulent feast had already been meticulously prepared.

I noted how late in the day it was. How much time had passed since I was taken? I couldn't determine, and I was uncertain how the king had managed to infiltrate the camp to secure my capture. I knew I needed answers, so as we sat down and he offered me food and drink, I adopted a pleasant demeanor, trying to appear as open as possible.

"I truly didn't intend for you to be handled in such a manner. I merely wished to meet you," the king explained, and I waited until he took a bite of food before eating myself.

"I believe you, but next time you wish to speak with an Omega, perhaps sending a letter to request a meeting would be more appropriate," I suggested, seeing the king smile.

While I couldn't recall his exact age, I believed he was a year or two younger than Cartan. However, there was something about his eyes that made him seem older, as though a more seasoned being peered through his azure gaze. It served as a warning for me to be cautious around him. His youth didn't diminish his intelligence.

"Omega, you possess a strong will, challenging an Alpha in such a manner," he remarked.

"Well, my sisters taught me to be confident."

"And where might they be?" he inquired, his cunning smile widening.

"I … don't know."

"Do not lie to me. Let's be honest. I want us to be friends," he declared.

"Friends? Does that mean you won't touch me?"

"Do not be afraid, Princess Kiandra. I have no desire to touch you. You already have an Alpha, and I don't want to make an enemy of Cartan."

"Then perhaps you shouldn't have taken his Omega," I pointed out.

"I admit it was a risky move, but I'm confident he will understand."

"How so?"

"Because while Cartan was successful in finding you princesses, he also lost them. Now none of us know where they might be," he explained.

"That's not true. I told Cartan where they might be."

"Yes? And has he found them yet?" the king challenged, causing me to stare at the food in front of me.

"No..."

"Exactly, and I think I know why."

"Why?"

"Because it shouldn't be an Alpha scouting for them out. It should be an Omega. Alphas share a deep connection with one another, as do Betas, but Omegas share one too," he elucidated.

"I'm aware."

"I don't believe Cartan is very motivated to find the other Omegas now that he has you," he insinuated.

"I think he is, because I failed to recognize the danger I put my sisters in. I genuinely believe he wishes to locate them to ensure their safety," I asserted. "You shouldn't doubt my Alpha. He will find them."

The king smiled, yet there was something dark lurking behind that smile that sent a shiver down my spine.

"You see, I don't actually doubt him, but I also know where his loyalty lies," the king explained.

"With you?" I asked.

"With his clan."

Chapter Forty-Five
Kiandra

I regarded the king curiously, uncertain of his intentions with his words.

"Of course, he is loyal to his clan," I replied.

"Despite them treating him as a low-ranking Alpha," the king pointed out.

"Well, I believe he has proven himself. What the others think doesn't matter to him. He knows himself," I explained.

The king nodded, looking at me approvingly. "You show deep respect for your Alpha. I appreciate it. It's good to hear that you Omegas still know what is best for you."

I wanted to roll my eyes at his words, but I remained still, not wanting to test my luck in the presence of this Alpha.

"But I am not an idiot," he continued.

"I never said you were."

"No, of course not, but you can count, right?" he asked.

"Of course."

"How many sisters do you have?" he inquired, and as soon as he asked, I sensed where he was leading the conversation.

I gulped. "Three."

"Is there another hidden one?"

I slowly shook my head. "No, my King."

"How many clan leaders are there? And let's not count the one who enjoys fucking ass," he growled lowly, making me gulp again.

"Three," I whispered.

"How many Omegas did Cartan not promise?"

"He promised away four."

"But we both know he intended to claim one for himself, leaving three available. Is he going to inform one of the other clan leaders that they will not receive an Omega?" the king asked, his words leading and his tone taunting.

My throat became dry, and I shook my head, fearing the worst. He had said he wouldn't touch me, but the way he was leading me along sounded very much like he wanted an Omega, regardless.

"Meaning Cartan is deceiving one of us, and since I know where his loyalty lies, I know who."

"W-Why help him then? Why not come for us yourself?" I whispered, finding it hard to meet his eyes.

"Because I didn't believe he would be foolish enough to deceive me. He knew what I provided him with, and why would I do the hard work when I can get someone else to do it?" he explained, his smile growing wider and making me glare at him.

"You just expected an Omega as payment," I mumbled, shaking my head.

"Of course. That's what he promised me in exchange for permitting him to cross the sea with my ships. But I always knew there weren't enough princesses. I was prepared to claim one of you if necessary," he elaborated.

"And now you have," I whispered, my voice trembling.

The king sighed, leaning to the side in his chair. "Do not cry, Princess Kiandra. I promised I would not touch you, and I will not. You are already claimed."

I bit my lip, uncertain if he was speaking the truth.

"No, I need you for something else."

"S-Something else?" I stammered.

"As I said, I believe an Omega is the key to

finding the others."

"My sisters…"

"No, either your sisters are deceased or have been taken by another Alpha," he groaned wearily.

"My sisters are intelligent. They can survive until they are found," I assured him.

"Then they must already have been fucked thoroughly by others."

I hissed at him, but he continued to smile, so I calmed myself, trying to remain composed. I needed to understand how the king had managed to take me and what his intentions were. That was the best way to protect myself and my child.

"If you don't want my sisters, then what do you want?" I asked.

"An Omega, of course, and you're going to help me find one."

"How? I don't know where there might be others."

"No, but I do," he revealed.

"What?"

He continued to smile, appearing entirely at ease as he leaned back in his chair. Then he gestured to the food in front of me. "Eat up. You will need your strength."

I wanted to ask more questions, but with a single look from him, it was clear I shouldn't inquire further. I fell silent and began to eat. When I had finished, he asked me to stand, and so I did. I followed him out of the dining room, still curious about something else.

"How did you take me?" I inquired.

"You were given a mild sedative, and I have business dealings with the clans. I used that opportunity to have someone capture you," he explained.

"You do know Cartan will come for me, right?"

"I do, and he will retrieve you. You have my word, Princess Kiandra, that no one will touch or harm you," he assured me.

I looked up at him, puzzled, but he sounded sincere as he spoke. Soon, we arrived at a set of grand double doors, and as the king pushed them open, I was ushered into the most magnificent place. My own home had a reasonably sized library, but it paled in comparison to the one I now beheld in the king's castle.

"This is the most extensive library you will find in Verocca, and..." The king began laughing, but I couldn't even turn my head to look at him. I was completely enchanted by the sight before me. "Feel free to explore."

The king continued to chuckle, and I realized it must have been due to the expression on my face. When he told me I was free to explore, I eagerly stormed into the library. I went to the first shelf, scanning the spines of the books. I felt the king approaching but was no longer focused on him. My curiosity had been piqued, and the king allowed me some time to take it all in. However, I soon sensed the tiny baby Alpha within me warning me to remain vigilant of my surroundings. I turned around to find the king standing very close to me, his charming smile belying the darkness beneath.

"Why have you brought me here?" I questioned, taking a step away from him.

"Because I don't believe you and your sisters are the last Omegas left in this world. I believe there might be an entire civilization left," he explained.

"What?"

"You must have come across it in your books. The Omega City?"

"It's just a myth," I told him. "I have never come across anything that claims to know an exact path to the city, or even its existence."

"I have."

"What?"

The king walked past me, moving down long rows of bookshelves, and I followed behind him, curious about what he might be searching for. Soon, he stopped, turned, and then handed me a large brown book with golden letters on its cover. I accepted it, and there, on the front, it read *The History of Omegas*.

"But this isn't about the city," I remarked.

"But it is," he told me. Then he gestured for me to follow, and we made our way to a large round table. He motioned for me to place the book down, and I did so. He flipped through the pages until he found the section that spoke of the disappearance of Omegas. I read through the text, surprised to find new information that I had never seen before.

"While I can see why someone might believe that Omegas sought refuge from the brutality they experienced, this doesn't necessarily mean they built a city for themselves. And even if they did, how did it go unnoticed?" I questioned.

"That is the intriguing part. But I have more," he explained before selecting another book titled *The Myth of The Omega City*.

He placed it in front of me, and my fingers tingled with anticipation as I scanned through its pages. He extended his hand, indicating I was free to touch and explore, and so I delved into the knowledge before me. I had read a bit about this, but I had never delved deeply into myths, as they often left you with more questions than answers.

However, from what I was reading, it genuinely seemed like this city existed. But how could one find it? More importantly, did I even want to find it? I glanced up at the king beside me, who smiled at me. Yet I suddenly found myself uncertain about seeking answers. If there was a city of Omegas, they had good reason to remain hidden. They *wanted* to remain hidden, and if I discovered their location, what would happen to them?

The king said he wanted an Omega, but I couldn't believe he would simply go to this city and politely ask for one or attempt to court one.

"Well?" he asked.

"Um, it does seem like it could be real," I admitted.

"I knew you would see it the same way as me," he praised. "But I also believe the only way to find this city is through an Omega."

"Oh?"

"Here, Princess," he said. He flipped through the pages until he found a passage that stated clearly only an Omega could locate the city. I was unsure if that was accurate or simply a way to dissuade anyone else from searching for it. However, it was evident the king believed it was up to me to find this enigmatic city. "So I will let you get to work. Your Alpha will probably arrive here in a day or two, threatening to destroy my home unless I hand you over, so we are both working under time pressure."

"Um, you could also just let me go, and I will return to my Alpha," I suggested with a tentative smile.

The king chuckled before patting me affectionately, much like one would a child. Then he walked away. Yet I wasn't entirely certain about my course of action. My heart urged me to explore the pages, to consume the information and satisfy my curiosity.

However, the voice of reason reminded me of the potential consequences for the hidden Omegas and me. I reached down to rest a hand on my abdomen. I didn't want any Omegas to come to harm, but I couldn't jeopardize my child's safety. I sat down in a chair, opening both substantial books and laying them side by side. I wasn't sure which one would lead me to the answers I sought, but I was determined to find out.

Chapter Forty-Six
Kiandra

A hand forcefully slammed down on the table, jolting me awake from my slumber. I glanced around, disoriented, and found an enraged king standing beside me. I blinked my eyes rapidly, attempting to shake off the remnants of sleep.

"Is something wrong?" I inquired, my voice dry, reaching for the glass of water provided for me.

The king ensured that I was fed and hydrated while I worked, though he didn't appear particularly pleased with me.

"You fell asleep," he pointed out.

"I've been studying night and day. It's no surprise I fell asleep."

"Yes, well, I know your Alpha is on his way here with an army, and in less than a day, he'll be surrounding these walls, demanding to see you."

"Then perhaps don't abduct his Omega," I muttered under my breath, hearing the king growl, and I lowered my gaze.

"What have you learned?" he inquired.

"Um," I flipped through the pages and shrugged. "Not much. It does seem highly plausible that this city exists."

"Yes, we established that."

"But some of these passages are written in riddles, speaking of something about the city being found where the sun touches the ground, and in that moment, you will see the city shine brighter than the very moon," I read aloud.

"I know what the book says! I've read it!" he snapped, causing me to look up at him, surprised.

"Then why do you need me?"

"Because only an Omega can find the city!"

"Yes, I understand that, but…" I trailed off as I flipped to a page I hadn't read yet, and that's when I noticed something.

Right on the pages were swirling lines that reminded me of something.

"What?" the king asked when I hesitated to continue.

I was about to answer him when my inner voice reminded me of the dangers of being completely honest with the king.

"I am trying," I admitted, attempting to be vague about what I had discovered.

"Try harder," he demanded. "Once your Alpha reaches us, I have no choice but to let him in."

I stared in shock at the king beside me. I hadn't expected that.

"What?"

"What?" he echoed. "You're not my prisoner."

"I'm not?" I questioned, not understanding why the king wouldn't attempt to stop Cartan from reaching me.

"Of course not. I don't want a war with the Black Desert, and if you provoke one clan leader, they all come running," he snarled.

"Don't you have the largest army?"

"The largest doesn't guarantee success. My father was foolish enough to antagonize one of the older clan leaders. I don't intend to make the same mistake," he informed me, and I blinked rapidly as I stared up at him.

He was certainly much wiser than I had initially assumed, and he didn't seem to share the same values as his predecessors. However, that didn't change the fact that he had abducted me. It was clear that you didn't defy the king, regardless of the circumstances, or he would come for you.

"I will do my best to find out as much as I can in the time I have left," I assured him.

"Just find that city," he snarled before leaving once more.

I glanced over my shoulder, watching him depart before heaving a sigh of relief. I wasn't certain if I could find the city, but that didn't deter me from reaching for a piece of paper I had close by, ready to take notes. As I worked, a smile gradually spread across my face. I followed the intricate lines throughout the numerous pages, noticing that the book was constructed in the same manner as the one in the castle on my island. I wondered if the same individuals had created both.

However, as I looked at the author's name, I was taken aback to see a horizontal line underneath the *i* in the name. It extended down to the bottom of the page, and I observed that this first page was thicker than the others. I grabbed a small knife, and although uncertain if it would yield anything, I began to carefully separate the page.

The page split in two, and I cut through it completely, creating two separate pages. As I unfolded it, I discovered another name written inside. It was undoubtedly a woman's name, but what brought a broad smile to my lips was the Omega symbol beneath the name, indicating it was an Omega who had authored the book. Could it be the same with my book back at the castle? Had she crafted that one as well? Why wasn't I surprised it had been obscured by a man's name? I shook my head before returning to my work, tracing the lines to each letter. While I transcribed them, I noticed they spelled out a word.

"Berachia," I read aloud, my mind struggling to

recall if I had ever encountered that word before.

I tapped a finger against the table when, suddenly, the doors behind me were thrust open. I glanced over my shoulder, noticing two guards at the library entrance. I stood up, realizing how late it had become as I gazed out the windows. Time had passed quickly, but when I hesitated to move, the guards approached.

"Omega!" one of them called out before gesturing for me to follow.

They urged me forward as we exited the library, heading toward the throne room. My Alpha's booming voice reached my ears even before we entered the room, and my heart raced at the dark timbre of it. It sent delightful shivers down my spine and brought a wide smile to my lips. The doors swung open, revealing my Alpha pacing in front of the king, who was seated on his throne. Clan leaders and a few Alphas were scattered throughout the room.

"I want her *now*!" Cartan bellowed. "How dare you think you can steal her away?"

The king appeared bored, as if he didn't consider abducting me from Cartan to be a problem. However, I couldn't stop smiling. Seeing him again felt like a breath of fresh air. Being separated from him for days had left me unsettled in a way I hadn't even realized until he stood a few feet away from me. I needed him as much as I needed air.

"I should fucking kill you right now!" Cartan growled.

"Your Omega and child are safe. They were fed and well taken care of. I simply borrowed her," the king explained.

"*Borrowed*?" Cartan roared, turning to the king. "You don't fucking borrow my Omega! You little—"

"Cartan!" I called out, and my Alpha spun around.

So did everyone else, but I only saw him.

He looked at me with wide eyes, and I rushed into his arms. In no time, he caught me, and I wrapped my legs around his waist, holding onto him tightly. His hands explored my body, checking for injuries without letting me go, and he inhaled my scent, making sure I was truly unharmed.

"I'm never letting you go again," he whispered in my ear. "From now on, you're always by my side."

His words filled my heart with warmth, and I clung to him even tighter before someone cleared their throat. Cartan reluctantly let me down on my feet and turned to the king.

"This will not go unpunished," he warned.

"Cartan, he didn't hurt me," I reassured him.

"I don't fucking care. This disrespect you've shown frees me from any vow I made regarding finding an Omega," Cartan snarled.

"That's fine. I didn't expect you to honor your word anyway."

Cartan didn't appreciate his integrity being questioned, and his growl darkened.

"That's why I retrieved your Omega. And tell me, little one, has your journey borne any fruit?" the king asked, turning to me.

"Not unless you know what 'Berachia' means," I replied. However, the king was a master of deception. His expression remained unchanged, revealing nothing. I couldn't discern whether the word held any significance for him, but he gave me a slight nod before dismissively waving his hand.

"You have your Omega now. You can leave," he said.

Cartan growled and moved forward, but I grabbed his hand, holding him back. Cartan turned to me, running a hand through my hair and pulling me close to his body. I could feel his entire frame vibrating with anger, but I understood the king's drastic decision. There weren't enough Omegas to go around, and Cartan was duty-bound to prioritize the clan.

I wasn't sure what Cartan's plans were regarding the king, but I knew for certain that starting a war with him would be unwise. The king was too cunning, too unpredictable, and the fact that he hadn't harmed me or used me to corner Cartan showed that he understood not to make an enemy out of my Alpha either.

"He took you," Cartan growled.

"Let it go. I'm fine, truly. It's not worth losing lives over. Let it be," I whispered and buried my nose in his chest.

An unsatisfied rumble emanated from Cartan, but I knew it was more crucial to him to get me back to his tent and into our nest. That's where I wanted to be as well. Cartan cast another warning glare at the king with his eyes before he lifted me, carrying me in his arms, and we all turned away from the throne room.

However, I peeked over Cartan's shoulder and saw the king smiling at me. I didn't like that smile, so I buried my face in Cartan's neck, seeking his strength.

Chapter Forty-Seven
Cartan

My Omega should never have been in this perilous situation. I was prepared to dismantle every brick of the city's protective wall if necessary to rescue her. However, instead of encountering resistance, the city gates were wide open, and the king himself stood ready to welcome us. Initially, I suspected it was a ruse, but that wasn't the case.

He gestured with his arm, signaling for us to leave the army outside. I insisted that the other clan leaders and a small group of fighters accompany us, just to be cautious. Though the king didn't seem pleased with the arrangement, he agreed without protest. I trusted the Alpha king very little, and I was ready to unleash my fury upon him. However, the moment my Omega appeared and I held her in my arms again, my anger dissolved. She was right. It wasn't worth sacrificing lives when she was safe and sound, along with the little Alpha growing inside her.

Once we were away from the city, back in the desert, and had set up camp for the night, I wasted no time tearing her dress away and lavishing every inch of her body with my attention. I meticulously checked for any injuries or signs of harm, but I found no bruises and no traces of any other male on her intimate parts. There was no indication she had endured any ill treatment, and she appeared strong enough to smile and writhe beneath my touch.

Barely a moment passed before she was climaxing for me, as eager for her Alpha as I was for her. I savored her taste before moving up her body and joining with her. She clung to me, her nails digging into my back and ass, urging me to go deeper and take her harder.

Her cries grew louder, spurring me on to claim her with all my might, holding nothing back. She shattered beneath me, calling out my name, and it made my body convulse with my release as I knotted her and filled her with my essence, marking her all over again. She panted in my ear as we remained locked together, but then she whispered the most precious words she could ever say, "I love you."

I pulled back, stunned by her confession, and she offered me the most radiant smile.

"What?" I whispered.

She reached up, her hands caressing my neck, sending delightful shivers down my spine.

"I love you," she repeated.

I had never imagined I would desire anyone's love. The person who should have loved me, wanted me, had never done so. Yet this remarkable Omega, with her sharp mind and inner strength, had somehow given me everything I had ever longed for. She completed me as an Alpha, and I leaned closer to her, gently brushing my lips over hers.

"I was never taught to love," I confessed, kissing her cheek and nuzzling her neck. "I'm not certain I fully comprehend the feeling, but everything you do to me makes me want to kneel before you and show my gratitude. You're my Omega, the one I didn't even know I was waiting for. There's no one I desire more than you, and I would tear down this world if anything were to happen to you."

I reached between us, caressing her stomach, ensuring she understood that my words extended to our child. Nothing would ever harm what was mine. I would always be there to protect them.

"You do know love," she assured me, causing me

to gaze down at her once more.

I shook my head.

"But you do, otherwise you wouldn't have come for me."

"Of course I would have."

"Not with an army, not with the threat of starting a war," she explained. "I would have been important to you because of what I can give you, and you would have come with words, a request to retrieve me. You wouldn't have promised the king's death. You may not speak the words, but you demonstrate them, and I desire that even more."

She pushed up to plant a tender kiss on my lips, and my entire body quivered. This Omega held me captive, and I never wanted her to release me.

"You have me, all that I am," I vowed. "Until the end of our days."

As soon as my knot released her, we mated throughout the night, ensuring she knew that I was wholly and irrevocably hers.

Chapter Forty-Eight
Cartan

"But that's only two," I pointed out to Tyros, who nodded.

"I'm aware."

"Then where by the Gods is the third?"

Tyros shook his head. "This was all the scouts brought back. They have been keeping an eye on them for a while."

"Why? I ordered them seized and brought here!"

"Well, it might be complicated with the eldest." He coughed uncomfortably and scratched his neck.

"Why?"

He reached out, pointing lower on the paper, and I read the report before reclining my chair in my tent, carefully examining every detail the scouts had provided.

"I see..."

"Will you tell her?" he asked.

"I will, but not tonight. However, we need to locate the third. She has been gone for far too long without anyone knowing where she is. I fear the worst," I admitted.

"We are looking. I promise you, High Alpha, we have everyone searching for her."

"The second one I want brought here," I informed him. "If she is on this side of the ocean, she should be relatively easy to capture."

"Shall I inform the other High Alphas?" Tyros asked.

"I believe we must. They will be furious if they slip through my grasp once more."

Tyros smiled a little. "At least you don't have another Omega to distract you."

"No, but the sisters are Omegas too, and from what I have now experienced, I know how hard they are to resist," I teased, hearing Tyros chuckle.

"I will let the other High Alphas know," Tyros said. He was about to turn away when my Omega stepped in, dressed in a dark-green stola, her hair braided. She smiled sweetly at us, then looked curiously between us.

"Why are you two in here? We are having a party," she reminded us.

"We are coming, little Omega," I told her, standing up, and she noticed me putting the report down.

"What is that?"

"Not important tonight. I will tell you later."

I walked over to her, wrapping an arm around her waist, and we left to go outside. We walked toward where the party was being held, but we had barely joined the festivities before people began exclaiming in worry, Alphas grew tense, and growling filled the air as a group of riders entered the camp at full speed.

I pulled my Omega closer, and a group of Alphas formed behind us, ready to defend her too. However, as soon as I saw the white lines drawn on the horses, I recognized who was approaching.

"Relax. They are not a threat," I assured them, yet everyone remained uncertain.

Soon, the horses slowed down, and the Alphas on them took in the sight of everything. The one in the front, with slightly greying hair and a broad smile on his lips, kept his eyes on me and my Omega.

"You do know they have every right to kill you for entering this way, don't you?" I teased.

"I had to see if it was true. It seems my son found his Omega after all," Kiran said.

"I certainly did."

"Son?" my Omega questioned and looked up at

me, and I smiled down at her.

It didn't take long for her to understand that this was the Alpha who had found me all alone in the desert and had saved my life.

"Oh!" she exclaimed, then smiled at Kiran, who slid from his horse.

My Omega was faster than me and hurried over to Kiran, jumping up and hugging his neck. I tried to suppress my growl because I knew my little Omega was just showing her appreciation, but it was hard not to want to tear Kiran apart. He was smart, though, knowing not to hug her back, but he smiled at me, understanding the respect that was given to him for being allowed to be so close to my Omega. However, I couldn't take it for long and quickly pulled her back to me. She wrapped her arms around me to appease me as I welcomed the group of riders.

"Join us," I told them, and the group quickly mingled with the rest. The other High Alphas weren't very happy to begin with, but they relaxed more and more as the riders showed no signs of aggression and simply wanted to celebrate that an Omega was finally among us.

However, late in the evening, I saw Tyros talking to the other High Alphas, and then Peros stormed away, which set me off a little.

"Why did he seem angry?" Kiandra questioned.

I had hoped to wait to explain it to her, but it seemed that wasn't going to happen, and I turned to her. "I believe we might have found two of your sisters. One of them is here, as you told me."

"Cassia?"

"Yes."

"Where are the rest?" she asked.

"Your eldest is still on the Rocky Island, but we

don't know where Solana is," I explained.

"What? How is that possible?"

"I don't know, but we will find out," I assured her before I kissed her on top of her head. "It will be okay, little Omega. I will bring back your family."

Kiandra clung to me even tighter, and when she looked up at me, I saw the endless trust she had in me. Though I knew she wanted to go search for her sisters herself, she allowed it to be my task and instead turned to Kiran to learn even more about him. It thrilled me to see how close they had already become, and I couldn't thank the Gods more for bringing my Omega to me. She was not just the woman I cared for more deeply than anything in this world. She was my goddess, the air in my lungs, and the reason my heart even beat in my chest. I would never let this Omega go. She was mine, and I would spend the rest of my life showing her why picking me as her Alpha was the right choice.

Chapter Forty-Nine
Marac

Allowing Cartan to take his Omega home had always been my plan. I only required her presence long enough to guide me in the right direction. When he took her away, I made my way to the library where she had been diligently working. I couldn't help but notice her uneasiness around me. The little Omega was clearly keeping something from me.

Over time, I had honed my ability to read people's expressions and intentions, distinguishing the genuine from the deceitful. I had learned to identify those who were trustworthy and those better suited for the wolves. However, this particular Omega had a vulnerability. Once she immersed herself in her work, the world faded away, along with her concerns. I noticed she had been taking notes, so I retraced my steps to the library, discovering scattered papers and even the small markers she had placed in the book she had been reading.

More importantly, the information she had given me—the name—was enough to set me on a path. It meant nothing to her, but I had heard that name before. It had featured in a fairy tale my mother used to tell me when I was a child. After perusing Kiandra's notes, I navigated the library to a section filled with myths and legends. There, I selected a thick book bearing the same name Kiandra had mentioned and brought it back to the table. As I opened it, I found the exact swirling lines as in the book she had been reading.

"Clever little Omega," I praised with a smile on my lips.

I walked out of the library, summoning a servant.

"Yes, my King?" she inquired.

"No one is allowed to enter until I leave the library. Bring me food and water," I instructed her. I noted the puzzled expression on her face, but she bowed, acknowledging my order.

Returning to the library, a smile remained on my face as I sat down and resumed studying the notes made by the Omega.

Epilogue
Kiandra

Months Later, deep in the Black Desert...

A sharp pain jolted me awake. I opened my eyes, gazing into the dark expanse of Cartan's chest, feeling an unfamiliar sensation. The pain subsided, but a lingering sense of unease remained. Everything seemed unnaturally quiet, quieter than any night I had ever experienced. Then, a deafening boom shattered the silence. While I had grown accustomed to the rainless storms that occasionally plagued the desert, this one felt more powerful than any I had previously encountered. Another thunderclap reverberated through me, and the pain surged once again, causing me to groan. Cartan stirred behind me, sensing my discomfort.

"What's wrong?" he whispered in my ear. I became aware of how damp I felt between my legs.

"C-Cartan, I think the baby is coming," I managed to gasp.

"What?" Cartan swiftly turned me onto my back, and I hissed in pain as another sharp contraction coursed through me.

"Get the healers," I whispered urgently.

Cartan reacted swiftly, leaving the nest and donning pants before exiting the tent. By the time he returned, I had been moved to an open area, where the healers could work more effectively. They encircled me, but Cartan found a place at my side, providing unwavering support as I brought our son into the world. The storm outside seemed to mirror my pain, growing fiercer and louder than any previous ones, drowning out my own screams. However, the moment our son cried out loudly, displaying his strength as he left my body, everything else fell silent.

The healers carefully severed the umbilical cord and wrapped our newborn in a soft swaddle before gently placing him in my arms. I turned my head to gaze up at my Alpha, witnessing the love in his eyes as he regarded both of us. He had often professed that he didn't comprehend the concept of love, but I could see it reflected in his eyes—for me, our pack, our clans, and most importantly, our son. I pulled him closer, our lips meeting in a tender kiss.

"I love you so much," I whispered, observing his eyes glisten with the happiness.

His purring began immediately, and he pressed his forehead against mine as the healers continued their work around us. In that moment, we felt nothing but each other. This was the power of a true bond—a love that would endure for eternity.

The End

ANNE T. THYSSEN

EVERNIGHT PUBLISHING ®

www.evernightpublishing.com

suppressed a moan of her own. Her horrid green gown felt several sizes too small as it chafed her taut nipples, and the heavy fabric combined with her kirtle meant she couldn't easily access the throbbing pearl between her legs, begging to be stroked.

All she could do was watch.

Watch and yearn and imagine.

Isla pressed her knuckles to her mouth as Glennoe shuddered and panted, his fingers tangling in Master Graham's luxurious hair as he thrust. They gazed at each other with lusty tenderness, the way Sir Lachlan and his ladies had, and envy nearly choked her. She wanted to join them. To have Glennoe's cock in her mouth, his fingers in her hair, and Master Graham's talented tongue buried in her wet cunt.

"Alastair," Glennoe rasped. "Feels so good...I'm going to spend..."

Master Graham continued to rub and squeeze the laird's swollen cock as he sucked and lapped at it. A moment later a raw, brutal cry echoed in the room as the laird's back arched and pearly seed erupted from the tip into his squire's mouth and onto his bearded chin.

Aroused beyond measure, a low wail of agonized need tore from her throat.

Time nearly halted. The two men looked at her with horrified dismay as they hastily disengaged, cleaned themselves with a linen cloth and righted their clothing, before walking toward her.

Isla couldn't move. Couldn't even flee as shamed guilt and unfulfilled desire turned her usually nimble feet to stone. She could only stare, her heart nearly thumping out of her chest, her cheeks hot enough to boil water.

"Lady Isla," said Glennoe, his face ashen. "We did not expect...that is—"

"Forgive me," she blurted. "I'm here to...the sword

lessons...I did not mean to watch. But I could not look away. I've never seen such *passion*."

The two men stilled and exchanged a glance.

"You are not distressed?" asked Master Graham warily.

Isla shook her head so hard her gable hood fell to the floor. "I have seen women kiss," she began, not wanting to reveal who, for that was Lady Janet and Lady Marjorie's tale to tell. "Not like friends, like lovers. If they kiss and touch each other, then of course there must be men who do the same."

"Indeed," murmured Glennoe, his tension easing a little.

"But...those women also kissed a man with the same passion. So I think some people like to kiss both. Do you only like to kiss each other, or, er...women too?"

It was a bold question, far too bold for such a short acquaintance. Yet she had to know. A husband who did not desire her would be most unwelcome, no matter how kind. She had *needs*.

"Both," said Master Graham, looking remarkably unruffled by the question. "Callum...my laird and I also enjoy kissing women. Bedding them."

"Do you bed them together? As three?"

His eyes widened. Then his gaze heated to pure sapphire. "We have not," he replied softly. "*Yet*."

Isla whimpered, pressing her thighs together in a futile attempt to ease the ache in her throbbing center. After what she'd watched and this wicked conversation, she desperately needed release.

"Would you like to sit, Lady Isla?" asked Glennoe as he held out his hand, his gray eyes glittering.

She stumbled forward like she'd made merry with an entire barrel of wine, near-feverish with lust. The laird's hand was smoother than hers but surprisingly strong, and she accepted his assistance gratefully as he led her over to the chaise. When she sat down on the cool beaten leather surface, a new scent teased her nose. Musky. Earthy...

Oh.

The cloth they had used to wipe his seed away rested on the low wooden table beside the chaise.

Isla bit her lip, her limbs trembling.

The laird frowned. "Are you frightened, lady?"

"No," she said bluntly. "I've never felt unsafe with you or Master Graham. But my cun..."

The word died on her lips. It was so commonly used, but some men pursed their lips if a noblewoman said it. While she didn't think that these two would chide her, it was never wise to assume anything.

Master Graham leaned against the fireplace. "Pray continue. Be honest and say your sweet little cunt is soaking wet and requires relief."

Isla nodded, almost miserable in her acute need. "It aches. I touched myself in bed this morning, but that is such a long time ago."

"Do you often do so?"

"Yes. It feels nice. I like to, even if it lands me in trouble. Actually, the thought of trouble has never halted me from doing something. But you know that already."

Both men laughed.

"Well," said Glennoe, his gaze approving. "If you wish to touch yourself, we certainly won't stop you. It shall be our secret. Or..."

"Or?" asked Isla breathlessly.

Master Graham smiled. "Or, you might ask Glennoe to assist. He has a wicked tongue, and if you've not had your cunt licked before, let today be the day you learn such pleasures."

Her body screamed '*yes*'. But her head warned caution. "Just that? I mean, I cannot do more."

"Just that," said Glennoe firmly. "If you wish. I would use my lips and tongue between your legs until you gain ease. Alastair would watch."

"Yes," she said. "*Yes.*"

"Then lift your gown," said Master Graham. "Now."

On another occasion she might have played coy; raised it slowly to tease. But her need was far too great. Instead, Isla yanked up her gown, kirtle, and shift, before spreading her thighs wide in invitation. The scent of her arousal perfumed the room, but rather than any dismay, both men gazed at her reverently. Hungrily.

Glennoe dropped to his knees between her legs, parted the bush of dark hair and exposed her tender pink flesh. Then, without further ado, he leaned forward and licked her.

Isla bucked at the intense jolt of sensation. But the gentle laird was ruthless as he dragged his tongue back and forth along her slick folds, circling her pearl, even penetrating her tight entrance and darting inside. It felt good. No, far better than good. *Divine.*

A ragged gasp escaped her lips. "More."

"Yes, Callum," rasped Master Graham. "Fuck her with your tongue. Lap up all that sweet honey."

Isla moaned. "Your cock is hard. Touch it if you want to."

The squire slowly pulled down his hose, revealing an enormous thick erection. As he began to caress it with those paw-sized palms, the lewd sight combined with the heavenly suction of Glennoe's lips on her delicate pearl, hurled her over the edge. Isla ground hard against Glennoe's mouth and chin as bright starbursts exploded behind her eyes, crying out with pleasure as she gripped the chaise arm and writhed in bliss.

Saints alive.

Only her best swordplay victory could possibly compare to that.

He'd finished second in his race and progressed to tomorrow's archery event. Alastair had brought him to a thunderous release with his mouth and hands. Now he'd made Lady Isla cry out with pleasure, and had the heavenly taste of her spiced honey on his tongue.

All in all, a splendid day.

Gulping air to calm his racing heart, Callum leaned against the arm of the chaise and watched Alastair handle his engorged cock, the strain of release denied apparent on his face.

"Will you spend in my mouth, Alastair?" he asked. "Then I'll have the taste of both of you there."

"Please do," said Lady Isla hoarsely. "The two of you together takes my breath away."

His squire stalked toward him like a rampant beast, and Callum went up on his knees to receive the thick length dripping with pearly moisture. One of Alastair's huge hands curled around his neck and gripped it, a show of dominance so arousing he shuddered.

"Suck me, my laird," growled Alastair, easing his cock into Callum's mouth.

Heady excitement rushed through him. Tasting his squire's cock, being ordered to pleasure him while Lady Isla watched avidly and touched herself...he'd never felt quite so *necessary*. So wanted. His hands moved up Alastair's thighs, one to circle the base of his cock, and one so he might stroke his heavy balls. Then Callum closed his lips around the warm, pulsing flesh, using his tongue to tease the underside of Alastair's cock, and hollowing his cheeks to increase the tug and pull. The earthy seed was delicious and he sucked greedily for more.

Alastair groaned, the smooth, shallow thrusts becoming

unsteady, rougher and deeper, until that glorious hardness fucked Callum's mouth. He breathed through his nose, kept his throat relaxed, unwilling to surrender even a moment of being owned in this way. The other man's sounds of enjoyment filled the room, but Callum could also hear fingers penetrating slick cunt, and the lusty scents of feminine honey, sweat, and seed hardened his own cock again.

Alastair turned to Lady Isla. "My laird's mouth is a priceless treasure, wouldn't you agree?"

"Yes," she gasped. "P-perfection. Now fill it. Make him take your seed. Every drop."

His squire thrust harder. "Heed the lady. Every drop."

Callum moaned, feverishly sucking and licking, and when he delved further between Alastair's legs to stroke his back entrance, a guttural roar nearly shook the furniture. Warm, sticky seed gushed into his mouth and he swallowed it down; Lady Isla's wild cry of release prompting his own to soak the front of his hose.

After carefully withdrawing his cock, Alastair sank onto the chaise next to Lady Isla. Callum swayed and sat back heavily on his arse, his head resting on the chaise. None were capable of speech.

It might have been minutes or hours later, but abruptly Lady Isla giggled.

Callum turned his head to glance up. "What amuses you?"

"I lied my way here from the castle for swordplay...not quite the swordplay I thought, though."

He didn't laugh. "You call yourself unconventional, but you are a jewel, Lady Isla. Rare and fine. Any man should be proud to have you on his arm—at court in a gown, or in hose and shirt with sword in hand."

"Just Isla in private," she said softly, as she rose to her feet.

"Then we are Alastair and Callum," said Alastair. "Are you...must you leave?"

"Ha! You might wish it soon enough; it's time for a sword lesson. Callum, put on fresh shirt and hose, and lend me some too, if you please. Alastair, would you assist me in removing my gown and kirtle?"

After a swift sponge bath Callum dressed himself, then selected some choice items of clothing for Isla and brought them out to her. She stood near the fire wearing naught but stockings.

God's blood.

Her body was so lithe. Long legs, flat belly, small breasts with surprisingly large nipples, and a tight arse. Her skin was Highland pale, which made the contrast of her green eyes, rosy nipples, and black hair and bush even more prominent.

"You are staring, Callum," she said archly as she tugged on the borrowed hose, but there was uncertainty in her gaze.

"Because you are beautiful."

"I am not. My mother and sisters are. Fair-haired angels all, with breasts and hips to cushion a lover."

"Not everyone seeks that," said Alastair as he watched her pull on a fine linen shirt. "Some find a wild lass with green eyes and a perfect arse very fine indeed."

Isla looked genuinely astonished. "Oh. Well. I...ah...shall we clear a space inside? Is there a private courtyard behind the cottage?"

Callum shook his head. "Nay. And close neighbors besides."

"Then in here it shall be. We don't need much space today, for I'll show you grip and stance to begin with. It may sound dull, but every tutor I've had spent a great deal of time on this. As I must be back at the castle before the supper hour, fetch your sword, please."

When Callum retrieved his longsword and handed it to her, Isla unsheathed it in one smooth, expert movement and examined it closely.

"Hmmm," she mused. "Good balance. Nice weight. But I must scold you for your care of it. How often do you oil the blade?"

Alastair coughed meaningfully, and Callum's cheeks heated.

"Er..."

"*Callum*. It must be wiped after each use. Sweat, blood, spit...all corrode the steel."

"It is rarely oiled for it is rarely used," admitted Callum, looking away in shame. What kind of laird avoided a longsword because it provoked so many memories of snarling lectures, cut and blistered hands, beatings, and cruel taunts? His father had eventually given up in disgust, instead loudly praising Red and the other lads in the clan for their fighting prowess. To Donald MacIntyre, only one skill had mattered: that with a sword.

Gentle fingers grasped his chin and turned his head, urging him to look at her.

"Have you had a bad experience?" asked Isla, her brow furrowed. "Tell me plainly. Perhaps a sound defeat? There is no shame in that; I have landed in the dirt with a sword tip at my throat more times than there are stars in the sky. But as Sir Lachlan used to say, *on your feet and try again. Tomorrow, you shall be better*."

"You had a far superior teacher, then," said Alastair with a dark scowl.

Callum sent him a quelling look. "No need to dig that body up—"

"Ah, a bad training experience then," said Isla briskly, yet her gaze was kind. "That is important for me to know, for now I understand where the reluctance stems from. Are you confident in your grip?"

He hesitated. "I believe so. My right hand is my strongest so it sits closest to the crossguard. But I have little force."

"That relies on where your weaker hand sits. For more force, it must be directly below your stronger hand. For flexibility, slide that weaker hand down to the end of the grip."

"Sounds too easy."

Smiling jauntily, Isla swung his longsword up in a perfect arc to rest on her right shoulder. If he tried that, he would lose an ear. But Callum couldn't stop staring at her pose, the expert grip, the long legs encased in hose, the fine linen shirt that in no way disguised her large pink nipples. Thoroughly distracting.

"Laird," she said patiently, "I've already removed your head in battle."

Alastair cleared his throat. "He's not going to be facing those pretty nipples in battle."

"More's the pity. I will admit to binding my breasts in the past. And wearing a longer, much coarser tunic. Now, show me your footwork."

"Or you could show me how it's done?" Callum asked hopefully.

"Very well. Stand back. There are several critical steps in sword fighting. Advance, retreat, sidestep, diagonal step and false step. First, I shall show you a proper advance..."

He watched in awe as Isla moved the sword from her shoulder to a fighting stance, the grip level with her cheekbone, then demonstrated steps going back, forth, and side to side.

"Do you stop to brace for an attack?" asked Alastair curiously.

Isla shook her head. "If I am moving, my opponent never knows what I am about to do. There is also less chance of them landing a deadly blow. But this does not mean you should dance about, tiring yourself. Every step must have purpose. Now. Both of you, fight with imaginary swords. Show me your feet. How would you sidestep to avoid an attack? How would you lure your opponent into a mistake with a false step?"

As a tutor, Isla was nothing like his father. Apart from her staggering expertise, she offered praise and encouragement as they repeated the same movements over and over until Callum was sure he'd be stepping in his sleep. It was humbling to know she taught him the easiest of skills, some she'd probably mastered as a child, for he could certainly see Isla convincing someone to teach her. Even more humbling that he would never reach her mastery of the sword, not in a thousand years.

But these lessons gave him the chance to improve himself, win the tourney and Isla's hand, and save his clan.

A chance for he, Isla and Alastair to be together for always?

Callum quickly suppressed the thought.

That would be hoping for far too much.

CHAPTER 5

The second day of the tourney dawned cool and cloudy after overnight rain, and did not grow warmer as noon approached.

Callum glanced at the men who stood to the left and right of him. Eighteen including his cousin remained for the archery, and while Red laughed and jested with the other entrants, most looked uneasy now that the king had announced the day's rules. Rather than everyone attempting to hit the center of one large target like a tree trunk, or a covered mound of earth known as a butt, they would be roving. James had arranged three targets of varying size and distance away, and each entrant would have three attempts to hit it with an arrow. If they succeeded, they progressed to the next target. If they missed...their tourney ended and they had to leave the field.

Oddly enough, archery was the event that concerned him least. With his average height and lean build, the short bow had always been his weapon of choice; fast, deadly, and best of all, it allowed distance between him and whatever he was trying to shoot. He had little chance with fists, mace, or battle axe, but bow and arrow...he could be quietly confident. Even the most judgmental members of his clan admitted that he had talent with this weapon, although they would never give it equal rank to skill with a longsword.

A warm, familiar hand settled on Callum's shoulders, and it took all his will not to lean back against Alastair, or even turn and rest his cheek against his squire's chest to hear the comforting thump of his heartbeat. After their lusty play with Isla, then his first sword lesson, he'd slept like a cat on a sun-drenched window seat last night. Probably why he felt so calm. Unlike many here, he was well rested and refreshed.

"Are you ready, laird?" murmured Alastair. "And by ready, I mean primed to crush all comers like they are fresh herbs and you a mortar and pestle?"

Callum's lips twitched. "Don't tempt the devil to spite me. With the dampness in the air, our arrows could fly in any direction."

"You have three for each target, so can correct if necessary. Your band of adoring followers—noble and commoner—expect great things."

At last, a laugh escaped him. "I shall endeavor not to disappoint."

Soon afterward a trumpet blast echoed around the field, and Sir Lachlan called the entrants to prepare for the start of the archery. Their first target was a straw man, wearing an old linen shirt with a large red circle painted on it, set at a distance of eighty yards.

One by one, each man drew back and released his arrow. All eventually succeeded in hitting the target, although a few were outside the circle, and some men needed a second attempt. Then Callum stepped up, took a single arrow from his quiver, and set it to his bow. Keeping his gaze unwaveringly on the red circle, he drew the string taut with three fingers, one above the arrow and two below. Then, with a deep breath to slow his racing heart, he let it fly. The arrow traveled toward the straw man so fast it was almost a blur, before embedding itself near the center of the circle.

The crowd applauded, and he allowed himself a small smile. A good start.

Their second target was much closer at sixty yards away but half the size; a fat cushion painted to look like a shield and held taut between two wooden poles with rope.

Again, Sir Lachlan arranged them in a line. "You have three attempts. If you succeed, you move to...the final target. If not, you must...retire from the tourney."

One by one each man released his arrow, although more needed a second attempt this time. A knight in front of Callum missed with his first and second...then his third. The crowd gasped as he let out a loud string of Gaelic curses and was unwillingly escorted from the field by two burly guards.

When the noise eventually waned, Callum stepped forward. Once more he set himself carefully, his gaze on the center of the cushion, before releasing his arrow. It flew straight and true, and pierced the middle of the false 'shield'. Only then did he allow himself a swift glance at Alastair, who grinned and nodded. When he looked at the pavilion, Isla raised her goblet in a discreet salute and even the king applauded.

But now came the third target, one that would take their full measure as archers. Although it sat at a distance of just forty yards, it was the size and shape of a goose, atop a wooden pole lodged in the ground. The other entrants grumbled among themselves as they formed a line, and even Callum gulped. Each time he blinked, the target seemed to grow smaller and move farther away. But he wasn't alone in these thoughts, for in the first fifteen archers, several required two arrows to succeed, and five more were forced to leave the field after all of their arrows missed the goose entirely.

"Next...the MacDonald of Carnoch!"

To the sound of loud cheers, Red unleashed his first arrow.

And missed.

Elation surged through Callum, but he forced himself to remain still and quiet. When his turn came, he could easily do the same. Besides, his cousin had not missed the target by much, perhaps a few inches at most.

Red's second arrow hit the outside of the goose, but rather than lodging in the taut stuffed fabric, it fell to the ground.

"Fail!" called Sir Lachlan.

Clearly shocked at the judgment, Red jerked around to glare at the king's champion. "How can you say that? My arrow was true."

"Nay. The rule is...an arrow must pierce and remain. You have one last chance, MacDonald. If you miss...you retire."

Callum's heart near pounded out of his chest as Red set his stance and took aim with his third and final arrow.

Miss. Miss. Miss.

The arrow flew through the air, the short feathers rippling in the slight breeze. Everyone understood the gravity of the moment; not a soul on the field moved or made a sound, not even the young children or those selling refreshments.

Miss. Miss. Miss.

The arrow thudded into the false goose.

Wild applause erupted, and the people chanted Red's name as they threw sprigs of purple heather onto the edge of the field. Red waved and bowed before turning and walking to Callum.

"Did you see that, cousin?" he said in a low voice, his eyes gleaming. "My arrow pierced that goose the way my cock will take Lady Isla's virginity. Hard and deep."

Callum's fingers clenched around his bow. "Do not speak of her so."

Red laughed and leaned down to speak directly into Callum's ear. "Oh-ho! Has the lady a protector in the little laird? Do not delude yourself, there is no chance you will take her to wife. Lady Isla and her coin shall be mine. She'll soon know who her master is, and if she is slow to learn...I've a whip to assist. That proud, defiant bitch will learn her place."

A startlingly feral snarl tore from Callum's throat; he jerked away from his cousin and threw his bow to the ground, wanting nothing more than to tear the man limb from limb.

Until a heavy hand clamped on his shoulder.

"Something the matter, Glennoe?" growled Sir Lachlan.

Callum gulped. Only a damned fool would succumb to Red's deliberate baiting. If he hit his cousin as his fists itched to do, he would be thrown out of the tourney and Alastair and Isla would rightly think the worst of him. The king's champion had just done him a great service, even if it did not feel like one.

Closing his eyes briefly to regain composure, he then turned and faced the judge. "Nay, Sir Lachlan. My bow... slipped from my hand, but all is well."

"Good. Rory MacDonald, you have progressed...to the stone put. No need to remain. Return to your tent. *Now*."

Red's lip curled, but he inclined his head the barest distance and walked away.

Abruptly Sir Lachlan turned to the royal pavilion and beckoned one of the men at arms. "Bring a new goose! This one has...too many holes."

Startled at the unexpected boon of time, Callum leaned down to retrieve his bow. First, he tested the tautness of the draw, before adjusting the leather guard protecting his left forearm. Slowly, his rage dwindled and his thundering heart calmed. In truth, Sir Lachlan had done him two services this day, far more favor than he deserved. But why? The Lord of Glennoe was certainly the least important title remaining, and it wasn't like he'd led an army for the king, built a splendid palace, or discovered some wondrous elixir to cure all ills.

"Our last entrant, Callum MacIntyre, Lord of Glennoe!"

Callum stepped up.

Now or never.

⚜

Would it be so wrong to heave Red MacDonald from the ramparts of Stirling Castle?

Alastair watched the man stalk back to his tent. Whatever he'd said to Callum, it had provoked a strong reaction. For a laird renowned as cool and calm and a man of peace to throw down his bow and appear ready to let fists fly...

He folded his arms, lest he get himself into trouble. Sir Lachlan had intervened on the field; to confront Red and spark that flint again would be unforgivable. Especially when it was Callum's chance to progress to the stone put event on the morrow. Plague take it, he could scarcely bear to watch, even though he knew how talented his laird was. Six men had already departed the field in defeat this day and after Red progressing by the narrowest of margins, it would be a travesty if Callum did not. Yet there was nothing he could do. Prayer seemed rather pointless, it wasn't like he and God were on particularly good terms.

The crowd hushed as Callum set his arrow and drew the bowstring back taut. A chill wind swept across the battlefield, ruffling his laird's shirt and hair, and it was enough to make Alastair wish he could paint or sketch. This was a moment to be captured, one of fierce concentration, courage, and leashed strength, representing the man that so few saw, but he knew intimately.

So very intimately.

Callum released the arrow, and as though guided by angels themselves, the tip pierced the goose so deeply that it rose in the air before tumbling to the ground.

All eyes darted to Sir Lachlan. He in turn gestured to the royal pavilion for the king's decision.

James laughed and thumped his hand on the wooden frame. "Glennoe, you have quite killed my goose! And just one attempt! What a fine arrow. I hereby declare you lord of the bow, and wish you good fortune in the stone put."

Noise erupted around the field, the din near deafening as the crowd clapped, stomped their feet, and yelled *Glennoe! Lord of the bow!*

Callum waved awkwardly; even from this distance his scarlet cheeks were clear to see. His laird was bashful at the public celebration of his victory, for it happened so rarely. In truth, it was galling that Callum could be feted here in Stirling for merely piercing a stuffed goose with an arrow, when everything he'd done for the MacIntyre clan was viewed with indifference at best and outright suspicion and disdain at worst. The clan measured success in one way: battles won and lost. Not kindness and self-sacrifice, meetings attended, ledgers balanced, or treaties negotiated and signed.

"Well, squire, it seems we shall remain in Stirling another day."

Alastair did not reply. Instead, with triumph and relief and aching need coursing through his veins, he ushered his laird into the privacy of the tent, cupped his face and kissed him forcefully.

Callum's hands gripped Alastair's shirt as he surrendered

for a long, sweet moment, before pulling away. "We can't. Not here."

"Forgive me," he rasped, swallowing hard against a rush of bittersweet lust, for it seemed this would forever be his lot: stolen moments of forbidden passion.

But for how much longer?

Wickedly unconventional Isla had allowed him to watch as Callum pleasured her. Had touched herself as he fucked Callum's mouth and spent down his throat. Yet he did not dare hope for more. As Callum and Isla, they might permit him to join their play. But if this tourney led to a wedding, and a new alliance with the cold and haughty Sutherlands, the Lord and Lady of Glennoe might feel quite different when the harsh reality of duty set in.

Would he ever truly belong somewhere?

"Lord of the bow!" came a voice from outside the tent. "It is Lady Isla. May I enter and offer my congratulations?"

"Of course," said Callum too-heartily.

She trudged in, one hand pressed to her belly, and Alastair frowned.

"Are you well, lady?"

Isla winked. "Alas not, Master Graham. I have a terrible stomach ache and fear I shall be resting this night rather than feasting with the king and queen, and honored guests in the Great Hall."

"Sad news indeed," said Callum solemnly, his eyes glinting.

"Very sad," echoed Alastair. "Be sure to have some, now what is it your mother recommends, laird? Boiled water with peppermint?"

"Aye. Peppermint for belly gripes."

"Thank you," said Isla, as her lips twitched madly. "Your concern is most kind. Glennoe, I wonder if you might show me your trusty bow? I should like to admire your grip."

Alastair pressed his fist to his mouth and coughed. Pure

mischief danced in Isla's eyes, she knew perfectly well the ribald meaning in her words. Plague take it, why did the woman who might overturn his precarious place in the world have to be so damned likeable?

"Here, lady," said Callum, picking up his bow and a single arrow, and settling himself into the correct stance for the benefit of anyone walking past the tent entrance. "See how I hold this at chest height?"

"Oh indeed," she replied, before moving closer and lowering her voice to the barest whisper. "I'll come to your cottage once the feast begins. My manservant Leith shall fetch me after he has delivered messages to Stirling, so less time than yesterday. I can offer some further swordplay advice, but nothing more. Much as I would like that."

Her cheeks went pink at those final words. All three exchanged heated glances; it seemed they remembered the previous afternoon's pleasures as vividly as he.

Alastair met Isla's gaze. "Why don't you hold the bow, lady? We should like to see your grip."

"I would enjoy that," she replied with such a falsely demure smile, he coughed once more.

When Isla demonstrated that she handled the weapon as well as any man earlier, she leaned close again. "I am curious, Callum. What did the MacDonald of Carnoch say to you after he succeeded with his final arrow?"

Alastair snorted. "Knowing Red, it would have centered around himself."

"You are acquainted with the laird? Oh, wait. Of course, you must be. Your lands are both in the Western Highlands?"

"Red's lands border mine to the north east," said Callum stiffly, all amusement gone from his face. "He is also my cousin. His mother is my late father's older sister."

"What did he say, Callum?" she whispered. "For I saw it angered and distracted you, and that cannot happen again."

"I'd rather not repeat something so vile. But Red would not be a good husband unto you."

Isla put her hands on her hips and glared. "Listen carefully, laird. I welcome friends who stand beside me or protect my back. But friends who stand in front of me in a misguided attempt to protect my maidenly eyes and ears will get a firm kick up the arse. I am a Sutherland. I know the twists and turns of court, and the worst impulses of men. I've heard the jests, and the threats. What do you think was said when my fall at St. Andrews revealed I was a lass? Do you think they cheered and said *well done, Isla?*"

Alastair sent his laird a stern look. "Tell us."

Callum rubbed a hand across his jaw. "Forgive me. I do not mean to belittle, only to spare you distress."

Her gaze softened. "You have a gentle soul. But I will expect my husband to share all with me. The good and the bad. To trust me, as I shall trust him."

Leaning forward, Callum beckoned them closer, so their faces almost touched. "He said a proud, defiant bitch needed to learn her place. With whip if necessary. See, I told you it was vile."

Alastair's stomach turned. He'd never liked Red. As the only son of the MacDonald laird, he'd been spoiled which had turned him cruel and spiteful. When he'd grown into a tall, bullish man and then became laird himself, those flaws only worsened. Red's decisions were made for the benefit of Red and no one else. He was about as far apart in character from Callum as it was possible to be; if Alastair had not known both men nearly his whole life, he would not believe they were even related.

"Hell-spawned devil," he snarled under his breath.

"Indeed," said Isla, as she handed back Callum's bow. "That is why it is even more important you improve your longsword skills, Callum. Expect a lad to visit your cottage."

"Good day, lady," Alastair bellowed. "We both hope you feel better soon."

"Thank you, kind sirs," she replied weakly over her shoulder as she trudged back outside to the field.

When they were alone, Alastair attempted a teasing grin. "Come, lord of the bow. The king will have another gold coin for you, then we must oil that sword of yours."

Callum's answering smile was grim at best.

The stakes were only getting higher.

❦

"Maybe I shouldn't go to the feast. Maybe the king would be impressed and offer further favor if I stayed and sat with you. He is difficult to read at times."

As her mother paced and pondered aloud beside her bed, Isla resisted the urge to shriek with frustration. Anne Sutherland had not coddled an upset, scraped knee, or belly gripe in her entire life; she had servants for that. But *tonight* she thought to play at cooing and fretting?

"I just need to rest, Mother," Isla replied, careful not to let any irritation show. That would only invite suspicion, and then she would never get to Callum and Alastair's cottage. "And have someone sing my praises at the feast. Who better than you?"

Anne nodded. "That is true. Your father will spend all his time discussing politics or battles, then jest that you could defeat the entrants in swordplay. Imagine that, your greatest flaw beside your wretched willfulness, pronounced as a virtue! No, you are correct, daughter. I must go and ensure they all know that despite your unfortunate looks, to take you to wife is to receive a great dowry, a great alliance, and with my own example and that of your sisters, an excellent chance of a fertile womb."

Under the quilt, Isla's fists clenched. "Yes, Mother. Dowry. Alliance. Womb. That is the best of me."

"Rest now," said her mother, but she was already halfway across the chamber. "Should you need anything, Morag will assist."

Aye, she would. As she always had, because Morag cared in truth, not when it made her look favorable in front of others.

After the chamber door closed, Isla counted to one hundred, then bounded out of bed and discarded her shift. From the bottom of her trunk she pulled Callum's hose and shirt that she had kept for this purpose, and after donning the hose, stood with her arms outstretched as Morag expertly bound her breasts with a length of linen bandage.

"He's a handsome one, that Glennoe," said the servant with a sly grin. "You should have told me it was him you liked. Leith says the king praises him often. Learned and steady. That is the kind of man a wild lassie needs; he can cool you, and you can warm him."

"Oh, hush," said Isla, rolling her eyes. Naturally, when she'd approached Leith for assistance, he'd told his wife. But not even they knew all of her mischief at the cottage.

All of her *wickedness*.

Leith and Morag had half the tale: a bold lady liking a laird and deciding to help him with sword lessons in secret. They certainly didn't know she'd spied on that laird being pleasured by his squire. Or that the laird had licked her cunt until she screamed in ecstasy. Or that she'd then touched herself while watching that laird suck his squire's cock and swallow his seed.

Not even her two loyal servants would assist if they knew that. Breaking the king's rule about assisting an entrant was bad enough, but doing so *and* disobeying her coldly pious mother and father to swordfight and perform lewd acts with two men...that was far too much troublemaking, even by Isla Sutherland standards.

"There," said Morag as she fastened the end of the bandage with a small knot. "How does that feel? Firm enough?"

Isla nodded and pulled the shirt over her head. After Morag braided her hair and twisted it into a tight ball at the nape of her neck, Isla donned a short cloak and one of Leith's soft velvet caps. "Young lad?"

"Aye. Now run. Leith has more messages than he thought; the king asked if he might add a few private letters to his satchel. I believe one is for the bishop. If you don't leave now, you'll be out for the entire evening and then your mother will have all our heads on a pike."

Leaning forward, she wrapped her arms around Morag. "I wish you were—"

"Here now, don't be sniffling all over me," the servant replied, patting her arm. "I've mending to do and a large dish of marzipan to eat. Away with you."

Blowing her a kiss, Isla dashed across the chamber before peering out the door into the wide, torchlit hallway. About twenty feet away, Leith leaned against the cool stone wall, his fingers drumming impatiently against his satchel, and she closed the chamber door, then hurried over to him.

The silver-haired man smirked. "You're looking remarkably well for someone with belly gripes."

"Shhh," she replied archly. "You're as tart-tongued as your wife."

"Except she gets a roaring fire and a dish of marzipan. You conceded to all her demands, didn't you?" Leith said with a mournful sigh.

Isla shook her head at the theatrics and dug into her cloak for a large handkerchief-wrapped square. "I brought you some, before you groan like an old oak tree in the wind."

He brightened, tore the handkerchief away, then devoured the entire sweet treat in two bites. "Mmmm."

"May we proceed?"

"We may," said Leith happily, as they descended the steps and crossed the inner close of Stirling Castle.

The sun was just beginning to set, giving the golden lime-washed gleam of the Great Hall a peach hue. Deliberately, Isla lifted the collar of her cloak and widened her step as the lads did. The last thing she needed was someone glancing out one of the windows and recognizing her.

The armed guards at the gate made her throat as dry as a desert, but they merely inclined their heads and waved them through with a polite, "Leith. Laddie."

When they were far enough away for privacy, Isla exhaled unsteadily. "That was easier than I thought."

Leith shrugged. "I come and go frequently with messages for your father and mother, but now the king is making use of my fine thoroughbred legs, the guards are especially courteous."

"I'm convinced Morag wed you for those legs alone."

"Quite overcome at the turn of my calf, she was," he agreed fondly. "And my hedgerow eyebrows."

Not for the first time, envy surged at the deep, abiding love Leith and Morag had for one another. Twenty-five years they'd been wed, and although she knew their lack of children hurt their hearts, it had never stopped them lavishing care and affection on each other, or waifs in their path.

Could she have a marriage like that? With a man like Callum, it certainly seemed possible. Aside from Leith, he was the kindest, warmest soul she knew, with a magical tongue and a brilliant brain. Alastair would be quite a different husband; protective, earthy, and raw. He wouldn't softly chide a tart wife, he'd be a stern master who ordered her onto her knees to take his cock in her mouth until she swallowed every drop of his seed. Or tease her swollen pearl mercilessly with his fingers while whispering lewd things in her ear, but withhold release until she begged and begged...

Isla nearly stumbled on the path.

Saints alive. Where had *that* thought come from?

She was a strong, unconventional young woman, as Morag had said, in need of a learned, steady husband. Not a rough and brawny squire with blue eyes to drown in and paw-sized hands that could both tenderly caress a cheek or possessively grip the back of a neck.

I want both. Together.

This time she did stumble, only halted from a face-first tumble down the steep path into Stirling village by Leith curling a hand under her elbow.

"Here now," he said with a furrowed brow. "You're not actually ill, are you?"

"No," she mumbled. "Quite well."

Ha. But she could hardly confess to her manservant the things she'd seen and experienced at that cozy cottage nestled near the bottom of this hill. Or that her increasingly wicked and forbidden wedding night wish was not just her husband bedding her...but her husband and their lover.

Really though, she didn't have time to ponder a wedding night, not when she had no idea who would win the tourney. Her heart and soul screamed for Callum, and he'd been nothing short of magnificent with bow and arrow in hand, but there was still the stone put and the revels to navigate before the final event of swordplay. Good men had left in defeat earlier, and vile men like that MacDonald of Carnoch had succeeded. Such was the nature of a tourney.

All she—all *they*—could do was take each day as it came.

"Here ye are then, lassie," said Leith as he halted outside Callum and Alastair's cottage. "I'll be back to fetch ye before nightfall; I have no wish to walk that hill with naught but moonlight to guide my way. Besides, we must return before the feast ends—"

"Or Mother will have all our heads on pikes, I know, I know," Isla replied with a faint grin.

"I'll knock thrice on the door. Teach him well."

"I shall," she promised.

Her very future depended upon it.

CHAPTER 6

"I'm rather envious at the care you are lavishing on that blade. Are you hoping to impress me or Isla?"

Alastair glanced up from where he sat on the chaise, polishing his laird's sword to a gleaming shine. "I want it to look like the weapon of a champion."

Callum tilted his head. "You didn't answer my question."

What was he supposed to say?

Yes, I wish to impress her. Also not just watch, but pleasure your future lady wife. Fuck her until she screams herself hoarse then hold her in my arms as I held you.

"Of course, I wish to impress. A poorly kept blade will hardly find favor with a swordfighter."

"Alastair. I know you desire Isla. You don't have to conceal it to protect me. In fact, I wish you wouldn't because I don't want any secrets between us. Unless your desire for me has cooled?"

He stilled. Callum was rarely so blunt. Then again, this was an unusual situation. "No," he said forcefully. "Never. But while I do lust for her, I won't make trouble or insist you choose...look sharp, laird. A lad approaches the front door."

"Then we should let the lad in," said Callum, smoothing his linen shirt, and his hair, for about the twentieth time.

It made Alastair want to kiss him; to disturb that perfect surface. Yet now he wanted to do the same to Isla. To leave his mark on her, let all and sundry know she was his and he would fight beside her unto death.

"Welcome lad," he called as Callum ushered Isla into the cottage.

She grinned and bowed. "Why thank you, kind sir. I see you are doing good work there."

Alastair gave the sword blade one last rub with the rag, twisting it one way and the other to ensure no oil spots or finger marks remained. "I pray it shall be deemed worthy of a warrior."

Isla discarded her cap and cloak, then sauntered toward him. His breath caught at her sheer sensuality; the confidence she had when wearing hose rather than the gowns she hated. Naturally, his thoughts turned carnal, imagining Isla naked on her hands and knees in front of him, his fingers tangled in those pitch-black curls, teasing her sweet cunt while his thumb penetrated her arse to heighten release...

"Why Alastair," she purred, raising one winged black eyebrow. "Whatever were you thinking just now?"

A polite lie slid onto his tongue, but much like Callum didn't want secrets between them, he didn't want a lie between him and Isla, even a small one.

"Lewd things."

"Oh?" Isla replied, looking interested rather than offended. "Such as?"

"You, naked, on your hands and knees. Your hair tangled about my wrist. Teasing your wet cunt while I press my thumb deep in that perfect peach arse of yours," he said abruptly.

Absolute silence filled the room. Then she pressed her thighs together.

Alastair's lips twitched. Isla was indeed a hot-blooded lass. "'Tis a shame we have little time today. After you teach Callum, we could have taught you."

"We have time," Isla whispered. "The king gave my manservant Leith private messages to deliver also. He'll be back to fetch me at nightfall so I return to my, er, sickbed before the feast ends. His wife Morag is guarding the chamber from concerned visitors."

"Well then. Callum? Shall we strike a bargain with the lady? Sword lesson for pleasure lesson?"

His laird joined them in the space cleared for practice. "Only if you wish, Isla. I am grateful you are here at all, for I know the risks you are taking to help me."

Isla smiled. "Oh, I wish to. Very much. As to the risk...all the more reason to do as much as I can in the time that I have. So let us dance, Callum. Today I will show you the best ways to defend yourself. Alastair, fetch your sword. I need you to be the devilish beast that he may face on the battlefield."

He handed her Callum's sword before unsheathing his own and taking up a stance in the center of the room. "One devilish beast at your service, lady. Do you require sounds? A few growls or snarls maybe?"

Isla giggled, and the delight on her face, warmed him to the core. "But of course. Callum, watch closely."

"Yes, lady," his laird replied, brow furrowing into that endearing look of complete concentration.

"Now. You remember the correct grip, your right hand closest to the crossguard, your left directly below it for the most force? Good. Then let us begin with the best stance; holding the sword beside your head, the hilt level with your cheek. This is especially helpful when you are unsure of your opponent, for it allows you to move easily into attack or defense. See?"

Alastair's jaw dropped as her sword flashed about his body and head, cutting and thrusting with such precision, such control, he felt a slight breeze when the steel passed by his flesh. He'd known she would be good—anyone praised by the legendary Sir Lachlan would have to be—but Isla was a master. She wielded the sword as though it was part of her body, yet every movement had purpose, control, and aggression; nothing loose nor lazy, no wide arcs or extravagant flourishes here. In true battle, this lady would have your head or innards on the ground before you'd even raised your arm.

"Well, sir?" said Isla, as she stepped back and rested the sword on her shoulder.

Alastair dropped to one knee. "In this, I yield."

"How did you even do that, Isla?" asked Callum.

She patted the sword hilt fondly, like it was a small child. "I learned from the best. Years and *years* of practice. I was gifted my first wooden sword aged four and pestered everyone to teach me. Leith first, then an indulgent uncle who wanted to annoy my father. Later, a few Sutherland men at arms, followed by a gentleman from Rome hired for my brothers, all whom I bribed with coin. When I heard about Sir Lachlan's training school, I told my mother and father that I needed to go to St. Andrews to learn piety. Instead, I encountered my toughest and most gifted tutor, honing my skills for months before...well, you know what happened."

"I thought that only strength mattered," said Callum slowly. "But you demonstrate that speed and skill can triumph."

Isla's expression turned serious. "Let me be clear... strength does matter. However, it is not the only path. Great swordfighters have strength *and* speed. Strength *and* skill. And they are often fighting an opponent who has none. Also, the line between victory and defeat is very narrow. It could be *one* move you did or did not do, and the same for your opponent. It is easy to become tired and lose concentration. Perhaps be fooled by a false step, take too long to respond, or allow the other to get too close."

Alastair gazed at her in awe. If anyone was unclear that swordplay was Isla's passion, hearing her speak, seeing the way her face lit up, watching her demonstrate her expertise, would end that uncertainty. She was a truly remarkable woman.

Yet this knowledge brought with it unwelcome feelings, the kind he did his best to quell each and every day. That his whole life was a lie. That he knew nothing, was nothing, and would amount to naught. Aye, he looked the part of devilish beast. But what else did he have to offer? Behind the oak door remained the little boy he'd once been: starving, abandoned, trying desperately to belong, the one who'd mastered no skill as a grown man but fucking and massage.

Eventually, Alastair cleared his throat. "How then..." he said hesitantly, the words bubbling up from somewhere deep and dark inside him, unable to be halted, "how do you keep fighting when all is against you?"

"Not *all* is against me," said Isla, reaching out and gently squeezing his free hand. "I am not hungry, penniless, or without a home. My family might see me as no more than a body to sell for favor and position, but Morag and Leith care. Sir Lachlan, Lady Marjorie, and Lady Janet kept my secret and urged me on. Many men would have mocked my offer of help, sure a woman could teach them nothing, but you and Callum accepted. Rays of sunshine can find their way to light even the loneliest path."

That made him flinch. Callum and Lady Maude were his rays of sunshine, the only two people who had ever cared for him. He wanted their happiness and prosperity more than anything, but the key to that was Isla. And while he felt a fledgling trust and affection for her alongside the lust, the Sutherlands loomed as a cold, malevolent force behind her. They did not believe in tender sentiment, and were renowned for opposing the unconventional. Not in a thousand years would they countenance their daughter's husband bedding another man. What if a marriage, the dowry and alliance hinged on his removal from Glennoe Castle? It wasn't as though he was an actual MacIntyre...

"Enough talk," Alastair growled, despair awakening a true devilish beast. "*Fight.*"

Isla's steady gaze held far, far too much understanding. "Very well, Master Graham," she said softly. "Let us dance."

Pain. So much pain in Alastair's eyes, Isla could scarcely bear it.

But if she'd learned one thing being around Highland men her whole life, it was that they loathed to share what hurt or grieved them. They brooded, then either fought or fucked.

She wanted to know what haunted Alastair, to hold and soothe him the way Morag held her when she raged at injustice. But he did not want that. Fortunately, she could be an opponent—with more than enough skill to play until he grew weary, or disarm him if necessary.

"I said," she repeated, challenging Alastair with a haughty raised eyebrow, "let us dance. Callum, I hope you are watching carefully, for I am about to show you how to manage a devilish beast with a burr in his paw."

The squire scowled and took up his stance. Then he lunged.

Isla delicately sidestepped, easily deflecting his blade with her own. But Alastair wasn't a fool, and when he turned, he attempted to deceive her with a false cut left before thrusting right. She nodded in approval even as a simple flick of her wrist turned the attack away, her blood heating at the familiar and arousing sound of steel kissing steel. "Better."

"Don't you dare be kind," he snarled. "Pity me at your peril."

In response, she pointed her sword tip directly at his throat. "I pity no one on the battlefield."

Again and again, the squire lunged and retreated. What he lacked in honed skill was bolstered by a power she knew all too well: pure stubborn hurt. Alastair had the heart of an ox and would keep trying until injury or his legs collapsed. Each time she parried his blade, and when he began to tire, she performed a downward cut followed by a straight thrust that would have gutted him had she not halted the movement.

Alastair took a shuddering breath, pausing to dash a shirt-sleeve against his damp forehead. "I should thank you for allowing my innards to remain beneath skin."

Isla inclined her head then turned to Callum. "An important lesson. The only place for a wide arc or flourish in sword-play is on the stage with a wooden weapon. On the battlefield they leave your chest and belly exposed for a death thrust. Understand?"

"Yes, lady."

At last, Alastair became more watchful, using his advantage in height and reach with an admirable downward thrust.

"Ah," she said as she deflected the blow, her sword shuddering at the impact. "Now you are thinking like a fighter. But still too slow, beast. You wish to conquer me? Move swiftly."

The angry hurt eased from his face. Now, his eyes glittered like sapphires, a wicked grin lifting his lips as they circled each other. "You invite a conquering, Isla?"

"And what if I did?" she shot back, forcing him to retreat and defend against a flurry of slashing blows before stepping out of his reach. "What if my desire to conquer halts at the bedchamber door, where instead I wish to surrender and be conquered most thoroughly...by not one man, but two?"

Alastair stumbled, his sword clattering to the floor.

Isla winced, not at the sound but at her recklessness. How often had Sir Lachlan scolded her for making her move too soon? Ugh. She'd been so caught in the thrilling dance of learning an opponent, the rasping shriek of clashing blades, the heady scent of sporting sweat and leashed power, that she'd blurted words that could never be unsaid.

She sheathed her sword and leaned it against the wall. "I mean...er—"

"I feel like I've learned a great deal today, watching a master swordfighter at her work," said Callum, clasping his hands. "Telling me is one thing. But you *showed* me, and I am most grateful. I believe you deserve...a reward."

"Oh?" she said huskily, her nipples hardening to a point that made the linen binding unbearable.

"I believe the bargain was a sword lesson for a pleasure lesson, Alastair?"

"Aye. And as the lady is the victor, she must decide her spoils."

Pure excitement swirled. In a world where she often had no choice at all, how marvelous it was to have a voice in her own destiny. And each time, these two men made her feel safe; to explore and learn, to speak openly of her needs and desires, all while remaining free from retribution or unwanted attention.

"I should like kisses," she said slowly.

"Where?" asked Callum casually, as though they discussed a cloudy sky rather than where on her naked body she wished to have his mouth.

"My lips. My nipples. Oh, and my pearl stroked with two fingers. Also..."

Alastair raised an eyebrow. "*Also?*"

She folded her arms. "I am the victor, am I not?"

"Aye. Tell us plainly, then."

"Before...you talked of me on my hands and knees, your fingers tangled in my hair and your thumb in my arse. I should like to know what that feels like."

There was a brief silence.

Then Alastair's gaze scorched her from head to foot. "As you desire."

"Shall we undress you, Isla?" asked Callum politely, but he could not disguise a growing bulge tenting his hose.

"Yes. Oh yes."

The men set to work, lifting her borrowed shirt over her head, before sending her into a slow spin to remove the tight linen binding her breasts. All the while they stroked and caressed, and by the time her taut nipples were freed from their linen dungeon, Isla panted for breath, already desperate for release.

As promised, Alastair curled her braid around his fingers and tugged until her scalp prickled delightfully. Then his hard, hot lips were upon her, kissing and nipping at the sensitive place where her neck met her shoulder. If that weren't wondrous enough, Callum leaned forward and brushed his lips against hers, back and forth, coaxing her mouth to open for him so he could dart his magical tongue within. Saints alive. Not even her lewd dream had prepared her for the sensation of being pleasured from all sides.

Soon Alastair slid his free hand around her ribs, and cupped her breast. Like an expert baker he gently kneaded the slight curve, before taking her nipple between two fingers and squeezing it to a heady point just below pain.

"Mmmm. More."

"Suck her nipple, Callum," rasped Alastair, and Isla shuddered. She couldn't see him, but his voice in her ear and his big hands on her body were a wicked delight.

She bucked at the first lash of Callum's tongue, gasping when his hot, avid mouth engulfed the taut peak and sucked it firmly. He attended to both her nipples until they darkened from rosy pink to the color of wine, and even a light puff of air seemed too much.

Just when Isla was about to beg for her throbbing cunt to be eased, the two men led her over to the chaise. She was quickly stripped of the remainder of her clothing, then placed on her hands and knees. With anyone else, such a vulnerable position would be unthinkable. But she trusted Callum and Alastair, for they had both demonstrated they cared about her well-being and comfort. Always offering choices. And that only heightened her desire and affection for them.

Instinctively, she arched her back and parted her thighs. They made her wait until a needy sob tore from her throat, then at last, Alastair's thick thumb delved into the slick folds of her cunt and wet itself thoroughly before smearing her own honey across the tight hole of her back entrance. Over and over his thumb dipped and smeared, and unable to remain still, Isla rocked to meet it in an attempt to hurry penetration.

Callum laughed as he circled her nipples. "I believe the lady wishes your thumb inside her."

"I am equally certain she wishes you to stroke her pearl," said Alastair.

Isla hissed in frustration as she gripped the chaise arm. "The lady wishes you would both stop talking and start pleasuring."

The slight sting of a punishment swat to her arse made her moan, but that was naught compared to the burning stretch of Alastair's thumb entering that forbidden hole for the first time. Much like her need to be the conqueror and the conquered, this indescribable sensation was two sides of a coin. Pain and pleasure. Confusing and clarifying. Something her body both welcomed and rejected. Then she couldn't think at all, as Callum's hand delved between her legs to cup her mound and rub her aching pearl. Each time he rubbed, Alastair tugged her braid and thrust his thumb shallowly into her arse, and the feeling of restraint, of being surrounded and taken, was her undoing.

An abandoned cry tore from her throat as release hit like a storm-tossed ocean, both lifting her up and overwhelming her completely.

She'd thought she knew ecstasy.

Once again, these men had proven her wrong.

⚜

Much like a diamond, Isla had many sides. The cool-headed swordfighter. The impish mischief maker. The courageous woman navigating the treacherous waters of a world made for wealthy men as best she could. But this day he and Alastair had seen a new one...

The submissive lover.

Callum had greatly enjoyed licking Isla to a screaming release in their previous lesson, and sucking Alastair's cock in front of her had only heightened his arousal. Neither could compare to this, though: he and his squire working *together* to pleasure her. The way they had teased her with words, with touch...he'd felt closer to them both. As though they truly could exist as three rather than a forced choice of two.

Callum's breath caught.

Isla and Alastair in his heart and in his bed? And all delighted to be there?

Even the thought made his cock throb, and he bit back a

groan, needing release more than he needed food to sustain him.

On the chaise Isla trembled a little, and they removed their hands from her body. She turned onto her back, and Callum drank in the glorious sight of her flushed skin, swollen nipples, and wet cunt, pleased she did not move to cover herself.

Eventually she blinked at them with dazed eyes. "I think my name is Isla."

He smiled. "'Tis a pretty name. Rare and precious. Is there a story behind it?"

Isla stretched like a cat and pointed her toes. "No heartfelt tale, I'm afraid. My grandfather was Lord of the Isles, and my family sought to flatter him. A wasted effort, considering the king seized the estates and title when I was nine."

"I still like it. Almost as much as you soundly conquering Alastair with your sword."

"Ha," said his squire. "I am quite certain, my laird, that I could conquer you with my *sword*."

Callum moaned. Usually Alastair called him laird, but sometimes in tender or lusty moments it was *my laird*; not a term of deference, but possession. It both warmed his soul and aroused him to the point of pain. Yet in the freedom and privacy of this cottage, he desired so much more. To have that ownership demonstrated in full measure, not just with words or hands or mouth, but Alastair's cock buried deep inside him. "Please," he said hoarsely, the way he'd begged that long ago night. "*Please*."

Isla sat up and bit her lip. "What are you going to do?"

"I'm going to fuck Callum," said Alastair bluntly. "We'll retire to the bedchamber."

"But I want to watch," she whispered. "Not spy...*watch*. Like when he sucked your cock. May I?"

Alastair turned to him. "Can she?"

Callum shuddered as his cock jerked. "Yes."

"Then we'll fuck here, on this chaise. Isla, kneel on that cushion for the best view. Come here, Callum, so I might undress you."

Never had he thought undressing to be an act of torment until this day. The removal of his shirt and hose, his shoes and stockings, each took a thousand years as Alastair stroked and licked each newly revealed part of his body. Neck and chest. Inner thighs. The underside of his knees.

But not his cock. No, his lover deliberately went around the engorged, seed-damp length now bobbing against his abdomen.

"*Alastair*," he gritted out, provoked beyond endurance, for he could feel Isla's hot gaze as much as his squire's masterful touch.

"Fetch the oil."

With unsteady hands, Callum reached down for the bottle of light oil Alastair had used to polish the swords. "Here."

"Bend over."

At the first penetration of Alastair's oil-slick finger into his arse, he gasped in delight. Gentle to start in preparation for a rough fuck later, just the way he liked it.

"Does it feel odd to you?" asked Isla abruptly. "The way the stretch burns but you don't want him to stop because the more he strokes the nicer it is?"

"That's...exactly...it..." Callum stuttered as Alastair added a second finger and pushed them in deep. "But when...*oh*... when it's his cock, it feels even better."

Moments later, Alastair pulled his fingers free, and Callum nearly wept at the loss. Until he was handed the bottle of oil.

"Prepare my cock," Alastair ordered as he nearly tore off his own clothing. "Isla, I see you there, unable to sit still. If you wish to come and assist...do so."

Isla nodded eagerly and shuffled forward. "What must I do, Callum?"

Taking her hand, he turned it over and poured some oil into her palm. Then he did the same to his own hand. "Cover his cock in oil. It eases the way inside in the absence of honey from a cunt."

They smoothed the oil all over Alastair's huge length. Never had he seen his squire's manhood so hard or so thick, the damp head almost purple. He couldn't wait to have all of it stuffed inside him, owning him, filling him with seed as he found a shuddering release.

"Enough," gasped Alastair eventually.

Callum sighed in relief. "How shall we fuck?"

"I'll sit on the chaise. You'll sit on my cock. That way Isla can touch you...if you'd both like that."

Isla brightened further. "My hands are already oiled. Can I, Callum?"

"Aye," he said, taking a deep breath in an attempt to stop himself releasing his seed there and then. First, he and Alastair working together to pleasure her, but now she and Alastair working together to pleasure him? God's blood. Perfection.

"Up here, Callum."

He rose to his feet and Alastair pulled him close, one hand at the back of his neck, one pressing against his arse, his lips captured in a hard, brutal kiss that left him panting to be taken.

"Please," he said again, unashamed to beg. "Don't make me wait any longer."

Wordlessly, his squire sat on the chaise, before carefully turning him so he faced away. Then, those huge hands at his hips, he was guided down onto Alastair's cock.

Callum groaned at the burn; even with the preparation, two

fingers were nothing compared to this enormous length and the way it stretched his tight hole. But the oil eased the way too perfectly, and Alastair relentlessly worked his cock deeper and deeper, a little more each time. Just when Callum thought he could take no more, Isla distracted him by stroking his inner thighs, his heavy balls, and the sensitive tip of his cock.

He shuddered, the delicate touch such an erotic contrast to the rough penetration. "Isla..."

Pure wickedness lit her eyes, and agile as a cat, she climbed his body, rubbed her taut nipples and wet bush against him, then kissed him sweetly. Next, she rose on her toes to kiss Alastair as well, before retreating back down onto the cushion to close her strong, sword-wielding hands around his cock.

Callum bucked, his guttural cry echoing in the room. He would not survive this, it felt far, far too good. Yet soon it was even better, as with his feet braced on the ground, and Alastair's hands guiding him, he began to move up and down on his squire's length, each action ending with Isla handling his cock.

Up. Down. *Squeeze*. Up. Down. *Squeeze*.

He tried to stave off release but it hit him with the force of a Highland storm, and moments later his roar of ecstasy echoed in the room as he gushed seed all over Isla's hands, even landing some on her breasts. Then Alastair bit his neck and thrust hard, once, twice, before spending deep inside his arse, and Callum cried out helplessly as more seed jolted from him.

Exhausted, utterly sated, he sank back against Alastair's chest. One brawny arm wrapped around his waist, and Callum tilted his head so he could rub their cheeks together. Isla stared at them, her face the portrait of yearning, and without hesitation he held out his arms. She burrowed against him, her head falling forward to rest on Alastair's shoulder, and Callum let out a long, slow sigh.

This. This was paradise.

He and Alastair and Isla together.

Eventually, Isla moved back, looking woebegone. "I must dress. Leith will return for me soon. Will you help me with the linen binding?"

Indeed, grim reality beckoned for them all.

He needed to practice with Alastair what Isla had shown him with the sword, rest, and also prepare for the stone put event on the morrow. If he did not progress from that event, nothing else would matter.

"Of course," said Callum, regretfully easing away from Alastair.

With a cloth and warm water from the wooden bucket near the fire, they each cleaned themselves and then dressed. Callum reluctantly picked up his sword and unsheathed it. Unsmiling, Alastair picked up his, and they circled each other, offering the poor cuts and thrusts of frustrated men. Isla's corrections came in the sharp tone of a frustrated woman. The room seemed darker and colder, the rules imposed by others and an uncertain future stealing the pleasure and peace they'd found together.

If he succeeded in this quest, he might have the world.

If he failed...he could well lose everything.

CHAPTER 7

"Smile, daughter!"

Isla bared her teeth at her mother as they stood outside the royal pavilion in anticipation of today's event: the stone put. "Is that better?"

Anne pinched Isla's elbow. Hard. "You have been out of sorts all morning. Are you still unwell? I shall order the royal physician to send an elixir if you are."

"No," she muttered, repressing a shudder at the thought. "I feel much improved."

"Then smile. No man wants to see a scowl on a woman's face, especially yours. We want the men to desire your hand in marriage, not run screaming from the field, especially when this wretched tourney has cost us such a staggering amount of coin."

Isla pressed her lips together.

I am the only person who wants to run screaming from the field.

How much more of this could she take? The previous evening, Leith had returned her to the castle and Morag had helped her undress and tucked her into bed with mere minutes to spare, before her father and mother walked in.

That she must continue this charade, when all she wished for was to ride back to Callum's castle at Glennoe and enjoy a life of swordplay, lusty bedsport with her husband and lover, caring for their children and the clan...unbearable.

Children.

Isla stilled as the word settled in her mind.

Until now, she'd not seriously considered them. Even as wee lass, news of her older sisters in yet another confinement had never provoked any enthusiasm to be a mother herself. But with Callum and Alastair...suddenly she could see a new and different future. Little ones with books and sweetmeats and wooden swords creating merry havoc in the nursery. Children with fair hair and gray eyes; brown hair and blue eyes; ebony hair and green eyes. Any combination, really. Because they would all be cherished no matter what they looked like or their talents. All encouraged to pursue their dreams and true love, none belittled or ignored or abandoned. And they would witness equality, their mother respected and *seen*.

"Isla!"

She jumped and glanced guiltily at her mother. "Yes?"

"The king and queen approach," Anne hissed.

Isla sank into a curtsy, her gold-embroidered brown velvet gown swirling around her legs. Today promised to be unusually warm; already she could feel sweat gathering under her gable hood. Others in the crowd might envy her being in the royal pavilion, but with so many people in an enclosed space, the stench of food and overheated bodies could be nauseating.

"Ah," said the king with a friendly smile. "Lady Isla and her dear mother. Good morrow to you both. Lady Sutherland, would you indulge my queen in some advice about her wardrobe? She admires you so."

Anne inclined her head, but irritation flashed in her eyes. "It would be an honor, Your Grace."

"My thanks. Lady Isla, shall we greet your suitors? Just twelve left vying for your hand."

She forced herself to nod. It annoyed her when the king spoke as though she had a choice, when she did not. In truth, she hated the trite words and pretty lies of court, the never-ending intrigues and hypocrisy. Give her plain-speaking, honest men any day. "Certainly, Your Grace. If I might ask one boon...have mercy on my complexion and do not ask me to tarry long in the sunshine. Freckles are the very devil and lemon juice is not nearly successful enough in removing them."

James quirked a knowing eyebrow at her pitiful excuse. But ever the gallant, he held out his arm. "Of course. I would be a poor sovereign indeed if I did not protect such a delicate Scottish flower."

"Your Grace!" called a liveried servant as he ran forward clutching a short scroll. "An urgent message from the bishop."

The king frowned. "I must see to this. Hmmm..."

"Might I assist and escort Lady Isla to meet her suitors?" said Lady Marjorie Ross, rising from her cushioned chair in the pavilion.

"I would be most obliged, madam," said James, kissing her hand before marching away.

Isla glanced at the other woman in relief. Sir Lachlan's convent-raised wife was of a similar age yet startlingly beautiful, with brown hair, blue eyes, and lush curves. But Lady Marjorie was also sweet and delightfully pert, a woman brave enough to defy the queen's edict to wed an English border lord and instead follow her heart. That she also loved and lusted after Lady Janet only made her more interesting. "Good morrow, my lady."

"Good morrow," said Lady Marjorie with an impish grin. "I'm happy to be ill all over the shoes of any man you dislike and blame it on my belly."

"That is a very kind offer," said Isla, smiling in return, "but Sir Lachlan would rampage if he thought you were unwell."

"Alas, yes. He is even more protective now I'm with child. Shall we walk?"

The two women linked arms and made their way to the center of the field where the twelve remaining men stood, awaiting the start of the stone put. This event celebrated pure strength—in two groups of six, each man would throw a large and heavy-looking river stone twice. The best eight would receive a third throw, but only six would advance to the revels.

The sheer size of the other entrants compared to Callum had Isla's stomach roiling. For the past few days, she had refused to consider him not progressing. Now, the fear was bone-chillingly real.

Isla swallowed hard. "I do not favor this foolish event. Throwing a rock. Bah."

"I am praying for your favorite. Janet is also," murmured Lady Marjorie.

She glanced sharply at the other woman. "My favorite?"

"Come now. We have seen the way you look at Glennoe. *And* his squire."

A hot blush scorched Isla's cheeks. "Er..."

Lady Marjorie giggled. "Aha! That is the face of a lady who has broken more rules. I heartily approve. May I add," she said, her voice lowering to the barest whisper, "it is quite, quite wonderful having a husband and a lover. To be part of a trio. Stay strong. Happiness is there for the taking."

"I want that," Isla blurted. "But..."

"No buts. Just greet your suitors like they all matter to you. From my experience, no one must know the plan or preference. Not by a twitch."

Isla nodded at the wise counsel. "Aye."

When they reached the men, they first greeted a young

border lord. Somehow Isla smiled and made conversation, and did the same for two battle-hardened knights, the laird of clan MacLeod, and the wily, silver-haired Lord Spalding. Yet then came the MacDonald of Carnoch, and knowing what he'd said about her, and that neither Callum nor Alastair could abide him, she couldn't even muster a smile.

"Carnoch," said Marjorie coolly. "I see you are ready to heave the stone put all the way to the village. But you have misplaced your shirt. Or torn it, maybe?"

The laird, clad only in hose, chuckled as he bowed with a flourish. "Come now, my lady. We are about to perform great feats in the sunshine and a shirt might impede my throw. Highlanders are not usually so modest. Wouldn't you agree, Lady Isla?"

She barely refrained from spitting on his bare feet. No doubt many women fell prey to that smile and those broad shoulders, but to her the laird was less appealing than a serpent. Especially when compared to the finest of men like Callum and Alastair.

"I say His Grace declares the rules of the tourney and would not speak against him," Isla said sweetly. "But cry to no one if the sun and wind turn you as red as a holly berry."

Carnoch scowled. "I do not cry. Other men will, as you'll soon see."

"We are eager to see fine throwing," said Marjorie, dismissing him with a turn of her head. "Ah, Glennoe! How do you fare?"

Callum stepped forward, Alastair at his side, and both men bowed. "Well indeed, Lady Marjorie. And you?"

"Excellent."

"Lady Isla?"

At the sound of her name on his lips, Isla clasped her hands so she did not throw her arms about Callum, the kind, affectionate laird who had watched her swordplay and assisted her to a powerful release the previous evening. The man whose hard cock she had handled, whose seed had splashed upon her naked breasts as his low roar echoed in the room. Nor could she embrace his squire, the blunt, sensual beast who had yielded to her sword then introduced her to such forbidden pleasures; the master who owned her and Callum both.

"Glennoe," she replied, holding out her hand. "I am well, and wish you good fortune this day."

"I shall need it," Callum said ruefully as he took her hand and squeezed it. "Alas, Master Graham cannot heave the stone in my place."

"Do not fret, lady," said Alastair, his gaze caressing her when his hand could not. "My laird is ready."

Marjorie coughed and tugged Isla's arm. "Glad to hear it. Do not let us keep you from your preparation. Come along, dear lady, still more suitors to greet..."

Isla couldn't help a glance over her shoulder as she was purposefully ushered away. Of course, she hadn't been able to say that she cheered only for Callum. Or that she resented each moment away from him and Alastair.

God willing, she would have another opportunity to say so.

※

"This tourney may go straight to purgatory."

His laird's words were too quiet for anyone but him to hear, but the sentiment was louder than a bellow in the tent. They had returned here after speaking with Isla, unwilling to wait and fret with the other men. Or watch bloody Red strut about.

Alastair paused in kneading Callum's shoulders, an activity probably assisting him more than his lover. If he didn't do *something*, he would go mad. "You finished second in your foot race and were named lord of the bow. All is proceeding to plan."

"What if I am the first man in stone put history to not even lift it, let alone hurl it? The devil-spawned thing is the size of a crofter's hut."

"Aye, it is large and heavy," he replied solemnly. "But you do not have to defeat all the men here. Only two, to get a third throw. Then two again to progress to the revels. One step at a time, my laird."

Callum rubbed his face. "I keep thinking of Isla. It is getting very difficult to say nothing in public. About my feelings, I mean. I would never speak of our private time with her, but an action may betray me. A glance, or holding her hand too long."

Alastair looked away. At least Callum, with lands and castle and title could glance at Isla and hold her hand. Unlike an orphaned squire who possessed only what the MacIntyre clan chose to bestow upon him. It was poison to feel like this but he could not halt it; such was his frustration and resentment that he had to remain silent rather than publicly declare in word and deed that Callum and Isla belonged to him. Never could he wed either, nor drape them in jewels and fine cloth for he had no coin to purchase such items.

He'd always loved Callum. But since meeting Isla, his yearning for a permanent home and family had only strengthened. How did one man say to another after twenty years of close friendship and a few rough fucks in times of emotional turmoil, that he wanted—he *needed*—not the crumbs but the whole feast? That he wanted to claim him forever, in bed and out? That he wanted to claim Callum's prospective lady wife as well?

Only the worst fool in Scotland would dream of such a thing.

Probably the worst fool in the entire world.

Alastair grunted. "They'll think you a gallant. As long as you say nothing about Isla's true self. You cannot reveal her dreams or desires, for then they'll wonder how you know."

"Even the thought of her wedding another...being bedded by another...they won't know her," said Callum fiercely. "She'll never be permitted to sword fight or wear shirt and hose again, and that will kill her soul."

"That is *exactly* the thought you must hold close when you reach for that stone. For only a mighty effort on your part will prevent such a bad end."

Callum turned, his gaze troubled. "What if Red—"

Alastair's hand shot out and grasped his laird's chin. "Do not speak of him or think of him," he murmured. "He is one of twelve. Think of Isla and me. As I thought of you all night, sleeping in my bed alone when I should have been lying next to you. Are you still a little sore, my laird, after taking my cock deep inside you? Do you remember how it felt to have Isla kiss you so sweetly, to hold her in your arms?"

"I remember," said Callum hoarsely. "Every moment. It was so good."

"Then heave that stone with all the strength and courage I know you possess, and such lusty play may happen again."

"Very well," said Callum, lifting his hand to rub a thumb against Alastair's skin, his gray eyes solemn and yet glittering with heat, too. "*Master* Graham."

A trumpet blast shattered the intimate moment, and Alastair scowled before letting his laird's chin go, and rubbing his shoulders one last time.

When he and Callum walked to the roped area where the others waited for the stone put to begin, they passed many empty spaces where tents had once stood. Servants from the royal household removed them after an entrant retired from the tourney, and it was a stark reminder at how fleeting success could be. A feted champion one day, defeated the next. Although Callum had performed marvelously well so far, he was glad that this was the last event on the open field. His laird much preferred to be indoors; thankfully both the revels and sword fighting would be held in the Great Hall.

Sir Lachlan beckoned them closer and held up a length of rope with small knots at equal distances apart. "Each throw will be measured. I will decide...the best four...in each group. Any dispute will be decided...by the king. Those waiting their turn...must stand well back. First six. Take up your stone!"

Alastair and Callum moved away, for Callum had been drawn in the second group alongside Red. Once again, the king had added a difficulty to this contest; not only did they have to hurl the stone a great distance, it had to remain in the narrow rectangular area allocated to each entrant, or would be judged a failure. Their sovereign may have forbidden jousting, but he was certainly making each man work hard to progress. Really, Alastair welcomed such rules. Any event where mind mattered just as much as strength assisted Callum.

One by one, the men picked up their stone for the first throw. Each took a few running steps before heaving it forward, and the many ways used actually gave him hope. Some threw from their chest, others attempted a two-handed put from above their head, but only two of the six balanced the stone in their right hand, tucked it against their neck, and used their whole body rather than just the strength of their arms.

Alastair leaned down so he might speak directly into Callum's ear. "I do not think many of these men have thrown a stone put before. Look how little distance they got in their first throw."

"Apart from that young knight, Sir Leslie Hay," muttered Callum. "And Lord Spalding. He fools many with his silver hair and amiable smile, but I have negotiated with him and he is *cunning*."

"Let us see what happens in the second throw. If the others learn from their mistake."

They did not.

Every attempt was thrown the same way as the first. One lord's put rolled out of his area, and was declared a failed attempt. As his first throw had been poor, Sir Lachlan declared his tourney over. Five men remained, only four would be permitted one more chance.

The air was heavy with tension as Sir Lachlan and his men at arms measured the remaining puts. While Sir Leslie and Lord Spalding were the clear winners of the group, the remaining three appeared almost in a row. Plague take it, if he felt this way now, when he cared about none of these men, how would he be when it was Callum's time?

Eventually, Sir Lachlan beckoned the five remaining men to stand in a row next to him. "We have a decision. The four men...who shall progress...are Lord Spalding. Sir Leslie Hay. Lord Ruthven of Perth...and the Ranald of Clan Ranald."

The cheers and applause were deafening; it seemed at the first hint of sunshine all of Stirling and the surrounding towns and villages had gathered to watch the event. But Alastair felt for the knight denied a further throw by mere inches, now forced to leave the tourney. The walk from the field, with only his squire for company and a few thousand eyes upon him, probably seemed the longest and loneliest of his life.

After the stones were moved back to the throw line, the ropes pulled tight, and grass and dirt pressed back down to a reasonably flat surface, another trumpet blast sounded and Sir Lachlan gathered the second group.

Callum held out his hand. "Would you bind my wrist?"

"Gladly," said Alastair, before swiftly wrapping a length of linen around Callum's right wrist to support and strengthen it for his throws. "You know the prize that awaits you. Go forth and heave that damned stone."

His laird attempted a smile, but there was no disguising the paleness of his cheeks, or the rigid set to his shoulders. "I've just seen two men forced to leave the tourney; one for a failed throw, and one because his put was an inch too short. But I shall do my best."

"That's all I ask. All *we* desire."

Callum tested his wrist binding, then took a deep breath. "Pray for me."

"Nay. *Cruachan*," Alastair replied forcefully, the MacIntyre battle cry, for this event would be a stern test of Callum's character. Especially with his devil-spawned cousin at his shoulder, willing him to fail.

A glance at the royal pavilion informed him that Isla, the king and queen, Lady Marjorie and Lady Janet, and the Sutherlands all now stood ready to watch. An eerie hush settled over the crowd.

The time of reckoning had arrived.

๑๕๛

Callum had been placed fourth in the row of six, which unfortunately gave him prime viewing of all the other men. Including his cousin, who had been placed third.

"Greetings," said Red, his lips smiling but his eyes cold, as he easily shifted his stone between hands. "How do you fare this day? I must admit, I did not expect the sun to shine on Stirling like this. I do appreciate you keeping your shirt on, however. No one wishes to see skin as white as snow or a lad's limbs on a grown man."

"Red," he replied stiffly, as he glanced down his roped area. God's blood it seemed narrow. How had the men in the previous group kept their stones within it?

"Oh, you don't wish to talk? How unfriendly, when we are family. Here I was prepared to share some advice, even."

He glared at his cousin. "I need no advice from you."

"Because Alastair Graham has offered instruction? *Callum*. You'll never rise to greatness if you surround yourself with lowborn scum. Look what happened to the old king. Bedded men as well as women, took advice from tailors and masons... and was murdered in a barn. Some say a fitting end for such ungodly weakness, I say God will judge those so wretched that not even their own family want them."

Callum's fists clenched so hard he could have crushed the river stone to powder. First vile words about Isla, now sly insults and threats directed at him and Alastair. But a surrender to rage was no path to victory. Sir Lachlan would probably not intervene a second time; to succeed in this event he had to shut Red out of his mind.

At last, the stone put began for the second group. The first two men achieved no great distance with their throws, then Red stepped up and passed them by several yards, heaving the river stone as though it were a velvet cushion.

Sweat dampened Callum's temples. But he set his stance as Alastair had taught him many years ago at Glennoe; the stone balanced in his right hand against his neck with his fingers spread. Elbow high, left foot forward, yet all weight on his right foot.

The stone was heavy. Too heavy. Already his arm ached.

Throw the damned thing.

Moments later he drove hard from his hips, rocking his weight from his right foot to his left as he heaved the stone. It flew a short distance, hit the ground, and flopped forward.

Hmmm.

Not terrible; better than the first two entrants, but well short of Red's effort. The two men following him both bettered his distance, leaving Callum in fourth position. If they remained this way, he would progress. If one of the first two men improved, he would be the one trudging from the field in shame.

Each stone was measured, then all returned for their second throw.

Callum permitted himself one glance at Alastair, who briefly tapped his elbow, and lifted it. His squire had always scolded him about that, even as a young lad.

"Ready, Callum?" said Red, grinning like a wolf now. "Fourth position, you must be very anxious. Lady Isla is keeping a close eye on you, how does it feel to be pitied so?"

"Maybe it isn't pity," he replied.

Red blinked. "Of course it is. What else would she feel for you?"

Fortunately, he did not need to answer, for Sir Lachlan demanded silence before the second throws began. The first man's distance appeared similar to his first. The second man bettered his. Red stepped up and effortlessly heaved his stone at least a yard further. Gah. Every day it became so much easier to hate him. Then it was Callum's turn. Again, he set his stance, although this time he purposefully lifted his elbow higher. The stone scraped his neck and his wrist shook under the weight, but he gritted his teeth and heaved it forward with all his might.

A better throw than his first, but he had to wait and see how the last two men fared.

Eventually Sir Lachlan took measurements, then cleared his throat. "I have a decision. The four men...who shall progress are: the MacDonald of Carnoch. Sir David Erskine. Lord Hamilton of Arran. And Callum MacIntyre...Lord of Glennoe."

He'd done it! He'd cleared the first obstacle.

Callum gulped in air as the crowd cheered and when he looked over at the royal pavilion, Isla beamed at him, which dulled his aches and pains a little. Now Sir Lachlan was directing his men to widen the roped area to allow for eight men rather than six, so Callum took the brief respite to hurry over to Alastair. "Well?"

"That second throw was much better," said his squire, as he took Callum's arm and began expertly stretching his shoulder. "Higher elbow. Do that again, and you'll be dancing with Isla tomorrow at the revels. One more throw, that's all it is. Better than two other men. You can do this, my laird, I know you can."

Once again, he wanted to wrap his arms around Alastair for his unwavering support. "I couldn't have got this far without you. I—"

But the trumpet sounded and Callum had to return to the roped area. This time he was placed seventh in the row; blessedly, Red would throw at the other end in second. None of the other men spoke or smiled, but Callum did not hold it against them. He had no desire to speak either. What would they discuss? The unusually warm day, like Englishmen with no conversation did?

In truth, the wait was agonizing. The sun in his eyes, his skin itchy with sweat and his stomach churning with anxiety at being so close to progressing and yet so far. Finally, the men began to heave their stone puts. Barrel-chested Sir David Erskine, who offered a loud grunt but not much distance. Red, with a throw that flew like a spear rather than a stone and landed a jaw-droppingly long distance away. Lord Spalding, who grinned as though it were all a lark, and casually landed a very decent throw. Sir Leslie Hay, who beat his chest with a closed fist, picked up his stone, and proceeded to heave it just as far. Lord Hamilton of Arran, a handsome behemoth who let out a roar and sent his stone past Red's. Lord Ruthven of Perth, a startlingly tall but lean man who struggled with the stone but managed to heave it about equal to Sir David's.

Now it was his turn.

Callum dashed his shirtsleeve across his face, but sweat still dripped down his forehead and into his eyes. Even balancing the stone on his hand made it ache, like he held up a damned mountain, and his fingers slipped as he wedged it against his neck.

Please, please do not let it drop at my feet.

Everything felt wrong. His knee trembled, his heart thundered, and for a moment he couldn't catch his breath. Not even his elbow would stay high, and when he heaved the stone it landed on the grass with a dull thump...in what looked like the worst throw of all.

Despair hit him like an arrow to the chest, and he sank onto his haunches.

His tourney over. Alastair and Isla lost to him, all because he couldn't throw a stone properly. No wonder his father had rejected him in favor of a nephew better in all ways...

"A failed throw!"

Callum blinked, trying to clear the fog in his mind. But the sharp words weren't directed at him. The eighth man in the row, the Ranald of Clan Ranald, had just heaved his stone put outside the roped area. With great dignity, the laird bowed to the royal pavilion and Sir Lachlan, before he and his squire departed the field.

Seven entrants. Six places.

Sir Lachlan gestured for his men at arms and their measuring ropes. The king walked from the royal pavilion, the queen on one arm and Isla on the other, to inspect the process.

"The first three," said Sir Lachlan, "are clear. Lord Hamilton of Arran. The MacDonald of Carnoch. Sir Leslie Hay. But the remaining four...must be measured."

It took forever.

God's blood, could they not just end his misery and declare him the loser?

Eventually, the king clapped his hands, breaking a silence so profound they could practically hear the grass growing under their feet.

"I have a decision on this most excellent event! My gratitude to all for their efforts, however just six men shall progress to the revels. Sir Lachlan informed you of the first three, Lord Hamilton of Arran, the MacDonald of Carnoch, and Sir Leslie Hay. The second three, in a very, very close finish decided by less than an inch...are Lord Spalding, Lord Ruthven of Perth...and Callum MacIntyre, Lord of Glennoe."

Utterly shocked, Callum's knees buckled and he sprawled onto his arse. Yet he still heard Alastair whoop in triumph, and saw Isla applauding wildly until the queen sent her a quelling look.

Just like the first group, less than an inch and a failed throw had been the difference between success and failure. But he'd made it through to the revels.

It was enough to make him believe in miracles.

CHAPTER 8

"Isla's not coming, my laird. If she could escape the castle, she would be here. It is as pitch black as her hair outside."

Sighing glumly, Callum retreated from his position beside the street-facing window to the chaise in front of the fire. Anyone with a cool head would tell him that two long visits to this cottage had been risky enough; a lady could only claim visiting a friend, or illness, a certain number of times before invoking suspicion. But his heart still hoped to see Isla before the revels so they might celebrate his miraculous progression from the stone put. Tomorrow among the music, dancing, pageantry, and six remaining suitors vying for her hand, he and Alastair might not be able to speak with her at all.

"I know. I so wished to see her, though. Did you notice how swiftly Lady Sutherland ushered her away after the stone put? The countess doesn't like me at all."

Alastair set down his wine goblet. "Her opinion has naught to do with liking, and all with your power compared to the others. But the tourney rules have been set, and she must accept the outcome and any decision the king makes.

You have a supporter in him. He has given you more of his time than he offers to others. Especially Red."

Callum nodded. "That is true. Alas, though, the king is a practical man. He will think of his realm first and foremost, not a lady's wishes, no matter who her family is. And he certainly won't choose an unimportant laird from the Western Highlands above an alliance that suits his purposes."

"Bah. James has a soft heart for those he cares about. You remember the scandal and trial after Sir Lachlan's secret marriage to Lady Marjorie. She was supposed to wed an English baron, but they live with Lady Janet at St. Andrews. I would wager a large sum all three in a bed. And the king allows it. Remember that."

"Lady Janet was his mistress, and is still a beloved friend," said Callum as he leaned back against the chaise and drummed his fingers impatiently on the arm. "Sir Lachlan is his champion. It is hardly the same situation. I haven't fucked the king. Or fought at his side."

"Glad to hear you haven't fucked him. I should dislike having to shove our sovereign into the River Forth."

Callum stifled a grin. Alastair shied away from tender sentiment, and much preferred to show he cared with touch or deeds rather than say it.

And he did care. But was it love? Or just his own heart foolishly wishing that close friendship and hot lust took the final step forward to forever after?

"Devilish beast," he said instead, stealing the opportunity to lean over and kiss his squire on the cheek as he yearned to do more often. Naturally Alastair took control of the moment, cupping the back of his neck and mastering his lips, before plunging his tongue deep. The only other person Callum could imagine enjoying such intimacy with was Isla. Unlike Alastair's hard lips, hers were soft and plump, but they also made him forget his own name.

A sharp knock at the door jolted them apart.

Frowning, Alastair rose to his feet. "Sounds urgent. Could be from the castle."

Callum silently lit another candle and handed it to him. A weapon as well as illumination; few things slowed evil intent like hot wax to the face, then Alastair would have time to unsheathe his dagger and stab.

Slowly, cautiously, Alastair opened the cottage door. "Yes?"

"Saints alive, let me in. It's cold out here."

Callum leaped to his feet. "Isla!"

She grinned and twirled in her short cloak, hose and shirt. "Yes, 'tis I."

"You walked alone?" growled Alastair. "That is dangerous."

"Of course I didn't. I joined a group of lads who had finished their duties and decided to go and visit a tavern for some ale and amiable company. However, I will require an escort part of the way back, though."

"All the way," said Callum. "You are far too precious to risk and don't have a sword."

Isla tilted her head, then wound her arms about his neck, and kissed him.

Sweetness exploded in his mouth, and he immediately surrendered to her questing tongue. Even with the binding he could feel the slight swell of her breasts, and he cupped the firm perfection of her arse and rubbed his cock against her.

Isla eventually moved away, panting for breath. "I've been waiting to do that for hours. You did so well at the stone put. I was very proud."

"Hardly well," said Callum, his cheeks heating. "Pure good fortune assisted me today."

"It doesn't matter *how* you progressed to the revels. It only matters that you did."

"What I told him," said Alastair.

"Because you are a great and wise devilish beast," replied Isla with a wink, as she danced over, went up on her toes, and kissed him passionately also.

Callum swallowed hard at the erotic sight. While he loathed the thought of Isla wedding another tourney entrant, oddly he didn't feel a whit of jealousy at the affectionate lust between his lover and his potential wife. Just an overwhelming urge to join them, discard all clothing, and pleasure both however they wished.

When Isla stepped unsteadily back from Alastair and removed her short cloak, he thought maybe she agreed. But then she gazed at him, all humor gone. "Fetch your swords. We must commence your lesson at once."

Quickly, he obeyed her order. Alastair moved furniture to clear a space in the center of the room, then lit extra candles so it appeared bright as day. Callum kept his own sword, while Isla took Alastair's.

"What will you teach me this night?"

Isla swung the sword up and rested it on her shoulder. "I have shown you grip, footwork, stance, and ways that a person who is smaller in build can defend themselves against a much larger opponent. But today I must show you how to attack. If you surprise your opponent, whoever they are, you may have just enough time to defeat them. Ready?"

Callum took a deep breath, firmly suppressing the old sweat-inducing fear and shame that holding a sword invoked. This was the only way forward, and Isla cared so much she would risk all to visit and help him in the dead of night.

"Ready," he replied, settling into the stance she had taught him.

"Begin," commanded Isla.

Callum nodded and attempted a short slashing stroke, remembering to keep his chest and belly protected. But before his sword was even in front of his face, Isla sharply blocked him and the clash of steel on steel sent a shudder down his arms. "That was swift..."

"Yes. Your opponent will expect to be the aggressor, the one who decides the speed and direction and so forth. They will also expect you to allow their attack then defend against it. No. They are wrong. You need not wait until a cut or thrust is nearly complete to block it. In fact, the faster you respond, the less power they have. Understand?"

"I do."

"Now, I shall attack you slowly. Halt me."

Again and again, Isla attacked. Again and again, his response was ponderous and weak, and the third time his sword clattered to the floor.

Frustrated despair dropped his shoulders. "I'll never learn this."

"Yes, you will," said Alastair. "But you must fight as though she is Red whom you loathe, not Isla whom you like. Remember all those insults. Take that rage and use it. Isla is an expert with sword in hand, not a delicate flower. Treat her thus."

Callum stared at his blade. Then at Isla. "Forgive me. I am poor at—"

"No," she snapped, her green eyes flashing. "Not poor. Your grip and footwork are most adequate, and your excellence with a bow and arrow is testament to your strength and awareness of what is happening around you. There is only one reason you cannot improve your swordplay...and that is because you heed the man in your mind who long ago decided your worth and ability based on your size rather than your skill. We are near the same height. You are larger than me. If I can do this, you can also. But you must *believe*."

Callum didn't wince at the scolding; the words were far too familiar even if the tone was Isla-fiery rather than Alastair-gruff. Really, he owed his squire a thousand favors for not storming away in disgust when he wallowed in bad memories. Especially when Alastair's own childhood had been so terrible. His closest friend might be the most steadfast in the realm.

"My late father is the man in my mind," Callum confessed. "He often told me I was worthless. Too short. Too delicate. Soft in head and hands from reading rather than fighting. My cousin Red was his favorite."

"Wrong," she replied fiercely. "Wrong. Wrong. Wrong. Now pick up that damned sword and show me Callum MacIntyre. The learned scholar who negotiates trade. The lord of the bow. The lover who brings such pleasure. Show me him with sword in hand, for he is worth all the treasure in the kingdom."

As he leaned down to grasp his sword, a flame sparked in his soul, cleansing the shame that had festered there for so long. Filling him with determination.

"Aye, lady. Let us dance."

୧୬୬

His heart in his mouth, Alastair watched Callum pick up his sword and prepare to fight.

It did sting a little, well, more than a little, that something he'd said so often to his laird was only now being considered properly. Callum yielded to him so very sweetly on numerous matters, especially in bed. But he'd never been able to convince him of his worth, to remove the mocking voices of his wretched father, Red, or those in his clan who would be guided by such absurdity, and help him see the man that others admired.

Isla had convinced him. Easily.

Once again that poisoned thorn of doubt sank into his skin. Was he no longer useful?

He'd spent most of his life striving for that, so never again would he be abandoned. In the past twenty years, although Callum and Lady Maude had always made him welcome at Glennoe, he'd still felt like he didn't fully belong. While he had his and Callum's longstanding friendship in his favor, Isla was an exceptional woman. Strong and skilled. Beautiful, lusty, and sensual. And she could give Callum what he could not: coin, a powerful alliance with her clan, and children. But her family would be an obstacle to his happiness, not to mention the king. James might accept the one man, two women trio at St. Andrews, but it could be much harder for him to see two men and one woman, and be reminded of his late father. The relationship between James and the old king had been about as complicated as Callum and the old laird's.

Far too much to ponder for a simple squire.

A loud clash of steel jolted him from his bleak thoughts, and his heart twisted with both pride and despair at the delight on Callum's face when he retained the sword in his hands rather than having it dislodged onto the floor.

"Better. Much better," said Isla as she circled Callum. "But do not stand still. It is much harder to remove your innards when you are moving. Not skittish, like an ill-tempered horse, but purposeful. Confuse me. I think I know what you will do next...make me doubt myself. It is similar to one of your trade negotiations. Quick wits win the day."

Callum stepped left then right before thrusting straight ahead, but Isla easily deflected the blow with a flick of her wrist. "I am too slow, still."

"Yes," she replied gently. "Behave as a hawk. Circle to learn the landscape, then swoop to strike. Use your opponent's arrogance against them. Most will not wait to learn your strengths and weaknesses, they will only see an advantage in height or reach, think that means an easy victory, and move to deliver the final blow. That is when they are most vulnerable. Would you not agree, Alastair?"

He grunted. "If your opponent is larger, he may not be able to change course so easily. Like a ship approaching rocks."

"I could not have described it better," said Isla, darting forward with a downward cut that almost removed Callum's arm. "Yes! See what you did there? A neat sidestep that saved your arm. You are heeding my words and learning; I did not turn my wrist away. A larger man might be on his knees weeping right now, although I must remind you that the tourney rules only permit blunted swords. I am more dangerous than your opponents will be...Alastair, would you come and play the part of devilish beast once more? I need to correct Callum's elbow."

Alastair nodded. "He always drops it."

"That he does. We'll have to start punishing him," Isla purred, as she handed him back his sword and moved to stand next to Callum.

Callum blushed but readied himself into his battle stance again, and Isla slid two hands under his elbow, lifting it, and moving his forearm back and forth, turning both wrists to show him easier ways to move the weapon without losing power. Over and over they pressed swords, upward cut, downward cut, diagonal slash, until Callum became more comfortable with the adjusted arm position and held it without assistance.

"Fight," commanded Isla.

Callum lunged at him, but his blade was too upright, and with Alastair's height advantage, he easily blocked the move.

"Too high," said Alastair. "Cutting my ear will not stop me. And if you drop that left elbow, I will trap your arms near your body with my reach, and enjoy sliced Callum for supper."

Isla nodded. "He's right. Again."

They hunted each other then pounced; swords clashing once, twice, thrice, the shrieking sound overloud in the room. Yet this time his laird held firm, and they stared at each other through the frame of two steel blades.

"Better, Master Graham?" asked Callum as they turned in a slow circle, each breathing hard and dripping with sweat.

His cock jerked and began to harden. "Adequate, my laird."

"Ha. Damned by faint praise. What say you, Isla?"

When she did not reply, they both turned their heads to look at her. Isla's cheeks were flushed, her chest rising and falling...and one hand rested between her legs.

She bit her lip. "Forgive me. But watching your exertions...the improvement...then the way you eat each other up with your eyes..."

"It makes your cunt wet?" asked Alastair.

"*Yes.*"

"You need release?"

"At once," she replied, spreading her thighs a little.

Alastair shook his head before walking to the chaise to sheath his sword, Callum right behind him to do the same. "Alas, you must wait."

"*Wait?*" Isla stared at him in shock, and Alastair almost smiled. Indeed, a lady well used to servants obeying her commands. But this night, if she wished for pleasure, she would have to *earn* it. She had taught them skills in sword fighting. Now it was his turn to teach her about pleasing a man. Or this night...pleasing *men*.

"Indeed. You have been the master, but now you must be the student. Callum and I will both attend to your needs... after you learn how to suck our cocks."

Isla quivered. "I suppose you'll ask me to be naked for this lesson. So you might spend your seed over my breasts and rub it into my nipples. And spank me for misbehavior."

So that was what the naughty lass wanted, was it?

"Not ask," Alastair growled. "Insist. And yes, you well know the punishment for impatience."

She sucked in a breath and sauntered toward them, kicking off her shoes, before halting beside the chaise to peel off her stockings and hose. Soon her spicy wetness scented the air, and his mouth watered to taste her. No matter that he was beneath her in every way the world would measure, Isla Sutherland would fully surrender to his tongue this night.

"Kneel on the cushion, Isla," said Callum. "You'll be warm enough in front of the fire."

With a slight sway of her hips, Isla walked to the cushion and gracefully sank to her knees. Then she loosened the ties at the neck of her borrowed shirt, yanked it over her head, and tossed the garment away. Last of all, she rested her hands atop her head so they might attend to the length of linen binding her breasts.

When she was completely naked, her creamy skin almost golden in the firelight, Alastair placed one hand on her narrow shoulder. Her flesh was like silk, warm and smooth, and he dragged his callused palm along her collarbone.

Isla arched her back in an unspoken demand for him to stroke her jutting nipples. In response, he trailed his fingers between her breasts, down over her belly as though he meant to cup her dewy mound. Instead, he circled back, all the way up to grasp her chin and turned her head this way and that, as though inspecting her.

"What do you think, Callum?" he rasped, rubbing his thumb along her plump lower lip. "Will our cocks fit in this pretty mouth?"

She whimpered, and meeting his gaze, her green eyes glittering in challenge, delicately licked his thumb.

A willfully disobedient lass.

"I think we need to undress and find out," his laird replied, adjusting the fit of his hose around a large bulge as he moved to stand next to Isla rather than behind her.

To torment her further, Alastair leaned forward and kissed Callum, gripping the back of his neck in the possessive way his laird enjoyed. Then he removed his clothing and gestured for Callum to do the same.

"Stroke your cock, my laird," said Alastair as he handled his own thick length. "Show the lady how you like to be touched and what she'll soon be sucking."

Isla moaned, her body near-swaying on the cushion as she struggled to follow his rules. The curious little kitten wanted to touch and taste; need was plain on her face.

Showing her mercy at last, Alastair reached over and took one of her hands, then guided it down to wrap around his engorged cock. Callum did the same.

"Now," he bit out, stifling a groan of pleasure at the sensation of her rough palm encircling him. "Now we begin."

☙❧

Every day, she envied Callum at the way Alastair respected him in public, and mastered him in private. Those hungry kisses. Teasing touches until he begged. Rough fucking that left him sated and dripping with seed, before being tenderly cradled. She had provoked Alastair repeatedly, hoping intemperate words or brazen behavior would lead to the same for herself, yet he had always resisted.

Until now.

Saints alive, the way he'd just touched her, treating her not as a highborn lady, but a lusty woman with desires he knew just how to ease. Even better, he would not gift her pleasure, but insist she earn it. Any warrior knew the greatest victories were those fought hard for.

Isla knelt on the cushion, the fire warming her naked skin, a thick, engorged cock clasped in each hand. Yes, her nipples and cunt throbbed in righteous fury at being neglected, but knowing that Alastair would decide if she had earned a reward and would be permitted release, only heightened her arousal.

"What must I do?" she murmured.

Alastair settled his hand atop her head, his fingers parting her hair to massage her scalp and ease the ache of her tight braid, and she almost purred. The squire often massaged Callum, and to receive the same strong yet tender touch was thrilling. With him, she wasn't forced to choose between warrior or cosseted lover. She could be both, and that was wondrous indeed.

"Lick the head of each cock, Isla. Kiss it. Then take it between your lips and suck."

"You will...ah...go slowly?"

His gaze softened. "Just the head. As it is your first lesson, neither of us will fuck your mouth. You decide how much to take; if it becomes overwhelming, then draw back and use your hand."

"We'll tell you when we are close to spending, so you might rest our cocks on your breasts," added Callum. "You do not have to swallow our seed."

"Very well," she said, gazing up at Alastair. Then, keeping her eyes on him, she dragged her tongue against the head of his cock.

His breath hissed between his teeth, and Isla shivered in delight. How exciting to know, that even naked on her knees and ordered to kiss and suck two cocks, she still held such power.

Eagerly, she learned the size and texture of Alastair's

beast-sized cockhead with her lips and tongue. It was stone-hard, yet the skin felt soft, and the pearly moisture dripping into her mouth tasted almost salty. Earthy. Then she moved her head and did the same to Callum. His cock wasn't as thick, but longer in length, and he tasted muskier. As promised, they remained still, but the ragged gasps and guttural groans at her ministrations boosted her confidence.

Isla returned to Alastair and took the entire head of his cock into her mouth, until she could close her lips around it.

"Yes," he breathed. "Now suck. There's a good lass. Use your tongue on the underside, and your cheeks. Harder. Like that...just like that. Clever Isla..."

Warmed by the praise, sinking into a dreamy, intimate world of mouth and cocks and hands, she slid her fingers to the base of each shaft and began stroking the heavy balls dangling underneath while she sucked. Moving from one cock to the other and back.

Callum shuddered. "You are...a fast learner, Isla."

She smiled and took him deeper into her mouth, until his hand clenched her shoulder and he moaned. Then she returned to Alastair, handling his cock as she sucked and lapped at him.

"I'm going to spend," he bit out, the hand in her hair tugging until she arched her back. "Cup your breasts."

Isla lifted and pushed the small mounds together as best she could. Alastair gripped his cock and rubbed it in the narrow furrow, and as he found his release with a low roar, warm seed gushed onto her breasts. He anointed her taut nipples with the silky, sticky mess, teasing and pinching them, and Isla whimpered as jolts of sensation arrowed straight to her wet, aching cunt.

"Spend, Callum," commanded Alastair. "Cover her with it."

Now she held the laird's gaze as he roughly handled his

cock, and soon his pearly seed trickled down from her collar-bone, his cry of release still echoing in the room.

Kneeling there, the fire warm at her back, the scent of lust heavy in the air, and dripping with seed, Isla trembled. Never had she felt like she belonged, that she had a sanctuary where she could be her true self in every way and indulge her most wicked passions. But here with these two men, who yielded to her with sword in hand then ordered her to pleasure them...it felt like she'd finally found her home.

Tears she never cried gathered in her eyes. "Alastair," she said hoarsely, near mindless now with need. "Callum. *Please*..."

Alastair crouched down and guided her onto her arse with her legs stretched out in front of her. "Aye, my lady, you've earned your reward. Fetch another cushion for her head, Callum."

Soon she lay on the woven rug in front of the fire, her thighs spread and feet flat on the floor. But to her surprise, Alastair lifted her legs and gently pushed them back toward her breasts, making her hold onto them. Now her slick folds and back entrance were fully exposed to his glittering gaze.

"I'm going to feast on this sweet cunt now," he rasped, licking his lips. "Callum, suck her nipples. Suck them until they are harder than diamonds."

Isla closed her eyes, her breathing shallow pants. "Hurry. *Hurry*."

But she received neither boon. Instead, Alastair's hand curled around her mound and administered a sharp smack. She groaned as the delicious sting worsened the throbbing of her swollen pearl.

"Impatience, lady?" said Alastair in a steely tone.

"N-no," Isla choked out. "No...Master Graham."

"Better."

A word she had often said to them in swordplay. How

reassuring it was that he remembered and understood: before she had been the conqueror, now she wished to be conquered.

To add to the occasion, even gentle Callum tormented rather than eased her; smoothing her hair with one hand while the other drew patterns on her skin, purposefully avoiding her seed-splashed breasts or the top of her mound.

"How wet is our captive?" asked Callum, as though inquiring about the weather.

Alastair smiled. "Sight and scent says the lady is soaked. But only with touch can I be sure."

Almost lazily, he petted her bush, before pressing one finger deeper, parting her slick, petal-soft folds and stroking them. Isla whined at the too-delicate touch, but in her current position she lay perfectly, wonderfully helpless.

Callum flicked her right nipple with his thumb. "Isla is behaving now. Shall we reward her?"

"*Aye.*"

The word hung in the air like fine mist. A heartbeat later, Callum's lips fastened about her nipple, Alastair's tongue laved her cunt, and a shriek tore from her throat as her body bucked in release. Yet even when the first harsh spasms weakened into gentle pulses, the men offered no respite. Callum moved next to Alastair, leaning down to tease her back entrance with his tongue before pushing it inside her. Alastair pressed on her pearl with his thumb, and her hips writhed on the cushion as a second release crashed over her.

Her head too heavy to lift from the cushion, she sensed rather than saw them move again.

"I...I can't," she whispered dazedly. "Not a third time."

"You can and you will," said Alastair. "With Callum's finger in your cunt and mine in your arse...oh, look at that, my laird. Another trickle of honey at the thought of both of us inside her."

Isla sobbed. "When Callum wins the tourney...on our

wedding night...will you take me together? Not your fingers...but your cocks?"

Silence dropped like a heavy shroud and she inwardly cursed her wayward tongue. Once again, too soon.

Then Callum cleared his throat. "Is that what you truly want, Isla? A husband and a lover in your bed?"

"Not any husband or lover," she corrected. "Callum MacIntyre and Alastair Graham. If...if that is what you wish also."

"You really want me too?" asked Alastair slowly, his gaze wary yet glimmering with raw craving. "Why?"

"I should not like to choose between a masterful devilish beast and a sweet scholar. I want both. I *need* both. So much."

The laird nodded solemnly. "We'll not make you choose. Will we, Alastair?"

"Nay." Taking Callum's hand, Alastair swirled his middle finger in her honey, before slowly and gently pushing it just inside her cunt. "On our wedding night, Callum will take you here."

Isla cried out as the laird's finger swirled and found a small, rough spot that sent fierce darts of pleasure shooting through her whole body. "Y-yes."

"And I will take you here," Alastair continued, wetting his finger thoroughly and then easing it inside her tight back entrance.

She writhed; the double penetration too intense a sensation for her already overwhelmed body. Yet when those two fingers became four and began a slow, sensual duel, rubbing and caressing each other through the thinnest of internal walls, her head fell back and she screamed in ecstasy.

Soon, so soon, her world would be perfect. A husband, a lover, a new family to begin.

Nothing could come between them and happiness now.

Surely.

CHAPTER 9

"Wake up, Isla."

"No," she mumbled, quite content to remain exactly where she was, naked on cushions in front of the fire, with the arms of two equally naked men wrapped around her.

In all honesty, she wasn't sure if she could move. Her limbs were heavy, her skin sensitive, her mind at peace after Alastair and Callum had ruthlessly and relentlessly pleasured her for hours. The only place she should be was right here, cradled between them.

"Isla," said Alastair, curling his hand around her shoulder and gently shaking her. "You must return to the castle. Before anyone notices you are gone."

She sat up, utterly forlorn at the reminder. With both the revels and sword fighting remaining in the tourney, six men were still determined to win her hand in marriage. If her family, the king and queen, or the other entrants knew she had given Callum sword lessons, and that she had pleasured—and been pleasured—by him and his squire...there would be nowhere in Scotland for her to hide. "I know," she replied dully. "I hate to leave you both, though."

Callum kissed her neck until her toes curled. Then he rose to his feet, tugging her with him. "We'll wash and dress you. Then walk you to within a stone's throw of the castle gate."

After a sponge bath, they bound her breasts with the length of linen, and helped her with her shirt, stockings, and hose. Then they dressed themselves.

"What about your hair?" asked Alastair, frowning.

Isla gasped. "Oh no! Morag braids it very tightly and coils it to fit under my hat. I'm terrible at braiding, when I try to do it myself they are loose and lumpy. Devil take it, I can't return with my hair unbound."

"Allow me," said Callum.

"My braiding is better," said Alastair.

"I think not, old man."

Isla stared at them, torn between laughter and surprise. "How? Who taught you?"

"My mother has very long hair," said Callum. "She said everyone should know how to braid."

Alastair sniffed. "Based on some of the bird's nests we see in the Highlands, not nearly enough do. But I shall braid yours. Fetch the ribbon, Callum."

The laird did so, muttering darkly the entire time, and continuing on as Alastair sectioned her hair into three parts.

"Isla needs it pulled tight, Alastair."

"I am pulling it tight."

"Tighter. Like a rope, not a drunken caterpillar climbing her head."

"Any more advice," growled Alastair, "and you'll be taking a swim in the River Forth."

"Even swimming I could braid better," said Callum, rolling his eyes.

Her shoulders rocked with giggles. "You two."

Alastair spanked her arse. "Stand still or it will be a lumpy braid...there we go. Done."

Isla patted it with her fingers, then turned and beamed at the squire. "As good as Morag! I am most grateful to the Lady of Glennoe. And you."

Once she'd covered her hair with Leith's cap and pulled on her cloak, they lit two torches and set off for the castle. The night air was cool, and light rain dampened them all, but it wasn't that making her shiver. Only a need to hurry back to her chamber before anyone discovered the rolled-up clothing and carefully arranged pillows in her bed were not a person.

"Don't come any further," she said, when the castle gate was about fifty feet away. "I don't want anyone to recognize you. But I'll see you at the revels...after that just two little swordfights, Callum, and we three can return home to Glennoe."

The laird grinned wryly. "Yes. Two little swordfights. Good evening...*laddie*."

Alastair clapped her on the shoulder as men often did to greet or farewell each other, then he and Callum walked back down the steep path toward Stirling.

Taking a deep breath, Isla sauntered toward the torch-lit gate, as though a lad without cares. Two men at arms watched her approach and stood to attention, blocking her way.

"State your business," began one of the men, before pausing and peering at her in the low light. "Wait. I've seen you afore. Ain't you Leith's lad?"

"Aye, sir," said Isla, deepening her voice as best she could.

"What are you doing out at this hour?" he continued with a suspicious glare. "No messages to run."

She gulped. "A personal errand."

The second guard tilted his head, his eyes cold. "In the dark of night?"

"T'was the only time the lassie could meet me," Isla blurted.

The first guard snorted and shook his head. "Ye left the castle for a fuck? Daft wee lad. Plenty of willing women here. If a companion is needed, I'll find ye one."

"That is er...kind of you."

"Nay. Leith has been generous. Now get your scrawny arse to bed. You'll be working hard at the revels, that's a fact."

"Wait," said the second guard.

Isla froze, her heart threatening to pound out of her chest. "Yes?"

"Ye did spend outside her? We'll not have guests leave Stirling lasses with broken hearts and swollen bellies."

"No cock," said Isla honestly, her cheeks hot. "Tongue and fingers. Just as well the walls were stone, for she fair shrieked like a Highland wind."

Both men chuckled, and the second guard cuffed her shoulder, almost sending her sprawling onto the ground. "Good lad. You'll have sweet dreams with the taste of cunt in your mouth. Go on, then."

"Aye sirs," she replied, inclining her head.

Isla forced herself to stroll across the inner close toward her chamber, although her neck dripped with sweat. Next, she removed her shoes, climbed the stone steps, and hurried down the thankfully empty torch-lit hallway leading to the Sutherland lodgings.

Hardly daring to breathe, Isla eased the well-oiled wooden door open before latching it behind her. All she had to do now was cross the chamber and slide into bed. If she could remove her shirt and hose and put on the fresh shift she'd tucked under the quilt, no one would be any the wiser.

Slowly, so slowly, she tip-toed across the chamber. Fortunately, the path was clear; no rugs to trip over or chairs to scramble around. Nearly there, nearly there...

A hand clamped on her shoulder and roughly jerked her around. "You thought to rob the Sutherland, laddie? I'll gut you like a fish...what the devil? *Isla?*"

"Father," she croaked, truly fearful. "Ah...good evening..."

Lord John Sutherland glared at her, his silver-touched brows drawing together. "Where have you been, daughter? What mischief have you made now?"

"None, I swear," Isla replied, unable to meet his gaze.

"Liar," a voice hissed to her right, and before she could move, Anne Sutherland grabbed her right arm and twisted it painfully behind her back. "*Liar*. I note you did not answer your sire. Where have you been?"

"I just...needed some air."

"Dressed as a lad?" her mother spat, before jerking her arm higher. Her *sword* arm.

Isla flinched but stared defiantly ahead. "Shall I attend the revels with a broken arm, Mother? How should I respond to the king when he asks about such an injury?"

"I'll respond for you. That you are willful, foolish, and disobedient. Who were you with?"

A boulder lodged in her throat at the dangerous question. "No one."

"I'll find out and kill the wretch myself," said her father, cold as ice. "Easy enough to dispose of a body with the cliffs and river nearby."

Isla bit her lip hard enough to draw blood. Silence was her only friend here. If they knew who she'd been with, what she'd done, the consequences would be vicious and terrible for Callum and Alastair. Her father remained wealthy and powerful because he brutalized his enemies and shunned forgiveness. No one in Scotland would take the side of a minor Western Highlands laird over the Earl of Sutherland.

"Was it one of your suitors, Isla?" asked her mother, her gaze abruptly and deceptively kind. "Must we ask the king to cease this tourney, because you've already surrendered your maidenhead to a great lord? Such men easily turn a woman's head. Tell me which one. Tell me who I shall embrace as my new son."

"I am virgin, still," she snapped.

"But not unawakened," Anne replied, her voice hard once more. "I know that blush. Who has given you pleasure? Who dared touch what does not belong to him? Answer me, daughter, or you will regret it."

They stared at her; an earl who ruled with a fist of iron, and a beautiful countess with a heart of stone. Inside, little Isla, the youngest child who had always craved their love and approval, fought older Isla, the woman eager to leave them and their cruel intrigues behind.

"I was alone," she insisted.

"You disappoint me," said John. "A liar and a whore. But I'll find out who, and he shall pay dearly for his sins."

Anne nodded. "That clothing shall be examined to discover the weaver, and you'll be watched day and night until your wedding. We'll learn all your secrets. Now go to bed. I cannot bear the sight of you."

Somehow, Isla retreated to her corner of the bedchamber without stumbling. Soon, she huddled in her bed, cold and alone in the darkness but unable to sleep for worry.

Callum and Alastair did not know it, but they were now in grave danger. How could she warn them without being caught or landing Leith and Morag in trouble with her?

For the first time in her life, a task seemed...impossible.

※

Stepping into the Great Hall was like stepping into another world.

Barely suppressing a gasp of admiration, Alastair allowed

his gaze to travel the length and breadth of the enormous space. Colorful ribbons fluttered whenever anyone moved past them, intricate tapestries hung from the walls, large urns held bouquets of wildflowers, and the usual trestle tables had been pushed aside to allow for rows of wooden benches covered with velvet cushions. Servants walked about carrying trays with pewter goblets of wine, mead, and small ale, others offered pastries, dried fruit, marzipan squares, and almond comfits. As the revels and swordfights would only be viewed by high-ranking courtiers and selected envoys; this aspect of the tourney was very much the king showing Scottish hospitality to the world.

He turned to Callum as they followed a large group of well-dressed men into the Hall. "Adequate."

His laird snorted. "You've never seen anything so grand. Admit it."

"I admit nothing. What do you suppose you'll have to do this day? The minstrels are up in their gallery, but I see instruments next to the king and queen's dais as well."

"Which instruments?"

"Hmmm," said Alastair, craning his neck a little. "Harp, flute, pipe, lyre, and lute. You are skilled with flute and lyre. As long as His Grace does not choose an instrument for you, or make you stand on your head to play it, of course."

Callum sighed as they found a less crowded space next to a fireplace. "At this point, nothing would surprise me. The king does enjoy keeping us on our toes. I don't want to stare... but how are the other men faring? Are they happy or anxious?"

Alastair glanced around. Red held one corner of the Great Hall, telling an eager group of courtiers a rather bloody tale of a stag hunt. Lord Spalding sipped from a goblet of wine while sharing jests with several beautiful ladies. Lord Hamilton of Arran stood with his arms folded on the other side of the Hall, his impatience unmasked as he spoke only to his squire. Sir Leslie Hay and his squire were admiring a tapestry of a unicorn and scantily clad maiden frolicking beside a loch. And Lord Ruthven of Perth, taller than everyone in the room, was devouring a handful of pastries with his squire.

"Well enough," he replied reluctantly. "I believe they all think to progress to the sword fighting."

A flourish of trumpet notes sounded.

"His Grace the king! Her Grace the queen!" bellowed the herald.

Everyone in the hall turned as the royal couple entered; the king resplendent in scarlet satin doublet embroidered with gold thread, black hose, and ermine-lined cloak, his chains of state gleaming in the mid-morning sunshine that streamed through the pairs of tall windows. The queen wore a cream velvet gown embroidered with silver, and like the king, her clothing was also lined with ermine. She near-dripped with jewels; her gable hood and girdle were studded with pearls, and she also wore an elaborate sapphire necklace and many rings. They nodded to those they passed, before settling on carved chairs at the center of the dais, in pride of place on the north wall. If any were unsure before, this confirmed it. The revels weren't for Isla at all, but a stage for Scotland.

"The Earl and Countess of Sutherland! Lady Isla Sutherland!"

The great lord of the north strode into the hall like a king himself, his wife's hand resting on his sleeve. They were night and day; he with silver-touched black hair and dressed in blue so dark it appeared black, while she wore yellow with gold embroidery and looked like a sunbeam. A *cold* sunbeam.

Alastair frowned. Both Lord and Lady Sutherland were smiling but the geniality looked forced, and their gazes darted about the Great Hall as though searching for something. Behind them, Isla walked alone wearing an embroidered gable hood and rose-pink gown, a color that reminded him so much of her nipples that he ground his teeth against a rush of lust. Yet Isla did not nod or smile at anyone. Instead, she stared directly ahead, her shoulders rigid. Even when she and her mother and father took chairs to the right of the king and queen, Isla did not look at the tourney entrants or the honored guests, only the king.

All was not well.

He folded his arms to stop himself marching forward and tossing courtiers out of the way to discover what pained her. Yes, Isla hated wearing a gown and gable hood, but this seemed far more than that annoyance. The magnificent lass who had easily defeated him with her sword, kneeled at his feet and taken his cock in her mouth, sobbed her pleasure at his touch, cuddled against his chest, and giggled at his hair braiding...had vanished.

Alastair leaned down to Callum. "Our lady is unhappy."

"Yes," muttered his laird grimly. "With us?"

"I don't think so...she is not looking at anyone. Only the king. It is very odd."

"The earl and countess are looking at us, though...I think this is how a rabbit feels just before it is torn apart by hawks."

Alastair nodded. "I'm thankful to have never faced the Sutherland on the battlefield. Or his lady wife for that matter. Could they know about the visits?"

Callum hesitated. "I'm not sure. They are staring at several men in that manner—"

The king clapped his hands and rose to his feet. "Welcome to my Great Hall! Queen Margaret and I are delighted you have come this day to watch the revels. Six men remain in my tourney to win the hand of Lady Isla, and shall entertain us all first with a tune on the instrument of their choice, then a dance with the lady. As my queen is most accomplished in both arts, she will assist me in deciding the final four to progress to the sword fighting."

Margaret preened at her husband's praise. "I have seen the best of the English court," she declared. "Now I wish to see the best of the Scottish."

The king smiled indulgently. "I assure you it will be merry. However…"

"Standing on my head," Callum groaned softly. "As you said."

Alastair didn't reply, already his heart had sunk to his shoes. What would James demand this time? At least they weren't the only ones reluctant to hear the news, murmurings around them revealed the other entrants were equally wary.

"However," the king continued. "For the tune, each entrant must be accompanied by his squire. He may sing or play an instrument, but they must both take part. A good husband, worthy of Lady Isla, shall have a range of skills and the trust and respect of those closest to him."

His spirits soared. At last, rather than just applaud or encourage or massage, he could truly assist his laird in winning the tourney and Isla's hand. Lady Maude had taught them both to dance and play instruments in her solar, and those times were some of the happiest of his childhood. The old laird had disapproved, shunning anything he deemed 'soft' but thankfully had not forbidden either activity.

"Excellent," called Lord Spalding. "Who shall entertain you and your lovely queen first, Your Grace?"

"Sir Leslie Hay," announced the king. "Followed by Callum MacIntyre, Lord of Glennoe, yourself, Lord Hamilton of Arran, the MacDonald of Carnoch, and to finish, Lord Ruthven of Perth. My lords, lairds, ladies, and honored guests from Scotland or abroad, please do sit and be entertained."

The young knight looked a little ill at the thought of

performing first, but he played the pipe more than passing fair, and his squire sang with a deep and powerful voice. When they finished, applause rippled around the Great Hall.

Now it was their turn.

"They were very good," muttered Callum as he chose a wooden flute, while Alastair reached down for the lute.

"We'll be better," Alastair replied. "Now is not the time to be modest; the king and queen must have no choice but to choose you as one of the final four."

All eyes were upon them as they returned to the center of the Great Hall, apart from Isla who glanced, but just as swiftly looked away. Irritably, he stared down at his lute, cradling the pear-shaped instrument against his chest. His left hand curled about the long neck, while the fingers of his right hand plucked at each course of strings, the first a single, then five pairs.

Plague take it, what was wrong? Did she have regrets about the hours they'd spent together?

Did the lady regret submitting to an orphaned, penniless squire? Had she decided, as most did, that he was unworthy of her time and affection?

The thoughts clawed at him, and he plucked the bottom string too firmly, causing a discordant note to echo in the Hall. Several men laughed, devil-spawned Red the loudest.

Mortified, Alastair gritted his teeth then met Callum's gaze.

"Begin."

※

Before he performed, Callum inhaled and exhaled slowly, allowing himself one glance at Isla. Alastair was correct, she did look unhappy. Not sad, though. More like she wished to find a dark chamber and stab a cushion sixty-five times.

There might be a reasonable explanation, but at this moment his stomach roiled with dread.

No. He needed to take control. Like archery, playing music was something he could do well. He and Alastair had often entertained his mother as she sat embroidering in the solar or working in her herbal chamber. '*A merry tune*' she would say. '*To lift my spirits and give praise unto God.*'

That was the answer. Something to show Isla they cared, something to make her smile.

Callum met Alastair's gaze. "A *merry* tune," he whispered, before settling the flute near his lips.

His squire nodded. Shortly afterward, Alastair began tapping his shoe heel on the floor, a sharp and constant sound to keep them in time.

It was much easier to move about with a flute. As Callum's fingers danced up and down the wooden instrument, a kind of mist descended, blocking the other men and the Great Hall. He could see the king and queen, but played only for Isla. With a flourish of deep, low notes, he stomped forward as though in a temper. Then with a deliberately large side step he unleashed a flurry of high notes, complete with a twirl and heel kick behind him, the other side of the argument. Back and forth he went, low to high, temper to playful, and soon several ladies including the queen herself were giggling and clapping in time with Alastair's heel taps. Greatly encouraged, Callum made his movements even more expressive, and soon the sound of laughter from other guests and envoys was too loud to ignore.

He returned to Alastair and they began a musical duel, several notes from his flute challenging several notes from the lute. His squire remained in place, heel still tapping, but Callum circled him using several of the foot movements that Isla had helped perfect. Front. Back. Diagonal. False step.

"What a sight to behold," called the king delightedly. "Musical swordplay!"

Only then did Callum permit himself another glance at Isla. This time she met his gaze, the tiniest smile at her lips as she clapped a few times, before turning away again. Now certain that something was amiss, Callum moved forward so he played directly in front of the dais. God's blood, it was a contrast, the genial approval of the king and queen, and the frigid, false smiles of the Sutherlands. How had a warm, bold, unconventional lass like Isla survived in such treacherous waters?

He completed one final high note flourish on the flute, Alastair did the same on the lute, before both sank to one knee.

The king stood, applauding wildly. "Marvelous! What a spectacle! Glennoe and Master Graham have laid down a mighty challenge to the other entrants, have they not, my queen?"

Margaret nodded, her cheeks flushed and eyes bright rather than her usual petulance. "Very enjoyable. It... reminded me of Richmond Palace."

Callum bowed. "Thank you both."

"And what say you, Lady Isla?" asked James cheerfully.

Her smile was thin at best. "Good, Your Grace."

"Indeed," he replied, looking a little surprised, before turning back to Callum and Alastair. "Sit, with my compliments. You have earned your wine this day."

A servant took their instruments and then directed them to an empty, cushion-covered bench, and they sat down gratefully. Another servant brought goblets of wine and pastries, and they gulped down the light repast as Lord Spalding and his squire each fetched a lyre.

Callum's spirits flagged a little when they played well together, although they rose again when Lord Hamilton of

Arran and his squire performed poorly with the same instrument. Alas, then came Red, lugging a harp into the center of the Hall. While the squire played, Red sang an old Scottish ballad, and nearly everyone in the room had tears in their eyes as they stood to applaud at the finish.

"Sewer rat," he muttered.

Alastair's lip curled. "Your cousin did not play an instrument at all. Should be tossed out on his arse."

"That would be too much good fortune. But here is Lord Ruthven of Perth. He and his squire both have lutes."

What proceeded was rather like the performance of small children; great enthusiasm rather than talent, and from the expressions of those around them, the applause at the end was relief rather than appreciation.

The king rose to his feet. "Thank you for your efforts, my lord. Let us all pause for wine and entertainment, then the dancing shall begin. Lady Isla, I hope you are well rested, for you must dance with six men this day, in the same order as their musical performance."

She curtsied. "As Your Grace wishes."

The wine soon flowed in the Great Hall, a long procession of servants filling and refilling goblets until jests became more ribald and laughter even louder. Fortunately, more trays of food that could be eaten from a linen napkin rather than a plate or trencher came from the kitchens as well; soft white bread with butter, hearty pasties made with beef and venison, sliced wheels of cheese, and cherry tarts. Soon afterward, Peter the Moor, the king's African drummer who often traveled the country with him, performed to thunderous applause.

After Peter bowed to the royal couple and departed the Hall, the minstrels in the gallery began to play once more, and the entrants and guests returned to their seats.

"Sir Leslie Hay," said the king. "*Dance*."

Callum gritted his teeth as the knight whirled Isla about the floor with confidence and skill. It seemed certain he would be one of the final four and when their music came to an end, the young man returned to his seat with a grin that near split his face.

Alastair leaned close. "Dance well, my laird. And find out what ails our lady."

"I will."

The king beckoned him forward. "Callum MacIntyre, Lord of Glennoe."

When Callum joined Isla, she sank into a curtsy. "Glennoe."

"Lady," he replied, taking her hand and squeezing it.

A tiny shake of her head told him he'd erred, and his brow furrowed as the minstrels began a rousing and familiar Highland tune.

"I was discovered," muttered Isla through a falsely bright smile as they held hands and stepped four paces right, then left. "My father and mother are watching for my lover..."

They broke apart, turning a full circle, before joining hands again.

"Did they hurt you?" he asked.

"Not really. Furious, though. My sire wants *blood*."

With opposite hands clasped over their heads, they stepped toward each other then back, once then twice. "He knows it is us?"

"Not yet. Be careful."

Callum's heart swelled. "You care a great deal."

"Aye," she said, glaring at him as they broke apart and turned again.

"When we are wed," he murmured as they skipped eight paces right, then eight paces left. "You'll be free to choose. Clothing. Hair. Swords. A husband and a lover in your bed. This I swear."

Isla deliberately stumbled against him. "I cannot visit this night. Win my hand. I beg you."

The minstrels ended with a great flourish, and more reluctant than he'd ever been in his life, Callum let go of Isla and bowed. She curtsied with a cool smile, before returning to the dais.

"Your Grace," laughed Isla. "Do forgive my clumsy misstep. Glennoe deserved better than a crushed foot. May I have a moment before the next dance?"

"Of course, of course. Glennoe, sit and rest that injured foot. I know as a gallant like myself, you shall not limp too noticeably."

Callum stilled at the gleam in their sovereign's eye. He knew Isla's story was a lie?

God's blood. There were far too many intrigues at court for his liking.

Heart pounding, he returned to Alastair and sat down. "Isla was discovered. That is why her father and mother watch us all like bloodthirsty hawks. They know she has a lover, but not who."

His squire cursed. "Is she well? Did they hurt her?"

"She couldn't say much, but is eager for this tourney to be over. I just hope you are correct when you say the king favors me, for he well knows Isla did not step on my foot."

They sat in tense silence as the remaining four entrants danced with Isla, each demonstrating varied grace. Once the king had conferred with the queen, he clapped his hands for quiet.

"We have seen great talent in music and dance this day. But I have made my decision. The four men to progress to the final event on the morrow, the sword fighting, shall be..."

As one, all in the Great Hall leaned forward to hear.

"The MacDonald of Carnoch against Sir Leslie Hay. And Lord Spalding against Callum MacIntyre, Lord of Glennoe."

Torn between elation at progressing and dismay at his opponent, Callum rubbed his jaw. The wily older lord had fought on many battlefields, and as he'd proven in the previous events, age had not dimmed his vigor at all.

He would be a formidable opponent indeed.

CHAPTER 10

Yesterday the Great Hall had been a genial stage of laughter and merriment. Today had a different air altogether: pain and humiliation.

"If the longswords weren't blunted, Red would have killed him by now."

Alastair nodded grimly at Callum's whispered words as they watched the battle raging in front of them. "Aye. I wonder how long the king will permit this to last. It is clear to all that one is superior."

Although Sir Leslie Hay was a rival, the suffering he endured at Red's hands made Alastair wince. The longsword tip might be blunted, but the blade remained sharp, and Sir Leslie's clothing had been torn, his arms and chest a mass of shallow cuts. If someone other than Sir Lachlan was overseeing the fight, or someone other than the king had provided the swords to ensure no trickery, he hated to think of the bloodshed that might have occurred.

The other mercy was Red and Callum being kept apart in the first round. He suspected it had been deliberate on the king's part, and was grateful beyond measure. His laird needed a fair fight to gain further confidence after Isla's lessons.

Isla.

As always, she sat on the dais with her father and mother alongside the royal couple. Today she wore a gown of stark white velvet embroidered with silver and lined with mink, a silver girdle at her waist, and a pearl-studded gable hood with a white satin veil covering her hair. Not a gown Isla would have chosen; never had she appeared so cold, highborn, or untouchable. This was the Sutherlands declaring their ancient bloodline and that their youngest daughter would be a virgin bride.

It irritated him no end that they'd not had the chance to speak with Isla, even in a group. He wanted to know she was well, *truly* well, for it was hard to imagine her family forgiving a transgression without brutal consequences. While Callum would fight for her, he needed to reassure her that they both cared, that they would both cherish and stand with her wholeheartedly from this day forward.

At last, Sir Lachlan stepped forward to halt the sword-fight. However Red, like the weasel he was, managed to land one final blow that left his opponent sprawled on the floor, bleeding from a fresh cut to his side.

The king stood and rang a large hand bell. "Sir Leslie has fought admirably and brings honor to his name and clan. But I must declare the battle over and the MacDonald of Carnoch the victor."

Applause swept through the hall. With no thought for Sir Leslie, Red left him lying on the floor being attended by his squire, and instead walked to the dais. He bowed to the royal couple, then dropped to one knee in front of the Sutherlands.

"My lord. My lady. I have proven myself many times this week, and seek a blessing to wed your daughter when I win the second swordfight."

Lord Sutherland laughed. "*When*. I admire such confidence and wish you well, MacDonald. It will take a strong husband to curb Isla's willfulness."

"Yes," said Lady Sutherland, her lips pursing. "She needs to learn proper wifely ways."

Red and the countess exchanged a significant look, and Alastair's fists clenched. Neither of them even glanced at Isla. She might have been a wooden box for all they cared.

The king rang his bell again. "I now call Lord Spalding and Callum MacIntyre, Lord of Glennoe to fight."

Alastair turned to Callum and massaged his shoulders one final time. For the swordfight he would wear shirt and hose, but the hose had been trimmed at the ankle to leave his feet bare, so he did not slip on the floor.

"Lord Spalding is an experienced swordsman," he murmured, "but his right shoulder is troubling him. He clutched at it after the stone put. Now is the time to be ruthless. I expect it of you. Isla expects it of you. *Red cannot be permitted to win this tourney.*"

"I know," said Callum simply.

"Good fortune, my laird."

They stared at each other so long he almost forgot himself and kissed Callum. But the last thing this day needed was a hue and cry from the Sutherlands about MacIntyre sin and immorality.

Callum smiled and squeezed his hand. Then he turned and walked to the center of the Great Hall. A servant handed him his blunted longsword, and he tested the weight and grip, slashing left and right before carefully resting the blade on his shoulder as Isla did.

Alastair stifled a grin. His laird almost looked...*calm*. All the hours of training with Isla, salt baths for his feet, and the foul-smelling poultices applied to his limbs to draw out aches and pains, had not been in vain.

Next, Sir Lachlan ordered Callum and Lord Spalding to clasp hands. "As in the first fight, the rules are thus: no blades to the head. On my command...you halt at once. A man who loses...his sword thrice, is defeated. I insist on a fair fight. Any trickery...will be punished harshly. I am the king's champion. *I will know*."

Both men bowed to the royal couple, then to Sir Lachlan.

Moments later, the first clash of steel echoed in the Hall.

Alastair couldn't watch. Yet he couldn't look away. Lord Spalding had an ease of movement that came from experience; his cuts were graceful yet deadly, and it was only Callum's nimble feet that allowed him to avoid the slashing blade.

"Attack," he muttered. "Faster. Remember what Isla said. Do not let him decide the pace and direction. And it's his shoulder. His damned shoulder. Make him stretch it."

As if he'd heard, Callum lunged with a sharp upward cut, forcing Spalding to defend at an awkward angle. A heartbeat later he lunged again with a straight thrust, and Spalding's sword clattered to the floor.

"One point, Glennoe," said Sir Lachlan, as applause sounded.

The men readied themselves; Callum looking more relaxed and Spalding a little tense. But the older lord was far too cunning to be surprised a second time, and lunged at Callum with a sharp downward cut. This time it was Callum's sword on the floor.

"One point, Spalding."

Alastair hissed at the result, and when he met Callum's gaze, he touched his elbow. Plague take it, if Callum lost this battle because he neglected to keep his elbow high, he would chain it to his laird's head himself.

Callum understood though, for this time he stood in the stance that Isla had taught him with his sword grip next to his cheek, his elbow high and steady. He and Spalding circled each other and his opponent lunged, but Callum did not allow him to complete the cut, forcing the other man onto his back foot with a deflection before attacking swiftly.

Again, Spalding's sword clattered to the floor, and now he glistened with sweat.

"Two points, Glennoe," said Sir Lachlan.

Alastair bit his tongue to prevent commands spilling from his lips; orders for Callum to finish his opponent, to remove a limb or maybe an ear. All they needed was one point, just one, and his laird would face Red for Isla's hand. Callum had come so far. He'd always had skill, but had lacked in confidence. Travelling to Stirling, meeting bold, unconventional Isla and exploring lust as a trio had been the key to turn that. They both needed her. And she needed them in return.

Callum lunged, and his blade tore a little of Spalding's linen shirt. The older man attempted to fight back, but his right shoulder hung loosely and his cuts were becoming weaker, his sword trembling as it met Callum's.

"Take him," Alastair snarled. "*Take him.*"

Spalding hopped from one foot to another, before bringing both arms around in a strong horizontal slash. Alastair gasped as the blade missed Callum's side by less than an inch, but now his laird had an advantage, for the other man's arms were close to his body, his wrists angled downward. Using his shorter height, Callum crouched a little, then struck upward with a strong cut, lifting Spalding's sword out of his hands and spinning it away onto the floor.

"Three points," announced Sir Lachlan. "Glennoe wins!"

A brief, eerie silence filled the Hall as the guests and envoys realized the renowned courtier expected to win had been defeated. How could a short, slender Western Highlander have conquered the great Lord Spalding?

Others weren't befuddled, though. The king and Isla were

applauding, as were Lady Marjorie and Lady Janet, both seated down on the wooden benches, and sporting huge grins. Eventually more and more people joined in, a few even stomped their feet in appreciation of the unexpected win.

"How splendid," said James, his eyes gleaming. "The battle for Lady Isla's hand shall be cousin against cousin; the MacDonald of Carnoch, and Callum MacIntyre, Lord of Glennoe. We will halt now for a light repast and music from my minstrels, to allow the two men time to catch their breath. But mark me, friends, there shall be a victor and a wedding this day."

The Great Hall erupted in cheers, but Alastair remained silent. Yes, there would be a victor. Then, saints willing, he, his laird, and his lady could return to Glennoe and start their new family.

It was long past time for Red MacDonald to receive his comeuppance.

☙❧

One more victory, just one more.

Isla clasped her hands in an attempt to calm herself. Callum had fought so well against Lord Spalding, but it had been exceedingly difficult to stay in her chair and not leap about when he scored a point and shake her fists when his opponent did.

Yet after this rest would come the final— and largest— obstacle to happiness: the MacDonald of Carnoch. She'd never liked the red-haired Highlander and her initial dislike had soon grown into loathing. Everything about him was vile; his character, his manners, the way he treated others. The MacDonald wouldn't be a husband who offered choice, he would only humiliate and oppress.

"So, daughter," said her mother, leaning close. "Soon you

will be wed to Rory MacDonald. How happy you must be! A strong, handsome husband to give you fine sons. He will ensure you are an obedient wife who brings honor to his clan and your own."

Isla frowned. "The tourney is not over."

"Surely you do not think Glennoe will win? How foolish."

"Not think," she said. "Believe with my whole heart."

Anne laughed, the sound without warmth. "There is no chance of such an outcome. None whatsoever, my dear."

"You don't know that."

Her mother's eyes gleamed with malice. "But I do."

Isla froze. She knew that look. The careless spite of a woman who did as she pleased and suffered no consequences because her husband was a powerful man and the king needed their goodwill. "What have you done?"

"Merely ensured you will wed in the best interests of the Sutherland clan. A poor nobody who lusts after men is no use, even if he had a fine weaving house."

Saints alive.

Someone had recognized the MacIntyre cloth of her borrowed shirt and hose.

Black spots danced in her vision, but Isla forced herself to choke out the words once more. "*What have you done?*"

Anne glared. "No need for theatrics, Glennoe will be quite well by morning," she snapped. "It's just wine with some powdered Lily of the Valley."

"He'll not drink it. Not a gift from you," she replied in relief.

"Which is why I sent it to him, and his squire, with your best wishes and compliments."

No!

Pure horror cleaved through her body. Quickly followed by a surge of rage, and Isla stood to leave the dais. Anne tried to grasp her wrist, but after years of sword fighting, she knew exactly how to twist away from such a grip.

Nothing mattered but getting to Callum and Alastair.

Uncaring of the audience, Isla stormed from the Great Hall then ran as fast as she could across the inner close to the castle proper. At least living in Stirling Castle the past week, she knew where the various chambers and antechambers were. Thankfully there were few rooms available for guests, so if fortune smiled upon her, she would find her men before they drank the poisoned wine.

In the long hallway, she began pounding on doors. Both the first and second chambers were locked, but the third swung open to reveal Alastair, scowling darkly and holding a goblet.

"Isla?" he said, his frown easing to concern. "What is the matter?"

She snatched the goblet and hurled it onto the floor, wincing at the sound of pewter meeting stone. Then she pushed past him and hurried into the room. Oh no. Callum was drinking! "Put that down!" she screamed. "Spit it out. *Spit it out*!"

The laird's eyes flared and he thumped the goblet down on a side table. "Not from you, then. Who sent it? What was in the wine, Isla? Do you know?"

Tears spilled down her cheeks. "My mother. Lily of the Valley. You both must retch it up. Please."

Alastair cursed. "I only took a few sips, but Callum nearly finished his wine...my laird, what do you need from the medicine satchel?"

Callum sank to his knees. "It only takes a little. We must both retch. There is a small bottle of boiled water, and packages of powdered milk thistle, peppermint, and chamomile. A pinch of each. Hurry."

While Alastair prepared the herbal tonic, Isla dashed to

the corner of the room to fetch the copper chamber pot. Utterly indifferent if her awful gown became dirty, she knelt next to Callum. "Here. *Retch*."

Terrible sounds filled the chamber. When Alastair joined them, all she could do was rub their backs and sponge their foreheads as both men attempted to purge the poisonous plant from their body before it took hold. Eventually they sat back, their faces ashen and sweat dripping from their temples.

"The tonic," whispered Callum.

"Sip, don't gulp. There you go," said Isla, trying to remain calm as she held the bottle for them to drink from, but she shook with rage and fright. *Poison*. Her own mother had attempted to harm Callum so he would lose the swordfight he had trained so hard for, and Alastair as well so he could not fight in his laird's place. She'd always known Anne Sutherland had a heart of stone, but such an unspeakable act could not be borne.

"Here now, lassie," said Alastair gruffly, sliding a brawny arm around her shoulders. "Takes more than a little poison from your lady mother to halt us. Callum is the son of the most skilled healer in the Highlands, and she taught us well."

Isla buried her face against his chest and sobbed. It felt wrong—she loathed crying and rarely did so—but she couldn't stop the flow of angry tears. The MacDonald already had a height and weight advantage over Callum; if he won the fight because of damned *poison*...if the king tried to force her to wed that rodent...

She would slice out their innards. With a smile on her face.

"Dry your eyes, Isla," rasped Callum, taking her hand. "It might not be so bad; God willing I have retched up the wine in time. Only because you ran here in that gown and gable hood and heeled shoes...I am most impressed."

"Don't jest," she choked out. "This is unforgivable."

"Aye, it is. But you did not poison the wine. You do not benefit from such an act. My ire is not directed at you."

Isla shuddered, still unable to comprehend the evil that had been done in her name. "I could petition the king for more time. If he knew what had happened..."

Alastair rubbed her back, a remarkably soothing gesture. "He'd want proof. Your mother would only deny it. If Callum or I did become sick, they could claim bad meat or some such thing. Then others will say Callum is too scared to fight that festering turd."

She sniffled. "The MacDonald really is a festering turd. I hate him."

When Callum finished the bottle of herbed water, he lay down on a woven rug, one hand absently pressing his stomach. She moved so he could rest his head on her lap.

"Alastair, come join me," mumbled Callum, closing his eyes, and allowing his hair to be stroked. "This is very pleasant."

"Hush now," she replied. "Let that root—"

"Milk thistle, peppermint, and chamomile. I'm certain if you teach her swordplay, Lady Maude would teach you herbs," said Alastair idly.

Callum coughed. "The world is not ready for that much havoc."

"Ha. Just wait until you have a daughter who wishes to learn from mother *and* grandmother," she said in amusement.

His eyes flew open, and he struggled to sit up. "A daughter?"

Isla almost groaned. As usual, she spoke far too soon. "I know most men wish for sons, but daughters are special, too."

"Aye, they are," said Alastair as he took her hand and kissed it, making her gasp. "So you want children, Isla?"

"I never did before," she said honestly. "But now I can see

them in my mind. Little ones with gray eyes...and blue eyes. In a nursery with wooden swords and books and instruments, causing mischief aplenty for their mother and fathers. A true family. Not just blood, but choice."

Alastair reached for Callum's hand as well, before clasping them with his own. "A family of four thus far, for I know Lady Maude would welcome you into her heart, but with more to come. I believe we should pledge here this day to protect, cherish, and defend each other. In sad times and merry. What say you?"

"I do so pledge," said Callum, holding their hands tightly. "This day and every day henceforth. An unbreakable trio, equal partners all."

Isla gazed upon the only two men who had ever fully understood and accepted her, who had shown her such pleasure, the only two men she would ever love. Then she reached under her gown sleeve and withdrew three green hair ribbons she had secretly fastened about her wrist. "I do so pledge to protect, cherish, and defend, in sad times and merry. Now and forever. I hope you'll accept these as a token of my favor. As in the days of old. I thought...I thought we could each wear one."

"Aye," said Alastair, swallowing visibly as he wound her ribbon around his wrist and did the same for Callum. "Now the world will see we are three."

A knock came at the partially open chamber door. "Glennoe?" said a guard's voice. "The king requests Lady Isla return to her chair, and that you prepare to fight."

Isla kissed both Callum and Alastair's hands. "Fight for us. Fight for our family."

They stared at each other for an endless moment, their eyes conveying words their lips could not. Then Callum slowly rose to his feet. "I'm ready."

When Isla returned to the Great Hall, she curtsied to the king and queen but ignored her mother completely.

"Daughter—"

"Do not speak," she snarled. "You are the worst woman I've ever known. The worst mother. Fortunately, good shall triumph and your spite, your *evil* will not succeed. Now, you are dead to me. I renounce the Sutherlands and shall think of you no more."

Anne gasped in outrage, but Isla turned her shoulder away. This woman she'd tried so hard to please, had begged for attention and love from, was now as insignificant as an ant.

Please God, let Callum win.

༺✦༻

After Isla departed, Callum waited for a few minutes with Alastair in the chamber. Neither spoke, but their hands remained clasped, the narrow green ribbon binding them to Isla even when she wasn't with them. Then, they disengaged and walked side by side back to the Great Hall.

Never had he felt such fury.

He'd endured many slights in his life, but tried to remain fair and just. To improve himself and the lives of the others around him. The only reason he'd entered this tourney was to save his clan from destruction; that he'd not only found the woman of his dreams, but also renewed and strengthened his love for Alastair, was a wonderful addition.

However, as so often happened in his life, there were those who conspired against him and wished him harm. And as always, curse him to purgatory, Red stood at the center.

In childhood, it had been Red who encouraged others to throw stones, to mock Callum's English mother and humiliate him in front of his father. As a grown man, that spite and greed and selfishness had only become worse.

However, today's act was beyond all.

He'd seen the look that Red and Lady Sutherland exchanged after he defeated Sir Leslie. One that spoke of an unholy alliance. But never had Callum thought it would be an attempted poisoning that would unleash this need for vengeance. In the Great Hall he had to be more than a man of words; for a chance at love and happiness he'd scarcely dared to hope for, was on offer. Three points stood between him and victory over his cousin. And nothing would stop him. Not insults, not threats, not trickery, and certainly not his roiling gut.

Callum winced. While he hoped his retching and dose of herbed water had been enough to halt the flow of poison into his body, it was hard to be sure. He had nearly downed an entire goblet of wine, and Lily of the Valley was a harmful plant. Certainly not deadly like Belladonna, English Yew, or Water Hemlock, but still enough to make a body very ill. God forbid he succumb to any sudden body purges during the fight. That would be a woeful tale to follow him for the rest of his life.

"My laird..." said Alastair, with a gentle squeeze to his shoulder. "Is there anything you need?"

"Just those I love," he whispered.

His squire stared at him, tenderness and fierce pride in his eyes. "Good fortune."

The king rang his bell, and the guests and envoys took their seats. "Welcome back. This tourney started with thirty men, and now just two remain, each hoping to win the hand of Lady Isla. To my right, the MacDonald of Carnoch!"

Loud cheers sounded in the hall, and Callum gritted his teeth. If they knew Red as he did, would his cousin still have this support? It was hard to know with the wheels of favor in the Scottish court ever-turning.

"And to my left, Callum MacIntyre, Lord of Glennoe!"

Generous applause followed, alongside some raucous whoops, and he stifled a smile. Yes, everyone else expected Red to win, but Isla and Alastair, and his unexpected supporters Lady Marjorie and Lady Janet, would urge him on every moment of the swordfight. Maybe even the king as well.

Sir Lachlan stood between him and Red, an immovable man-mountain of judgment and justice. "Clasp hands."

Red smirked and held out his hand. "Cousin. At least you are well used to defeat, having enjoyed it for a lifetime."

"Cousin," Callum replied, clasping it for the least time possible, before stepping back.

"The rules of engagement...have not changed," said Sir Lachlan. "First man to three points...shall be the victor. Stop and start...on my command. No blades to the head. Trickery or misdeeds...shall be punished harshly. Here are your longswords."

Red took his and strolled to the center of the Great Hall, waving to the guests seated on benches either side of him. Callum glanced at Isla then Alastair; both nodded in encouragement. Bolstered by their support and the green ribbon wound around his wrist that symbolized their trio, he set his stance. Left foot forward, both hands gripping the sword hilt next to his right cheek. Isla had tutored him, Alastair had massaged him, now it was time for his part.

The king rang his bell. "Begin!"

Red swung his sword in a wide arc. "Come to me, cousin. Show everyone your measure, small though it may be."

Ignoring the taunt, Callum circled him and attempted a few false cuts, just to see what Red would do. While his cousin was much taller and stronger, his feet did not move overmuch. Red expected to win easily with a series of single blows. Because of Isla, Callum now knew ways to halt that. It would take speed, graceful footwork, and near-perfect timing;

not to mention a few miracles for him to not curl up on the Hall floor with belly gripes as his herbal tonic fought its own battle with the plant poison.

But he had a chance.

Callum lunged and swung his blunted sword in a sharp downward cut. The clash of steel echoed in the Hall, and the shudder that went through his arms almost provoked a stomach purge, but he'd surprised his cousin. That much was clear.

Red laughed as they circled one another. "How are you feeling? Quite well?"

"Well enough to leap through a valley of lilies," he replied, baring his teeth.

His cousin's eyes widened, before he attacked with a straight thrust. Yet as was forever his trouble, Callum dropped his elbow and his attempt to deflect was weak. Red lunged again with a horizontal strike, and Callum's sword fell to the floor.

"One point, MacDonald," said Sir Lachlan.

Emboldened, Red fought as he'd done against Sir Leslie, trying to overwhelm with a flurry of cuts. Callum blocked the first, the second, the third...but the fourth was one of those swooping hawks that Isla had spoken of, and again it was Callum's sword on the floor as the guests and envoys cheered for Red.

"Two points, MacDonald," said Sir Lachlan.

The words sounded like a reprimand. Callum didn't need to look at Alastair or Isla to know they would be almost clawing their chairs not to intervene.

Speed. Footwork. Timing.

Think, Callum.

Red circled close. "One point away from my wedding night. I shall enjoy breaking the little bitch. Even more so knowing you care for her, and she you..."

With a feral snarl, Callum swung his sword hard in a right upward cut. Caught flat-footed, Red's block was clumsy, and when Callum tried again from the left, his opponent's sword dislodged from his hands onto the floor.

"One point, Glennoe!" Sir Lachlan bellowed.

Fury darkened Red's face as he collected his sword, then lunged with a straight thrust. However, this time Callum neatly stepped aside, then diagonally. As Red's arms were up, exposing his belly a little, Callum brought his sword around in a horizontal slash. His cousin wasn't quite swift enough to block it, not only receiving a cut to the arm for his trouble, but losing his sword once more.

"Two points, Glennoe!" said Sir Lachlan, a tiny smile lifting his lips. "The next point...shall decide the victor."

"Weak, mewling scum," spat Red. "Son of an English witch and friend to the lowborn sinner. I'll have your woman, and your lands soon enough. You'll always be nothing and no one."

Callum laughed. It hurt his stomach, but the shock on his cousin's face was worth the discomfort. "You bray like a mule. Always have."

Roaring the MacDonald battle cry, Red rushed forward. His intent was clear: while his sword tip might be blunted, he intended to maim with the blade.

Speed. Footwork. Timing.

An odd sense of calm washed through him, clearing his mind and easing his stomach. The world around him seemed to slow, while he became swifter. Gripping his longsword tightly, Callum advanced and swung hard in an upward cut, before Red had completed his downward thrust. Their blades screeched and hissed, but Callum had planned for this and absorbed the agonizing shudder. Then he stepped and cut again and again without halting. Left. Right. Horizontal. Upward. Downward. Every movement hurt and his back was drenched in sweat, but he didn't permit his cousin to attack. Instead, Red was forced to defend and defend until he actually began to retreat.

And stumbled.

Strike as a swooping hawk.

Callum almost heard Isla's command in his ear. Lifting his sword above his head, he swung it down from right to left with all his might, dislodging his opponent's sword. Red fell onto his arse, unleashing a guttural wail of despair as his weapon tumbled to the floor, the hilt bouncing once, twice, before settling with a noisy clatter.

For a long moment the only sound in the Hall was Callum gasping for breath as he mopped the sweat from his forehead with a shirtsleeve.

And then it came.

A soul-stirring sound he'd never heard before, one that started as a murmur and became louder and louder until it near lifted the roof of the Great Hall. "*Cruachan. Cruachan. Cruachan!*"

The king and queen, the guests and envoys, bellowing the MacIntyre battle cry...for him.

Tears blurring his vision, Callum raised his sword in acknowledgment. But his gaze darted between his two loves, Alastair and Isla. Who even now were running to him with arms outstretched, their joy plain to see.

To celebrate his triumph.

Needing to feel them both in his arms, he waited until he was swept up in the tightest embrace imaginable. Then he tilted his head back, and roared his victory:

"*CRUACHAN.*"

CHAPTER 11

Now, he believed in miracles.

Alastair pressed his fist to his mouth so he didn't bawl like a babe at the sight of Callum and Isla standing in front of the altar in the king's chapel, hands clasped, as the Bishop of Stirling joined them in holy matrimony.

In truth, his heartbeat still had not slowed after the events of the afternoon. Drinking poisoned wine. Isla running to warn them. The terrible purging with the sweetly affectionate aftermath. Then the swordfight, where Red had surged ahead with two points, before Callum rallied to defeat him.

Without a doubt, his hair would be silver on the morrow.

Once the ceremony was complete, the king rose from his chair, his face wreathed in smiles. "My heartiest congratulations to Callum and Isla MacIntyre, the Lord and Lady of Glennoe! There is but one more act to complete...a formal written alliance between the MacIntyre and Sutherland clans, full payment of dowry, and pledge of future support without interference. I ask that each of you present bear witness as

Lord and Lady Sutherland come forward and acknowledge this decree from their sovereign."

Alastair's eyes widened with admiration. A royal decree. Approval for the marriage, couched in such terms that the Sutherlands could not protest nor renounce it without committing offences against the crown. The great warlord and his iron lady from the north might be furious with the tourney result, and that their misdeeds had failed, but they had no choice but to sign the document in front of the bishop and so many witnesses.

With stony faces, the Sutherlands did as they were bid, then retreated.

"Excellent," said James. "Now, let us go and celebrate in my presence chamber. Master Graham, you may join us on this special occasion."

Alastair's gaze met Callum and Isla's; his own frustration mirrored in their eyes. Much as they were grateful, the three of them wished to be alone. But unwilling to slight the king, they followed him to the presence chamber along with Sir Lachlan, Lady Marjorie, and Lady Janet.

All accepted a goblet of wine. None sipped from it.

James grinned at Callum as the seven of them stood in a small circle beside a window, the setting sun giving them all a peach-like glow. "You aged me at least ten years, Glennoe. What say you?"

Callum hesitated. "Might I ask a question, Your Grace? A delicate question?"

"I cannot say you shall receive an answer, but yes."

"I feel like this week I have been shown favor. Granted small boons. Had secrets kept."

The king exchanged a glance with Sir Lachlan, and his grin widened. "Do you now?"

"Why did you help me?"

"Why did you help *us*?" added Isla boldly.

"Because," their sovereign said softly, his expression now solemn, "I believe in justice, of right overcoming wrong. But more so, I believe in the courage of men and women who fight for love, even if they break the rules."

Lady Janet snorted, yet she glanced affectionately at the king. "Aye, but you'll never know this until *after* the great trial. His Grace reveals no plans. But he does know the happenings in every hallway of his castles."

"And I recognize steps...taught to my best student," added Sir Lachlan, staring pointedly at Isla. She blushed.

Alastair coughed, unable to halt the boldest question of his life. "So you are not against a trio, Your Grace?"

"I find it hard to imagine His Grace denying love when he believes in it with his whole heart," said Lady Marjorie softly.

James sighed, and just for a moment looked so lonely, that Alastair's heart ached for him. Aye, he had sacrificed much for his country; the burden of Callum's duties as laird was light compared to their king. "I do believe in love. It marches on even when all about you may falter. And if you find it you must hold it close, lest it be lost forever. So go. Go, you *three* and enjoy your wedding night. And when you return to Loch Etive, give my regards to Lady Maude. Tell her...tell her I now consider the debt repaid in full."

All three stared at the king, their jaws about resting on the floor. Then Alastair dropped to one knee. "God save and keep ye, James, King of Scots."

Callum bowed low, and Isla curtsied. "God save and keep you."

"I wish you safe travels," said the king, inclining his head. "When I next visit the Western Highlands, I shall expect a warm welcome at Glennoe."

"It would be our honor to host you, Your Grace," said Callum, bowing again.

When their sovereign walked away, Alastair, Callum, and

Isla bid farewell to Sir Lachlan, Lady Marjorie, and Lady Janet, then took the opportunity to dash for the door. They must have looked a sight as they ran out of the King's House, crossing the inner and outer close at pace until they reached the Stirling Castle gate.

Alastair glanced at Isla as they went through the forework tunnel. "Can you manage the hill in those shoes and that gown?"

She kicked the satin shoes away, tore off her gable hood and veil and gave it to a very bemused guard. Then she hooked up the train of her gown, and gazed at him expectantly. "Carry me, devilish beast."

He scooped her up, and when she curled an arm about his neck and settled against his chest, he murmured, "A demanding wife shall face consequences."

"Yes," she said hoarsely. "Hurry."

All three nodded and smiled at those who offered congratulations as they passed on foot or on horseback. But they did not halt on their way to the cottage; not when privacy beckoned and no restrictions stood in their way. Soon they would just be a husband and wife and lover at last able to share a bed.

Callum opened the door and ushered them both inside the blessedly quiet cottage.

"Well..." said Alastair, as he set Isla on her feet. "That was a month in a day."

"How are you feeling, Callum?" asked Isla anxiously.

Their laird nodded. "Surprisingly well. This might sound strange, but just before I won that final point...I became calm. My head cleared and stomach settled. All that mattered was a future with those I hold closest to my heart. Those who bring me joy and comfort and support. Those who I pleasure and who pleasure me in return, exactly how I want and need it. I love you both. So much. I cannot wait to return to Glennoe and begin a new life, a new family together."

Quite overcome, Alastair stepped forward and curled his hand around Callum's neck, mastering his lips in a heated kiss until his laird surrendered with a moan. Then he did the same to Isla until she melted against him, whimpering.

But eventually she stared up at him and shook her head. "Nay, Alastair. You cannot just show us. You must tell us of your love."

He swallowed to dislodge a boulder of emotion from his throat. "It is...difficult to express tender sentiment in words. Lust is easy. I give orders without thought. But my heart was trapped behind a wall after being abandoned as a child. Having no coin, no land or title, no blood clan...it leaves a scar. A deep one."

Isla took his hand and linked his fingers with hers. "All will be well. You are under my protection now."

Alastair's eyes burned, even as his lips twitched. "Is that so, lady?"

"Aye. Callum is, too. Woe betide anyone who threatens my men."

"I love you," he said rawly. "I have loved Callum my whole life. To have one great love is a blessing beyond all...but two? A family of my own? I cannot think to deserve such happiness."

Callum stilled and tilted his head. "You spoke of a blood clan, which makes me think you do not feel that you truly belong with the MacIntyres. Is that because of your name? Do you wish to be known as a Graham, or nay?"

He blinked. "Graham might be my surname, but I do not hold any great attachment to it. Not after what they did."

"Then formally pledge yourself to me. Pledge yourself to the MacIntyres and become one in name as well as deed. Be the husband of our hearts. Isla and I need you, Alastair. Our happiness cannot be complete without our master."

Alastair's eyes burned again, but this time the mist turned into tears that trickled down his cheeks. "That...that sounds like forever."

"It is," said Callum seriously. "If that is what you wish."

"Aye. More than anything."

Isla and Callum wrapped their arms around him and they stood in that cool, silent room as three people in love. Then Isla peered up at him, a mischievous twinkle in her eyes.

"Now you've said, it is time to show. Take me to bed, my MacIntyre men."

Fierce lust surged through him. Aye, this night he would bed the husband and wife of his heart most thoroughly. It was his sacred duty, after all. To love and cherish them for as long as they all should live.

Alastair took Isla's hand, and Callum's, gently leading them forward. "To the bedchamber, then."

◈

It was her wedding night.

As Callum lit candles in the bedchamber, Isla stared at the bed in front of her in consternation. While being conquered rested easily on her shoulders, tonight added the uncertainty of something altogether new: it would not just be penetration with fingers or tongues, but those huge cocks inside her. At the same time.

And she was a wife now. Would that change anything? Would the lusty play she so enjoyed, the blunt talk, the submission, the unashamed nakedness, the worship of their bodies, the pleasure for pleasure's sake...halt now if the purpose was the creation of children?

"I can almost see your mind turning, Isla," said Alastair,

resting his hands on her shoulders and massaging them until she relaxed with a sigh. "What troubles you?"

"My future as a wife," she said slowly. "If it will be as I hope."

Callum took her hand and squeezed it. "It shall be how you desire, Isla. We are all new students in the school of marriage. I know there'll be much to learn and things we'll do wrong. But if we talk to each other with truth, open hearts, and kindness, then we shall overcome any obstacle."

Isla smiled. "You hold such wisdom, and Alastair is a rock of strength. I was afraid of marriage, because I never thought, not even for a moment, that a man would understand me. That he would welcome my unconventional nature. And now I have not one but *two* men who accept me for who I am. Do you know how rare and precious that is? I love you both with my whole heart. Yet I do have a concern. I wish to be Isla the wife, and one day a mother. But I do not want to stop being Isla the lover and friend and protector. Isla the swordfighter. And I know...I know the clergy and court have certain thoughts on this. About a woman's place..."

Alastair snorted. "The clergy and court have certain thoughts about many things. Including that it is immoral and shameful for two men to love each other with hearts and bodies. We don't believe that, nor do we seek to change you or suppress your spirit. In bed, you submit, for it gives you great pleasure to do so. However, you are always free to make your desires plain, or to decline an act."

"My weavers will make you hose and shirt to fit," added Callum. "And if you wish to practice swordplay every day; to train my clan and be the warrior Lady of Glennoe, then it shall be so. None of us are conventional people, and that alongside love, will be our great strength."

"Then I am most content," said Isla, beaming at them

both. "And now I wish very much to be bedded by my husbands."

Callum and Alastair exchanged a wicked grin. Then slowly, far too slowly, they began to undress her. Girdle. Gown. Kirtle. Shift. Stockings. All the while they caressed her, stroking her shoulders and belly and inner thighs until she thought she might scream with want. At last, they guided her over to the biggest bed and settled her in the center, before removing their own clothes.

To provoke them, Isla pinched her own nipples before licking a fingertip and sliding it down between her legs to tease her pearl. Retribution was swift; Callum secured her hands above her head, and Alastair gave her cunt a sharp smack.

Isla quivered in delight. How wonderful it was to have lovers who knew exactly what made her wet and needy...and provided it.

"You see, Alastair?" said Callum, circling her nipple with his fingertip. "We have a very wicked wife. A wild Highland lass, indeed."

"Aye," said their squire, as he leaned down to kiss her. "She'll need pleasuring often. And discipline. 'Tis the only way."

"Bed me now," Isla demanded, moaning when she received another smack. "*Please...*"

Alastair trailed his fingers over her breasts, down her belly, until he could thread them in the crisp dark hair between her legs. Isla parted her thighs wide and lifted her hips so her mound rubbed against him. But her devilish beast would not permit that, and his fingers retreated to caress her hip instead.

"Noooooo," she wailed.

Callum kissed her neck and stroked the sensitive skin of

her inner thigh, making her gasp. "The scent of you," he whispered. "It makes my cock so hard."

"Then fuck your lady wife," Isla whispered back. "She needs it."

"Greedy lass," he replied, gently pushing a single finger inside her wet sheath and moving it in and out until she writhed on the bed. Then Alastair added a finger as well, and Isla's whole body arched as she cried out in sweet release.

She hoped to be taken, but her husbands continued to torment her with their fingers; Callum pushed a second inside her, while Alastair painted her swollen pearl with her own honey, before leaning down to suck it off. Soon she bucked, soaring to the stars as pleasure shook her to the core.

"Fuck me," Isla begged, when she eventually regained her senses. "*Please*."

Alastair nodded. "Callum, lie on your back. Isla, get on your hands and knees and take his cock into your mouth. I'll prepare your cunt and arse with some oil. We shall do this very, very slowly."

Prowling up her laird's body like a cat, Isla kissed him, flicking his lips with her tongue until he sucked it into his mouth. Then she slithered down, took his cock in her hand, and lapped at the damp head.

Callum groaned. "Yes."

Soon it was her groaning around Callum's cock, as Alastair worked two oil-slick fingers into her cunt, and two into her arse. Even with her wetness and the oil the stretch still burned, but it promised such ecstasy she pushed back against Alastair, trying to force him deeper inside her.

He brushed his lips against her back, and Isla shuddered with need. "Please," she said again. "Don't make me wait anymore."

"Brace your hands on Callum's chest, and take his cock inside your cunt," Alastair commanded. "*Slowly*."

Sitting astride him, Isla took his cock in one hand, fitted the head to her entrance, before easing down upon it. Callum's fists gripped the quilt, his jaw clenched, but he did not thrust upward and she appreciated his restraint as her body rebelled against a brief stinging pain before adjusting to an overwhelming feeling of fullness. Soon, he was balls-deep inside her.

Bracing her hands on his chest, she rocked a little to find a more comfortable position.

They both gasped.

Well. Little wonder those in power wished to restrict this act. Hard cock moving in wet cunt felt very good indeed. Then Alastair's oiled fingers pushed into her arse once more, and Isla shuddered at the jolt of hot, tingling sensation that arrowed between her legs.

"I'm going to enter you with my cock now," said Alastair gruffly. "If it is too much, just say."

Isla nodded. "I will."

She bit her lip as Alastair's cock pressed against her tight hole, a whimper of discomfort escaping as he pushed the engorged head inside her. But Callum distracted her by pinching her nipples, and that sharp edge of pain seemed to lessen the burning stretch as Alastair's thick length penetrated her arse inch by inch.

"God's blood, Alastair," said Callum, moaning. "I can feel your cock nearly rubbing against mine."

Isla sobbed. "So...full..."

Alastair kissed her neck. "You're doing beautifully. Just a little more. There now."

Panting, Isla balanced on a blade of pleasure and pain. Yet her men didn't thrust, just held themselves deep inside her cunt and arse as they kissed her, tweaked her taut nipples, pressed her pearl with a thumb. Eventually her breathing slowed, the rigidness left her limbs, and she circled her hips a little.

Oh. That felt *good*.

Even better, Callum and Alastair both gasped.

Isla smiled. Much like she'd still held power on her knees sucking two cocks, she still held power with those same cocks buried deep inside her. She did not lose herself in any way, only gained pleasure.

Again and again she circled her hips, and as she moved more freely, her men began to gently thrust. Sometimes one then the other, sometimes together, and she could *feel* a wild storm gather low in her belly as the promise of an explosive release teased at her senses.

"More," she begged. "Faster."

Callum gripped her inner thighs as his thumb teased her pearl, Alastair curled one arm around her so he could cup her breast and pinch her nipple, and both began to fuck her hard. The storm built and built, and she cried out, needing release more than her next breath. Her men thrust deeply, once, twice, and at last the wave crashed over her, rough and overwhelming and perfect, and she screamed in bliss. Moments later, the low, raw sounds of her husbands' ecstasy echoed in the chamber, and her cunt and arse were filled to overflowing with hot seed.

Carefully, Alastair and Callum withdrew from her body, and they lay on the bed embracing, still shaking and struggling to catch their breath.

"Saints alive," said Isla weakly. "That was...that was..."

They merely held her closer. Indeed, no words were necessary.

She had found her forever.

Loch Etive, Western Highlands

Callum tapped his heels on his horse's flanks, urging the stallion on. They were only a few miles from Glennoe Castle now, and as the familiar scents of mountain and loch soothed his senses, his yearning for home grew even stronger. Not to mention a yearning to show his new wife, the warrior lady in shirt and hose with her arms wrapped about his waist and her cheek resting on his back, the castle and lands where she would reign alongside him and Alastair.

This was the moment he had waited so long for. The start of a glorious new chapter in the manuscript of his life, with his wife and the husband of his heart by his side. There would be difficulties, he well knew that. And he would probably never be able to be as affectionate in public with Alastair as he would like. But the people of his clan would soon learn that their laird, lady, and squire, stood together as three. A love that had been forged in the fire of a royal tourney would not be torn asunder by anyone.

When they reached the ridge about a mile from the castle, Callum pulled up his horse and gestured down. "There, Isla. Glennoe."

She sucked in a breath. "It's beautiful. So peaceful and unspoiled. I see fishing boats, but do you swim in the loch as well?"

Alastair laughed as he brought his mount to a halt beside them. "Aye, when we are feeling adventurous. It's a sea loch, so very cold and very deep in places. But plenty of fish, and game in the hills. You'll never be hungry."

"And so many people! Look, all gathering near the castle."

His heart pounding, Callum exchanged a grim glance with Alastair. God's blood, not today. Had Red sent a raiding party? Had the Campbells? It seemed a terribly rash action when in his saddlebag was a copy of the king's decree and his alliance with the Sutherlands, but there wasn't a moment in Scottish history where something being rash had halted action. Sure, he had gained six trained men at arms as part of Isla's dowry, but they followed behind with the wagon carrying Isla's trunks, her beloved servants Morag and Leith, and the gift of cloth from the king. More Sutherland men would be sent to help guard his lands, but they would not arrive from the north for a month, at least.

If anyone had harmed his mother...he would show them no mercy. The days of being crushed under the weight of fear, past shadows and expectations, and lack of belief in himself were over. He was worthy. He did have skill. And each day he would only be bolstered by Alastair and Isla's loving care.

Callum clicked his tongue, and his horse cantered forward, well used to this path that led down to the castle.

"You are tense, husband. Do I need to unsheathe my sword?" asked Isla in his ear.

"Maybe," he admitted. "I know not why people in the clan have gathered, unless there has been trouble. Before we left for Stirling, my weaving house was razed to the ground in a raid. Both Red and the Campbells have long wanted these fertile lands for themselves."

"I am ready to fight," she said fiercely. "No one shall threaten my laird's home or lands. Especially not a wretched *MacDonald*. And your clan—"

"Our clan."

"*Our* clan will learn to value all skills. Warrior and scholar, protector and healer."

"That is what I needed to hear," Callum replied. "It strengthens me no end to know I have yours and Alastair's love. We three shall achieve great things."

As they neared the castle gate, he and Alastair both eased

their horses into a trot. Then the applauding began. And the loud cheers. Women waved ribbons and linen cloths, their faces wreathed in smiles, and men stopped work to raise a triumphant fist.

"Welcome home, laird," called one silver-haired man as he stepped out of his hut. "'Tis a grand day to be a MacIntyre!"

"Hail our laird," yelled a young lad from the shore of the loch as he tugged a small fishing boat behind him. "The man who defeated all comers, including the MacDonald. Cruachan!"

A small boy bounded up. "Is this the new Lady of Glennoe, laird? The one who fights with swords?"

Isla leaned down. "Aye, laddie. I am Isla MacIntyre, formerly a Sutherland. Do you like my fine clothes?"

The boy's eyes bulged, a huge grin split his face, then he turned and called to a group of other lads behind him: "It's true! The lady wears hose!"

Abruptly the crowd parted to reveal his mother in a deep blue gown and silver girdle, her fair hair unbound and fluttering in the wind. "My son."

Callum dismounted from his horse, assisted Isla down onto the ground, then strode forward to take a knee for her blessing. "Mother. I am glad you are well. When I saw the gathering..."

Maude rested a hand on his head, murmuring words in a language he did not know, before tugging him to his feet. "Let me look at you."

"Aye." Callum stood still at the familiar command, and she clasped his face in her hands, her violet gaze searing into his soul. Then she dipped into a curtsy.

"All is well," said his mother with a sage nod, a beaming smile lighting up her face. "And all will be well. Now, introduce me to your wife."

Callum held out his hand, and Isla walked over to join

him. His mother's eyes softened as she looked Isla up and down, before clasping her face in the same manner.

"Ah, yes," she murmured. "A fierce and loving heart. You are most welcome here, Lady of Glennoe. God's blessings upon you this day and all those to come. But you require shirt and hose to fit, so visit me in the solar this night for wine and comfits and I will take your measurements. We shall have such fun, you and I. A daughter at last. My heart is full."

"Thank you, lady," said Isla, her voice quavering a little.

"Maude. Or Mother."

"Thank you...*Mother*."

Callum cleared his throat, before he joined the two women in gaining misty eyes. "I ask that you also bid Alastair welcome, Mother. Alastair *MacIntyre*."

Maude beckoned Alastair closer, and he took a knee in front of her. She took his chin in her hand, tilting it this way and that, before placing her hand atop his head. Then she turned to Callum. "'Tis long past time you claimed the son I found, Callum. Long past time. Welcome home, Alastair MacIntyre."

Callum stilled, staring at his mother. She stared right back, one haughty eyebrow raised, all the knowledge in the world gleaming in her eyes. For they both knew she meant far more with the word *claimed* than Alastair having a permanent home with the clan.

"I...er...yes. Foolish," he replied. "But that mistake has been mended, and forgiveness granted. As you said, all is well. Now we must rest, after a week's tourney and two-day ride from Stirling."

Maude winked. "Indeed. Rest, my dears. I shall enjoy hearing all about the tourney in time. Especially how you defeated Rory MacDonald in a swordfight."

He nodded. "I promise you will. Almost every detail. Then perhaps you'll tell us what debt the king owed you."

"I promise I will. Almost every detail. Now go. *Rest*."

Callum held out his left arm for Isla to take. Then he rested his right at the small of Alastair's back, and they made their way into the castle as the trio that they were.

Home.

They were finally home to the place that would witness their family, their children and their joy in the many years to come. But best of all it would witness the powerful love between a shy and scholarly laird who had found strength, a bold lady swordfighter who had found acceptance, and a brawny orphaned squire who had found his place in the world.

All was well.

All would be well.

Love had declared it so.

⚜

Need more Glennoe Highlanders?
Purchase Book #2, Her Wicked Highlander (Lady Maude's
story) <u>HERE</u>

Excerpt of HER WICKED HIGHLANDER © Nicola Davidson

Glennoe Castle, on the shores of Loch Etive
　　Western Highlands
　　March 1505

. . .

Many would find it exceedingly odd, a woman of forty-two summers kneeling naked in supplication at her bedchamber window. For Lady Maude MacIntyre, it was a daily ritual.

A full year ago, death had finally dragged away the cruelest husband in Scotland. But while she continued having the visions that lit such a clear path for others, her own future remained stubbornly hidden and her most fervent prayer unanswered.

Clasping her hands, Maude arched her back so the rising sun bathed her skin in enchanted light. Then she lifted her beseeching gaze upward.

"For twenty-six years, I did everything asked of me. Wed a laird I neither loved nor desired to conceive my Callum. Fostered Alastair, and raised both into fine men. Sent them to the royal tourney in Stirling to win dear Isla and the love of the clan…"

Her head dipped, tears trickling down her cheeks.

"Mistake me not, I have much to be grateful for. My boys found bliss in a trio and I'll be a grandmother in autumn. I heal others mostly without impediment and the MacIntyre clan now enjoys peaceful prosperity. But I beg thee…after a life of marital misery, may I not discover love for myself? To know pleasure and comfort in the arms of my chosen man?"

As usual, the heavens remained resolutely silent.

In despair, Maude snatched up her brocade robe and dressed. Thankfully no one was here to witness such weakness; bad enough to be English in the Highlands, let alone possess white-blond hair, unnatural violet eyes, and visions that had first occurred in her sixteenth summer. If she'd been anyone other than the laird's wife, and now the laird's mother, certain villagers would've long ago drowned her in the loch.

A harsh knock on the bedchamber door jolted her from such bleak thoughts, and Maude slowly stood. After crossing the room, she opened her door to the startling sight of a stone-faced MacIntyre guard with a hissing, clawing child dangling from his meaty fist.

Saints alive. Sorcha Wright.

The poor mite appeared much younger than her eight summers; red hair a tatted mess, tunic threadbare, and face smudged with dirt. But since her father and mother had been killed in a raid back in August, Sorcha insisted on staying in their mountain dwelling next door to her uncle.

The child didn't roam. Why would she be out at this hour?

Maude's neck prickled. "Yes?"

"Lady," said the guard with a curt nod. "I found the bairn wandering in the clearing, so brought her to the castle kitchens. But she ran straight to your herb garden to *steal*."

"Did not," spat Sorcha, as she attempted to bite the guard. "Just needed some lavender. To help."

"Help who?" asked Maude, her heart now thudding frantically.

Sorcha's blue gaze was equally fierce and terrified. "Uncle Keir. He's injured verra bad."

Maude gasped.

No. Please no.

Keir Wright was the enormous, ebony-haired Highlander she'd been forbidden to tend or even speak to, due to her powerful attraction to him. Every battle scar Keir gained, every illness he'd endured had been agonizing, knowing he suffered without treatment solely because of her husband Donald's spiteful jealousy. Then, two years ago, Keir had broken Donald's nose in a brawl, been dismissed from his post as captain of the guards, and banished to live on the cold and rugged slopes of Ben Cruachan. That had been the worst blow, being unable to see him each day. But even after Donald's passing, Keir had stayed away and she didn't know why.

Now he was badly injured. What if he died?

No. Not while there was breath in her body. For this time she *could* go to him. Tend him as she'd always longed to do. Perhaps even find out the truth.

"Leave Sorcha with me," said Maude abruptly.

The guard's lip curled. But he nodded, dropped his burden with an unforgiving thump, and left the room.

Crouching down, Maude tried to smile reassuringly at Sorcha. "Can you tell me what happened?"

The child scowled. "I'm no thief."

"I know. But if you tell me what you saw or heard, I can decide what's to be done."

"Uncle Keir always puts out food for me. But not last night. So today I opened the shutter and jumped through a window in his dwelling. He lay on the floor, all shivering and sweaty. When he was out hunting, his foot slipped on gravel and he slid down a ridge. A big rock cut his leg and it's bleeding lots. He said to fetch the blacksmith because ye won't tend him. So I thought if I just got some lavender..."

Maude winced, the words a dagger to her heart. But how could she explain cruel husbands to a little girl? "I'll help him."

Hope dawned in Sorcha's eyes. "Truly?"

"Yes. I'll pack my herbal satchels then inform the laird that I'll miss morning chapel and be away for a while. You shall go to the kitchens to wash your face, and eat your fill of buttered bread and small ale."

"Don't take charity," said Sorcha, raising her small chin.

"That wasn't a request," replied Maude, hardening her voice. "Go."

The child turned and sprinted away.

Her stomach churning relentlessly, Maude halted and pressed a fist to her lips. But she couldn't shatter now, not when there was still a chance to save Keir. She needed to behave like a vastly experienced, steady-handed healer, not someone terrified of losing their lover.

He's not your lover. You've never even kissed, despite all those prayers for it.

The thought hit like a bucket of frigid loch water, and rather remarkably, cleared her head. Swiftly, Maude discarded her robe to dress in her special healer's tunic, a dark brown ankle-length garment made of heavy linen and secured at her waist with a girdle, and a warm cloak. When tending patients, she opted for comfort and ease of movement, so never wore a petticoat or hood, and certainly not a gown of costly fabric with a train. Then she stuffed her sturdy leather satchel with a second tunic, fresh shift, and woolen stockings, for it remained icy cold on the mountain in early spring.

Next, she hurried into the adjoining chamber that served as her apothecary to fetch supplies. The pungent scents of peppermint and ginger were soothing, although the clutter of parchment and quills, leather-bound Latin medical texts, ancient recipes, countless jars, pestles and mortars, and half-open drawers of cut, dried herbs no doubt alarmed others who didn't understand her methods.

But what to take?

Maude added several jars to her satchel: coneflower salve to treat wounds, lavender to heal and relax, peppermint to cool. Also bog moss to halt bleeding, yarrow for fever, and white willow bark if his pain was unbearable.

"Lady Mother. We hear you go to Ben Cruachan?"

Maude dropped an assortment of fresh linen bandages into the satchel side pocket, then glanced up to smile briefly at her beloved family who all stood in the chamber doorway. Fair-haired, scholarly Callum, the laird of Clan MacIntyre. His ebony-haired, swordfighter wife Isla, who never wore gowns, only shirt and hose. And their lover Alastair, like hewn rock behind them, brown-haired and brawny. "My sons. Daughter. Yes. I am urgently needed for a serious injury."

Alastair folded his arms. "Keir Wright?"

"Indeed," she replied, more sharply than intended. "And none of you may even consider forbidding it. Keir is not ill-tempered, even though he broke a nose."

Callum made a frustrated sound, an hourly act for a Scottish laird. "I'm aware. That is why I had Gavin invite him to return to the village. *Twice*. But Keir refused."

Maude grimaced. As Gavin MacTier had replaced Keir as captain of the guards, she wasn't entirely sure the message had been delivered with the goodwill intended. Yet Keir remained on the mountain. "He did refuse."

"Imagine that, a Highland man stubborn as an ornery bull," Isla said pertly as she cradled the slight swell of her belly. "They're usually so reasonable and obliging."

"A truth," said Maude, unable to halt a snort.

"Here, now," chided Alastair, as both he and Callum sent Isla looks that made her cheeks pinken.

Oh.

Maude sighed. In the past she might have sworn Keir gazed at her like that—gruff tenderness and fierce lust together. But obviously she'd been mistaken, for he'd never come to claim her.

Callum cleared his throat. "Guards will accompany you, Mother. Oh, and here, a letter arrived from the king."

Brightening, she took the missive and added it to her satchel. Her longtime friend James's twice-monthly letters always entertained with their outrageous bawdiness, court news, and whatever learning he currently held close to his heart. It would be a treat to read once Keir was better. "Thank you. As for guards, they may accompany me to the clearing and no further. You know I don't permit others underfoot when treating a patient. I'll be quite safe and shall return in three or four days. Blessings on you all."

The trio looked unconvinced, but understanding her ways, eventually nodded. Maude kissed each on the cheek before hurrying from the herbal chamber.

She only prayed it wasn't too late.

To lose Keir before they'd even had a chance... unthinkable.

ALSO BY NICOLA DAVIDSON

A Rake, His Patron, & Their Muse (#1)

An Earl, His Valet, & Their Wife (#2)

A Lady, Her Lord, & Their Duke (#3)

<u>Regency Standalones</u>

Seven Sinful Nights

Duke for Hire

Her Virgin Duke

Mistletoe Mistress

Joy to the Earl

Once Upon a Promise

<u>Medieval Scotland</u>

<u>Glennoe Highlanders</u>

Wicked Passions (#1)

Her Wicked Highlander (#2)

Scandalous Passions

<u>Tudor novellas</u>

His Forbidden Lady

One Forbidden Knight

<u>Paranormal</u>

<u>Medieval Wolf Kings</u>

Wolf Duke (#1)

<u>Contemporary</u>

Ladies First (erotic short stories)

ABOUT THE AUTHOR

USA Today bestselling author **Nicola Davidson** worked for many years in media and government communications, but hasn't looked back since she decided writing erotic historical romance was infinitely more fun. When not chained to a computer, she can be found ambling along one of New Zealand's beautiful beaches, cheering on the All Blacks rugby team, history geeking on the internet, or daydreaming. If this includes dessert—even better!

Her books have appeared in *USA Today, NPR*, and *Entertainment Weekly*.

Keep up with Nicola's news on Twitter (@NicolaMDavidson) Facebook (Nicola Davidson—Author) Instagram (@NicolaDauthor) or her website www.nicola-davidson.com